PERCIVAL GYNT AND THE CONSPIRACY OF DAYS

PERCIVAL GYNT AND THE CONSPIRACY OF DAYS

MONDAY
8:06 AM
APRIL 9, 20018

A NOVEL BY
DREW MELBOURNE

RUESDAY BOOKS

This novel is a work of fiction. Probably. If the events depicted herein were to actually take place 18,000 years from now, the author would be well and truly gobsmacked. Or long dead. More likely the latter. Any references made to real-life, modern-day persons or organizations should not be interpreted as an endorsement of or by those persons or organizations, nor as a 100% guarantee that such persons or organizations will continue to exist 18,000 years from now. But let's be honest: There will always be Walmarts.

Visit the author's website at www.drewmelbourne.com.

Published by Ruesday Books.

Paperback ISBN 978-0-9998748-0-6
eBook ISBN 978-0-9998748-1-3

FIRST PAPERBACK EDITION

10 9 8 7 6 5 4 3 2 1

For my Dad
and his perpetual motion machine

CONTENTS

PART IV

IN WHICH OUR HERO IS LURED
INTO STRANGE MATTERS
BEYOND HIS AGENCY

Top 5 News Downloads for April 9, 20018

5   Church of the All-Mother Bans Sorcery on 14 Worlds

4   Paranoia, Toxic Masculinity, YouTube Fuel Resurgence of Nth Realm "Space Nazis"

3   Beloved Magician Illuminari Laid to Rest

2   New Settlers to Commemorate 20th Anniversary of Gynt Massacre

1   Celestial Governor Zell Wins Re-election Uncontested

You may also be interested to know

237   Husband and Wife Slain, Child Abducted in Slidetown Province

Today's Weather

Auspicious

1 | THE 8:05

Slidetown Station was that morning more than usually overpacked with ne'er-do-wells, with schemers and scalawags, ruffians and rakes, and all manner of bottom-feeders between. Poor Percival Gynt was wedged in so tightly at the front of the train platform that he scarcely had room to open up his broadsheet edition of *The Daily Internet*.

A recorded message from the station master played across the loudspeakers to mark the hour. The pleasantly mechanical voice intoned, "The time is now 8:00 AM."

Crammed in to Percival's right slouched a hipster-wizard, wearing one of those wink-wink ironic pointy wizard hats that had been making their way back into style. When Percival's paper half-brushed against his arm, the wizard turned and sneered and looked like he was about to say something, then apparently thought better of it. Instead, the wizard averted his gaze down to his shoes and pulled his retro-cool stars and moons robe around himself all the tighter, and he muttered an "I am awesome" charm as quietly as he could to himself.

"The next train to arrive on Track 3 will be the 8:03 Express to Lunar Colony."

The heavily armored, faintly rotting Grimsoul bounty hunter to Percival's left was oblivious to his fellow commuters' almost-exchange as he sucked down the last of the grape drink from his rapid-reuse juice box. Grimsoul bounty hunters are feared the galaxy over for their vicious depravity, but they do enjoy sucking liquid through tiny, bendy straws.

"Next to arrive on Track 4, the 8:05 Express to Planet's Core."

And Percival, squeezed in between these two characters, on a platform that was that day full of characters, was neither vicious nor feared nor hip nor pointy-hatted. Nor thankfully did he need a special charm to render himself more awesome.

Percival was still a young man then, thin, light brown skinned with an unruly mop of dark brown curls, handsome perhaps if not for his hawkish nose and almost too large eyes. They were too full of curiosity, his mother had once told him.

This being a workday, Percival was dressed smartly in a tailored three-piece suit, gray with pink pinstripes, paired with rose-gold cufflinks and a sky-blue tie. A handkerchief of matching blue was folded and tucked neatly into his breast pocket. His favorite hat, the gray bowler, was pulled down tightly over his curls. A long black umbrella hung from his left arm in case of rain.

"Remember: Unattended packages will be vaporized by Province Police."

Percival held *The Internet* open as wide as he could in front of him, folding it over now and then to scroll through the articles. *New Settlers to Commemorate Twentieth Anniversary of Gynt Massacre*. And why not? thought Percival. Have a party. Light it up. Let it burn.

"Excuse me, sir."

Percival turned his head. This was not the mechanical voice of the station manager.

Behind him then, pressed up tight against him in the crowd, was the loveliest young woman whom Percival had ever been pressed up tightly against. She had glittering green eyes and long, wavy black hair and a demure, but optimistic smile. Beneath her lavender traveling cloak, her clothes were a mash of long abandoned fashions, all straps and scarves and synthetic fibers. There was a thoughtlessness to her attire that to Percival suggested a woman of true substance.

He did not notice the small stone in her necklace, which seemed to burn from within with its own golden fire.

Percival arched an eyebrow and allowed a confused half-smile to creep across his face. He wasn't sure why such an obviously interesting person would be speaking to him of all people. He'd been playing the role of mild-mannered accountant too long.

"Hullo," he sputtered. Then, after a second to think, he added cannily, "Have I dropped something?"

The mysterious young woman in the lavender cloak pulled in closer to Percival, reaching one hand up around his neck and guiding his ear down to her so that she might whisper to him.

Her breath was warm against his cheek. She smelled to him of distant and long forgotten meadows.

And in a hushed tone she asked him, "Are you honest and clever and kind and forgiving, and does danger always seem to find you?"

"I..." Percival paused. As you might expect, he didn't have a proper answer prepared for such a question, but he was absolutely certain that the correct words, chosen at this precise moment in time, would mean the difference between a thrilling new adventure and a right slap in the face.

"I need to know," she whispered with urgency. "I don't have much time."

He looked into her eyes, and behind their beauty he could see fear. He could see someone who needed his help. "Yes?" he answered with a transparent lack of confidence. He took a moment to steel himself before repeating, "Yes. Yes, tell me what you need."

She didn't answer. Instead she leaned into Percival and kissed him softly on the lips, which Percival speculated was a sort of answer on its own. And while he may have been momentarily surprised by her forwardness, Percival was not one to question a good turn. He slipped a hand through the locks of her hair and another around her waist, and he kissed her back.

If his eyes were open just then, Percival might have noticed that the golden light from the young woman's necklace intensified as he kissed her. But they were not, and he did not.

The hipster-wizard glanced at the pair of them and then across to the Grimsoul bounty hunter, and he rolled his eyes. Caught by the wind, *The Internet* flapped away across the tracks.

The young woman, whose name Percival still did not know, jerked away from him suddenly. He opened his eyes to see her staring back at him with regret. She was holding his hat in her hands.

"Then I'm sorry," came her response at last as she backed away into the rabble crowd.

"Wait!" Percival shouted after her, attempting to push past the Grimsoul bounty hunter with no success.

She mouthed the words "I'm sorry" once more before he lost sight of her.

"But that's my favorite hat!" he called out, exasperated, now to no one in particular.

And then the crowd parted, not in front of him but behind, as two Province Police in full riot response gear emerged just a few paces from Percival. They wore crimson armor and crimson skull masks and green-glowing goggles and badges of tarnished gold, and they held their Mark 12 semi-automatic Smith & Wesson ion pulse cannons at the ready.

The officers spun up their weapons' autocyclotrons to prime them for fire. One snarled at Percival. The other shouted, "Halt!"

But Percival needed no such direction. He stood fully halted at the platform edge, pointing half-heartedly in the direction that the young woman in the lavender cloak had disappeared with his hat.

"M-My mum gave me that hat," he stammered.

With weapons trained, the two officers conferred. "Surveillance confirms known associate," one said. "Suspect must be neutralized," said the other.

Percival did not like the sound of that one bit, so as the officers raised their pulse cannons to attack angle, he yanked the umbrella from his arm and opened it as a shield in front of him. The officers fired, but the concussive blasts dispersed against the umbrella's triple-reinforced microweave fabric.

Percival grinned. "And everyone said I was mad to buy an umbrella from an arms deal—"

The snarling officer fired again, and though the blasts still had no effect, Percival took a half-step back on instinct, a half-step off the platform.

And then a curious thing happened: As Percival slipped backwards off the platform edge, all the sounds of the station seemed to fade away. The two officers were clearly speaking to Percival as they advanced, probably offering to vaporize him quickly if he stopped resisting, but Percival could no longer hear what they were saying. Nor could he hear the taunts and jeers of the crowd, who disliked cops, but disliked scrawny men in suits who kissed pretty girls even more. Nor, thankfully, could he hear his own semi-pathetic, semi-girlish scream as he fell backwards to the tracks below.

In fact, the only words that Percival could hear were these, echoing like the voice of God Himself or Herself through every loudspeaker in the station:

"Now arriving on Track 3, the—"

And just like that, Percival knew what to do.

The drop from the platform to the tracks below was not quite three meters. The umbrella helped to slow his fall a bit, but Percival still counted himself extremely lucky as he landed on both feet. From overhead a pair of pulse cannon blasts rained down, one just grazing Percival's right jacket sleeve. Percival turned and dived across to the far tracks, narrowly dodging the incoming 8:03.

"—8:03 Express to Lunar Colony."

Percival rolled over onto his back and crowed, while passengers on the 8:03 pressed their faces to the glass to gawk at this young fool. His glee was not long lived though as the station master followed good news with bad:

"Now arriving two minutes early on Track 4—"

Percival could see the headlight of the 8:05 racing towards him at an alarming speed. He pulled himself up to his feet and fumbled through his pockets for his Apple Watch.

"—the 8:05—"

Percival swiped through the apps menu frantically. "Alarm, phone, camera, music, TV, internet...

"—Express to—"

He swiped faster. "...pocket light, mirror, magnifier, voice recorder, email, games..."

"—Planet's—"

"...calculator, navigator, meat thermometer," then finally, "TIME STOP!"

He tapped the screen and the entire universe ground to a halt around him. The hulking 8:05 Express sat motionless a few meters ahead of him, its brilliant headlight nearly blinding at that distance. Up on the far platform, commuters stood still as a photograph.

And his screen display began to count backwards from six.

The Apple Watch Time Stop app was originally bundled with the 19947 model. The thinking had been that it would be easier to take still pictures if the things you were taking pictures of were, in fact, still. And what better way to ensure a still subject than to pause all motion in the entire universe for as long as necessary to snap your picture?

Unsurprisingly, this app turned out to be wildly impractical. First off, as it turns out, the very act of pausing the universe subtly rewrites several key cosmological constants necessary to keep reality in one piece. In other words, stop time enough times, and you may find that gravity's not there when you start up again.

And second, the Time Stop app is a tremendous drain on battery life.

For both of these reasons, the Time Stop app was limited to six second bursts starting with a 19948 OS update, and discontinued all together in the year 19950.

Percival purchased his 19949 Apple Watch with original OS off eBay last fall. Coincidentally, that model was also the only one that came with a pocket light, and Percival was forever losing his loose change down between seat cushions and under his couch.

Five.

With no interest in wasting time, Percival quickly pocketed his watch and directed his attention to the matter of making his way up out of the track well before time restarted and the train could splatter him to messy pulp.

Four.

It was just under three meters from the tracks back up to the platform. With a short run, a jump, and a reach, Percival was able to catch the hook of his umbrella on the platform edge.

Three.

The umbrella held as he scrambled up the side of the platform.

Two.

Percival dragged himself up onto the platform and collapsed, exhausted, hugging his umbrella tight to his chest. The paused commuters who loomed above him were in for a bit of a shock.

One.

With his umbrella as a cane, Percival pushed himself to his feet. And the world around him began to move again.

"—Core. Our apologies for the early arrival time."

A wrinkly nun, a Sister of the All-Mother, cursed at him as he appeared seemingly from nowhere. "God hates teleportation!" she added as she wagged her finger in Percival's face.

Percival nodded politely as he backed onto the 8:05 train, destined for Planet's Core.

"Next stop: The Sorrow Point."

Percival let out a sigh of relief as he squeezed a seat between two elderly superheroes. He took his watch back out and checked the battery power. "Almost empty," he muttered as he swiped through to the email app.

He held the watch up to his lips, and he began to dictate a letter. "Dear Mum, I seem to have gotten myself into a spot of trouble."

Percival glanced up as the slide doors opened at the far end of the train car. Two Province Police emerged from the car adjoining. These two were bigger and meaner than the ones Percival ran from on the platform. One had a robotic third arm protruding from his sloppy gut.

The other held in his arms a gun that made the Smith & Wesson ion pulse cannon look like a Smith & Wesson ion pulse BB gun.

Excessive, thought Percival. He continued his dictation more quickly now. "I may not be able to make it for Sunday dinner. I'm sorry for that, and I want you to know..."

The officers were nearly to him now. They pushed aside a young straight couple from Lunar 3 and trained their weapons on Percival.

"...that I love you very much, and I hope to see you again soon."

The officers stood over Percival, pulse cannons aimed at his head. They primed their weapons.

Percival faked a smile for them. "Warm regards, your son Percy." He tapped the send icon and closed his eyes. Finally, Fate had found him. "Go ahead, then. I've had a good run."

Percival waited patiently for the end to come.

No such luck.

2 | TO PLANET'S CORE

The officers did not kill Percival Gynt, though he rather suspected that they wanted to. In those days most Province Police were absolute lunatics. They were common thugs recruited off the street, armed and trained to keep the other thugs in line. And they relished every opportunity to line-keep that they were given.

That he had not yet been line-kept himself suggested to Percival that someone higher up had plans for him. Now, that might mean tea and crumpets with the Celestial Governor, or it might mean a slow, torturous execution televised galaxy-wide on MTV3.

If given the option, Percival would remember to request the crumpets.

He was brought off the train at Sorrow Point Station in shackles. The fat, three-armed officer prodded Percival along with his confiscated umbrella.

Outside the train station the officers had a cruiser waiting. It was sleek and black with white tail fins and gull-wing doors, and it bobbed gently as it hovered over the pavement. The officers shoved Percival into the back seat, then climbed in up front.

The fat one switched on the sirens with his third arm, and in another moment they were off, dodging between the rush hour traffic that filled the intraplanetary tunnel on route to Planet's Core. They sped past rocketmen and cargo vans and hover-trikes and all-terrain Chevy SpiderMechs™.

The cruiser's quick flips and turns buffeted Percival from side-to-side in the back seat. The officer with the outsized gun occasionally glanced back from the wheel to lend a snigger. Percival knew that it would only make matters worse to complain, so he kept quiet and he kept his thoughts to himself.

His thoughts were these:

First, Percival considered whether he had made the wrong choice spending his final moments of freedom on an email to his mother. She was, after all, not expecting him till Sunday. And what would she do till then? Percival's silence would have saved her six futile days of worry.

And in the meantime, there were others who would question his absence far sooner. Yes, on reflection, he would have been far better served dictating a quick message to his employers at Henderson, Glorp & 11010, who were no doubt already speculating as to the circumstances behind his uncharacteristic tardiness.

Henderson, Glorp & 11010 was a small accounting firm located on the far side of Lunar Colony, where Percival served as a junior associate. The firm's business consisted primarily of keeping its rich clients rich via ever more creative misreadings of the tax code. One summer Percival set up four hundred and seventy bank accounts for a single client to skirt local disclosure regulations. Though such work bordered on the unscrupulous, Percival felt a certain loyalty to his employers who had hired him straight out of university. Mr. 11010 in particular had always been kind to him, to the extent that his programming allowed.

Percival was an excellent accountant, and he hoped that if he was tortured and executed on live television, his co-workers would miss his contributions to the bottom line.

Second, despite all efforts to the contrary, Percival found his thoughts drifting back to his mystery woman in the lavender cloak. Even now, after she had absconded with his hat, he could not help but look back fondly on their kiss. Though perhaps he was not best suited to judge, it had seemed genuine to him. And the look in her eyes, that desperation, did not seem an easy thing to fake.

But why had she approached him only to flee so quickly? If she'd needed his help, why hadn't she said more? Why take his hat?

He assumed that she was fleeing the same officers who had then accosted him. What had they said? "Surveillance confirms known associate." Was that it, then? Was the kiss simply a ploy to deflect the officers' attention? To throw another target in their path?

If so, it had worked, Percival noted ruefully. He was a prisoner on his way to face judgment, and she was free and likely halfway to Lunar Colony by now.

Still, if she was innocent... Percival pondered the possibility. If she was being pursued for crimes that she did not commit, perhaps a little gallant martyrdom was called for.

Third, what real danger was he in? He had not been "neutralized" by the Province Police. He was surely on his way to Central Precinct now, which would mean protocols and paperwork and enough kilometers of red tape to keep him safe till the truth came out.

After all, for every thug in uniform, there were a dozen bureaucrats back at Central Precinct who, if given the option, would rather *not* fill out another forty-page weapon discharge report in triple triplicate or attend another six-hour use of force hearing.

And Percival had even helped some of them with their taxes.

Fourth, his spirits finally eased, Percival began to construct an anecdote around the events of the day:

His brief encounter with the mystery woman. His near escape from Province Police. The bumpy ride to Central Precinct. The hours spent waiting in a lonely hallway as the officers process his release papers. The inevitable apologies from lifeforms-in-charge.

It was a story he would enjoy telling Mother at Sunday dinner.

Percival smiled. Everything was going to be fine.

"We're here," the owner of the outsized gun announced matter-of-factly.

Percival looked up and out the cruiser window, and his smile vanished. Wherever *here* was, it was plainly not Central Precinct, or even Planet's Core.

Where Percival had expected to see the great floating megastores of the planet's capital city, those garish, ad-smeared monuments to consumer greed backlit by the scarlet light of the GE MagmaStar™, he instead saw a shadowed expanse of fog-bottomed cavern lined with mile after mile of neon-lit, graffiti-tagged warehouses. Where he had expected to see commerce and hustle and commotion, he found only a chill hush.

"Yoo get out here," the fat one growled.

It seemed that Percival had missed a turn.

3 | *THE VOID FAERIE*

The officers dragged Percival out of the cruiser and into the fog. He did not protest. Torture it was then, but not to be televised. Percival did not know this place, but its purpose was plain enough to him.

This was the place that you don't come back from.

The officers led Percival through a narrow break between two of the buildings and into heavy shadow. They marched him back to the cavern wall where, after Percival's eyes adjusted to the low light, he could discern a steel door built into the stone and tagged by some vandal with the words "Vargoth Gor is not dead." Percival did not know who Gor was, but at that moment he envied him.

The owner of the outsized gun removed a gauntlet and pushed the flesh of his palm flat against the steel door. Percival heard an audible thunk from within, and the door slid open. Inside, he saw only black.

"Gimme yer hands," the fat one said, and Percival complied. The officer used a tool from his belt to unlock and remove Percival's shackles.

"Thank you," Percival muttered as he massaged his wrists, though he understood that the officer was less interested in Percival's welfare than with the safety of those shackles. They intended to leave him there, but the shackles were getting a reprieve.

"Inside," the owner of the outsized gun commanded.

Percival stepped into the black. Behind him the door slid shut. "Thunk," he whispered in time with the door's locking mechanism.

Percival closed his eyes and took a slow breath. He chose to think of this place not as a trap, but a puzzle. It was the Thursday Sudoku. Difficult, but not *very* difficult.

The air around him was cool, perhaps air-conditioned? He tapped his foot twice. The floor was hard, probably metal like the door.

He opened his eyes and turned back to the sealed door. He felt on either side for a light switch. No good. But he wasn't without light.

He reached into his jacket pocket and withdrew his Apple Watch. There was no signal, and the battery was nearly dead, but if he was lucky... Percival thought of loose change between his sofa cushions, and he smiled.

He thumbed through the menu and selected the pocket light feature. A weak beam issued from the face. It would have to do.

The wall and floor were clean and white. The ceiling was high, further than he could make out in the flickering watchlight.

He turned and ventured forward into the room, which proved to be large and essentially featureless. A dozen paces in, his eyes locked on a point in the distance. A blue glimmer in the endless dark. He approached with caution.

Nearly a hundred meters from the structure's entrance, someone had hung an old-fashioned birdcage. The cage was round and domed and made of brass, and it was covered with a hood of thin gauze that could not entirely conceal the blue glow that issued from within. With his free hand, Percival removed the hood.

Though it had wings of a sort, the creature inside the cage was no bird. It was a wretched thing, not quite a half meter tall, with a twisted spine and crooked legs that barely held its weight. Its "wings" were tattered flaps of flesh, hanging limp from its distended arms. Its face was monstrous, a great wrinkle where its eyes should be and a mouth full of thorns. The blue light shined like a sea of neon from beneath its flesh.

Percival was fascinated.

Up close and uncovered, the creature's glow was bright enough that Percival barely noticed when his own light source flickered out. He slipped the useless device back into his pocket absently without taking his eyes off the creature.

"What are you, then?" he asked, not anticipating an answer. He had a suspicion though. The thrill of life and possibility was slowly returning to him.

Percival leaned in closer to the creature and he whispered, "Percival Gynt is an accountant."

The creature did not react.

Percival leaned in still closer, and again he whispered. "Percival Gynt lives in apartment 4D at 1636 Traveler's Way in Slidetown Province on the exterior surface of a planet called Sanctuary-8."

No response.

Percival studied the sad creature. Did it even know he was there? This would be the test. He leaned as close as he possibly could to the cage, his lips nearly kissing the bars, and he whispered these seven words with solemn determination:

"Percival Gynt has never known true horror."

The creature quivered and let out a helpless wheeze. The sea beneath its skin began to churn, and the blue was swiftly blotted out by inky phosphorescent white. Percival shielded his eyes, for the light was even brighter than before. Even as he turned away, the image of the ghoulish creature was still burned into his retinas.

Thunk.

As Percival wiped the spots from his eyes, the door at the end of the room slid open. A small man entered, he of dwarven proportion, wearing a dapper suit and a sour expression. He stopped just inside the door to adjust the knot of his red power tie.

"You have a void faerie!" Percival shouted across to the small man with more than a hint of admiration.

Behind Percival the white light was fading. Behind the small man the entry door slid shut and locked.

"You know, I've never seen a void faerie before. They're a bit miraculous, aren't they?" Percival allowed his thoughts to unspool out loud in the encroaching dark. "Didn't think you could get one if you weren't a smuggler or a space pirate or a, um... I don't know... smuggler of space pirates?"

Darkness swallowed the small man as the bright white beneath the creature's skin gave way again to soft blue.

"How does the rhyme go?" Percival called into the dark. "Blue in the darkness, white when you lie, red if there's danger..."

Percival's voice trailed off. He feigned to forget the rhyme's conclusion. What sort of man was he up against? He wanted to hear the stranger say the words, to hear his tone. To glean his character. Somewhere, some distance away in the dark, the small man took his bait, finishing Percival's rhyme with grim flatness:

"...and black before you die."

Lovely, thought Percival. Bureaucrat.

The small man clapped his hands twice, and the room was full of light. From a hundred meters above, massive banks of florescent bulbs bathed the room, and finally Percival could see where he was.

He stood in the middle of an enormous underground hangar. The space was octagonal, and at every obtuse corner sat a hulking rusted machine, a relic of the planet's centuries-old tunneling fleet, each drill pointed upwards towards an open shaft.

Behind him all light was gone from the void faerie's skin, leaving it a sickly gray. It made a pathetic half-choking, half-hissing sound in Percival's general direction.

The small man approached, pulling a folded sheet of paper from his pocket as he walked. Percival slipped his hands into his trouser pockets and waited.

By the time the small man had reached Percival, he had unfolded the sheet of paper to a full A1. The small man tapped the page, then held it out at arm's length, widthwise, for Percival to see.

Percival was looking at the image of two Province Police forcing their way into an apartment in Slidetown. No, "looking" wasn't the word. He was watching them, watching them break down the door and storm inside with weapons drawn.

The flat has been upturned. Drawers have been emptied. Mirrors have been broken. Tables have been overturned. A couch has been torn apart.

The lead officer points to one door near the entrance, while he continues wordlessly towards the back. He climbs over the remains of the couch, surprisingly stealthy in his bulky red armor, and reaches a door ajar at the far end of the room.

He pushes the door open with the tip of his gun. It won't go all the way, so he slides in, gun ready.

He gasps. At the foot of the bed, blocking the door, lie the bloody remains of a human being, a woman. His head jerks up. He nearly fires. Parts of the husband lie in a pool of blood on the bed. Blood is smeared on the floor, on the walls, on the ceiling.

Across the room, the window is open wide. The officer steps cautiously over the dead and takes position by the side of the window. He counts backwards from three to calm himself. Then in one swift movement he steps out in front of the window, jerks his head and gun outside, looks down the fire escape, looks up, looks side-to-side.

The officer begins to climb outside as his partner calls out to him.

"Sir, we have a problem."

The officer climbs back in, glares at his partner.

The partner fumbles with his helmet, revealing the face of a frightened rookie. "I mean an even bigger problem." He holds up a picture in front of him, glass frame smashed:

A man and a woman and a hollow-eyed ten-year-old boy.

Percival recalled reading something about this in the morning download. He repeated the headline quietly to himself. "Man and Wife Slain, Child Abducted in Slidetown Province."

With his video complete, the small man lowered the paper.

"Did..." Percival knew what he had to ask, but he didn't want to say it, didn't even want the thought in his head. But, however reluctantly, he forced himself to form the words: "Did the woman on the platform have something to do with this?"

The small man frowned. "My name is Fred," he told Percival without answering his question. "I work for the government."

"Oh. Um." Percival thought for a moment. "Did the woman on the platform have something to do with this... Fred?"

This amused Fred mildly. He allowed the faintest twitch of a smile to half-form at the very corner of his mouth before suppressing it entirely.

"The woman on the platform was Millicent Lamb. At least, that's the name she gave to her employers. She arrived on Sanctuary-8 three weeks ago, looking for a position as an *au pair*. She had an excellent resume but passed over several enviable opportunities with wealthier families at Planet's Core to accept an opening with Martin and Joanne Cooper of 17 Fisherman's Court, Apartment 31S in Slidetown Province. The Coopers required someone to help them care for their son Kevin, a boy with special needs. Martin and Joanne Cooper, who are now dead. And Kevin, who is now missing."

"Millicent Lamb." Percival said the name to himself. It didn't sound right. "You said the boy had special needs? What sort of special needs?"

"That's classified."

Percival started to chuckle, then realized that Fred was not making a joke. "Oh, sorry."

Fred continued. "This woman who calls herself Millicent Lamb, have you ever met her before today?"

"No," Percival answered.

"And did she tell you anything about herself? About where she was headed?"

"No."

"About the boy?"

"No."

"Just stopped for a quick snog and went about her way, then?"

Percival chose to ignore Fred's cheap taunts, his whole line of questioning, and to instead test a theory of his own. "The boy in the photograph, he looked sick. Was he?"

Fred didn't answer.

"Province Police working hand-in-hand with mysterious government agents? Witness interrogations conducted in forgotten, out-of-the-way locales? Exotic supernatural creatures procured to ensure my veracity? He was more than sick, wasn't he?"

Fred didn't answer.

"I don't think you're trying to catch a killer, Agent Fred. I don't even think you're worried about the boy. You're just trying to cover up whatever it is you did to him."

Fred didn't answer.

"What did you have incubating inside of him? A new drug? A new curse or poison? What weapon did our government see fit to secret in that scared little boy?"

Fred struggled to maintain his cool. "You're off-base, Gynt," he spat. "This *isn't* about the boy."

Percival smirked. "You're lying."

And in that moment the white light of truth ignited behind Percival with all the fury of an angry god. The tiny man threw his arms up to shield his eyes. He fell to his knees, cowering from our silhouetted hero.

"All right. All right!" Fred confessed as the faelight began to fade. "We have a special interest in the boy, yes. That much is true. But it's not what you think. We were *protecting* him."

"Protecting him from what?" Percival demanded.

Fred shook his head as he pulled himself from the floor. "I don't know. It really *is* classified. But whatever the threat, it endangers us all."

"So what now?"

"We need your help," Fred muttered glumly.

Percival checked his ear for wax. "Sorry?"

"We need your help," Fred repeated with the same defeated tone.

Percival glanced behind him to the void faerie. Still gray. Maybe it was broken?

"We're running out of leads, we're running out of time, and we need your help, Percival Gynt. Will you help us?"

Percival grinned. "All you had to do was ask."

"Good. We don't have a great deal of time left to us, so I will attempt to be both thorough and succinct.

"There is a woman in my office who collects stories about you. Some tell of the wunderkind accountant, yes. But there are *other stories* of Percival Gynt. Of how you survived the Gynt Massacre. Of the crimes of Alexander Eeps, the Christmas Machine heist, the haunting of the Hartford, and more. In short, Mister Gynt, I know who you are. I know what you're capable of. And today I need your help."

Percival nodded for Fred to continue.

"The woman who called herself Millicent Lamb is gone. She departed Lunar Colony approximately twelve minutes ago, stowed away aboard a cargo freighter headed for the Lower Rim."

"If you know where she is, why don't you—?"

"She doesn't have the boy. She may not even know where the boy is, but she's our only lead. We could capture her, interrogate her, but we can't be sure that she'll cooperate.

"But there's you. She reached out to you. By design or by coincidence, the two of you seem to have made a connection. Perhaps we can use that connection to our advantage.

"All we want to do is to make sure that the boy is safe. Our intentions are essentially honorable." Fred eyed the void faerie, perhaps afraid he might be challenged on this point. He continued, "If you can convince the girl of that, of our good intentions, then we may still be able to save the boy."

"So you want me to chase this woman down for you, and—"

"Talk to her. Convince her to turn herself in. Convince her to help us. Convince her to do the right thing."

"And if I can't?" Percival asked.

"Then an innocent boy will die. And perhaps others."

Percival thought carefully. "I have terms."

"Terms?" Fred was not prepared for a negotiation. "What terms?"

"If I do this, I do this alone." Percival was firm. "You give me a fast ship, and you send me on my way. I'll intercept the freighter and talk to the girl, and depending on what she says, I'll decide what to do next.

If I sense for a moment that you're up to something underhanded, I'm done."

"No."

"Sorry?"

"No," Fred repeated. "No, we can't just give you a ship. We'll partner you with one of our men. He'll be there to assist, and to..."

"I don't need a minder," Percival insisted.

"Maybe yes, maybe no. But you're getting one nonetheless."

"Fine, but I need someone... subtle."

Fred smiled. "We have someone in mind."

"Someone subtle?"

Fred's smile broadened. He wisely refused to answer that question in the presence of the void faerie.

4 | PLANET'S CORE

Planet's Core was originally built as a refuge during the Last Great Intergalactic War. While the Nth Realm scoured the universe for Jews, telepaths, and other so-called "impure creations," a coalition of the enlightened joined together to construct secret sanctuary cities deep within a dozen uninhabited worlds. While war raged across the galaxies, millions of the hunted huddled together in these dark and quiet spaces, waiting for their fates to be decided.

Even after the War ended and the Nth Realm was momentarily defeated, many of the hunted were reluctant to return to their old homes where friends and neighbors had so readily turned against them to side with the Realm. Instead, they chose to build new communities within these sanctuary worlds. These were artists and artisans and intellectuals with high-minded goals. They had just survived an unprecedented galaxies-wide genocide, and in the wake of incalculable horror, they were desperate to believe that Utopia too was possible.

And for one too brief moment, it was. They lived communally, creating great works of art and science and wizardry and sharing all the fruits of their labor with their brethren. They lived without malice or greed.

But then the bankers came. Then came gentrification. Then came corporations and property taxes and thirty millisecond thought-pushed adverts that make you feel hollow and worthless if you don't drink the right beer or drive the right car or eat the right double cheeseburger with extra bacon.

One by one, then ten by ten, then by the hundreds and the thousands and the millions, the original refugees were pushed out of Planet's Core and the other cities like it in favor of wealthy off-world investors.

Their spirits broken, the twice-dispossessed settled slums like Slidetown and Sorrow Point, where endemic poverty begat crime and bigotry and all the other social ills that the survivors had long hoped they'd left behind.

Planet's Core, by contrast, now has three Walmarts.

Percival sat at a small round table in the corner of the cafe, sipping a lactose-free Grande Cinnamon Dolce Frappuccino while his Apple Watch charged from the wall socket. Outside, a video billboard floated past playing an advertisement for Viagra-cut-with-Ecstasy:

"Ask your doctor if Viagra-cut-with-Ecstasy is right for you."

Time to go. Fred had told Percival to wait for him here in this Starbucks, but that was nearly an hour ago, and Percival had only ever been able to stand Planet's Core in the briefest of doses.

When the time came, Percival was confident that Fred could track him down no matter how far he strayed. And so he stood, unplugged and pocketed his watch, and took a final swig to finish off his Frappuccino.

As Percival lowered the cup from his lips, a curious thing caught his eye, a bit of scratchiti carved into the table ringed by Frappuccino perspiration.

As before: "Vargoth Gor is not dead."

Though the words were no clearer this second time, Percival was certain that their return was no coincidence.

"All right," he said out loud. "I'm willing to concede the point. But who's Gor?"

The crude scratches stubbornly refused to answer.

"P. Gynt? Is that you?"

Percival looked up to see a man he did not recognize, a

businessman perhaps, blond, about his age, in a slate gray suit. The stranger smiled and clasped Percival's shoulders gregariously.

"I'm sorry—?"

"Clay Watkins. From University! We were lab partners once. How have you been doing? I heard that you'd been living off-grid? Are you working in this complex? My firm is just down the way. Oh my, but you seem to have snagged your jacket. What have you been doing with yourself?"

Percival nodded his head slowly and allowed a weak grin. "Absolutely," he replied.

Though Percival did not recall a "Clay from University," he could not discount his existence either. Over the years, Percival had secured abundant headspace for facts and figures by purging the memory of similar oafs and bombasts.

"Well, that's good to hear," Clay carried on. "We must have dinner one of these days. Have you met my wife?"

Percival shook his head.

"Here's my business card." Clay pulled a card from his inside pocket and flicked it to make it play: Clay on electric guitar while the name of his firm scrolled behind him. "Quite good, don't you think? It says we're edgy, but compassionate. Here, take one, I've got thousands."

Before Percival could protest, Clay slipped the card into his breast pocket behind his handkerchief. Percival frowned at this breach in etiquette and turned to exit.

"That's the Percival I know!" Clay called after him. "Always good for a stomp!"

Outside, Percival took a long breath. The Core's bleached, reprocessed air burned the inside of his throat. Still better than being trapped in a Starbucks with Clay from University, Percival thought.

It was just then that the weighted end of a rope ladder came smacking into the side of Percival's head. He recoiled, clutched his ear, and let out a little "augh" sound. But when he looked up, he smiled.

The craft from which the rope ladder had descended was beautiful, an orb of riveted brass, perhaps five meters across, with a stained-glass eye and luminous branching wings that perfectly refracted the scarlet light of the city's MagmaStar.

From the open hatch, Fred called, "We don't have all day, Gynt!"

Percival climbed up the ladder into the ship's cramped hold.

"This isn't government issue," Percival noted as he helped Fred pull the ladder back inside.

"No, no. The Wisp here was seized from a clan of Grimsouls during a recent drug trafficking sting." Fred noted Percival's sudden frown and added, "But don't worry. They're all dead." He paused, then corrected himself. "Dead again, I mean. You don't have to worry about them coming back for their property."

"Drug smugglers. Of course. I suppose that's where the void faerie came from, then?"

"Oh. No. The void faerie I bought at market on Sanctuary-1," Fred explained. "Found a merchant there who breeds them."

"Hmm. Don't suppose you have a spare I could take with me? As long as you have a source..."

"Ha. Not a chance. A single one of those creatures is worth more than my salary. Had to empty my men's pensions just to afford mine. You want one, you can go and buy your own."

"Right then," said Percival, allowing the matter to drop, "I suppose it's time to meet the partner?"

Fred pointed up a shaft in the ceiling. "Up there. He's waiting for you."

"You're not coming?"

"This is my stop," Fred replied.

Percival looked down through the open hatch to see that they were now drifting low over the capitol building. So graceful was the ship, Percival hadn't realized they'd been moving.

Fred shook Percival's hand, offered a stiff-lipped "Godspeed, Mister Gynt," then took a short hop through the hatch to the roof below.

As the ship rose, Percival watched Fred adjust the knot of his red power tie and disappear through a door into the capitol.

Percival closed the hatch and headed up.

The shaft opened up into the Wisp's main compartment, a claustrophobic box of lights and switches about two meters in diameter.

There were two seats bolted into the flooring. Of these, one was already occupied. Though his back was turned, Percival could immediately discern something familiar about the occupant.

"Hullo," Percival offered.

His partner turned, rising from his chair. An alien. Percival didn't recognize his species. He was rotund but imposing in his bearing with rough brownish-green skin, saucer-wide eyes, and a froggy-mouth stretched across his overlarge head. A mechanical third arm protruded from his sloppy gut.

"Oh. It's you."

The officer was dressed casually with a black T-shirt pulled tight over his chest, the word "COP" spelled out in big white letters that danced for emphasis.

"Um," the officer replied.

"Yes, I don't quite know what to say either," Percival commiserated.

"Um," the officer repeated.

"Quite awkward, yes."

The officer froggy-frowned, then bent down to one side, and stood up again holding Percival's umbrella out in front of him. "Name's Um. Officer Um. Sanctuary-8 Elite Corps."

"Ah." Percival accepted his umbrella with a polite nod. "Yes, of course. And I assume you know who I am by now."

Um returned to his seat. "I been briefed."

"Wonderful." Percival took a seat in the chair next to Um's. "I just want to impress upon you that this is a very delicate operation, Officer... Um."

Um pulled a lever, and the craft began to accelerate towards an open shaft in the Core wall.

"When we're in the field, it's imperative that you follow my lead," Percival added as the Wisp picked up speed. "Hang back, let me do the talking and, above all..." Percival's teeth rattled as the Wisp emerged from Sanctuary-8 at ten times the speed of sound. "...don't shoot anyone."

Um smiled a broad froggy-grin. "I can try."

Gravity hit Percival like a wall as the Wisp broke atmosphere. Um turned the dial for superlight, and they were gone.

5 | THE LONELY MUTT

Officer Um proved poor company. He did not speak again for the duration of their flight, nor did he appear overly troubled to listen. Indeed, despite all his best efforts, Percival Gynt arguably knew less about his new partner on arrival at their destination than he did prior to their departure from Sanctuary-8.

Despite requests, Um showed no interest in identifying his species, no interest in relating the story of how he acquired his mechanical third arm, nor the slightest interest in telling Percival where he bought his animated "COP" T-shirt, though Percival suspected either Old Navy or the Iblis-Yzjzyax Confederacy.

But, for the record: Indulian. From the cybersmith of Outer Perexia. Old Navy.

Both parties were genuinely relieved when the Wisp touched down on the surface of refueling asteroid AA31-Esson-B. The asteroid was perhaps a quarter kilometer wide and surrounded by hundreds of parked, docked, and tethered ships. A simple weather charm provided atmosphere. Artificial gravity assigned a top to the asteroid on which was built a fueling station, a gift shop, and a Classic McDonald's diner.

The queue for the McDonald's single occupancy loos extended out the front door and twice around the asteroid.

On descent, Percival noticed another piece of Vargoth Gor graffiti scrawled across the diner roof. This he accepted without question or comment.

"Do you know the name of the freighter we're looking for?" Percival asked as he climbed out of the hatch.

"The Lonely Mutt," Um grunted as he followed. "Y'know ya got a tear in yer jacket, right?"

"Six hours of silence, and that's your conversation starter?"

"Noticed it when we was leavin' orbit. Figured if I brought it up then, yoo'd take it as an invite ta yack the whole way."

Percival frowned as he regarded his jacket sleeve. He had forgotten. One of the officers had grazed him as he'd dived for safety in the track well back at Slidetown Station. The jacket was salvageable, maybe, but hardly presentable.

Percival handed his umbrella over to Um, pulled off his jacket, emptied out the pockets, and stuffed the contents into his waistcoat and trousers.

Um cleared his throat for effect.

"All right, all right." Percival bunched up his jacket and dropped it into a nearby waste recycling unit.

First the hat. Then the jacket. It was like playing strip poker with the universe. And the universe was winning.

Percival snatched back his umbrella.

"Now then," he inquired. "Care for a Big Mac?"

Um shoved his way through the loo queue and into the diner, ion cannon in hand, and he shouted as loudly as he could, "WHICH A YOO LOSERS IS CAP'N A THE LONELY MUTT?"

A hundred bystanders looked up from their extra value meals in abject terror. A few edged towards the queue.

"S'okay!" he added with a froggy-smirk. "I'm a cop, see." He tapped his T-shirt, and the letters danced for emphasis.

From outside Percival could hear screams. He ignored them. Instead, he continued circling the asteroid. Freighters are big. Hard to miss. Just stay alert and...

A dozen meters up and right in front of the gift shop, tethered to a titanium docking post by a centimeter-thick plasma tractor-anchor, hung The Lonely Mutt. It was large and bulky and battered and, conveniently for Percival, emblazoned with the words "THE," "LONELY," and "MUTT" in big, bolted-on letters.

Two Grimsoul bounty hunters, both armed with really sharp knives, stood guard at the post.

Percival approached. "Excuse me," he asked, "but are the two of you by any chance guarding the Lonely Mutt?"

The Grimsouls looked at each other and seemed by some silent exchange to agree to remain silent.

"I was sent by the authorities. For the..." And here Percival shifted into his ultra-subtle voice. "For the package." He added a wink for good measure.

Again the Grimsouls regarded each other, but this time the conclusion of their silent exchange was altogether different. The Grimsoul to Percival's left sprung forward with his really sharp knife. Percival dropped onto his back to dodge the blow, then kicked up hard into the Grimsoul's gut with both feet, knocking him backwards.

As Percival lay prone, the second Grimsoul crouched and dove for him. Percival rolled to his side and opened up his umbrella to block a knife thrust. Percival rose as the Grimsouls recovered.

Percival wiped the perspiration from his forehead. "How about this?" he suggested. "You drop your knives, and I drop my umbrella..."

The Grimsouls snarled and waved their blades.

"...then if it rains, we'll be even."

Next, both Grimsouls came at him in a coordinated strike, one high from the left, the other low from the right. Obvious. Percival allowed himself a half-step back, then flipped his hold on the umbrella, hooked the arm of the airborne Grimsoul and sent him slamming down on top of his partner.

Percival closed his umbrella and took another step back as the Grimsouls pulled themselves up again. It was at this moment that Percival realized he had an audience. A small crowd had gathered to watch the fight, several recording the event on their Apple Watches.

"If you're trying to do something secret," Percival told the

Grimsouls, "that's done. This'll be all over YouTube in a few minutes. Better run along and tell your boss, before he reads about it on the blogs."

The Grimsouls seemed to agree, stepped back, grabbed the tractor-anchor and began running up it to the ship. Began but did not finish, because of the two kill shots, one through the chest of each, that sent them falling back down to the ground with a crunch, crunch.

The crowd of onlookers parted for Um, ion cannon smoking, a big froggy-smile on his face.

"Don't worry," Percival reassured the bystanders. "His shirt says he's a cop."

In the original patent application submitted by GlaxoSmithKline, back before any of the focus-grouping or user-testing was done, the remorseless killing machines that we now know as Grimsouls were called "MegaMurder Corpisoids." In fact, GSK was so excited by the "MegaMurder Corpisoids" brand that they applied for an intergalactic trademark on the name, not just in the category of necromantically-reanimated, bio-genetically-reengineered, cybernetically-augmented soldiers-of-fortune, but also in the categories of comic books, wall posters, breakfast cereals, puffy stickers, and grade-B7 nerve toxins.

You can perhaps imagine the GSK shareholders' disappointment on discovering that they'd been beaten to the IP punch by their rivals at Pfizer, who had not four days earlier registered a competing trademark for their new line of MegaMurder Porpisoids, the universe's first necromantically-reanimated, bio-genetically-reengineered, cybernetically-augmented porpoises-of-fortune.

But it was GSK that had the last laugh. After the MegaMurder Porpisoids ate the Pfizer board of directors, their sales plummeted, and the rebranded Grimsouls went on to become the most successful necromantically-reanimated, bio-genetically-reengineered, cybernetically-augmented anythings-of-fortune of all time.

This wasn't the first time that Tarot had felt the cold muzzle of a gun pressed up against her temple. Her own father once held her hostage on intergalactic television, though that was as part of a magic trick. But here the rules weren't so very different: stay quiet, stay calm, and wait for your moment.

Sadly, that moment would come too late for ship's captain Jerry Klieg. Jerry was a kind-hearted man, to the extent that he had not jettisoned Tarot out of his airlock when he could have, the moment he'd found her stowed away on his ship. And now he was an open-hearted man as well, to the extent that there was now a gaping hole in his chest, carved out with a Grimsoul's blade. Jerry was dead on the floor of his own cargo bay, a corpse between crates of funions and cheese puffs.

The Grimsouls felt no remorse, the remorse part of their brains having been extracted back at the factory to make room for dual-processing, laser-directed targeting computers.

There were three of them there, three Grimsouls assembled in the cargo bay. The first, who we can call Mister One, was hunched over Tarot, gun to her temple, growling through dead teeth. The second, Mister Two, was crouched atop a funions crate, licking his blade clean. The third, Mister Five, stood motionless before Tarot, head limp, jaw slack, brain switched off, with an Apple Watch hanging by a cheap lanyard from his neck.

Through the watch came a synthesized voice designed to mimic 20th Century Earthman James Earl Jones.

"Where is the child?" it demanded.

Tarot, curled on her side, eyes closed, lavender cloak wrapped tight around her, declined to answer. Wait for your moment, she repeated to herself. Wait for your moment.

"I do not toy, woman, and I do not let sentiment cloud my judgment. Tell me where the child is, or I shall leave you to my agents for their amusement."

Wait for it...

"And you know what the Grimsouls will do with you. They so love their playthings."

Wait for it...

"They love them to pieces."

Wait...

With a loud whirr, the inner airlock doors spun open, and Percival Gynt stepped out into the cargo bay, umbrella open like a shield. Behind him Officer Um primed his ion cannon.

"Um..." Percival allowed his voice to trail off as he assessed the situation.

"Gynt?"

"No, no." Percival snuck a look back at his partner. "I was just working out what to say."

Um frowned and took aim.

From across the cargo bay, the synthesized voice of James Earl Jones cried out, "Rotate 270 degrees!" and Mister Five, brain still disengaged, shuffled mechanically to face our hero.

"Who are you?" barked James Earl Jones.

"My name is Percival Gynt, certified public accountant, and this is Um..."

"Spit it out!"

"...and I've come for my hat."

On the cold metal floor, concealed within the folds of her lavender cloak, Tarot clutched a familiar bowler tight to her chest, and she smiled.

Percival advanced towards the Grimsouls with Um close behind, ion cannon at the ready. Mister Two, high atop his funion crate, took aim with his knife. Mister One grabbed Tarot by the hair and pulled her half to her feet, gun pressed hard against her cheek.

From Mister Five's chest, James Earl Jones chose his words carefully. "You're here for... your... hat?"

Percival nodded as he approached Mister Five. "I love that hat. My mum gave it to me." He folded his umbrella closed.

"Your... mum?"

Percival leaned down to stare into the watch display. On the screen it read "CALL FROM 0001."

Percival turned his head back to Um. "Seems to be having trouble forming sentences. I think it might be broken."

"I... am not... broken," James Earl Jones fumed.

"You know, on second thought, I'll take the girl too. Dead or alive, I think." Percival turned his back on the Grimsouls and winked. "Um, if the Grimsouls haven't left in thirty seconds, shoot the girl."

Tarot bit her lip. It was a trick, surely.

"No! No! *We* will kill her!" James Earl Jones insisted. "We will torture and kill her till she gives us what we want."

Percival walked back towards Um, umbrella over his shoulder. "Well, that's the point, really. You're not going to kill her if you need information from her. And you're not going to get information from her if we kill her either."

"We will kill her, and you, and then we will kill your families!"

Percival half-smiled. "You really don't know who you're dealing with, do you? Ten seconds."

Mister One and Mister Two looked to Mister Five and the watch for commands. "There will be no refuge for you anywhere in this galaxy, Mister Gynt! For you or your froggy friend!"

"Five." Percival turned back towards the Grimsouls. "Four."

"By the Giant's Eyes," James Earl Jones grumbled. "Activate Time Stop."

The three Grimsouls vanished from the cargo bay, leaving poor Tarot to fall backwards gracelessly onto her bum. Percival rushed to give her a hand up, while Um turned to a control panel by the airlock door and began typing.

"You weren't really going to shoot me, were you?" Tarot asked as Percival pulled her to her feet. She flashed a tentative, conspiratorial smile.

Percival grinned. "Of course not."

"Yeah," Um corrected from the control panel. "Pow, pow."

"No," Percival struggled to reassure Tarot. "Um's kidding."

"Nope," Um insisted, one froggy eye raised from his work. "Not kiddin'. Pow-pa-pow-pow."

Percival let his umbrella clatter to the floor and turned back to Um frustratedly. "BUT... I... *WINKED.*"

Um nodded. "Yeah. Yoo winked. As in, 'I'm one a them cheeky types that's capable a anything.'"

"For the love of the All-Mother, that is the absolute opposite of what winking means! What planet are you from that you can't understand the meaning of a simple wink???"

Um frowned. He did not enjoy being yelled at, not by anyone, and most assuredly not by this scrawny, tawny, squishy thing. But he remembered his orders, so he swallowed his pride and answered Percival as honestly and as succinctly as possible:

"Indulia."

Percival arched an eyebrow and began to string together all the syllables necessary to respond "Induliwhatnow?" But it was then that he saw him, poor Captain Klieg, eyes wide, dead and forgotten between the crates.

"Oh."

"He seemed like a nice man," Tarot offered. "He told me a bit about his wife Karen. She's part werewolf."

"We should..." Percival's voice trailed off. He looked to Um. "What can we do?"

Um turned away from the control panel. "I alerted system authorities. They'll clean up. We gotta get back ta Sanctuary-8 with the girl."

"Tarot," she corrected.

Um blinked.

"That's my name. I'm Tarot. Like the cards."

The alien began again. "We gotta get back ta Sanctuary-8 with Tarot."

Tarot shook her head. "I can't go back. Not yet."

Um frowned at Percival. "We gotta get back ta Sanctuary-8. That's the job."

Percival bent down over Captain Klieg and slid his eyes shut. "Part werewolf?" he asked as he studied the man's blood drained face.

"Just the wife. And just—" Tarot held her thumb and forefinger a centimeter apart. "Just a little part."

Percival stood. He'd made his decision.

"Miss Tarot-like-the-cards, would you allow me to buy you a milkshake?"

6 | *THE CONSPIRACY OF DAYS*

Tarot pushed Percival's bowler back to him across the tiny table. "I'm sorry for nicking your hat, Mister Gynt," she told him, barely managing a straight face. "I didn't know it was from your mum."

"Actually..." Percival began, admitting a smirk. He picked up the hat, flipped it around, dusted it off, and handed it back to her. "Actually, why don't you hold onto it for a bit? I think it looks better on you, to be honest."

Tarot blushed as she pulled the hat on. She felt a bit foolish, but it was true. And Percival noticed for the first time the curious stone that hung from her neck and the golden fire that seemed to dance from within.

"Where did you—?"

A waitress-bot set down two strawberry milkshakes between them. Tarot raised the bendy straw to her lips and drank quickly.

Percival took a moment to appreciate the woman before him in all her his-hat-wearing, strawberry-shake-slurping, mysterious-stone-burning wonder. And he frowned.

"I'm going to misjudge you," he said plainly. "I want to apologize for that while I can."

As she lowered the straw from her lips, Percival could see it again. The fear.

"I need to know what's happening if I'm going to help you, Tarot. I need to know everything. Absolutely everything."

She nodded. "There's a lot to explain."

"Perhaps you could start by telling me who Vargoth Gor is, and why everyone seems so certain he's not dead."

Tarot grinned. "You've seen it already? That's interesting. The graffiti, it's a sort of a taunt meant for Gor's enemies. *Her* enemies. She cast a spell a number of years back, planted the meme into the minds of vandals on a thousand inhabited worlds, and then enchanted the words so that only her enemies could see or hear them. Now that—"

"Hold on a moment. *Only her enemies?* I've never even heard of this Gor person."

"It doesn't matter, Mister Gynt. If you can read those words, that means Vargoth Gor has heard of you."

"Oh."

"Do you remember the magician Illuminari?"

"The entertainer? The one who just died? With the great long beard and the pointy hat?"

"The same. Illuminari was my father. But—"

"Oh, I'm sorry."

"But more important than who he was to me, is who he was to the rest of you. You see, while all of you were shopping at Walmart and watching the telly, Illuminari was the man who saved the entire universe from utter annihilation.

"The thing about magicians is that they always keep their greatest secrets to themselves. It's only ever after a magician dies that the truth begins to come out. And that's what's happening now. That's what's happened with the child on Sanctuary-8 and, in a way, that's what's happened with Vargoth Gor. The universe is about to discover Illuminari's greatest magic trick was the trick they never saw.

"He called it *The Conspiracy of Days.*

"Vargoth Gor was an enemy of my father's, many centuries back, born on a world that no longer exists. That's why you've never heard of her. She was a rival magician, but unlike my father, she wasn't content with the adoration of the crowd. She demanded their absolute devotion. Their obedience. My father and Gor clashed many times over many years, matching magic against magic, up until the day that father tricked Gor into the singularity at the heart of a raging MagmaStar.

"And there Gor stayed, inside the MagmaStar, twisted inward on herself in unimaginable agony, neither alive nor dead, for many years."

"Vargoth Gor is not dead," Percival repeated to himself.

"Exactly. Not alive, but *definitely* not dead, for years and years and years.

"Then, eleven years ago, a threat emerged more terrible than even Gor could conceive. A thing awoke in the dark of space, an ancient mechanical thing. A thing as old and terrible as the universe itself.

"My father called it the Engine of Armageddon. Claimed that it was built by God Himself at the beginning of time. That it was placed into the universe for just one purpose. To awaken at the appointed hour and end us all. To open its unblinking eye on the whole of creation, and to uncreate it.

"You see, a starship has missiles and cannons and smart bombs, but those weapons are like pebbles to the Engine. The Engine would simply travel from system to system, gaze upon a world, and in its sight that world would cease to be."

Percival shook his head. "You're talking in past tense, as if this has already happened. Surely, we would have heard if the universe was ending. If whole planets were being destroyed..."

"That's just it. The Engine doesn't simply destroy worlds. It reaches backwards through time and gobbles up history itself. Eleven years ago, the Engine of Armageddon awoke and devoured a third of the universe, and no one remembers because none of it ever happened."

"That's..." Like a good accountant, Percival ran the numbers. "That's what? Fifteen, maybe sixteen thousand inhabited worlds. There would have been casualties in the trillions."

Tarot nodded. "A million million dead, and no one to mourn them."

"But the rest of us are still alive. Your father stopped this thing? Destroyed it somehow?"

"Stopped, yes, but never destroyed. The Engine is indestructible.

That's what *Conspiracy of Days* means. It's the trick that Illuminari played on God Himself. The universe was meant to end eleven years ago, Mister Gynt. Every day since has been my father's gift to us. But the end is still inevitable. All my father did is delay it for a time."

"Delay how?"

"It was the greatest piece of magic my father ever worked. And he couldn't have done it alone. He had his beloved assistant Lora at his side and his young apprentice Mouse. And—"

"And he freed Gor from the MagmaStar."

"Yes. The four of them together devised a plan to stop the Engine. You see, the Engine itself is just a machine. Indestructible, yes, but ultimately lifeless. But within the Engine there resides a presence, an animating spirit that my father called the Rider. The Rider is pure, unyielding evil. But pluck the Rider from the Engine, and the machine becomes inert.

"As it turns out, the ritual to separate the Rider from the Engine is fairly simple. The real problem was, once you extract the Rider, what do you do with it? How do you contain pure evil?"

"How *do* you contain pure evil?"

"In a prison of innocence. Illuminari crafted a child, absolutely pure of heart, and he bound the Rider deep within it. And then he hid the Engine, and he hid the Rider."

"Kevin Cooper..."

"Yes. That's what they're calling it this year. The child doesn't age, so they had to move it every so often, relocate it from family to family. My father's illusions helped to conceal its location and its true identity, but after he died, those illusions started breaking down."

"You came to Sanctuary-8..."

"Because I knew the child wasn't safe anymore. I wanted to be there to protect him."

"But you couldn't."

"They have the child. They only need the Engine now."

"They? They who? Are we talking about Vargoth Gor? The Grimsouls?"

"I wasn't there when they came for the child. I was coming back from the market, a bag of groceries in each arm. I saw shadows moving in the window and a glimpse of something. A cyborg maybe, half made of flesh and half of gold. And..."

"And?"

"And upon his chest, a symbol. The broken cross."

"Space Nazis?"

"I don't think they call themselves that."

"Are you sure? I think I read that on *The Internet.*"

Tarot shrugged. "Well, whatever you want to call them. They were loyalists to the old N^{th} Realm, perhaps foolish enough to believe that they can use the Engine as a weapon. Or perhaps they've decided the universe isn't worth purifying. Whatever their motive, we have to find them and stop them."

"But we don't know where they are, do we? They could be anywhere in the entire universe by now."

"We may not know where they are, but we know where they're headed. They'll be after the Engine next. If we can get to the Engine before they do, maybe we can stop them."

"Do you have any idea where the Engine is?"

Tarot smiled and sucked down the last of her milkshake. "Not a guess. You?"

7 | EIGHTY-TWO PERCENT

Magician's Station was in the precise middle of nowhere. This is no hyperbole, but rather a literal statement of fact. Or, if you can wrap your head around the concept, a literal statement of non-literal fact.

Thanks to a clever bit of spellwork performed by the late Illuminari, the only way to reach Magician's Station by starship was to navigate a steady course that led you absolutely nowhere while simultaneously avoiding everyone and everything in the entire universe. And even if Tarot was correct that the universe was now a third smaller than it had been eleven years ago, that was still an awful lot of universe to avoid.

Um was not thrilled about this detour, even after Percival explained that a location that is nowhere is by definition not-not on the way back to Sanctuary-8.

Magician's Station was, as Tarot explained it, her father's home in his final years, the ultimate hermit's retreat. And if there was a clue to be found anywhere in the universe as to the location of the Engine of Armageddon, it would surely be here.

The station itself was a great rusted cube, at least a kilometer to a side, inscribed with ancient runes, slowly turning within a pair of fast-spinning rings of blue-white fire.

Percival held up his watch to the window glass as the Wisp drew into orbit. No signal. And apparently it was now Tuesday.

Um stared into the rings of fire and growled, "So what's the trick, then? Password? Secret entrance?"

He looked across to Tarot who had taken Percival's seat at the controls. "That'd be nice, wouldn't it?" she mused.

"You tellin' me I need ta fly this crate straight through them things?"

"Quick as you can, if you please. Those rings will slice through this ship like a knife through jam."

"Gynt?"

Percival smirked. "Don't look to me as the voice of reason. If the lady says we fly through, we fly through."

Um grumbled as he began the calculations for entry.

Percival pocketed his watch and leaned down next to Tarot. "All right, but seriously," he whispered, "How are we really getting through?"

"I wasn't kidding. We need to fly in."

"Oh, come on. You're telling me that your father, greatest magician in the history of magicians, etcetera, dodged through flaming rings on his way back from the pub every night?"

"Feels about right for him. But no. I'd assume he had a teleportation charm worked out for coming home from the pub. You don't happen to have a teleport in your back pocket, do you?"

"Don't be silly." Percival reached into his back pocket with a grin, pulled out his watch, and dangled it by the fob in front of her. "God hates teleportation."

"This is insane!" Tarot protested as Percival screwed on his spacesuit helmet.

"No, no," Percival corrected, holding down the vocal transmit button on his suit. "Your plan was insane. My plan to launch myself out the airlock through two gyroscopic flaming rings as I freeze all motion in the universe for six seconds, allowing me to slip through safely to the surface of the cube is just good sense."

Tarot fumed, "Even assuming that you could clear the rings in six seconds, a prospect which I find deeply mathematically suspect, you'd still need to find a way into the cube, and you'd still need to figure out how to shut off the flaming rings so that we can follow you in. Now how do you propose to do that?"

"Um..." Percival thought for a moment, finger on his vocal transmit button. "Brilliantly?"

Tarot didn't smile, not even a little, which was a challenge, because she dearly wanted to. Instead she put out an open palm and with a commanding tone she ordered, "Give me the watch."

"What?"

"He was my father. It was his station. His magic. Once we're past those rings, I have the best chance of figuring out how to open it up and get the rest of you in.

"So. Give. Me. The. Watch."

Percival shook his head. "I'm not going to let you—"

"Oy! If the two a yoos is done flirtin'..." Um looked up from the navigation computer with froggy-disdain. "I'm 82% sure I can fly us through them hoops."

Percival could feel the fight pour out of him like water from an overturned bucket. He dropped his watch into Tarot's hand.

Tarot closed her fingers around the face and looked up to Percival. "Thank you," she whispered.

That was enough.

Percival wrestled with his helmet, finally pulling it off on the third try. He flung it to the ground, pulled Tarot into his arms, and kissed her as if nothing and no one else had ever mattered to him.

Um snorted. "Eighty-two's great odds. Nobody's kissin' me..."

He was rightly ignored by both parties.

Um ran through the math again as Percival triple-checked to make sure that Tarot's spacesuit was secure.

"All right. Computer says when we jettison ya from the airlock, yoo'll be travelin' roughly one hundred thousandth the speed a light, so—"

Percival fake coughed.

"About thirty meters per second. We're a half-kilometer from the hoops' outer edge now, so that gives ya sixteen seconds or so before ya burn ta crisps."

More fake cough.

"We measure the width a the hoops ta be an average one hundred fourteen meters in diameter, which means it'll take ya just under four seconds ta pass through—"

Tarot tapped the vocal transmit button. "I'm sorry, did you say *average?*"

Um nodded. "Ya cross any point where they're wider 'n one hundred fourteen meters, yoo'll need just over four seconds."

"So, you're saying that I need to activate the watch within thirty meters of the giant mystic rings of fiery death."

"Yoo'd be safer if ya waited till yoo was under ten."

"Count down from fifteen and then stop time. Check."

Percival placed a hand on Tarot's shoulder. "We'll patch your vocal transmit though to the Wisp. If you need us to pull you out, we'll pull you out."

Tarot nodded. The two men climbed back up into the cockpit and took their seats at the controls. Um eased the ship over onto its backside, angling the airlock like a gun towards the cube.

"Can't believe yer lettin' us shoot yer girlfriend through spinnin' hoops a fire," Um guffawed.

"It seems that you were correct about me, Officer Um." Percival closed his eyes and took a deep breath. "I'm one a them cheeky types that's capable a anything."

The whole ship shook as Um opened the airlock, rocketing Tarot into the void.

"Can you hear us?" Percival asked through the shipboard radio.

A half second of static preceded Tarot's response: "Do you want to know why I took your hat?"

"I honestly don't," Percival answered. "Focus on the rings." Tarot was a drifting speck on the ship's monitors.

"I cast a spell on it."

"You can tell me later. Just—"

"I was so scared."

"I know you were."

"But I'm not now. The spell—"

"Three seconds, Tarot."

"It was an 'I'm not alone' charm."

With those words, Tarot vanished into the fire. Percival's eyes darted from monitor to monitor, searching for some sign of life. But she was gone.

Um frowned. "This is basically the opposite a my orders, by the by. Instead a returnin' the lady ta Sanctuary-8, we jettisoned her inta space ta be roasted alive. Best case, we aided and abetted her escape."

Percival only half heard Um. He was still staring at the monitor output, still hoping that they might reestablish contact. "You really think she might have escaped?" he muttered. To Percival, this would have come as fantastic news.

"Nah," Um replied flatly as he stood. "I'm gonna take a leak. Let's give it five. Then if we haven't heard nothin', we can try flyin' in after her."

Um climbed down to the hold, leaving Percival alone in the cockpit. Should have just gone with the 82% odds, Percival thought. Eighty-two's not bad.

Percival spoke into the radio: "Tarot?"

Static.

"Tarot, I want you to know that I know what it's like to be alone. When I was a boy, I lost everything. My friends. My family. Even people I didn't like very well. It's amazing how much you miss the people you don't like very well, once they've gone.

"They were all killed. Were all butchered, really. And everything after that, for a long time, seemed like a dream. Fragmented. Sort of floaty. And every pleasure, every joy that I felt, felt fleeting. Impermanent. Like it could and would be stripped from me in an instant, and there was nothing I could do to stop it.

"Maybe that's why I grew to like numbers so much. Math is fixed.

Forever. The tax code has its own impersonal logic. It can surprise you, but it can't betray you."

Percival took a breath. He didn't cry, though he knew crying might make him feel better.

"I know what it's like to lose a father. How everything must seem upside down and backwards and inside out right now. But if you can promise me that you're alive, I can promise to be your tax code. I can promise I won't betray you."

Static.

Percival stood and reached into his pockets for his handkerchief.

And the rings of fire extinguished.

From the radio: "My tax code? Really, Gynt?"

Percival smiled, calling down to the hold, "Good news, Um! Our 82% chance just shot up to one hundred!"

8 | *POINT OF INGRESS*

It should be made clear that there were many moments over the course of this adventure that Tarot experienced doubt. Doubt in herself, doubt in her own resolve, and most acutely, doubt in the rightness and efficacy of her ultimate mission. One such moment came on a Tuesday in the early hours as she found herself falling sideways through space at the precipitous rate of 32.41 meters per second, threading between two enormous storms of blue-white fire while all motion drained from the universe save her own. For six seconds, all that mattered in the universe was her, falling.

And it was then, in that moment, that Tarot considered the very real possibility that she had made a horrible, horrible, irrevocable, horrible mistake.

And then that moment ended. Time resumed, and Tarot came crashing down into her father's station, first headlong, then shoulderlong, then backlong into the deep, rusted-out crater of a Deathward rune. She let out a light "augh" noise meant just for her, and she picked herself up.

She allowed her white-knuckled grip on Percival's watch to loosen slightly. The battery was low, but the device was undamaged. The same could be said for Tarot herself, minus an aching shoulder. The spacesuit's double-reinforced impact-resistant microweave had done its job. That or possibly she had died and the Deathward rune had revived her. She chose not to analyze the situation too closely.

Instead she gently massaged her shoulder, and she muttered an "it's not that bad" charm to herself, and she reached up her good arm and pulled herself out of the crater.

The station's artificial gravity extended to its exterior surface, which was helpful. Tarot didn't have to worry about accidentally kicking herself off into space in some random direction. She'd once heard a story about a shuttle mechanic who died that way. Eventually.

But not drifting off into deep space was both the start and end of her good fortune. The surface of the station was a square kilometer per side and all six sides were dense with runic encryptions on varying scales. Some, like the Deathward rune, were hundreds of meters wide and deep across the surface, while others were small and intricate. And there were runes within runes. The Deathward itself had hundreds, maybe thousands, of smaller runes carved into its interior. And any one of them might be encoded with the magic to turn off the rings or to open a passage into the station.

Or perhaps none of them were. This was after all a hermit's retreat, and Tarot's father had always been, at least in her own compromised estimation, a bit of a bastard. He was exactly the sort to build an unenterable building and then laugh at anyone who deigned to mount a break-in.

Tarot considered her options. She could search the surface of the station for days looking for the right rune and maybe find something or maybe not. Or she could give up now, switch off her oxygen-recycler, and save herself the wasted effort. Or...

Tarot held Percival's watch up and examined its features in the blue-white ringlight. No signal. She smirked, flicked off her spacesuit's radio link with her free hand, and whispered a "four bars, please" charm.

And then she made a phone call.

"Yes," came a voice on the other end, male.

"I'm on the station surface now. Can you tell me how to get inside?"

"We were supposed to meet at AA31-Esson-B. Why did you leave without us? Whose phone is this?"

"Never mind whose phone this is. The plan was to get into the station. Well, I'm standing on top of it. How do I get in?"

"Which side are you on?"

"The Deathward side. Right by the edge of the runecrater."

"All right. Let me consult my map."

Tarot could hear a rustling of papers over the line. She smiled to herself, imagining some fumbling slapstick.

"Twenty meters west of the north-most edge of the Deathward, you'll find a Glyph of Ingress."

"Ingress? Are you sure that's a word?"

The man on the other end of the line responded with more rustling.

"Never mind, never mind. And how do I turn the rings off?"

"Yes, of course. There's a control panel on the interior of the hatch door. The code to disable is... 3-1-21-12."

"Cute," said Tarot, in a tone to indicate that it wasn't.

"Oh. Heh. Every once in a great while, the old man would surprise you with his sentimentality."

Tarot ended the call with a thumb press. "Just seems morbid to me."

She took a moment to scroll through the phone options and delete the call record before turning her attention to her contact's directions. She circled the Deathward till she reached the top of the symbol, and then she estimated twenty meters west.

There on the surface of the station was etched a circle, approximately one meter in diameter. "Can it really be this simple?" Tarot asked herself.

She traced her finger along the groove, and as she did a blue light followed. When the circle was complete, the interior rotated ninety degrees and floated a meter and a half upwards.

Tarot checked, and sure enough, there was a control panel on the underside. She inputted the code 3-1-21-12, and the station's rings extinguished.

Breathing a sigh of relief, she switched her suit's radio link back on.

As she did, she caught Percival in mid-sentence. "—alive, I can promise to be your tax code. I can promise I won't betray you."

She smiled as she considered this bizarre notion.

"My tax code? Really, Gynt?"

9 | *MIDGE'S CLOSET*

One word that well described the interior of Magician's Station was peculiar. Another, incongruous. And a third, absurd. Though it was certainly a space station by function, which is to say by its we-are-in-the-middle-of-outer-space-and-inside-this-thing-and-thankfully-not-dead-ness, by design Magician's Station was something else entirely.

The station's winding halls were lined with dark paneled wood, and the floors were green grass. Daisies sprouted along the foot of the walls.

Illumination came in streaks of blue-white flame flitting through the corridors. The light surged and faded as the flames hummed by overhead, the sound echoing and recombining like music through the station.

And everywhere, in the walls and in the ceiling and in the doors and in the moldings, were carved the most intricate arcane symbols. What was their purpose? Percival wondered. Were they defenses? Curses?

As Tarot explained it, most were simply warnings written in a very ancient script. Or jokes, maybe? After all, how many people could there be both smart enough to decipher the symbols and stupid enough to have come here uninvited to read them?

Percival patted her on the shoulder. "Just you, I suppose."

Tarot smirked, but the point was not lost on her. She had translated the marks on the first door they came to as "Warning: The Uninvited Will Be Unassembled." Probably just bluster, she'd reminded herself.

But she didn't share that translation with her companions.

Still, Um was uneasy. He eyed the hatch they'd come in through, still open a few meters back. Thanks to a weather charm, the station maintained its atmosphere even with the hatch open, but the three had agreed to keep their spacesuits on "just to feel safe." In Um's case, the spacesuit wasn't helping.

"Yoo don't need me fer this part, do ya?" Um asked via their suits' direct radio link. "Maybe I should wait back on the Wisp?"

Percival leaned over to Tarot and whispered through the link, "Is it possible that Officer Um is afraid of magic?" Of course, he knew that Um could hear him just as well as she.

That was the point.

Tarot answered Um first. "You shouldn't worry. Any spells my father cast to protect this place will have been broken with his death."

Um scowled and counted down on three squat fingers as he recapped, "Hoops a fire. Streaks a light. Weather charm."

Then Tarot answered Percival. "Yes. Definitely afraid of magic." And with that, she pushed her way into the Unassembled Room.

Percival followed, and Um followed Percival, however reluctantly, gun first. Overhead, the streams of fire followed too, whizzing in and out in turn.

The room was large, Percival noted. Too large to fit inside the station without supernatural encouragement. The vaulted ceiling would have extended some dozen meters out beyond the station's outer hull if normal physical laws were in effect.

And all throughout the room hung strings of wooden beads, perhaps a million beads or more, draped at every angle, some so low as to be in easy reach and others hung within an arm's length of the ceiling.

Percival took one bead and slid it a few centimeters along the string. "Prayer beads?"

Tarot smiled but shook her head. "Try again."

Percival slid the bead back and grinned. "Oh, that's lovely."

"What's lovely?" Um asked, raising his gun.

"It's an abacus." Percival surprised himself with an unplanned giggle. "The whole room's an abacus. A gobsmackingly enormous abacus. An abacus with the computing power of—"

Percival did some quick math on his fingers. Um and Tarot waited patiently.

"Well, with the computing power of a first-generation personal computer circa the late 1900s, but that's still rather brilliant for a room full of beads."

Um asked, "That enough computin' power ta record the location a this Engine-thing yer worried about?"

Percival folded his arms, looked around, took it all in. "Yes. Yes, of course it is. But I wouldn't have the first clue how to decode it." Then, turning to Tarot: "You don't happen to have a magic-abacus decoder ring on you, do you?"

"No, but we've still got plenty of station to search."

And search they did, through room after room after room of impossibilities. They searched the Room of Whales and the Clockwork Room and even the *Casablanca* Room, where it felt like they were stepping through the original film, and then later through the unfortunate 2042 remake. They searched the Room of Infinite Baked Beans twice, just to be certain. They searched Illuminari's Room of Pointy Hats, where they found pointy hats, and his Room of Pointed Questions, which was evidently empty, by which time they were all of them beginning to tire of the search.

"Is this gettin' us anywhere?" Um grumbled to no one in particular.

Across the room Percival's shoulders slumped and, without turning to face Um, he responded, "Officer Um, remind me again: Would you rather that we saved the universe or that we followed your orders to the letter and let the universe and everyone and everything in it die?"

"Yoo think I'm some moron, don't ya? I suppose yoo'd rather we futzed around disobeyin' orders *as* the universe ends?"

Now Percival turned, quite flushed, stepped forward, and threw a finger in Um's face. "But do we really know what your orders are? Why do I suspect that you know more than you're letting on?"

At this point Um had taken all that he was willing to take from the scrawny, tawny, squishy thing. He shoved Percival back with his mechanical arm and growled, "Yoo think ya can take me in a fight, Gynt?"

Tarot seized this figurative and literal opening to interpose herself between Percival and Um, offering this excellent suggestion as she did: "Gentleman, perhaps we should finish this conversation *outside* the Room of Pointed Questions."

Both men nodded sheepishly.

Back out in the hallway, Percival felt like a fool. Um did as well, though his alien features did much to mask his embarrassment.

Tarot apologized and explained, "Sometimes my father found it helpful to use a questioning charm to force out questions that needed asking. In my experience, those charms work by forcing out a lot of questions that don't need asking first."

"Yes, well, I can't say I liked losing my temper back there," Percival confessed. He extended his hand to Um, who offered up his mechanical counterpart with mild indifference.

After the shake Percival continued, "And Um did make a good, um... point... in there. This search is getting us nowhere. I don't mean to be negative, but I've been doing some math and..."

Um frowned. "Please don't do math."

"Well, it's what I do, and it's just that with the size of this station, the volume we're talking about, figuring a roughly estimated one kilometer per side, that's give or take a billion cubic meters of station that needs searching. That's not just looking for a needle in a haystack. That's—"

Now Tarot cut him off. "We know."

"Do you? Because I have this friend, Midge Jha. A very nice woman, excellent typist. Lives like a grade schooler. She lost our concert tickets in her closet once. It took us an afternoon of sorting through to find them. Her closet. And now we're talking about searching... let's say, conservatively, 250 million closets. And we're not even sure what we're looking for or even if the-thing-which-we-do-not-know-what-is is even here to be found."

"Yer right," Um agreed. Finally, the skinny thing was talking sense. "Let's get the lady back ta Sanctuary-8, and we can sort the rest from there."

But Tarot was only listening to Percival. "So, what are you suggesting?"

"Well, Officer Um here is rather good at hacking into things. Probably." Percival glanced at Um for some sign of agreement or disagreement and, getting neither, continued, "So if we can find an access panel to a central mainframe, maybe he can find the piece of information that we're looking for. Or find the location of the piece of information we're looking for. Or find the location of something that will tell us the location of the..." Percival trailed off. "Well, you get the idea."

"Computer. Yes. Lovely. But the only one we've found so far has been made of string and beads, so unless the officer learned hackery at the heel of a costume jeweler—"

"Well, that's not entirely true," Percival corrected. "If I recall correctly, there was a control panel on the underside of the entry hatch where we came in. I'll lay odds that it's tied into a central network. If memory serves, there was a touchpad on the control panel. No letters, of course, but I suspect that Officer Um—"

"...likes it when people talk about 'im like he ain't standin' right here? Not in particular. But fine. Fate a the universe rests in my hands. Makes sense. I got more 'n most. So I'll go back ta where we came in. See if I can't hack inta the computer system. In binary, no less. Find out what I can about this place, about this Engine, and where any Engine-related secrets may be hidin' from us. Fer the best. At least up there I'll be a quick scramble from the Wisp. No offense ta yer late father, miss, and maybe it's just me, but this whole place smells like death."

"Actually, it is just you." Percival waved his hand in front of his visor. "Literally, you. Your olfactory is self-contained within the spacesuit. You're just smelling reprocessed air."

Um mostly ignored Percival, turned his back on him, and tromped off the way they'd come. His only response, a muttered "it was a metaphor" over the radio link.

Percival and Tarot watched him go. "Are we sending him topside by himself?" she asked.

"Makes sense to split up. You and I as well. We're all on the link together. He'll let us know if he's found anything. Meantime, we might as well cover as much ground as possible."

"Hah." Tarot gave a little smirk. "So I'll take the 125 million closets on the left, and you take the 125 million on the right? Easy."

Percival brushed a gloved hand across Tarot's helmet. "And we'll meet in the middle for milkshakes."

Over the link: "Augh. Y'know I can still hear yoo, right?"

10 | THE BLUE LIGHT

Topside, Officer Um made short work of the station's security firewall. As you might have guessed, Um was a much better hacker than the late magician was a computer programmer. But Illuminari was a man who knew his limitations, and the sole contents of his computer systems turned out to be:

- code to turn off flaming rings: 3-1-21-12
- two recipes for beef stroganoff
- brief video of dog skateboarding
- one text file reading: "I curse you to unending torment"

Um scowled beneath his helmet. "Well, that's probably just fer Gynt."

"What's for who now?" Percival asked over the link. Percival was, at that moment, climbing down through pitch blackness, down a rickety ladder that he'd found at the back of a linen closet. Hardly the cleverest idea he'd ever had. He'd hoped he'd stumbled onto a secret passage to the lower levels, but the further down he climbed, the more certain he was that this was some sort of a trap. An infinite ladder down the side of a bottomless pit.

There are few ways to die more ignominious than of starvation, on a ladder.

"Hey, Gynt. Are yoo bein' tormented?" Um asked over the link. "And… d'ya think what's happenin' ta ya is gonna stop… or … the opposite a that?"

"Hmm. No to the first and third questions." Percival could see a prick of light down below. He grinned. "And yes to the one in between."

"Oh," Um replied glumly. "Well, nevermind, then." He turned back to the control panel and restarted the dog on a skateboard video for a third time. "Must be a clue in here somewhere."

Elsewhere, Tarot was stripping off her spacesuit. She had kept hers on in solidarity with the boys, but it just seemed foolish while she was on her own. The atmosphere was clearly breathable, the extra weight would simply slow her down, and Tarot knew exactly where she was going.

For unlike Percival and Um, Tarot could read the writing on the walls. And, yes, some of it was magical. For instance, a few of the runes she'd seen reversed station gravity with a slap. And, yes, some of it was meant to scare off that rare brilliantly stupid trespasser. One of the more intricately carved symbols translated as "your malicious machinations will get you marvelously masticated."

But most of the symbols etched across the walls weren't warnings either. Rather they were markers, simple way signs, meant to guide a weary, drunken magician through the station and back to his quarters after a long night spent drinking at the pub.

Percival hung from the bottom rung of the rickety ladder, legs dangling out the bottom of the hole, and into a room of pure shimmery white. Directly beneath him, about four meters down, floated a linoleum block no more than a half-meter to a side. The room extended another four meters below that. And beyond that, it appeared a second hole and a second ladder led further down.

"This doesn't seem like a good idea," Percival said to himself as he considered whether to let himself fall.

"What doesn't seem like a good idea?" Tarot asked absently as she flipped through the pages of her father's final journals. She'd patched the suits' radio link through the station's intercom, so Percival's voice boomed from above.

"I'm hanging from a ladder over a room with a floating block of kitchen tile in the middle of it. Any idea where I am?"

"Sounds like the bottom floor of the ship. In all six-directions." Tarot closed one book and opened another. "If you think of the station as a set of nested boxes..."

"That's the smallest one down below. I get it." Percival swung an arm up to the next rung. "Doesn't seem like there's anything to see down here. I'm going to head back up."

"Good idea," Tarot replied. "I think I found what I was looking for."

Somewhere else, just then, a blue LED light switched on.

And a seismic wave slammed through Magician's Station. Percival's right hand came loose, and then his left. He fell, his helmet cracking hard against the side of the linoleum cube, but he couldn't grab the side in time. Instead he kept on falling straight down, but now with the sensation that he was being lobbed up into the air, almost reaching the far shaft, his hand outstretched, before falling back down towards the cube again. And his helmet bounced against the cube once more.

Crack!

As gravity lobbed him back the way he'd come, Percival shouted, "I HAAATE FIZZZ-IXXX!" into the link. It was the sort of impassioned non-sequitur that would have properly vexed his companions if they weren't otherwise embroiled.

Only Um saw what had hit the station: a smoldering red asteroid, perhaps a hundred meters across, strapped with massive golden engines and a cargo pod emblazoned with the broken cross. And the cargo pod was opening.

Um looked up at the Wisp floating overhead, rope ladder trailing, perhaps the least threatening starship in the galaxy, all glass and brass and glittery bits, and not a weapon on her. And yet it was their only way off the station, so Um made a dash for it.

Out of the pod marched a dozen N^{th} Realm shock troopers armored in black and gold and red, the blue-eyed, blond-haired or blond-furred master races of a dozen worlds, united by hate and their thirst for conquest.

Um leapt into the air, grabbed the rope ladder and scrambled up arm after arm after arm as fast as his flabby frame could take him.

He was ten meters from the ship's hold. Then eight meters. Then six. The shock troopers calmly trained their weapons. Five meters. They were each of them armed with a Magnum Heat-Seeking Agony Rifle, arguably the most sadistic weapon ever designed. Four meters. The Magnum Heat-Seeking Agony Rifle's payload is a self-separating cluster of smart-shrapnel, coated with neurotoxins that scramble the central nervous system, simultaneously tripping all of the victim's pain receptors and initiating a full body evacuation. Three meters. And while the shrapnel is shredding the victim's body, a necromantic curse keeps the victim alive, conscious, and acutely aware of what's happening. Two meters. It's really very, very painful. One meter. Which is why you can't buy one on most planets without a valid hunter's license.

Um threw himself up into the hold with an exhausted gasp. Ha. Ha. Ha. He'd made it. He hugged the end of the rope ladder to his chest. Stupid N^{th} Realm shock troopers.

And then the heat-seeking payload of twelve Magnum Heat-Seeking Agony Rifles shot up into the hold and eviscerated Officer Um.

Um died. Eventually.

11 | THE GYNT MASSACRE

Percival sat on the floating linoleum cube at the center of Magician's Station, feet dangling into the anti-gravity, helmet now in pieces in his lap, bleeding from the back of his head.

He applied pressure with one hand, which helped a little. He was in shock. He knew he was in shock. But knowing he was in shock, he didn't much care that he was in shock.

He didn't know that Um had been killed. Didn't know what happened to Tarot. His radio had broken on third impact with the cube. Um's had died when the smart-shrapnel sliced through it. Percival had only heard the first of Um's terrified screams.

In this small way, he was fortunate.

The station shook. Percival didn't know what was happening outside. Didn't care. He was trapped at the bottom of a six-way pit. He had a choice of exits, four meters above in two directions, with no way to reach them. Didn't care.

Didn't.

"Sit still. Be quiet. Absolutely silent. And don't move from this spot, no matter what you hear. Do you understand?" The man with the scratchy beard repeats, "Do you understand?"

The little boy shakes his head. He is sat on a cold rock. It is dark here, save for the dull glow of the man's pocket watch. They are in the part of the cave that you can only get to by crawling, the part the grown-ups have told him he must never go. But now he has to stay here.

Is he being punished?

"No. No. You're a good boy. A good boy. You stay here until Daddy comes back."

The man shoves the pocket watch into his son's hands and closes them around it. A soft light slips out through the boy's fingers. Then the man turns, leaves, crawls sideways to get out like a funny caterpillar.

The boy does not laugh.

The little boy is alone. He does as he is told. He is quiet. And in the quiet, every echo finds him. There are screams. Screams of men and women and of children. And he hears the ripping claws and gnawing teeth and the pleas for mercy that end mid-word.

And a roar. A vicious, echoing roar that seems to come from everywhere and from nowhere. It does not sound like any of the animals that the boy has learned about in school. It is not a displacer beast or a lion or a cockatrice.

At times it sounds like a horrible old woman who only thinks she is an animal, and at other times it sounds like Hell itself has been given a mouth.

And the boy does not move. He does not shift a centimeter, and he tries to keep his eyes perfectly still.

For he knows that any move or sound will summon her.

And in the watchlight he can see the hole at the very straining edge of his vision. The caterpillar hole where his father wriggled away.

The hole that she will come through if she hears him.

He tries not to breathe. Outside, the screams have died. He cannot hear her roar.

He tries not to breathe.

Silence echoes. His chest is heavy.

He tries not to breathe.

And then a scratching at the hole. Like a fingernail or claw against the stone. He cannot turn his head or she will get him.

"We can smell you, little one. Come out and play with Mama

Alecto."

And then he sees it from the corner of his eye. Her talon, long and black and sharp like a knife, reaching out through the caterpillar hole and dragging back against the stone.

"Come out," she whispers, "for Mama Alecto has left space for you."

Sit still, he said. Be quiet. Absolutely silent. And don't move from this spot, no matter what you hear. The boy tries so hard, but his hands are shaking now, and his eyes are wet with tears, and it feels like his heart is ready to turn over in his chest.

"Come out, you delicious little thing."

His small hands tremble and tighten over his father's watch, the spaces between his fingers closing, and all is lost to darkness.

And in the darkness, he can hear her, clawing at the stone. Dragging her nails. Dragging herself through the hole.

In the darkness she pulls closer. Closer.

And then he hears her at his feet. "You shall know such joy," she whispers, "in between our teeth."

And a hand rises up his leg. It is not a human hand.

Percival Gynt knew death. He had known horror in his life. And by that measure being trapped at the bottom of a box in a box in a box was just a passing mathematical inconvenience.

He looked up to the hole in the ceiling above him. Four meters. Well short of a high jump, but perfectly reasonable for a long jump.

He removed each piece of his spacesuit and placed it on the left face of the cube: helmet fragments, gloves, boots, belt, spaceshirt, spacetrousers. He stood and unbuttoned his waistcoat, removing it and emptying the contents into his trouser pockets. He removed his cufflinks, pocketed them, and rolled up his shirt sleeves.

He folded his waistcoat neatly and set it down with the spacesuit parts on the side of the cube.

He loosened his tie, unbuttoned the top button of his shirt, and then flipped his tie back over his shoulder.

And then he crouched, and then he began to run. And with every footfall, his path twisted around the cube. Over the top, down below, and up again he ran, wrapping around the cube, faster and faster.

He grunted to himself. He is running through the night. Running through muddy water. And the beast is behind him. Can't stop. Faster. Faster.

And then he leapt out to the tunnel in front of him, ahead and not up, four meters, then three, then two, and he caught the last wrung of the ladder in one hand just as gravity caught up with him.

He dangled, groaned, and then with the strength of one arm, pulled the other up to the bottom rung.

He began to climb.

And below, a patch of blood was forgotten.

12 | WHAT HAPPENED TO TAROT

Tarot did not miss her father. She did not mourn him. Nonetheless, she felt a pervasive sadness overtake her as she read his final written words. The journals that lined the walls of Illuminari's study contained the magician's final verdict on the universe that he'd helped to save. A universe he alternately loathed and very loathed.

A universe in which Tarot was of, at most, passing significance.

This harsh truth was underscored by seven words found midway down page 85 of Illuminari's final journal, in an entry headed "Facts of Some Import."

These words were the words she had come for, though they were not the words she had hoped to read.

Tarot tore page 85 from the journal and set it afire with a subtle charm. She steeled herself as the ashes drifted downward to the waste basket.

The station shook again. Um and Percival's radios had both cut out to the sound of screams. She was on her own again. She clutched the small stone that hung from her neck. It was cold in her hand.

It would be difficult to start over.

Tarot left the study, headed back upstairs to where she'd left her spacesuit. Along the ceilings, the blue-white flames seemed to hum a childish, taunting melody.

She pulled her suit back on over her traveling clothes and opened the radio link to all frequencies. "If anyone can hear me, I have the answer. You do not want to kill me. Repeat: I have the answer."

She squeezed her helmet on over Percival's hat, screwed it down as tight as she could, and triple-checked the air seal. And she strongly considered buying a gun at some point.

There was a spiral staircase near where she stowed her spacesuit. She took it up four floors to the top level. It let out near the Room of Pointy Hats.

Under her breath she muttered an "I am not to be trifled with" charm as she stepped out into the hallway. No one in front of her. No one behind. "I am not to be trifled with. I am not to be trifled with."

Unimpressed, the blue-white flames whistled and jeered as they passed overhead. Still Tarot repeated, "I am not to be trifled with. I am not to be trifled with." The station shook again. She clutched the wall to steady herself. "I am not to be trifled with," she insisted, louder this time.

She rounded the corner towards the *Casablanca* Room. "I am not to be trifled with. I am not to be trifled with." And ahead of her stood three men she'd seen before: The Swordsman. The Cyborg. And the Golden Ape.

"Hello, Millicent!" The Swordsman smiled with all but his dead left eye. He raised his blade. "Funny seeing you this far out."

The Cyborg half-growled as his plasma fist charged. "Knew she wasn't just a nanny. Nannies don't kick like that."

Behind them the Golden Ape cracked her knuckles. "For some strange reason," she observed, "I have an abiding need to trifle with the young lady. Why do you suppose that is?"

They were N^{th} Realm. The elite. Evil to the core and immunized to her charms by a magic much stronger than her own.

Tarot dived back around the corner as the Swordsman lunged. She screamed into the radio link, "I HAVE THE ANSWER! I HAVE THE ANSWER!" Around the corner, the Cyborg clasped his mechanized, all-frequencies-radio-enabled ear drum and screamed in pain.

The Swordsman crouched low, grabbing Tarot by the ankle and flipping her down, face-first into the grass, and he dropped his full weight against her back, elbow first.

Tarot grunted. She could feel the Swordsman's blade slowly slicing across the double-reinforced microweave at her shoulder.

"Let's get you into something more comfortable," he whispered. And she could hear the others coming around the corner behind him.

And from the direction opposite, a voice. "Here's a question for you, gentlemen. If you were really genetically superior to the rest of us, why would it take the three of you to bring down one of us?"

A dozen steps away, still in shock, still bleeding from the back of his head, unarmed, unhelmeted, and thoroughly undeterred, Percival prepared to take a punch. "Let's rebalance those odds, shall we?"

Tarot whispered to the Cyborg over the radio link, "All right, boys. Now you're in for it."

13 | SHALOM, SCUMBAG

"This one looks Jewish," the Swordsman said, and as far as Percival knew it might have been true. He knew so little of his own ancestry. The Swordsman did not suffer this uncertainty. He'd been grown in a vat on Aryan Pod Colony 75 and educated by the Celestial Overmen and trained in sword fighting by the Archduke himself.

He'd been taught to hate Ant People and telepaths and Radioactive Nyorg Eaters, and he thought he understood why, but he'd never received an adequate explanation for why the Nth Realm hated the Jewish people. "Reason does not matter," the Archduke had once told him. "Only the hatred matters." And so he hated Jews, and if this curly-haired dandy was one of them, he would feel better knowing he had made the universe that much purer in his slaying.

Behind him the Cyborg fired off his plasma fist, sending it slamming into Percival's right shoulder and throwing him off his feet. Percival landed with a thump in the grass, but he felt neither impact. He grabbed the Cyborg's fist off the ground as he stood and guffawed. "You threw your fist at me! Now I have your fist!"

The Swordsman sprang forward and swung wide across Percival's chest with his blade. Percival pulled back, but the tip sliced his tie in two. Percival reached into his pocket and flung a cufflink ineffectually into the Swordsman's dead eye.

The Swordsman sneered. "You'll have to do—"

Before the Swordsman could finish his thought, Percival hurled the

Cyborg's fist into his jaw. It connected with a loud crack. The Swordsman spit a bloody tooth into the grass and smiled a broken smile. "Better."

The Cyborg and the Ape were closing now, leaving Tarot to clamor to her feet. "You're not going to like this, Percival!" she shouted with a finger on the suit's vocal transmit button.

The Swordsman punched Percival hard in the chin with his sword hand. Percival couldn't feel it, but he understood things were going badly as he staggered backwards.

"Not terribly, no!" he shouted back to her.

"Not that," she whispered. The Cyborg turned back towards her, having heard her over the link. "This," she said, slapping a defensive rune on the corridor wall.

And in that moment up and down reversed themselves, and Percival, Tarot, the Swordsman, the Cyborg, and the Ape all went tumbling up/down into the ceiling. Tarot, the only one ready for the reversal, flattened herself tight against the wall as two streaks of blue-white flame shot through the Cyborg and the Ape, their tune now nauseatingly discordant.

The Cyborg only lost his metallic left leg in this first volley, enough to drop him to the ceiling floor. The Ape was burned in half. A second volley roasted what was left of them. The Swordsman drove his blade down into the ceiling, cutting a streak of flame in half, dissipating it, protecting both himself and Percival. Percival thanked his savior with a punch to the back of the head.

Unfazed, the swordless Swordsman turned and grabbed Percival by what was left of his tie, yanking him forward and arcing him towards the oncoming fire. The streaks were coming fast now, merging into a sea of blue-white flame that parted only where the Swordsman had planted his blade.

Pinned against the wall, her spacesuit licked by passing fire, Tarot could only offer encouragement. She tapped her suit's vocal transmit button and shouted a "you have excellent balance" charm, and Percival teetered back onto his feet. He pushed himself into the Swordsman, arms up in front of him, and he shouted back to her, "And you have a distracting smile!"

The Swordsman shoved Percival back to regain his bearings. Percival reached into his pocket for his watch. This was getting out of hand.

Hmm, he thought to himself. No watch.

The Swordsman raised his fists. "I am going to hurt you. A lot."

Tarot tapped the wall rune again, and gravity corrected itself. Tarot and Percival and the Swordsman and some smoldering hunks of Cyborg and Ape fell down onto the grass below.

Above, streaks of blue-white fire danced merrily.

The Swordsman rose from a crouch as Percival lumbered to his feet. Percival grinned. "All right, now you're definitely in trouble."

"And why's that?" the Swordsman asked.

"Well, for three reasons, by my count. For one, I felt that. Which means I've about come to my senses. And two, you are definitely not getting your sword back now." Percival was swaying a little bit more than he liked, but his eyes were steady.

"And three?"

"Right. Right. And three... Um... This is really my favorite..."

"Is it?"

"Yes... Um..."

"Spit it out."

"Um," Percival smiled, "looks properly pissed off."

Behind the Swordsman, flat against his head, a Smith & Wesson ion pulse cannon whirred to life. Its owner, a certain Indulian peace officer, now alive, now naked, now with a hole in his gut where he used to have a mechanical third arm, took great pleasure as he squeezed the trigger.

After the flash and the boom, what was left of the Swordsman slumped to the ground. "Shalom, scumbag," Um growled, and he fired again at what was left of him.

The three of them, Percival, Um, and Tarot, stood over the smoking remains, a bit surprised to still be alive.

"It's funny. I hadn't realized you were Jewish," Percival offered in an attempt to break the silence.

"Yoo got that from, 'Shalom, scumbag?'"

"Well, that and your circumcised fourth arm."

In their defense, both Percival and Tarot were trying very, very hard to avert their gaze.

14 | THE RUNECRATER

Officer Um, like the enigmatic Vargoth Gor, was not dead. Which is not to say that he hadn't died, because of course he had, repeatedly, over the course of the preceding half hour. But getting dead and staying dead are two different tricks, and Um had only ever been any good at the first of these.

To review: A volley of smart-shrapnel had been fired into the Wisp's hold, simultaneously eviscerating Um's body, tripping all of his pain receptors, and forcing him to pee and poop himself quite vigorously. And then there was the business of that curse, the one which kept him alive and conscious and suffering while all of this was going on.

It was at minute three of the worst agony that any humanoid sentient has ever had to endure that Um managed to gather his wits about him. He lifted his pulse cannon with what was left of his right hand and fired straight up into the ship's navigational mainframe. The Wisp jerked violently to one side, knocking Um off what was left of his feet, then lurched, rolled, and dropped straight into the side of the station and exploded.

Finally, mercifully, Um died.

And that would have been the end for Um, except the ship crashed dead center into the middle of the Deathward runecrater, and the magic of the runecrater instantly began to knit Officer Um back together again the moment he died.

And so, a mere twenty seconds after his death, Officer Um found himself alive again, naked and mechanical-armless in the smoldering wreckage of the Wisp. Deathwards are powerful elder magics, but even a Deathward can't reanimate a mechanical arm or a pair of trousers. For his part, Um was well satisfied just to be alive.

Then he died again. Lack of atmosphere plus lack of spacesuit. Then, twenty seconds later, he was reanimated. Then he died again. Same reason. Reanimated again. Dead again. Etcetera.

By this point most of the shock troopers had gathered round to watch. All of them except the elite squad, the Swordsman and the Cyborg and the Ape, who had other business below. Um's unending torture was good fun for the rest of them. Twenty seconds dead, then maybe forty-five seconds gasping for air as his blood boiled in the pressure-less environment, then dead for another twenty seconds, on loop.

After he awoke from his sixth death, Um began to regain his focus. He grabbed his gun from the wreckage and pushed himself to his feet. He actually shuffled forward a few meters before he dropped again. The shock troopers smiled and applauded. And then he awoke from his seventh death and made it a few more meters. His eighth, and a few more.

Slowly and methodically, he carried himself out of the wreckage and across the runecrater. The shock troopers followed, intrigued. A few placed bets on how far he could make it in this state.

By his thirteenth death, Um had made it to the edge of the runecrater, just twenty meters shy of the entry hatch, still open. He looked back at his killers, who at this point were goading him on.

"You can do it!" one yelled. "We believe in you!" another added. "Drop dead!" cried a third, who had bet half a month's pay that Um would never make it out of the runecrater.

The second he stepped out of the crater, its magic would leave him. He would die and stay dead. He only had one chance at this, and he knew it. Then he died. Then he was reanimated, and he knew it again.

And then he was off. He started with a run, tumbled, fell on his face, pulled himself to his knees, began to crawl. There was no oxygen in his lungs, and the blood in his veins was evaporating, but Um kept crawling forward, even as his vision began to fade, even as the world got heavy all around him.

In his head he pictured his wife crying. He didn't have a wife, but if he did she would definitely be crying. He imagined his superiors and their dawning realization that without Um they had no hope. The universe itself would soon be over. Not enough. Time and space were vanishing around him. He would not come back a fifteenth time. Something else. Something else.

Gynt. Percival Gynt standing over him, unmoved, unimpressed. "As I expected," the scrawny, tawny, squishy thing declares with a sniff. "All rough and tumble when the stakes are for nothing, but soon as it really matters? Where do we find him? Where is the pride of Indulia? Taking a nap on the hull while the enemy gawks and jeers."

No, Um thought as he inched towards the open portal. I will not let that scrawny, tawny, squishy, swishy thing think himself better than me. Will not let him have the last word.

Edward Braun, who had considered becoming a horticulturalist before he was radicalized, turned to his fellow shock trooper, Fnn-12, and asked the obvious question, "I think he might make it. Shouldn't we all shoot him again, just to be safe?"

Fnn-12, eleventh removed clone of the notorious Franco Nicodemus Noon and frankly a bit of an idiot on account of the pattern degradation, just shrugged. "Our heat-seekers can follow him in, right? Let's just wait and see if he makes it. Castor has to lend me his wife if he does."

They turned back to Um just in time to see him fall into the open portal, down into the station and out of sight.

Castor swore loudly, and the others laughed. They lined up, readied their weapons, and took aim. "On three!" Edward shouted.

Fnn-12 looked over at Castor. "Don't worry, buddy. I'll give her back in the same shape I get her."

"One."

Castor kept his eyes on the target. "Funny."

"Two."

"Yes, sir. She'll be just as dumb and ugly as the day you married her."

"Thr—"

But just as the shock troopers began to squeeze their triggers, station gravity reversed itself and all twelve of them, their ship, and the wreckage of the Wisp were flung out into space.

Edward and Fnn-12 and Castor and the others died.

Eventually.

15 | FACTS OF SOME IMPORT

After three quick rounds of rock-paper-scissors, it was determined that Tarot should give Um her spacesuit so that they all had something to wear. Percival won, having thrown paper-paper-rock. Tarot, who would have preferred to keep the spacesuit for herself, lost, having thrown rock-paper-scissors in that overly predictable order. Um, who was passingly embarrassed to have lost his third arm in the crash of the Wisp but fundamentally indifferent to being naked, stayed out of the decision-making process entirely.

Once Um had trousers on, the talk turned serious.

"So," Percival summarized, "we have no spaceship, and this station is literally non-literally in the middle of nowhere."

"And the universe may soon end," Tarot added.

"And the universe may soon end," Percival repeated. "So where does that leave us?"

Um's reply, "Stranded on a space station?" wasn't meant as a joke, but Percival laughed anyway. It was more a nervous we're-all-going-to-die laugh than a cheery why-Um-you're-suddenly-quite-the-card laugh, but it felt good to laugh at anything, for any reason, knowing that this might be his last chance.

Tarot did not laugh, though she was glad that Percival still could. The stone that hung from her necklace flickered to life for the first time since she'd touched down on Magician's Station.

She pulled Percival's watch from the pocket of her cloak. "I may be able to use a charm to boost your watch's reception." She added, "Mind you, I've never tried anything like this before, but it should work in principle."

Percival nodded. "We're a bit out of our depth at this point. I suppose it's time to call in Agent Fred."

"Finally, some sense!" Um agreed as he pulled on the rest of the spacesuit. "All this jibber-jabber 'bout the Realm and engines and conspiracies. We gotta turn this over ta the government and the lawyers ta sort out."

"Oh." Percival considered the prospect for approximately one half of one half of one half of a second. "No, let's definitely not do that. What we need is..."

Percival thought. Tarot raised an eyebrow. "Yes?" she prompted.

Percival turned to Tarot. "Did you say you found what we were looking for? Over the radio link. Before the Space Nazis struck?"

"They don't call themselves that. But yes. Yes, I did. Except it won't do us much good if we can't get off the station."

Percival slid his hands into his pockets and prepared to be patient. "And..."

She tried again. "Except it won't do us much good if we can't get off the station *and* save the universe?"

"And the thing you found that we'd been looking for...?" Percival prompted.

"Oh. Well. It was just an off-hand remark in one of my father's journals, but he said—"

Before Tarot could finish her sentence, a voice boomed through the corridor, "ATTENTION, TRESPASSERS! WE HAVE SIX GE MAGMACANNONS™ TARGETING THE STATION! SURRENDER IMMEDIATELY, OR WE WILL BE FORCED TO DESTROY YOU!"

Um clicked the vocal transmit button on his suit. "It's comin' over the radio link too," he confirmed.

"Then we can respond," said Percival. "Tell them we're not trespassing, and see if that slows them down any."

Um nodded and repeated Percival's message over the radio link.

"We ain't trespassin'."

Tarot took Um by the arm. "I think I know that voice. Tell him I'm here. Tell him that Illuminari's daughter is with you."

"I'm here with Illuminari's daughter, if that helps."

"TAROT? ARE YOU THERE?"

"Tell him that I am."

"Wait," Percival interjected. "Who are we talking to?"

"A friend of the family," Tarot replied with a confident smile. "A friend with a spaceship."

"A spaceship with guns," Um pointed out. "I like 'im already." And then he added, through the link, "Yeah, she's here. Tarot, daughter of Illuminari, is here. Stand down. We're on the same side."

Percival gave Tarot a squeeze around the shoulders. "Did you hear that, Tarot? Um's on your side. A minute ago, he was ready to turn you over to the bureaucrats on Sanctuary-8 for interrogation and sentencing. But now we're a team!"

Tarot gave a little grin. "It's amazing what a Wormhole engine and a weapons battery will do for the group dynamic."

"MAINTAIN YOUR POSITION! WE ARE LOCKING ONTO YOUR POSITIONS! WE ARE COMING IN!"

Percival and Tarot and Um maintained their positions.

"We?" Percival asked. Tarot gave away nothing in her expression.

Seconds later, two figures materialized in the corridor ahead of them. One, a young woman with short blonde hair, perhaps twenty-five, with delicate features and brilliant blue eyes. She was dressed in tails and carried a black cane. The other appeared behind her, a man no older than thirty, short, smiling, boyishly handsome, with messy dark hair and thin-framed glasses. He wore a long leather coat over a rumpled button-down shirt and carried a holstered Magnum Conflict Resolver at his side.

"Mouse!" Tarot pushed past the woman and hugged the young man with a childish glee. He returned her hug awkwardly and gave Percival and Um a nod as he did.

The young man greeted her post-hug. "It's good to see you again,

Tarot. You must know how sorry I am about your father."

"I do."

Percival reached out a hand to the young man. "Percival Gynt. Accountant."

The young man accepted his handshake. "Pleasure to meet you, Mister Gynt. Name's Matthew Holden, and before you get any funny ideas, I can count on one hand the number of people in the universe who can still get away with calling me Mouse."

Mouse slipped off his glasses, folded and vanished them, as a grim expression drew across his face. "Eleven years ago, I thought I'd saved the universe. Apparently, I was wrong. Now I aim to finish the job."

It was a properly epic pronouncement, and Percival felt an immediate, visceral, unshakeable need to step on it. "You were Illuminari's apprentice, yes? A sort of boy sidekick?"

"For a number of years," Mouse obliged. "Now, I'm on my own. This is my lovely assistant, Halla."

On cue, Halla gave a showman's bow.

Percival gestured to Um. "And this is our lovely assistant, Officer Um of Sanctuary-8 Province Police."

Um tapped the vocal transmit button on his spacesuit. "Charmed. You got a spaceship or what?"

Mouse grinned. "I do like a man who gets to the point. Yes. The Prestige is orbiting overhead as we speak."

"It's funny. You showing up right after us," Percival said.

"We would have gotten here first," said Mouse, "but our ship is weighed down by its massive, massive guns."

If Um was holding down his vocal transmit at that precise moment, the others would have heard a strange noise, the Indulian equivalent of a school girl's giggle, but he was not, so they did not.

"Shall we go, then?" asked Percival.

Mouse looked to Tarot. "We're done here?" he asked.

"Yes," she replied, "I know how to find the Engine."

"That may be the best news that I've heard in eleven years," said Mouse. "Ready?"

Percival was not strictly, but before he could say anything, the five of them were someplace else.

It has been said more than a few times that God hates teleportation. But, as any follower of the Great and Terrible All-Mother could tell you, She hates a lot of things. Teleportation ranks, at highest, seventh on the list behind the undead, auguries, the evil eye, Viagra-cut-with-Ecstasy, worldly relations with lower invertebrates, and extinction-level events. In roughly that order.

The reason that God hates teleportation, per the followers of the Great and Terrible All-Mother, is that teleportation is impossible. Which is of course not to say that it *can't* happen. Impossible things are happening every second of every day somewhere in the universe. But there is certainly no physical law that allows for matter to move from one location to another instantaneously without traversing the intervening space.

This hasn't stopped scientists from trying to discover such a law. And some have come close. For instance, many thousands of years ago, humans discovered a method of disintegrating themselves, beaming the energy produced by their immolation over a great distance, and then using that energy to construct perfect clones of the dead would-be-teleporters. Gruesome in retrospect, but back then the clones of the inventors of this technique were quite proud of themselves/the people they were cloned from.

Some would also describe wormhole technology as teleportation. Wormhole engines allow starships to pass through folds of space and emerge light years, or even light millennia, away. From a primitive, Euclidean point of view, this might seem like teleportation. But when you understand the true geometry of the universe, this is no more remarkable than finding a shorter route to the market taking only back streets. Again, not really teleportation.

But another way of saying something is scientifically impossible is to say that it is possible, non-scientifically. Magicians long ago mastered the art of the vanish and reveal. Teleportation by magic is a well-studied discipline practiced by millions of magicians the universe over. And that, most of all, is the source of God's ire.

It's not the impossibility of the act. It's the arrogance of those who would defy the will of the universe, to make the impossible ordinary. But the All-Mother is Great as well as Terrible and would never be so petty as to hate any of her children.

Love the teleporter. Hate the teleportation.

The five of them, Percival and Tarot and Um and Mouse and lovely assistant Halla, stood in a clean white room with a single, sliding door.

"Welcome to The Prestige," Mouse declared with a hint of triumphalism. "Try not to muddy her up."

The door opened with a pleasing whoosh, and the five made their way out into the corridor. If possible, this corridor was actually cleaner and whiter than the teleport room behind them. Such a level of cleanliness suggested to Percival a mind either pathological or sociopathic. Hopefully the former.

Mouse led them to a lounge, clean and white, with a view of Magician's Station through a large bay window. He tasked Halla with collecting drink orders.

"Water's fine," said Percival.

"Water's fine," said Tarot.

Um, who was still wearing their last spacesuit, placed a finger to its vocal transmit button and requested, "Somethin' alcoholic. And strong. And... crunchy."

Halla left, and the others took a seat. The couches were covered in clear plastic and made a squeaking sound as they sat.

"Now, Tarot," Mouse began, "perhaps you should tell us what you found."

Tarot hesitated. How could she explain what she had discovered without making herself look childish? Without further exposing herself?

Percival slipped an arm around her shoulder and pulled her closer to him. "S'alright," he whispered, making Tarot feel even more weak-willed and foolish.

"In my father's journals, he wrote about the Rider and the Engine and about the Conspiracy of Days." She looked up to Mouse. "About you and him and Lora and Vargoth Gor, and what you did. He worried that after he departed, things might unravel. That precisely what's happening now might happen."

Mouse leaned forward. "And the Engine? Did he offer any clue as to where we can find it?"

"Yes. Sort of."

Mouse pressed her. "Explain 'sort of.'"

"Someone else knows. In his journal my father was quite clear that when he died there would still be one person left who knew where the Engine is."

"And that was...?" Um prompted.

"He didn't say. Didn't give a name, at least. But I think I know who it must be. In his journal he called this person 'the only one I could ever trust.'"

Mouse sighed. "Well, it wasn't me, I'm afraid. Much as I loved him, your father and I never had that type of bond."

"Nor me," Tarot whispered.

"Then who?" Percival prodded, for a moment letting his curiosity get the better of his compassion.

"It was Lora," Mouse offered. "It had to be Lora."

"His assistant?"

Tarot nodded.

"Take it from me," Mouse told them, "A magician has no greater confidant than his assistant. They have to be in on it for the trick to work. And no one can question how close the two of them were."

"And where is this Lora now?"

Tarot laughed weakly. Mouse shook his head. Percival glanced across to Um, who like him had missed the joke.

And so Percival asked, "Have I said something funny?"

"It's just that," said Mouse, "she's made herself rather busy these past few years, our Lora did. Started her own religion."

"Her own religion?" Um scoffed. "She ain't one a them crazies-with-daisies ya see at the spaceports, is she?"

"No, no. She's done a bit better for herself than that," Mouse explained. "You see, lovely assistant Lora has remade herself as the founder and High Cleric of the Intergalactic Church of the All-Mother."

Percival looked at Tarot, starting to understand. "But there's more to it than that, isn't there?"

Tarot nodded again, tears forming in her eyes. "She wasn't just Dad's assistant. He took her as his wife too. Lovely Lora, former assistant to the greatest magician in the history of histories, the one he trusted above all others, now holy leader of the most powerful church in the universe, a religion which teaches that all magic-users are abominations."

Percival took Tarot in his arms and hugged her to his chest. "I'm sorry," he told her as he stroked her hair, "but we've got to go see your mum."

PART

II

IN WHICH OUR HERO FINDS RELIGION
BUT LOSES THE GIRL

Top 5 News Downloads for April 10, 20018

5	Church Congratulates Celestial Governor on Re-Election
4	The Boy from Gynt: Where is He Now?
3	Officials Attribute AA31-Esson-B Footage to Swamp Gas, Weather Balloons
2	V4RG0THG0R1SN0TD34D
1	Governor Zell Promises Four More Years of Peace, Prosperity, No Civil Uprisings

You may also be interested to know

114	Internet Newsfeeds Surprisingly Easy to Hack

Today's Weather

Immaculate

1 | HER FIRST LAW

There were entire days when the High Cleric of the Intergalactic Church of the All-Mother did not leave her chambers, where she saw no one and spoke to no one. On those days her attendants would gather to her door and cup an ear to listen, to hear the mournful sobs of their most divine mistress muffled by her silken bed sheets and pillows.

The High Cleric carried a deep sadness in her heart. This was well known. It was a sadness that came, say the teachings, from her closeness to the deity. From her profound, existential awareness of the All-Mother and Her perfection and of the wallowing, disgraceful failure of the mortal races.

She, above all, understood mortal frailty, it was said. She alone understood the intraversable chasm between we and our creator. We were loved, and we were unworthy, and the High Cleric alone was burdened with the full and devastating comprehension of this truth.

It was only the High Cleric who understood the true meaning of the All-Mother's first law.

Sister Esme didn't care for the way the other attendants gathered by the High Cleric's door, though she was conflicted over whether she found such gatherings disrespectful or simply obsequious. Either way, she preferred to be elsewhere when the High Cleric was in one of her moods, in the orchards or in the library or down by the sea.

On this particular Wednesday morning, while the others were huddled outside the High Cleric's chamber, Esme was busy in the kitchen making sandwiches for the street children of South District. There were robots available to do the same work, but Sister Esme liked making a physical contribution to the cause. She'd been living rough herself before the Church took her in, so she knew it wasn't just the sandwich that mattered, but also that someone cared enough to offer it.

She lifted a piece of Swiss to her eye and peered through the hole. "Arr, I'm a cheese pirate!" she joked to herself, even though a piece of cheese with an eyehole is basically the opposite of an eye patch.

And then as she lowered the slice from her eye, she saw it, and she stifled a cry. There was a dead thing standing opposite her, on the far side of the counter, over by the doorway. It stood six feet tall, flesh rotted, jaw slack, in black leather, with an Apple Watch draped around its neck on a cheap lanyard. In its hand, a long, jagged knife.

"Do not be alarmed. I am here to see the High Cleric," said the voice from the watch that was programmed to sound like James Earl Jones.

What Esme did next, she did out of fear. She stepped back, crouching low behind the counter, quite reasonably, and then she lobbed the slice of Swiss across the room at Mister Five. It landed with a smoosh over the Grimsoul's right eye socket.

She was trembling now and starting to cry. She gripped a pair of cabinet door handles to try to steady her hands, but that just made the cabinet doors rattle. "Please don't kill me!" she whimpered as the Grimsoul clomped toward her.

On the street, if you're in danger, you find something sharp and you stab. Esme wasn't supposed to stab anyone anymore, and anyway she was reasonably sure that stabbing this creature would only make it angry.

She closed her eyes. "Please," she whispered.

She could hear the Grimsoul climb up onto the counter above her. "I am here to see the High Cleric," the voice repeated.

The creature was almost on top of her now. Even with her eyes closed, Esme could feel it looming above, the stench of death reaching down towards her.

"M-My first and true mother, you who see us for what we are..." She could feel the sharp of the creature's blade slide down along the side of her habit. "I who am undeserving of absolution..." The blade tripped across her cheek, scratch, scratch, scratch, drawing blood. "...ask only for the mercy..." The creature lifted Esme's chin with its blade, and she slowly, reluctantly opened her eyes to face him. "...of a swift and unflinching judgment."

The piece of cheese still hung from the creature's face. Esme let out a short, surprised laugh, which she immediately regretted.

"Be at peace," the watchvoice commanded.

Esme didn't know what to do with her hands, so she folded her arms and clasped them tight to her chest as she walked. In her head, instead of praying, she just kept repeating right foot, left foot, right foot, left foot over and over again.

Up ahead, the other attendants were crowded against the High Cleric' door, whispering like school girls.

Right foot, left foot, right foot, left foot.

One-by-one they turned to face Esme, who stood trembling, teary eyed, a bloody scratch against the brown of her cheek.

"You have to go now. You have to go back to your chambers," she told them all. "He's coming. You can't be here when he comes."

The others didn't know what to make of this. They stared, confused by what they were seeing, till Esme shouted, "YOU HAVE TO GO!"

And they ran, one nearly knocking Esme sideways as she fled.

And then she was alone in the hall, and she took her right hand, and she knocked three times against the High Cleric's door.

On the other side, silence. No one was to disturb the High Cleric's lament.

"I beg your pardon, Your Holiness, but there's a man come to see you. A dead man."

Behind her, the dead thing with the watch materialized.

"He's... He's come with a message for you."

She could hear footsteps to the door.

"He says that..." Esme looked back towards the thing, the slice of cheese still clinging to its face. "He says that the conspiracy is ending."

There was a silence at the doorway.

"He says that the conspiracy is ending... and that your child is on the move."

The High Cleric drew her door open to an eye's width and spoke. "Thank you, little sister. That will be all. You may leave the... gentleman with me."

Sister Esme wiped a finger across her bloody cheek. "Are you sure, Your Holiness?"

"Yes," the High Cleric replied tersely. "Run along now."

Esme nodded meekly, backed around Mister Five and, once she was clear of the thing, ran.

The High Cleric scowled at the Grimsoul through the crack of her door, and she hissed, "You bring me this message on a dead man's back? Tell me, Zell, in all the galaxy is there truly no one left alive whom you can trust?"

Esme didn't stop running until she reached the tower gates, stumbling through her final steps and catching herself against the bars. Her breaths were long and labored.

On the far side of the gates, tourists pointed and whispered. She snarled back at them, "What are you looking at?" And then she barked at them, twice, quite surprising herself as she did. It was enough to send them shuffling off about their days. Esme, for her part, was trapped in hers.

Above her, the All-Mother's first law was etched into the wrought iron:

THE ALL-MOTHER WILL NOT FORGIVE YOU

2 | UM'S IDEA

A half-galaxy away, Officer Um had a marvelously good idea. Since Tarot was so sure that the Nth Realm were the ones who'd abducted the boy, it made good sense to track down their ship and search it before heading out to find her mother AKA Mrs. Illuminari AKA the High Cleric of the Intergalactic Church of the All-Mother.

That ship, along with the remains of the Wisp and a dozen Realm shock troopers, had been flung out into the void when Tarot reversed gravity back on Magician's Station. By the time she'd reversed it back again, they were out of range and so continued outward along their deep space trajectory.

Without jetpacks, the shock troopers were quite helpless, unable to reach each other or the Wisp's wreckage or their own ship. They had recycling air supplies that would last them for weeks, and they were still armed and still in radio communication, but their ship was now at least a kilometer away from them and drifting further, and they had no food or water to sustain them. Death seemed inevitable.

Twelve minutes in, it was Fnn-12 who raised the possibility of a murder-murder-murder-murder-murder-murder-murder-murder-murder-murder-murder-suicide pact over the radio link. "Otherwise we're all gonna die of starvation," he griped, "like a dirty pack of Nyorg Eaters."

"Some of us still have things to live for," Castor reminded him, thinking principally of his wife, but also of his wife's friend, Jenny.

"There's still hope that someone will come looking for us."

Fnn-12 scoffed. "Do you really think we matter to the leadership? To the Archduke or Noon? To that accursed She-Ape? We're foot soldiers, Castor. Disposable. Valued only for our ability to march and shoot in straight lines."

Edward Braun, who had been walking when he started falling, and as a result had been slowly spinning head over foot while the others were simply drifting, interjected, "Listen, let's not fight. That's what they'd want, for us to fall into chaos. But we are the master races united. We're better than them, and we will find a way through this."

"Says the human cartwheel," said Fnn-12 with a snort. The other men laughed. "Forget it, Braun. I'm going to do us all a favor and put us out of our misery. You'll thank me in Valhalla." He turned his Magnum Heat-Seeking Agony Rifle first on Castor, who he'd never liked very much, and fired.

Castor let out a blood-curdling scream that echoed through all the other radios. Fnn-12 could hear the scream through Castor's radio, through Edward's, through his own, and through all the rest's as the smart-shrapnel tore Castor apart and the necromantic curse kept him alive.

"SHUT UP!" Fnn-12 shouted, turning on the others and firing. Edward, sensing the way the situation was going, pulled off his helmet and exhaled hard, hoping to die before the smart-shrapnel got him. Then the smart-shrapnel got him. Castor, who still had much of his right arm, turned his rifle on Fnn-12 and fired. Fnn-12 swore loudly into the radio link as his flesh shredded. More of the shock troopers fired at Fnn-12, and he fired back.

One of the shock troopers realized that kickback from his blast had actually pushed him in the direction of their ship. Given another minute or so, he'd be within an arm's reach. He couldn't believe his luck. He'd be able to climb back onboard, to power up the ship and save them all. He grinned inside his helmet. He'd be remembered for this. He'd be a hero. Children throughout all Fatherspace would know the name of—

And then Fnn-12 hit him with the smart-shrapnel. What's-his-name's eviscerated remains bounced off the side of their ship's cargo pod and out into the void.

Sometime later, they were all finally dead.

The Prestige approached the carnage with its weapons primed. The Prestige was an intimidating ship, less a spacecraft with six mounted cannons than six enormous cannons with an incidental spacecraft tucked between. Its hull gleamed white, every inch as immaculate as its interior, except for the places where shock troopers bounced and smeared across its surface.

From within Um pointed out the Realm ship, a smoldering red asteroid, strapped with massive golden engines and a half-open cargo pod emblazoned with the broken cross. "It's a mine ship," he told the others.

"You mean a mining ship?" asked Percival.

"Nope," said Um. "A mine ship. The ship *is* the mine. Asteroid's composed a radioactive isotopes. Ship extracts 'em, processes 'em, ingests 'em as fuel. The Nth Realm may be scum a the universe, but yoo gotta give 'em points fer efficiency."

Percival thought about this for a moment. "Good idea, I suppose, until you run out of fuel, and you've got no ship left."

"Well," Um shrugged, "I'd deduct points fer that."

Mouse frowned. "If the pair of you are finished scoring the handiwork of bigoted genocidal psychopaths, we should plan out our ingress."

Tarot pressed her nose to the glass, responding absently, "Are you sure that's a word?"

"We've been through that," answered Mouse with a bit of a sniff.

Since Um was already in a spacesuit and good with computers, the rest elected him to teleport into the open cargo pod and seal the door so they could port in after. While this was happening, Percival had his mind on the wreckage of the Wisp, a few kilometers in the opposite direction.

"All clear," Um broadcast over the radio link, his voice echoing through The Prestige intercom like a deep-throated, froggy-god. "Pod's sealed."

On signal Percival, Tarot, Halla, and Mouse ported into the cargo pod. It was a single room, large and open, with high ceilings and cold metal floors. Cots and footlockers and folding chairs lined the side walls, magnetically locked to the floor. The rear wall was a massive touch screen on which Um was presently pulling up crew profiles, a diagram of the ship, and other relevant information.

"Bring in a few more chairs, this'd be good for movie night," Percival joked, but no one else was really paying attention.

"Can you access footage from Sunday evening?" asked Mouse.

Um grunted, and a security feed filled the wall, a virtual mirror of the room they were standing in, except for the company of Nth Realm shock troopers and the two-day old timestamp running in the bottom right. As Um fast-forwarded, the shock troopers sped back and forth at super-speed, including the elite soldiers they fought on Magician's Station: the Cyborg, the Ape, and the Swordsman.

At 21:16:32.534 Sunday night, the Swordsman dragged glassy-eyed Kevin Cooper into the pod by one arm. Percival nodded to Um, and Um swiped a finger across the wall to turn the volume up.

The Swordsman turns the boy to face him, pulls his chin up to look him in the eyes. "We're sure that this is him?" he asks.

"It," the Ape corrects. "It is an *it*."

The two of them stand in the middle of the room with the boy and two shock troopers, Fnn-12 and one of the others. "You're kidding me!" Fnn-12 protests. "This is our secret weapon? Our key to dominance over the lesser races? Some doped-up tween with a sniffly nose?"

The Ape bends down next to the boy and paws through his hair. She answers Fnn-12 without turning to acknowledge him. "This *doped-up tween* is only one half of our weapon. This shell contains a great malevolence, the wrath of the gods, but it does us little good without the vehicle of that wrath."

Fnn-12 smirks. "So, what are we talking about here? Ten-speed? Maybe a bumper car of doom?"

"Ignore the shock trooper," the Swordsman cuts in. "He's 12th gen. Not good for much but shooting straight at this point. We should leave now. We need to be at the rendezvous by oh-eight-hundred."

The boy speaks inaudibly. Fnn-12 goes pale. The Swordsman looks to the Ape with concern. The other shock trooper stammers, "W-What did he say?"

The boy speaks again, inaudibly again, at most a few words, not looking at anyone or anything. "What is he SAYING?" the other shock trooper pleads, raising his rifle.

The Swordsman raises a hand and crouches down to eye level with the boy. He says it again.

The Swordsman repeats, "Only sky." He eyes the Ape. "Why does he keep saying that? What does it mean?"

The boy says it again. The other shock trooper panics, lifts his rifle to shoot, and Fnn-12 punches him in the teeth, grabs him around the neck, twists hard. The other shock trooper drops to the floor, lifeless.

Fnn-12 fires a cold stare at his superiors. "See. I do more than just shoot straight."

"Don't pay attention to anything the boy says," the Ape instructs. "Nothing he says..." She catches herself, corrects herself. "Nothing *it* says matter. We have our orders. We follow those orders."

Percival eyed Um and twirled his finger. "Fast-forward to oh-eight-hundred."

"We're here," calls one of the shock troopers.

The Swordsman has been sitting with the boy and now he pulls him up from his chair by the arm and drags him back to the pod door. The door slides up to reveal a blue cloudless sky.

And the Swordsman shoves the boy out into the blue. The boy falls from sight, limp, without struggle, without a sound. The Swordsman turns and walks back towards his chair as the pod door slides shut behind him.

He holds up a black envelope that he did not have a moment before. "Our new orders."

He pulls a black letter from the envelope and silently reads the message therein. Then he passes the letter to the Ape who does the same. The Ape nods to the Swordsman, then walks up to the screenwall and taps the screen three times.

"We can see you," she snarls, staring into the screen, staring out into the future. And then she reads aloud from the black letter, "Ythl. Ignus. Lom."

And the screen goes black.

Percival's eyes went wide. "Wait. What just happened?"

Beneath their feet, the asteroid began to rumble. Tarot looked to Mouse and then back to Percival. "It's a booby trap. They planned for this. We need to get out now."

Percival looked to Um. "Do we have time to... download... something to... something?"

Um spread his legs wide to steady himself as the rumbling intensified. "Yeah, and let's have tea and a quick nap. Mouse, you gonna zap us outta here or what?"

Mouse, who didn't like being called Mouse, made an exception under the circumstances, and triggered the return port. As soon as they'd fully materialized, he was out of the room and down the hall shouting, "EVADE! EVADE! EVADE!"

The ship rolled hard to the right as the asteroid the Realm ship was built atop exploded. The resulting shockwave sent the Prestige spinning, temporarily knocking out anti-gravity and sending Percival and the rest of them tumbling from wall to ceiling to wall down to the floor and back around again. Fragments of the asteroid pelted the Prestige's hull.

Halla backflipped off the floor and onto her feet, which struck Percival as a bit unnecessary. He lumbered up, clutching the small of his back, which he'd bruised. Tarot offered a hand to Um as she stood, but he just lay there, flat on his back. "Think I'll just stay here fer a few, if ya don't mind," he told them via vocal transmit.

The rest of them walked down to the lounge, where Mouse was waiting for them, staring out into the destruction. "How bad's the damage?" Tarot asked.

Mouse glanced back at her, "We'll be fine. The Realm ship is debris now. Nothing to salvage."

Percival scanned the debris field, his eye catching on a bit of the Wisp, a sliver of the hull that had been caught up in the shockwave. And floating just beside it...

"Ah! Things are looking up," Percival said with a grin. "There's my umbrella!"

3 | TRAPS

There are few planets in the universe with precipitation so severe that they actually require the purchase and use of an umbrella with triple-reinforced microweave fabric. Percival had been to two such worlds, although Jagrahr-4's Carnivorous Cancer Rain fell sideways so often he ultimately spent most of his time there indoors.

As it turns out triple-reinforced microweave umbrellas are far more useful when used as not-umbrellas, and that's where Percival found most of his umbrella's utility. In the past it had made an excellent shield, a passable grappling hook, an admirable poking stick, an exceptional "let's keep this door from closing all the way" wedge, a so-so parachute of last resort, a surprisingly functional radar dish, and an extremely convenient extender arm to reach things placed on the top shelf.

In Percival's experience, things placed on the top shelf were typically the best things, so he was grateful to have come across his umbrella in the debris field and happier still when Mouse was able to port it out of said field and onto the ship.

Once reunited, Percival grinned and gave his umbrella a hug and swore that they would never be parted again and instructed his inanimate umbrella to make a similar vow. When it did not, he feigned annoyance and began knocking it against the corridor wall so as to punish it.

Mouse watched this bit of silliness from down the hall, then turned to Tarot with a frown and asked, "Do we need him?"

"*I* need him," she answered.

Mouse shook his head. "You're making this harder than it has to be. At the end of our quest, one of two things will happen: Either the universe will no longer exist, or you'll be left in a universe where you've made some very hard decisions that you'll need to live with."

"I know."

"And if that happens, will he be able to live with you?"

Tarot looked away. "I'm not planning that far ahead," she lied, for the truth was too terrible to speak.

Elsewhere on the ship Um had found an access panel. And behind that access panel he had found a network access port. And behind that network access port he had found a series of alchemically-attuned, bio-electric radio relays, which he was now reprogramming with a broken-off fingernail to receive override transmissions from his spacesuit's radio link.

Just in case, thought Um.

"What do you think you're doing?"

Um turned his head quickly, not recognizing the voice over his shoulder. It was the girl, Halla, holding her cane out like a fencing blade in front of her.

"Didn't think yoo spoke," said Um, cautiously.

"Didn't think you... *vandalized*," she countered, a mischievous smirk across her lips.

"I don't know yoo people. All I got is Tarot's word, and she's an escaped fugitive."

"You know..." Halla flashed a smile and took a step closer. Then another. She let her cane slide down across the contours of Um's spacesuit. "...there *are* other ways to get to know someone."

"Heh," Um laughed nervously. "Yoo maybe got somethin' in mind?"

Halla grinned, snapped her fingers, and Um's faceplate went black.

"WAIT! WHAT'RE YOO—?"

Um grabbed his helmet and began unscrewing it. Halla flicked her cane down, fast, and the oxygen inside of Um's helmet turned to pure krypton gas, not a gas that Um could breathe. Luckily, he'd had some recent experience holding his breath.

Um flung his helmet to the ground just in time to catch a hard smack across the side of his head from Halla's cane. He clutched his cheek in pain, lurched forward, then charged hard into Halla, shoulder first, smashing her into the far wall. "WHAT IS WRONG WITH YOO?" he howled, an arm across her throat.

Halla's eyes went wide. She let out a helpless rasp. Um eased up just long enough for Halla to whisper a "zap" charm as she shoved the now electrified tip of her cane into Um's chest.

The jolt sent Um staggering back, and Halla followed after him, spinning, whipping a stiletto heel across his face and then the other and then the first again.

Um bounced against the far wall then dropped knees first, face second onto the floor. Halla shoved the tip of her still-electrified cane against the back of his head and held it tight as he convulsed and convulsed and then did not. Um was dead in a not inconsiderable pool of his own drool.

Halla bent down over him and whispered a "stop being such a baby" charm. Um drew in a sharp and startled breath.

Halla sighed as she stood, extinguishing her cane with a casual flick. She picked up the access panel that Um had removed and refitted it to the corridor wall.

"Ahoy!" Percival called out from the far end of the corridor. "What's going on down there?"

Halla did not answer. She simply bowed and backed away around the corner.

Percival jogged up to Um, who was by this point pulling himself to his feet.

"You all right?" Percival asked.

"I do not trust that lady," Um grumbled, glancing back over his shoulder.

"Oh. Yes, well..." Percival thought about this for a moment. "I suppose I don't either. Or her partner Mouse?"

"He's got some cool guns, but nah, not really."

"Do you trust Tarot?"

"You kiddin'?"

"Or me?"

Um frowned. "Not so far as I can throw ya."

Percival smiled. "Well, the good news is you don't seem to have a concussion. So tell me what happened."

"Don't wanna talk about it."

Percival slid his hands into his pockets, then asked smugly, "Was it your fault?"

Um shrugged half-heartedly and avoided eye contact. "We should get back ta the others. Make a plan."

Percival agreed.

Mouse set course for the so-called Great Cathedral, then homeworld of the Intergalactic Church of the All-Mother and home to its founder, the High Cleric. Eleven years earlier they had saved the universe together, but Mouse was under no illusions that the High Cleric would be happy to see him now. Of the four of them, understandably, she had had the hardest time coming to terms with what they'd had to do.

The Great Cathedral was a marvel of planetary engineering, a partially desublimated gas giant on the outskirts of the Aboolis system. The High Cleric had purchased the planet from the indigenous species for the sum of three billion and twenty-two space Euros, the exact amount she'd won in her divorce settlement. These moneys are referenced rather obliquely in the Church's holy texts as the First Donation.

As part of their deal, the indigenous species, a floaty, fleshy race of gasbags called the Fummers, accepted relocation to a small island on the dark side of their planet. There they used the High Cleric's money to start an ultra-successful, kid-friendly resort called Fum 4 The Whole Family™.

When the High Cleric realized that she was competing with the Fummers for tourists, she immediately declared visiting their resort a mortal sin. And that's the reason why everyone stopped telling the High Cleric that they were taking their families to Fum 4 The Whole Family.

Percival and Tarot and Mouse and Halla and Um gathered in the lounge to have a talk. Mouse sat first and Halla slid in next to him, under his arm. Percival and Tarot sat down across from them, knee brushing knee. Um stood by the door, froggy-eyes locked on Halla, froggy-lips frozen into a froggy-scowl.

She didn't seem to notice.

Outside, the ship's Wormhole engine folded space and time like a cheap napkin. It was distracting, so Mouse snapped his fingers and the bay window went black.

"So." Percival leaned forward. He looked into Mouse's eyes and asked, "What can you tell me about the Conspiracy of Days?"

Mouse removed his glasses, folded them, and vanished them in his right hand before answering. "I can tell you anything you want to hear, Mister Gynt. After all, I was one of the conspirators."

"Good. Number one. Tarot said the Engine unmakes things. Makes it so they never existed."

"That's correct."

"And because they never existed, no one notices that they're gone."

"Yes."

"But you lot did. You alone in all the cosmos. So my first question is: How did you manage that?"

"It was Gor. Did Tarot tell you why we released her?"

"You needed her help to contain the Engine."

"After a fashion. You see, Gor's planet was the first to go. At least, the first we noticed. Illuminari had removed Gor from space, folded her inside out, and trapped her within the theoretical gravity core of an active MagmaStar. Finished her off. End of.

"But then her world went. Then time was rewritten. And all across the universe, Illuminari's greatest enemy was forgotten. Illuminari's greatest victories, his most celebrated feats of heroism, his peerless reputation, vanished in an instant. And only Illuminari remembered what he had lost."

"Hold up. Why did Illuminari remember?"

"We didn't know at first. The old man was convinced that this was one of Gor's schemes, a trick. He tore open the MagmaStar and demanded that Gor undo whatever it was she did. Of course, Gor had no clue what Illuminari was on about. All she knew was that she'd been trapped and tortured for decades, and she wanted vengeance. So they set upon each other, and they fought.

"And this went on for days, spell against spell, from one side of the universe to the other. Ultimately, it was Gor who worked it out. She tried to summon one of her old weapons, her Apocalypse Wand, but it had been unmade. When she couldn't find the wand, she returned to her homeworld to look for it. And when she couldn't find her homeworld..."

"I suppose Gor was protected from whatever the Engine does because she was trapped inside the MagmaStar. But that still doesn't explain Illuminari. Why did he remember?"

"The most powerful magics... They bind caster and subject together, long after the spell is cast. Gor remembered the universe, and Illuminari remembered through Gor."

Percival frowned. That sounded more like a metaphor to him than the answer he'd been hoping for. Even if it was true, it barely made sense. This, Percival concluded, is why so many people hate magicians. He moved on.

"Number two. Gor and Illuminari remembered. All right. But how did they figure out what happened? How did they find the Engine?"

"Once they realized that something was happening, that the world was being rewritten around them, they set to tracking the change. Gor used her magic to create a Codex, a sort of Google Maps of reality that captured everything that was and everything that had been lost during his imprisonment. And Illuminari stored the Codex in the MagmaStar to shield it from further changes.

"Unfortunately, between Gor's release and the creation of the Codex was a period of days for which we have no record. We know now that the Engine was on the move, erasing worlds, rewriting history, but without Gor or the Codex in the MagmaStar... Illuminari later estimated that we lost eighty-eight civilizations during those Missing Days."

"And the Engine? How did you find the Engine?"

"Illuminari maintained a Secondary Codex outside the MagmaStar. By comparing them over time, we could track the Engine's movements."

"Follow-up. Where are the Codex and the Secondary Codex now?"

"I'm not sure."

"Disappointing, but all right. Number three. Who else knows about the Conspiracy of Days?"

"Besides us in the room? Lora. Gor. Anyone they told. Anyone Illuminari told. Anyone you told."

"And that's it?"

"And the Nth Realm, it seems. Perhaps the Grimsouls that Tarot told me about. I don't know who told them."

"Number four. Where is Vargoth Gor now?"

"I honestly don't know. Once Illuminari was done with her, perhaps he put her back in the MagmaStar. The old man wasn't known for his sentimentality."

"But you don't know?"

"That's what I said."

"Follow-up. Which MagmaStar?"

"I don't know. GE made a lot of them during the Fusion Boom. Doesn't Sanctuary-8 have a MagmaStar?"

"Number five. What about the boy?"

"The vessel?"

"Yes."

"What about it?"

"Am I to understand that you created him?"

"Yes. Well, no. No, not me, personally. That was Illuminari's work, the product of an ancient ritual, deep magics, with some help from his lovely assistant Lora."

"Follow-up. Why a boy? Why not a bottle or a magic circle or a bit of amber? Why create a human being, only to use him as a shell?"

"Let me ask you a question, Mister Gynt. How do you trap a shadow?"

"You tell me."

"Oh, come on now, Gynt. This is an easy one. Work it out."

"You..." Percival nodded reluctantly. "You trap it in a circle of light."

"You trap it in a circle of light. A prison of pure innocence for an entity of unfathomable evil. There was no other choice, Mister Gynt. No other option. In the end there was only the Shadow Trap."

4 | CALL FROM MUM

The Prestige came out of warp above the planet Ten at 12:02 PM. They were only a few hours away from the Great Cathedral now, but Mouse insisted that they stop to refuel. He also wanted a mechanic to take a look at his left tertiary reactor, which had been giving off strange readings since the Realm mine ship exploded, but he didn't want to worry the others with that particular piece of business.

"One hour," Mouse told the others just before porting them down into the middle of an outdoor market in a city in a country on a continent on the far side of the planet. The market was crowded with off-worlders, robots and mutants and angels and necroblobs and the occasional human. Some scowled as Percival and the others materialized between them.

"As a reminder, God hates the following things:" a helpful soul announced over the loudspeakers. "Teleportation. That is all."

The merchants were mostly natives, Tenners, purple and furry and thin with long tentacled noses. They sold food and drink and fine clothes and odd trinkets from their stalls.

"I could buy you a new tie," Tarot whispered to Percival, tugging on the stub that the Swordsman had left him back on Magician's Station.

"I'd rather we just got something to eat," he confided as he pulled off the remainder and deposited it in a nearby waste recycler.

Um eyed Halla, whom he assumed Mouse had sent along as a minder, then nodded. "I could eat. What about yoo, Halla?"

Halla shrugged.

"Right. Forgot ya don't talk."

Halla frowned and, perhaps sensing she was less than welcome, stepped backwards into the crowd and vanished.

Um turned back to Percival and Tarot. "That's better now, ain't it?"

"Just as long as they don't decide we're more trouble than we're worth and leave without us," said Percival.

Tarot wrapped an arm around Percival's and smiled. "You, sir, are worth every ounce of trouble that you bring."

Knowing what was coming next, Um turned his head quickly, covered his visor with one hand for safe measure, and growled, "Oy! Are we gettin' lunch or what?"

The planet Ten was originally called the planet Het which, roughly translated, means "best planet." The people of Het liked this name, but it didn't earn them any good will from the rest of the universe which, by and large, thought their own planets were also very good.

Then, in the year 19932, a scholar at Duke-DeVry University published a paper claiming that Het was actually the tenth oldest planet in the universe. The people of Het weren't sure if this was true, but it was a rather smashing claim. And since the other nine very, very, very old planets were either uninhabitable or very remote or, in one case, very smelly, it meant perhaps, by this one very narrow criterion, that Het really was "best planet" after all.

In 19934 the nations of Het got together and passed a joint resolution formally changing the planet's name to "Ten" in celebration of the planet's special place in intergalactic history. The new name had a basis in fact and was therefore less confrontational, but in every Tenner's heart it still meant "best planet."

When, in the year 19942, a scholar at Oxford FSU published a paper which provided ample evidence that Ten was merely the forty-fourth oldest planet in the universe, the people of Ten humbly declined to change their planet's name a second time.

"We should buy Um some new clothes," Percival suggested, between bites of his gluten-free Reuben.

Um looked up from his half-eaten nyorg appendix and shrugged. "It ain't like I'm naked. I got a spacesuit."

"Yes, but you're naked under your spacesuit," Tarot pointed out. "That can't be comfortable."

"Or hygienic," Percival added. "Particularly if one of us needs to wear that spacesuit after you."

"Okay, okay," Um relented. "I think I saw an Old Navy on the way here."

Tarot was about to call the waitressaurus over when the tune from *Jaws* began to play from her cloak pocket. This confused Tarot as much as anyone.

Um leaned forward. "Don't take this the wrong way, Tarot, but I got a feelin' something bad's about ta happen in yer... cape area."

Percival reached a hand out. "You still have my watch. That's..." His eyes were wide with alarm. His words, a puddle of defeat. "That's Mother's ring."

Tarot slipped the watch from her cloak. The screen text did indeed read "CALL FROM MUM." Tarot smiled a sly smile and lifted the watch to her lips, even as a pale and speechless Percival gestured for her not to. And she answered the call cheekily, "Hullo, Mum!"

Percival let out a helpless, open-mouthed squeak. His hand dropped to his lap.

On the other end of the watchcall, Fred snarled, "Hello, Ms. Lamb."

Tarot lowered the watch to her chest and joked to Percival, "You know, your mother has a very... deep voice."

Percival attempted to form words, but the world was all a bit swirly at that particular moment, and he wasn't sure if he was awake or dreaming or some unholy combination of the two. Um took a big bite of nyorg appendix and drank in Percival's discomfort like a fine nectar.

Tarot lifted the watch back to her lips, offering, "Don't you worry, Mrs. Gynt. I'm taking good care of your little Percy-Wercy."

Percival gulped down the last of his water and wiped away his flop sweat with a napkin.

"Oh, I'm so glad that you're taking care of my little Percy-Wercy, Ms. Lamb. Perhaps you'd be so kind as to put Officer Um on the line."

Tarot took the watch and checked the caller ID again. "Um," she said, "apparently Percival's mother wants to talk to you."

"Okay then," Um answered, reaching out for the watch, but Percival snatched it away before Tarot could make the exchange.

"Mother! I-I'm sorry for any confusion. That was... That was nobody. Nobody. Don't... I'm here now. I'm here." Percival turned away from the others and slumped forward in his seat. Um and Tarot shared a confused look.

"Now listen to me, you little ingrate! I gave you strict instruction back on Sanctuary-8. You were to apprehend Ms. Lamb and bring her back to me immediately! Not go gallivanting off with her to who-knows-where to do who-knows-what while the fate of the galaxy hangs in the balance! I know exactly who your mother is, I have her phone number, and I can arrange for a reunion between the two of you in one of two locations. Either I can track you down, put you in chains, and ship you to her, or I can send her to meet you. And your new girlfriend. Now, tell me, Mr. Gynt: Are either of those options preferable to you doing the job you agreed to and bringing me Ms. Lamb before matters get any worse?"

Um leaned across the table to the scrawny tawny huddled thing. "You okay, Gynt?"

Head still buried in his lap, Percival tossed his watch back onto the table. "It's for Um," he muttered weakly.

Um scooped up the watch curiously and raised the device tentatively to his lips. "Hulloo?"

"Officer Um," Fred began. "Please, for the love of creation, explain to me what's going on."

"Well," said Um, uncertain where to begin, "fer one, it sounds like Gynt has mummy issues."

On the far side of the galaxy, Fred counted backwards, silently, from ten. And he began again, "Why didn't you return with the girl, Officer Um?"

"I was usin' my discretion."

"Your *what*?"

"My discretion. It's a big word. I got a few."

"I heard you, Officer Um. I just had a hard time processing the words. Please tell me: Who was it who told you that you had the privilege of free will? Who lied to you, Officer Um? Tell me their name, and I'll have them hanged at dawn, but do not tell me that you're exercising your fictional discretion to make one more fictional decision that undermines my very non-fictional authority over this *anti-fictional case*!"

To this, Um chuckled.

"Mister Director, I'm gonna hang up on ya in a minute, but before I do, I want ya ta know why. I died twice in the last forty-eight hours, and I may die a bunch more in the next forty-eight. In the meantime, I only got three objectives: ta finish this tasty piece a nyorg meat, ta buy a new pair a trousers at Old Navy, and ta stop a pack a maniacs from reactivatin' a doomsday device that'll wipe out the entire universe, dawn ta dusk. And right now, my best shot at doin' that is a shiverin' little yutz with mummy issues called Percival Gynt. So, unless ya happen ta know the location a THE ENGINE A ACTUAL ARMAGEDDON, I suggest ya shut up, hang up, and go do somethin' more productive with yer time, *like think about how sad it is ya ain't tall enough ta ride none a the really good roller coasters*!"

With that, Um disconnected the call and let the watch drop onto the table with a stiff bounce.

"What?" he asked, but neither Tarot or Percival had said anything. Tarot was too busy laughing, and Percival was still clearly in shock.

"Um..." Percival said.

"Yeah, Gynt?"

"Um..." he repeated.

"Yeah?"

"Sorry," Percival apologized. "That's all I've got."

Outside the White Castle and five minutes later, Tarot was still laughing to herself the way that people do when the mere fact that they're still laughing becomes funny. Percival, for his part, had mostly recovered his wits. Thankfully for him, no one had asked him why he had become so anxious at the prospect of his mother calling him.

Um was feeling quite chuffed, but deep down was beginning to wonder whether he was losing himself. Whether the scrawny, tawny thing was starting to rub off on him.

And then he saw Halla from across the square, and he knew that everything was going to be all right, that he never made mistakes, and that this was going to be the best day of his life.

From across the square, Halla smiled an apologetic smile as she held up over her head a shiny, new mechanical third arm.

Before departing the planet Ten, Um stopped at the Old Navy and bought:

- o   one pair, socks
- o   one pair, underwear
- o   one pair, size 76 trousers with optional khakis-to-denim slider (default setting: "khakims")
- o   one brown belt
- o   one black XXXL T-shirt that read "Shhhh! I'm Undercover!" (tap for shush noise)
- o   one pair, climber's boots with 5 minutes of personal gravity per charge
- o   one red triple-reinforced microweave jacket with white racing stripes that was much too tight to zip

Once the ship was out of orbit, Um found himself an empty room, changed into his new clothes, and installed the new third arm that Halla had acquired for him.

According to the instruction manual, his new arm included the following features:

- one heavy blade, retractable, with flame sheath
- one light blade, retractable, with paralytic neurotoxin
- one meat thermometer
- bio-sensor array
- single-use personal force field
- death ray
- kung-fu grip
- instruction manual

Per the instruction manual: "Kung-Fu grip feature does not confer knowledge of kung-fu or any other martial art. Death ray should not be pointed at small children or instruction manual writers."

His new clothes and new arm brought Um some small measure of comfort, the latter plugging a quite literal hole in his being. Still, Um was troubled. After what he'd said to the Director, he was as good as fired and probably a fugitive. *And* the universe was probably going to end. *And* he'd had to say "thank you" to Halla, and she had kissed him on the cheek, and he wasn't sure whether he still wanted to kill her, which meant that the three elaborate ways that he'd devised to do the deed were likely wasted effort.

The third of these methods involved a rabbit, a top hat, and a Magnum Heat-Seeking Agony Rifle.

Sometime later, as the Prestige neared its destination, Um found Percival alone in the lounge, staring at the blackened viewing window like he could see through it. Or perhaps like he couldn't see it at all.

Percival looked up and nodded to Um as he entered. "Nice arm," he said, before turning back to the window. Um offered a mumbled "thanks" as he sat down, and he tried to see what Percival saw out the window.

"And thank *you*, by the way," Percival added, not turning to look at Um this time. "For taking our side against Agent Fred. I know you had your doubts about Tarot."

Had doubts? Still, he knew how Percival felt about her. "Ya know I was briefed, yeah? I played along like I was confused fer Tarot's benefit, but at some point yoo should maybe tell 'er who yer mum is."

"You mean before I invite her over for Sunday dinner? I'm trying to stay positive here, Officer Um, but the universe still existing on Sunday isn't a thought that I've spent a great deal of time contemplating recently."

"Suppose so. Still." Um thought about Halla for a moment. And then about a top hat. But then just about Halla again. "Maybe, right?"

Percival shook his head. "Can you imagine that conversation, though? 'Say, Tarot. You know how your mother is the founder of the largest and most powerful religion in the universe. Well, my mum's a raging b—'"

Before Percival could finish his thought, the lights in the lounge went deep red. Strange. Percival looked at Um, and Um shrugged.

Then, over the intercom, a cheery mechanical voice informed them, "Attention, passengers. Three heavily-armed foldships on trajectory to intercept. Remaining time to exist estimated at seventeen-point-nil-one seconds."

5 | ZOMWARD AND DOWN

In Euclidean geometry, the universe is defined in three dimensions: up and down, left and right, forward and back. People like Euclidean geometry because it's the geometry of the world they can see and touch and, when appropriate, lick. But Euclidean geometry is only a partial description of the universe we live in.

Because, besides up and down, left and right, forward and back, you can also travel ana and kata, cephal and nib, frisson and yon, pallow and nyuck-nyuck, frmm and 2.5, yellow and horn, Ford Motor Company Presents... Moventum™! and zom, or floops and shloop. Traveling in any of these eight higher dimensions will get you to your destination faster than simply going, say, forward, even if your destination appears to be in a straight, Euclidean line ahead of you. But just as you can't go left if there's a wall to your left, you can only go shloop if there's an unobstructed path to your shloop.

The easiest way to open a path through any of the eight higher dimensions is to use a Wormhole engine. Wormhole engines fold and realign space along your intended axis, thus allowing you to take superlight shortcuts through ordinary Euclidean space. Most starships that employ Wormhole engines maintain an interior Euclidean shell for the comfort of their passengers. That's a bit like shoving an egg down a soda straw without crushing it to bits. Not impossible, but you need a really amazing straw.

"An excellent investment!" says the egg.

But some starships are designed with less regard for a pilot's comfort and safety. Foldships, for example, have a cockpit the shape of a crumpled-up newspaper. Foldships are small, heavily armed, five-dimensional starfighters built in higher dimensional shipyards and optimized for higher dimensional combat.

Because of the peculiarities of their geometry, foldships can never enter Euclidean space. Foldship pilots don't so much board their ships as get fired into them from passing warp ships, and don't so much disembark as pull the ripcord on their pan-dimensional eject suits. And as painful an experience as boarding or piloting a foldship may be, pan-dimensional ejection is exponentially worse. Ilsum Yott of the Bluedusk Optima 1 once likened it to "standing up from a long, forced crouch only to be punched in the face by your own internal organs."

Of course, Yott was the rare pilot who found that sort of experience invigorating.

And now Yott was bearing frmmward on the Prestige with foldships Optima 2 and Optima 4 in tight formation to his ana and kata. "Fire!" he bellowed, and all three ships simultaneously unloaded their anti-matter wave cannons into the Prestige's right primary reactor.

This caused the reactor to overload and detonate. The resulting four-dimensional implosion/explosion tore apart all three of the ship's right cannons and cut a ship-long gash across the Prestige's hull, exposing the ship's interior to non-Euclidean foldspace. The ship's Euclidean shell burst, causing the interior to crumple, convulse, and finally turn itself inside out, expelling its contents out into higher dimensional space.

Said contents included Percival and Um, preserved in three dimensions by an unorthodox combination of Um's arm's single-use personal force field and, from Percival, what would in any other circumstances be described as an overly aggressive hugging style.

The three foldships swooped past their target and turned about for another run. What was left of the Prestige was now breaking apart, the three remaining engines separating off from the twisted body of the ship.

A tide of gravity pulled Um's force bubble zomward through the void. Perhaps, thought Percival, if we're close enough to the planet. Inside the bubble, he wrapped his arms around Um all the tighter. Behind Um's back he kept a white-knuckled grip on his umbrella, in case of rain. And he wailed into his partner's ear, "DON'T LET GO! DON'T LET GO! DON'T LET GO!"

Um, for his part, felt a preternatural sense of calm. He had, after all, died twice already this week. If he died here, precedent suggested that he would however improbably make his way back a third time. Plus, he had another trick up his sleeve. Or, to be more precise, in his trousers.

Um slipped a hand into his left trouser pocket and grasped a device he'd been carrying for just this eventuality, the radio transmitter from his old spacesuit, which he now turned on.

"Fire!" he growled into the transmitter, and one of the Prestige's broken off engines, the left tertiary, fired full force into the oncoming foldships, melting Optima 2 and Optima 4 into eight-dimensional, superluminal slag that streaked off into the void. In Optima 1, Yott pulled hard pallowward, just skimming the blast.

His friends were dead.

Just then, Um's force field, which had been to that moment a pleasant translucent blue, turned deep red, which Percival suspected was a bad sign. The Optima 1 spiraled around the left tertiary engine's blast, which was now giving out, and circled back towards Um and Percival, who were plummeting further and further away along the gravity tide. In the cockpit Yott clenched his teeth and wiped away his tears and locked onto our heroes with his anti-matter wave cannon.

Now Percival reached into his trouser pocket, and he activated Time Stop. That bought him six seconds to do... something. Think. Think. Ship's shredded. Tarot and Mouse and Halla and Tarot are dead. Force field's about to fail. Falling zomward. Caught in the gravity tide. Foldship's going to vaporize them. Foldspace is going to tear them apart.

Two seconds. Wait, no! Foldspace is empty. Need magic to fit an egg through a straw, but outside of the straw, the egg can just be an egg. No magic required.

Zero. Time started back up, and Yott's thumb pressed down on the trigger, firing his wave cannon. Percival shouted, "Drop the force field! DROP IT NOW!" which Um did without thinking, unexpectedly, implicitly placing his trust in the scrawny, tawny thing.

And suddenly they weren't in foldspace anymore, but back in normal, three-dimensional Euclidean space, in the upper, upper atmosphere of the Great Cathedral, plummeting through the clouds to their death.

Thinking quickly, Percival opened his umbrella, which was immediately ripped from his hands by the loud, buffeting winds. Percival let out a sort of a "BAGGH!" as his umbrella tumbled out of reach and as he and Um continued to drop like two shrieking stones through the clouds.

Through flapping, froggy-lips, Um shouted, "SOMETHING SOMETHING SOMETHING!" to which Percival responded, "YES! DO THAT!"

So Um did. As it turns out, "SOMETHING SOMETHING SOMETHING!" meant "MAYBE IF I FIRED OFF MY DEATH RAY A FEW TIMES, THAT'D SLOW US DOWN!" It did not, although the first blast did give Percival an awful scare. Cautiously, he slid around his companion until he was clung to Um's back. And the two continued to fall.

And fall.

And fall.

Four minutes later they were still falling through clouds, and if anything, those clouds were starting to get thicker. "WHY HAVEN'T WE HIT LAND, YET?" Percival shouted, though his voice was swallowed by the wind.

Um couldn't hear him, but took a guess at his question. "THIS PLANET'S A GAS GIANT! SURE, PARTS GOT DESUBLIMATED... THAT MEANS 'MADE SOLID'... BUT MOSTLY IT'S STILL JUST GAS! WHICH MEANS WE'LL

PROBABLY FALL RIGHT THROUGH THE CORE A THE PLANET AND THEN SLING-SHOT BACK THE WAY WE CAME!"

Percival nodded along to Um's explanation, though he couldn't hear any of it. When Um was finished, Percival tried again, "WE'RE GOING TO DIE, AREN'T WE?"

"YEAH, YEAH!" replied Um. "THAT'S A GOOD QUESTION TOO. MOST GAS GIANTS AIN'T GOT A BREATHABLE ATMO-SPHERE, BUT THE CHURCH CHOSE THIS ONE 'CAUSE IT'S MOSTLY NITROGEN AND OXYGEN, LIKE YOO HUMANS LIKE."

"WHAT ARE WE GOING TO DO?"

"RIGHT. US INDULIANS PREFER MORE NITROGEN AND LESS OXYGEN. TOO MUCH OXY BURNS MY LUNGS."

Percival was about to let go with another shout, but his throat was near raw. He stopped himself, took a moment to think, and then he grinned along with a dawning realization. "OF COURSE! THIS IS ONLY A *PARTIALLY* DESUBLIMATED GAS GIANT! AND THAT GAS MUST BE PRIMARILY NITROGEN AND OXYGEN! WE'RE GOING TO BE ALL RIGHT, UM! EVERYTHING'S GOING TO BE JUST FINE!"

Percival was clung to his back, so Um couldn't see the scrawny, tawny thing's expression or read its body language, but he knew when he was being properly hugged. "THAT'S IT!" he growled, just intensely enough that Percival could hear him past the wind. "RIDE ENDS HERE!" And Um engaged the artificial gravity units built into his boots.

The two tumbled to a bobbing float somewhere in the middle of the endless cloud. The winds were still fierce, but not so great that they couldn't shout over top of them.

Percival pulled out his watch and showed it to Um, who nodded vigorously. Percival swiped to the phone app and placed a call.

"PARDON ME, OPERATOR!" Percival shouted into his watch, "BUT I REALLY NEED A TAXI!"

Three minutes later, Um's gravity boots ran out of power, and the pair started falling again. No taxi just yet, though they'd been promised. "I have a good mind to call her back," Percival grumbled into the wind.

It took another seventeen minutes' worth of falling before the planetary rescue crew finally reached them, snatching them up with a pair of enormous robot monkey-foot-hands.

The rescue vehicle was itself a giant robot monkey, blue with whirling red emergency lights for eyes. Over loudspeaker, the pilot's voice boomed, "GREETINGS, TOURISTS! WELCOME TO THE GREAT CATHEDRAL AND ASSOCIATED ISLAND STATES! OUR APOLOGIES FOR YOUR TARDY RESCUE! TO MAKE THINGS RIGHT, PLEASE ACCEPT OUR COMPLIMENTARY DRINK TICKETS!"

Percival and Um held tight to the robot's monkey-toe-fingers as it rocketed upward through the clouds. Percival raised an eyebrow. Um shrugged.

"NEXT STOP: FUM 4 THE WHOLE FAMILY!"

6 | THE ENTERTAINERS

Some hours later the High Cleric of the Church of the All-Mother found her attendant dozing in the shadow of an old elm tree. For all the morning's traumas, Sister Esme now seemed at peace, and for a brief moment the High Cleric was hesitant to wake her. But these were grave times, and the High Cleric's heart was all but hollowed by a decade's grief and recriminations and whispered oaths.

The High Cleric jabbed at Esme's side with her pastoral staff until the girl woke, which did not take long. Four jabs at most. Esme winced in pain as she pulled herself to a seat in the grass, her back against the elm. The light of the noon sun was shining down through the branches now, and it took a moment for Esme to see the High Cleric and to understand where she was and what was happening.

"Little Sister of the All-Mother, I regret to say that I do not know your name."

"Esme," said Esme. After a moment's pause, she added a deferential "Your Holiness" and a quick nod.

"And, Esme," the High Cleric inquired, "how long have you been one of my attendants?"

"Five months and a few days, I think. I have not done the math."

"And before that?"

"Before that I was not," Esme clarified.

"Before that, what were you?"

"I was an orphan of South District, Your Holiness."

"I see. A vagrant?"

"And worse, Your Holiness. The church took me in and made me better."

"Saw many horrors, I suppose?"

"Many and varied, yes."

"Including death and dead men, I suppose?"

"At times, yes, Your Holiness."

"And in that time, did you ever know the dead to walk as men do or to threaten women with knives or to tell secrets?"

"None of those things, no. I knew my fair share of corpses, true, but they all seemed content to stay corpselike, which is to say quiet and... horizontal."

"And what do you imagine you saw this morning?"

"I wouldn't see it fit to speculate, Your Holiness. There was some matter that you deemed serious and private, and I accede to your wisdom as the voice of a righteous and unforgiving God."

The High Cleric smiled thinly, for this was the only proper answer to her question. "And when I found you here, little sister, you were sleeping in the grass. Should I judge by that and by your cool demeanor now that you were left untroubled by this morning's events? That you wear them as lightly cross your shoulders as you would a cloak of wishes?"

"Not at all, Your Holiness. From what I've seen and felt today, I am true and proper terrified. To the very core of me, I am. Both for my own life and for the lives and well-being of others. For the orphans now and the orphans to come. That I can sleep peaceably well is a learned thing, from my time on the streets. For I know, perhaps better than others, that I am a small thing adrift in a great large thing and that I shall not make a ripple no matter how hard I thrash my arms about. I sleep, because it makes no difference. Because sleep is easier than standing up with eyes wide open. Because I know now that the men of my nightmares are at worst shades of what's really out there."

The High Cleric frowned. This girl was perhaps too fatalistic for her purposes. Sensing her superior's displeasure, Esme forced a grin, adding, "Also, this particular patch of grass is super comfy."

A long time ago, the High Cleric had made the mistake of surrounding herself with idiots. Esme was not perfect, but perhaps not an idiot. She would have to do.

"Indeed. Within the hour, a trio of entertainers will arrive at the western gate, and they shall inquire as to whether they might perform a special engagement before the High Cleric. You will accept their offer and take them round the back of the tower and invite them to tarry in the larder until such time as I will come for them myself."

"You will meet them in the larder, Your Holiness?"

"Yes, Sister Esme. And you will not leave them unattended until such time as I arrive."

"I will attend them in the larder?"

"Yes.

"And, um...?"

"If you have a question, then out with it, Sister Esme."

"Will any of these entertainers be dead, Your Holiness?"

"They are not presently, Sister Esme, though we shall all of us surely become so in the fullness of time."

"In the fullness, yes, Your Holiness."

After the High Cleric took her leave of Esme, Esme stood and scratched the sleep from her eyes and brushed the dirt from her bottom, and she made her way to the western gate to wait for these mysterious entertainers.

There was a guard at the western gate named Franklin that Sister Esme knew in passing. He was an older man, all pudge and squints and "How d'ya do?"

Esme stepped up to his side and said quietly, "The High Cleric has asked me to receive three entertainers who will be arriving presently."

"Any three entertainers?" he asked with a sideways squint.

"Three specific entertainers," she clarified.

"And how will you know 'em?" he asked.

"They will offer a private performance for the High Cleric."

"Any three who offer a private performance, then?"

"Only these three."

"And how will you know the proper three?"

"It is said that they will come within the next hour."

"And if more come within the hour? How will you know which three?"

"I might not, I suppose. I simply intend to take the first three with me who meet these requirements."

"And if others come who meet the requirements?"

"Hmm. I hadn't thought of that."

The guard chuckled at Esme's foolishness. "I'd thought perhaps you hadn't."

"Well, in that case, perhaps you would be so kind as to have them form a queue inside the gate, in groups of three, in the order of their arrival, starting with the earliest to arrive standing at your side, on the grass just here, and the rest in order along the length of the fence? And then, should I have chosen the wrong three entertainers, I will return with them once I have made that determination, and escort the next three back."

Franklin thought on this for a time, punctuating his silence with the occasional "Hrmm" or "Mmmph" and at least one vigorous temple scratch. Then, at last, he concluded, "I suppose this seems a sensible pl—"

But before the guard could conclude his conclusion, a handsome young man on the far side of the gates interjected, "Pardon me for eavesdropping, but I believe that we're the three entertainers you were sent for. So, what do you say you let us in, and we'll put on a proper show for Her Holy?"

The young man wore a devilish smile quite at odds with his boyish good looks. He was short for one fully grown with a mess of dark hair and a pair of wire rim glasses that were, Esme suspected, only for show. And he dressed plainly. Surely no one would mistake him for an entertainer if not for his two companions.

The two women were both lovely, though hardly of a kind. She on the left, trying to dress like a man, with her short blonde hair and her showman's tails. She on the right, perhaps trying to look exotic or bohemian, with her straps and scarves and her purple cloak and that odd gray hat pulled over her long black hair.

"You're entertainers?" Esme asked, determined that she would not let in just anyone.

"Yes," the man confirmed. "We're entertainers. We entertain."

At which the one with the hat added, "Professionally."

"Yes," the man continued. "No mere amateurs, we. We have entertained for Kings and Queens and... Well..."

"Other nobility," the man-girl added flatly.

"And, frankly, they've always found us very entertaining."

"And what exactly is it that you do?" Esme probed. "How do you entertain people? What do you entertain them with?"

"Hmm." The young man pondered the question, then glanced back at his comrades for suggestions.

The man-girl shook her head. The hat-girl shrugged, offering, "Maybe we're funny?"

"Well that doesn't sound right," said Esme.

"We're jugglers," said the man-girl with a steely insistence that was decidedly *not* funny. "We juggle things, all sorts of things, and it's generally quite amusing. We've heard that the High Cleric is quite fond of juggling, and so we've come quite a great distance in order to do the juggling for her, and we're also very tired and don't like crowds or gates or sunlight, so we'd like to be taken inside now."

"If you're jugglers, where are your balls?"

"Pardon."

"Where are your juggling balls? Take them out and juggle me something," Esme prodded. "Entertain me."

The man shook his head. "We're not common street performers. Take us inside and then we'll show you all the juggling you want."

Esme took a long breath and examined the three of them again as she did. Then she looked to Franklin, who squinted back uselessly. "Franklin, you understand our plan?"

He nodded. "You take these three inside. Meanwhile, if there's anyone else comes claiming to be entertainers here to perform for Her Holiness, I line 'em up inside the gate, starting right here, and then back along the fence in threes, and if these three don't check out, you'll bring 'em back out with you, and then I'll hand off the next three to you, and so on, till we find the right ones."

"Very good," Esme replied, quite pleased with herself and with the old guard. Then she glanced at the three supposed entertainers and her smile faded. "This may take a while."

Esme led the visitors down a winding cobblestone path to the back of the tower. Could these three really be the ones the High Cleric had spoken of? They obviously weren't jugglers. But then, the whole "entertainers" story was likely a ruse. These three came here for the same reason the dead thing came here. Because something terrible was about to happen.

She looked back at them, now quiet and sullen. The one in the hat looked familiar. She was perhaps a few years older than Esme, which would put her in her early twenties. Had they crossed paths on the streets of South District? Or perhaps she spent time in the church?

"What are your names, then?" Esme asked without turning.

The three visitors looked to each other. They were getting lazier with their lies the more obvious it became that they weren't working. "I'm Michael Hauser," the man said. "And these are..." He gestured back to his companions, "Halo and... Cardz."

That got a reaction from the hat-girl. "Cards?"

"Cardz," he corrected. "With a z."

Well, Esme thought, at least none of them were trying to stab her.

The larder was a cavernous and inhospitably cold stone room located in the tower's deepest sub-basement, and it smelled of dead flesh. No one ever stepped foot into the larder who didn't absolutely have to. This, Esme speculated, must make it the perfect meeting place for those who prize secrecy or hate long meetings.

Esme herself had only been down to the larder once before, in her first weeks as a nun. She had been sent down from the kitchen to retrieve a tray of raw mutton on the day that the tower's artificially intelligent dumbwaiters had briefly turned vegan. She remembered the stench and the bitter cold and that the dumbwaiters were quite cruel until they were rebooted.

But there had been no dead men with knives. In retrospect, a good day.

Esme led her guests through one last door and down the narrow stairwell that opened onto the larder floor. It was as she remembered it. The familiar animal carcasses hung from the ceiling on hooks. Below each, a slab of blackest nullstone, stained with animal blood and radiating waves of cold. On a few of the slabs, a half-carved carcass or discarded cleaver remained from the morning's prep. And twelve artificially intelligent dumbwaiters lined the side wall, now properly mute and carnivorous.

Esme walked further into the room, rubbing her arms for warmth, deliberately separating herself from her guests. "I'm sure Her Holiness will be down to see you soon." She looked back to the others, still clustered by the steps.

Halo the man-girl scanned the room with a frown on her lips. "So, to say that you left things on bad terms might be a bit of an understatement?"

Michael the boy-man shoved his hands deep into his pockets and bounced on his heels to keep warm. "I don't know," he said, glancing about the room, "It's a bit homey, don't you think?"

"Do you think it's here somewhere?" asked Cardz the hat-girl. "Is it possible they hid it down here?"

Michael smiled wistfully. "That'd be nice, wouldn't it? Mummy and Daddy's own little side conspiracy. They really still loved each other and the whole intergalactic church and the 'God Hates Wizards' thing was just part of some cosmic cover-up? The most horrible piece of black magic ever conceived buried in the foundations of the Great and Powerful Church of No More Magic."

Michael spoke in the type of hush that echoed through a large room, and Esme was sure the three no longer cared about maintaining their cover or, presumably, about her existence much at all. Still, she wanted no part in this intrigue. She walked further back, towards the rear of the room and towards one particular slab on which a heavy steel cleaver lay. She saw her face in it and, for the first time, her new scar.

Cardz took Michael by the arm, whispering, "So how do we play this? Do we just ask her where the Engine is? Do we tell her everything?"

"Well, not everything, surely."

"You know what I mean. Do we tell her about Caul?"

Halo pushed in between them. "The plan won't work if we don't, will it?"

Michael walked away from the two of them, a frustration climbing up his chest and into his skull.

"Will it?" she pressed. "Matthew?" No response. "*Mouse?*"

He did not turn, but he answered her, in a tone tinged with defeat. "No, of course not. This has to be the way. She's not going to give up the location of the Engine unless she's emotionally compromised. It's a mistake to tell us where the Engine is. A mistake to tell *anyone*. She won't make that mistake unless she believes her son is in danger."

Tarot wiped a tear from her eye. "Or that there's a way to save him."

7 | FUM 4 THE WHOLE FAMILY

When Percival woke, it was night. Of course, where he woke, it was always night, so that didn't give him any real information about the time of day. And, of course, since different planets follow different clocks and calendars, such information wouldn't have been much use to him anyway.

In addition to not knowing what time it was, Percival also wasn't sure *where* he was or, more disturbingly, where his trousers had gotten to. He still had on his dress shirt and his boxers, thank goodness, and his socks, all of them dripping wet.

On consideration, he appeared to be in a bathtub, which suggested he was in a bathroom, and probably a very nice one from the size and general roundness of the tub. It is a truth of the universe that the poorer you are, the narrower your tub is. By contrast, a rich man's bathtub may be positively ovoid.

From above, soft neon lights shined in through a high skylight, pinks and greens. Again, the higher your skylight, the richer you are, and Percival estimated this one a good six meters overhead. There was also a sliver of light along the far wall. A cracked door, no doubt.

Trouserless, Percival emerged from the tub. He ran a hand back through his hair, also wet. Instinctively, he reached out for a towel in the dark.

"Here you go."

"Thank you?" Percival accepted a dry towel from an unseen hand.

The stranger's voice was calming, like a light breeze. Percival slowly mopped his soaked head as his eyes adjusted to the dark.

"Oh, you're most welcome, Mister Gynt."

Percival was mid-mop as his eyes began to process the thing that hovered before him in the dark. It was a purplish, fleshy, bobbing thing with a pair of long fleshy tentacles that ended in more tentacles that seemed a sad parody of fingers. Atop the main blob were a half-dozen eyes of varying sizes and along the front, a mouth big enough to swallow Percival whole. It blinked at him and smiled politely. *Enormously* politely, if one were to judge by the size of said smile.

"You're a—?" Percival began. "A—?"

"I'm a Fummer," the Fummer answered. "A proper son of Fum. I am here to answer to your every whim."

Percival thought really hard about the last thing he remembered before waking up in the tub. He remembered a giant robot monkey. Was that right? Had he dreamed that? And Um. And falling. Falling for a long time. And before that, the destruction of the Prestige. An explosion. Tarot. Tarot must be dead.

A familiar voice called from the other room, "If he looks like he's havin' a flashback, smack 'im!"

And on command, Percival was swatted across the chest with a limp tentacle.

"Um!" Percival turned to the doorway, shielding his eyes as he stepped into the light. "Um, what's going on here?"

Percival stepped out of the bathroom and into an enormous penthouse suite of the sort that most of us will only ever see in films. Or on TV shows that profile the sort of enormous penthouse suites that we only ever see in films. In front of him a short flight of stairs led up to a massive, four-poster bed that looked to be made of spun gold and also a second substance that Percival thought might have been spun plutonium, judging by its glow. To Percival's right was a full bar trimmed with neon and staffed by two Fummers. Beyond that, an empty dance floor. And beyond that, the penthouse opened out onto a massive gothic balcony overlooking two spuming waterfalls made of pure liquid oxygen and a fireworks display that illuminated the night sky with pyrotechnics in the shapes of famous cartoon characters of the past like Dora the Explorer and Snoopy and Alexander Hamilton.

The ceiling of the suite was a perfectly scaled reproduction of the Sistine Chapel, but with God replaced by the High Cleric of the Intergalactic Church of the All-Mother and everyone else replaced with Fummers. A sacrilege to be sure, though in the Fummers' defense, this mural was painted some years *after* the High Cleric had proclaimed their very livelihood a mortal sin.

To Percival's left was a full kitchen, again staffed by Fummers, and a full dining area and a giraffe for some reason and Um before a triptych of mirrors, being measured by a gaggle of Fummer tailors.

"Ain't this place great?" Um shouted from across the room.

Percival closed distance with his traveling companion quickly. He had a number of questions racing through his mind. Where were they? How had they gotten here? Why was he soaking wet? But the first that made it to his lips was this: "Why am I not wearing trousers?"

"Yer welcome," Um growled.

"I'm sorry?"

"Yer welcome fer savin' your life," Um clarified. "It was no big deal."

"I—" Percival sputtered, "I don't know what's going on. Can you please tell me what's going on?"

Um shrugged. "Yeah, well. Since ya said *please*. After we popped outta superlight, we was fallin' through the atmosphere fer a while. Turns out the oxygen content in the unprocessed air was a little much fer ya. Yoo passed out fer a while. Tried waking ya up with a cold shower when we got here, but that didn't work. Didn't figure it would, but I was bored on account a ya being passed out so long. And now the Fummers are fittin' me fer a new suit."

Percival just stared at Um, speechless.

"But serious, don't thank me or nothin'. I even thought ta take yer trousers off before we dunked ya, seeing as how ya had yer watch in there and whatever else technajawoosits ya normally carry."

Lest anyone take Um's turn of phrase in that moment to be a sign of low or limited intelligence, it should be acknowledged that the term "technajawoosits" accurately connotes a number of very subtle details surrounding the objects that Percival was then known to carry on his person.

"I'm sorry. Technajawhats?"

Um shook his head despondently. "Anyway, the Fummers felt real bad about our spaceship breakin' up in orbit, so they put us up here and agreed ta comp us fer the whole week. Nice, huh?"

Percival tried to force a polite smile, but it kept coming out as a grimace. "It would be... Officer Um... except for the unfortunate, unswerving reality... of the impending... doom... of the universe."

Um looked back and forth to his tailors. "Give us a minute, yeah?" The Fummers' idea of compliance was to slowly drift counter-clockwise while waving their arms and humming a tune that sounded strangely like that old Earth ditty, "Hey Ya."

Um shrugged.

"We have to get out of here, Um. We've got to go and find the High Cleric and tell her that her daughter is dead and that evil Space Nazis are after the Engine of Armageddon, which they plan to use to unmake the whole universe."

"I don't think they call 'emselves that, but yeah. I know."

"Also, I want my trousers back!"

"I know."

"Also, this song is *really* catchy! And I think I'd like to stay here and dance for a minute while you go and get my trousers."

And so Um did. And so Percival did.

In addition to getting Percival his trousers, Um also handed over his umbrella, which the giant robot monkey had also recovered from the planet's core, and which it had mistakenly believed was a third member of Percival's crew. In a rare moment of cheek, Um had confirmed the monkey's suspicions, identifying the inanimate object as Percival's dear wife Shoe.

Percival opened and closed the umbrella over and over as he and

Um walked along a moving sidewalk. "No worse for wear," Percival muttered, only half-listening to Um's plotting.

"Church says visitin' the Fummers is a sin, so they ain't got no direct flights back and forth, but there's a load of sinners in this galaxy, so we got plenty a indirect options. While yoo was out, I borrowed yer watch and got us a ride."

Percival lowered his umbrella and cocked an eye towards Um. "Smuggler?"

Um smiled. "Garbage scow."

Percival ran out of moving sidewalk and fell over. "I'm a professional!" he called out. "Ask important people! They know my work!"

And then to Um: "It's awfully comfy down here, by the way."

Though the Church considers it a sin to vacation at Fum 4 The Whole Family, they do not consider it a sin to collect the Fummers' trash, for a modest fee of course, and recycle it in the Holy Fusion Reactors that power their city. Anti-gravity scows arrive at the resort twice a day to receive waste and take it back to the Holy City on the far side of the planet. The scows are driven by Church zealots, so it's difficult to bribe them. Um found more success playing to their sympathies.

"Help!" he tweeted. "I crash landed on the wrong side of the planet! I'm surrounded by sinners! They smell like detergent! Please, won't some kind soul take me back to civilization! #blessed"

Within minutes, one of the drivers replied, "I'll be arriving at Dock 42 within the hour. If you're there, it would be my sacred honor to liberate you from these heathen balloon animals. #allmothertrucker"

The driver's name was Fabius Horbus. He was human mostly, perhaps a bit overweight, and he had tufts of gray hair growing in strange places, but he seemed like a genuinely nice man as he helped Percival and Um up into the cab of the scow. The outside of the scow stank like a rotten egg's nightmare, and the inside didn't smell much better. He explained, "Every time I finish a run, I need to take a bath in holy water to wash the stink of sin away."

"I will also need a bath," Percival confided, "to wash away the stink of... sin."

By the time the scow arrived on the far side of the planet, it was daylight. Of course, it was always daylight on the far side of the planet, so once again Percival was left with very little evidence with which to judge the local time.

After taking a moment to consider this conundrum, Percival asked the driver, "What's the local time?"

"It's nearly four," Fabius answered as he popped open the cab doors.

"Four in the morning or four in the afternoon?" Percival asked as he followed Um out onto a concrete dock.

"Would have to be!" Fabius conceded as he closed the cab doors again and lifted the scow back up into the sky.

"I liked him," Um volunteered. They both now smelled of week-old buffet.

The concrete dock extended from a crowded boardwalk out into a sea of liquid oxygen. From the end of the dock, Percival looked out past the crowds and the ramshackle buildings of South District to the great, gothic tower that loomed beyond. Like an enormous sundial, it cast its shadow over the district that morning-or-afternoon. No one in South District seemed to notice or care. They all just shuffled forward with their heads down, intent upon their journey, wherever they were headed.

Percival looked to Um and nodded and took a deep breath and pushed his way inward.

The guard behind the gate was middle-aged and chubby and graying at the temples with thin, squinty eyes. He was armed with a weapon that looked to Percival like the Smith & Wesson AK-71 Stun Baton, and he wore the standard portable force field belt they sell in the checkout aisle at Target. When Percival and Um approached, he raised his baton defensively and grumbled, "What d'you want?"

"We're here to see the High Cleric," Percival answered.

"Are you entertainers?" he asked.

Percival looked to Um in his "Shhhh! I'm Undercover!" T-Shirt and shrugged. "Sure."

The guard looked to his free hand, where he counted to two. "There are only two of you. Where's the third?"

Before Percival could answer, Um pointed to Percival's umbrella.

The guard narrowed his squint to such a degree that he was now essentially standing there with his eyes closed. "Looks like an umbrella to me."

"Her name's Shoe," Um explained. The guard accepted this on faith and drew open the gate for the three of them to enter.

"Please wait just here," he said, indicating a spot on the grass beside. "If the last group don't work out, Sister Esme will be back to show you to the High Cleric."

"The other group?"

"Pack of strange ones as I see it. Hardly entertaining to my mind. Particularly the one in that daft hat."

"Daft hat?" repeated Percival, at a volume louder and a speed more rapid than he intended. "Daft gray hat with a narrow band and a narrow brim and a bit of a divot in the top?"

"Amazing what the girls will wear these days, am I right?"

Percival turned to Um, gripping his arm, a smile on his lips and his eyes wide. Of course, Um's eyes were always wide and he didn't smile, so it was hard to gauge his reaction. Percival turned back to the guard.

"And this girl: Did she have long, wavy black hair and eyes that glittered like uncut emeralds and a smile that fills the room with light?"

"Um. Maybe."

With that faint hope, Percival sprinted a half-dozen paces towards the foot of the tower. Then Franklin hit him with a blast from his Smith & Wesson AK-74 Stun Baton. Then Percival fell like a ragdoll into the grass.

"He seems ta be doin' that a lot lately," Um confided to the guard.

"Runnin' off where he don't belong?"

"Nope." Um pointed to Percival's slack, snoring shape on the grass. "Just that."

8 | *SMELLING OF BAKED BEANS*

When Tarot heard her mother's footsteps echoing down the larder stairs, she began to cry. It had been eleven years since her mother had left them to found this Church, this Church that stood opposed to every quantum fiber of Tarot's being. Mouse wrapped an arm around her, and even icy Halla did not appear unmoved by the occasion.

On the far side of the room, Sister Esme was left to wonder who these strange people were who came seeking an audience with the High Cleric and then trembled and cried as she approached. Was this religious fervor or something more banal?

And then, in a flash, Sister Esme knew why the one in the hat had looked so familiar. She had seen those very eyes before, staring out from different sockets, out of the very head of the very head of her religion. There was only one reasonable conclusion to be made:

The High Cleric had a clone made of her named Cardz, who'd run off to become a juggler. But the clone was defective, so the jugglers were now returning her.

Also, they were looking for an engine and maybe someone named Caul. That part didn't quite make sense yet. Esme caught herself starting to speculate, to try to solve the puzzle of these strange visitors the same way she'd finished that jigsaw of the three kittens in a shoebox that was sitting out in the attendants' common area the week previous. In her head she repeated a mantra that had done her well on the street:

This is not your chicken. This is not your chicken. This is not your chicken.

By the time the High Cleric reached the foot of the stairs, Tarot was holding tight onto Mouse and crying rather profusely into his leather coat, her face buried in his shoulder. For her part, the High Cleric was stone-faced. And Halla glared daggers at the lot of them, for making her feel anything at all.

"Sister Esme," the High Cleric called. "You have done well. Please take your leave of us now, and speak of these events to no one."

"Yes, Your Holiness," said Esme. She did a quick curtsy and then stomped quickly past the entertainers and the High Cleric and up the stairs, moving faster and faster with each step.

This is not your chicken. This is not your chicken.

The last words she heard as she passed through the door at the top of the stairs were these: "I have had words with the Celestial Governor, and she has explained the situation in some detail. What I don't know is what you hope to gain by—"

Esme ran out the rear door of the tower and slammed it behind her, and she locked it tight with an old iron key and a trembling hand. She took a few short breaths to calm her frazzled nerves. Midway through her third calming breath, a shot rang out across the grounds, and she jumped a little, and she let out a little yip, and when she turned to look, she saw a man lying face down in the grass, smoke rising from his back. And further on by the gate, she saw some type of an alien with wide saucer eyes and a big froggy-mouth twisting one of Franklin's arms behind his back using some kind of a mechanical third arm.

Franklin shouted in pain. Esme closed her eyes, took one last calming breath, and then rushed forward into the fray.

"Drop yer weapon!" Um growled to the guard.

"Never!" the guard shouted back, between winces of pain. "Let me go!" He tried to reach back over his head and shoot Um with the Stun Baton, but his aim was miserable. He hit a passerby the first time, and then missed entirely the second.

Esme stopped over Percival and then shouted across to Um, "Let him go, or I'll punch your friend here in the head!"

Um looked at the girl, clothed in the white dress and habit of a nun, tiny fists trembling, brown eyes wide with fear. "I don't believe ya!" Um called back. "Yoo don't look the type."

Esme had been bluffing, but Um's condescension sent her right over the edge. She ploughed one balled up fist into the back of Percival's head after another. One, two, one, two, one, two.

"Augh!" Percival shouted into the dirt. He was awake now. Momentarily paralyzed from the neck down, yes, but quickly orienting himself based on the little information he could gather through his five senses. The sight of dirt as he tried to open his eyes. The smell of… also dirt. The taste of, blaugh, yes, Percival concluded, that's definitely dirt. The sound of shouts. An argument? And punches. Someone had definitely been punching him.

"Oh, I'm so terribly sorry," Esme apologized.

"S'alright," Percival replied pleasantly, his face still pressed down into the ground. "You hit like a girl."

On reflex, Esme kicked Percival hard in the ear. He let out a prolonged shout of pain into the dirt, while she bleated out another short apology. She rolled him over onto his back, and he smiled as he saw her. It would be wrong to call it love at first sight, but perhaps something close to trust or kinship. Percival felt an instant and broadly inexplicable bond with this young woman in that it could only be partially explicked by his recent head trauma and the slight blood loss out of his right ear where she kicked him.

"I'm Percival Gynt," he managed, in an uneven sing-song tone. "I'm here to save the universe from Space Nazis and evil spaceships and dead things with knives."

Esme did not trust easily. She had neither the inclination nor the desire to fall in love, nor did she share the giddy optimism or easy sentimentality of her Sisters. But she knew about dead things with knives, had lobbed a slice of cheese onto one's face, and logic told her that any enemy of such monsters must be a hero. However unlikely. However *exceedingly* unlikely. She felt terrible, and not just for the punching and the kicking. "My name's Esme," she said in her best, most comforting tone, "and I have one more thing to apologize for."

And then she shoved her finger up Percival's ear to try to stanch the bleeding.

"Aaaughh!" he cried out.

Um let Franklin go, and the old guard huffed his way to Esme's side. Um followed cautiously, keeping a distance and angle on the lot of them such that he could take them out with a single blast of his death ray should it become necessary. Percival included.

"Help me up," Percival rasped, and Esme helped him to his feet, hugging one arm close to her. Percival used his umbrella as a cane to keep himself steady.

"You need to be careful with this one," Franklin warned. "He tried to make a break for the tower. Wouldn't just wait in that spot we agreed on." And then his eyes shifted to Um. "And this one! Thinks he can take advantage of an old man with a cheap prosthetic and a kung-fu grip."

Um ignored the guard, insisting, "We need ta talk ta yer High Cleric. The fate a everything that's ever happened and everything that ever might rests in yer hands, Sister."

The High Cleric stopped a sentence mid-word when she heard the door latch lift at the top of the larder steps. She had been sitting on the stairs, her golden pastoral staff resting across her lap, her jewel-encrusted mitre hat set to one side. Her long black hair fell loose over her shoulders as it did in her younger days, when Tarot was small and her brother barely walking. She did not know whether she had the strength to put it back up again.

"Tarot?" Percival called down.

Down below, a ripple of shock passed through Tarot's heart. He was alive. How was he alive? "Percival, I'm here!" she called back.

Percival launched himself down the stairs, nearly tripping over the High Cleric's hat and then her staff and finally stumbling into Tarot's arms at the bottom of the steps and spinning her around twice for good measure.

At first they were talking over each other, explaining how each thought the other was dead, but after a few failed sentences, they deemed content merely to hold each other. And Tarot allowed herself to cry, just a little bit, but she smiled through her tears.

"Mother," said Tarot, still clinging tight to Percival. "This is Percival. He's my best friend." Percival wasn't sure if that was true or not, but he was happy enough to see Tarot alive that he wasn't going to argue.

Following Percival down the larder steps, though hardly with such vigor or drama, came Um, followed by Sister Esme and Franklin the Guard. The High Cleric seized her mitre hat and stood up, stuffing her hair underneath and adjusting her vestments to hang straight. She sniffed away the last of her tears and wiped away the smudges under her eyes.

"I'm not dead, neither," Um pointed out. "Again." He added a "'Scusing Yer Holiness," as he brushed past the High Cleric at the bottom of the stairs. Neither Sister Esme nor Franklin was so brazen. They waited further up the steps to either be invited down or, hopefully, dismissed.

"How did you survive the explosion?" asked Tarot.

"Um used his new arm to create a force field around us, which functioned like a Euclidean shell, allowing us to coast through foldspace into the planet's gravity well and pop out in the upper atmosphere. The planet's mostly gas, so we just fell and fell until the Fummers responded to our distress signal and sent a giant robot monkey to get us. They put us up at their resort while we recuperated. I think there was a giraffe? And then we hitched a ride with a garbage hauler Um met on Twitter, and here we are!"

"That's amazing!" said Tarot. "And also explains that smell!"

"And how did you survive?"

"We teleported."

"Oh. That story's shorter."

"Well, when we landed, we also had to do some walking."

"Oh, all right."

"God hates teleportation!" Sister Esme called down, more as a reminder than an impassioned condemnation.

"That's not right," the High Cleric muttered without turning.

"Your Holiness?"

"That's not right," she repeated, again softly. "God doesn't hate teleportation."

"Of course She does," Esme corrected. "Not as much as the evil eye or worldly relations with lower invertebrates, surely, but the sacred texts say..."

And now the High Cleric turned, and she looked up to Esme. "And who do you think wrote those sacred texts, little sister? The All-Mother doesn't hate teleportation. I do. And, if I'm being honest, I wouldn't even call it hate. It was always more a lingering annoyance than anything else."

"Your Holiness?"

"He'd stay out too late at the pub, as men do, till he was well past sober. And when he came home, he'd use this charm. This teleportation charm. Except he could never get the words right. Greatest magician who ever lived, but when he was drunk he couldn't spell properly."

The High Cleric laughed to herself, a joke just for her.

"He'd land in the wrong room, come crashing through a glass wall or fall and break his hip or come to bed smelling like baked beans. He could never just land where he was supposed to land. Never do what I asked him to do. Or not do what I asked him not to.

"So when I decided to start a church, I figured, 'Why not?' After everything he put me through. 'God hates teleportation.' It's silly, petty even, but then most religion is silly and petty. Don't get tattoos. Don't eat pork. Don't tell anyone about Xenu.

"I did it because I could. Because teleportation annoyed me, and I wanted to see if I could make people stop."

Esme bit her lip to try to stop from crying, but suddenly she was crying despite herself, and also her lip hurt. "You made it *up*?" she asked with a trembling indignation. It felt to her like her face might, at any moment, fall off into her throat. "You were married to a magician, and he smelled like baked beans, and you made it up?"

Percival gave Tarot a squeeze. Up the stairs, Esme looked like nothing more or less than a wounded puppy dog, her eyes wide and welling wet. The High Cleric between them looked on her attendant with unconcealable pity.

"I can't un-lie to you," she said, "but I can tell you truths that few know. I can share the secret of the First Law."

"I understand the First Law well enough, Your Holiness, and I can promise..." Esme forced her quivering lips into a scowl. "The All-Mother will not forgive *you*."

Esme turned and pushed past Franklin, who wasn't quite sure what anyone was talking about anymore, and she shoved her way out the larder door and let it slam behind her as she went.

Percival understood that this was a sad moment, so he counted down silently from ten before he interjected, "Sorry to be a bother, Your Holiness, but have you seen an evil spaceship from the dawn of time laying around here anywhere?"

9 | ESME

No one came to comfort Esme. In fact, in her whole life, no one had ever come to comfort her. Even the Sisterhood had only ever told her to stop crying, to stop being weak, to stop being scared or lonely or silly or wrong. After her years on the street, she thought the Church offered her a better way, but now she saw that they were only telling her what she had wanted to hear: That she was bad and broken and her sins were unforgivable.

Now, as she wept in the shadow of the great tower, she began to wonder if it wasn't the world itself that was bad and broken and unforgivable. But if it was, what hope did she have? What hope did tiny thrashing she have?

"Excuse me, young lady. You mustn't cry. Not out on the lawn like this, at the very least."

Esme looked up to find a distinguished-looking man looming over her, tall and thin and blond-haired, dressed in a noble's finery, a ceremonial saber slung at his side. He wore a gold-threaded sash across his chest and a red cape over one shoulder, and his moustache was thin enough to slice steel.

"Who are you?" she asked.

The stranger bent down next to her and placed a gentle hand upon her shoulder. "My name is Gregory St. George."

"I'm Esme," Esme sniffed. "Are you some kind of royalty?"

"I am," he said, "a duke. An archduke, in fact." He withdrew a handkerchief from his sleeve and he dabbed at her tears. "But we don't have to talk about that."

She reached her hands over his and pulled them down so she could look at him, this strange kind man. "Archduke Gregory," she said with a smile. "The Archduke of what?"

His expression flattened. "The Archduke of the Celestial Overmen of Aryan Pod Colony 75."

So swift and gentle was he that she did not feel it when he slid his saber in and out of her gut.

10 | THE CAULDRON

"So tell me, Mister Gynt," the High Cleric asked from her seat on the larder steps, "how long have you been seeing my daughter?"

Percival reached into his pocket for his watch. "Is it still Wednesday?" he replied, mid-scrounge.

"It is."

He checked his watch for the exact time. "Almost fifty-five hours, then."

"Well, you seem to have grown incredibly close in a very short time. That either speaks well of you or poorly of my daughter."

Percival grinned. "I like to think a little bit of both," he joked, giving Tarot's shoulders a little squeeze to let her know he was kidding.

"I'd always hoped that Tarot would marry young Mouse," the High Cleric admitted.

Percival glanced over at Mouse, who simply shrugged with his hands still in his pockets.

Just then Um made a guttural noise that sounded a bit like a throaty cough but was actually intended to replicate a human sigh. "Listen, I like family reunions as much as anybody..." This was a lie. "...but can we move this along? Engine, Armageddon, and all that."

"If we must have this conversation..." The High Cleric shook her head. "I'll simply tell you what I told my daughter. You're on a fool's errand. The Engine of Armageddon was hidden somewhere where no one will ever find it. Not you. Not the Nth Realm. Not whatever other factions have been vying to restore the accursed thing."

Percival reacted to the High Cleric's words with a mix of hurt and shock. And here he'd thought that he was making progress with the mother. "I think you have the wrong idea about us, Your Holiness. We don't want to restore the Engine. We want to protect it. The Space Nazis already have the Rider. If they get to the Engine before we do—"

"'The Rider,' he says. To me of all people. He doesn't know, does he? You didn't tell him?"

Mouse shrugged. "Not in so many words, no."

"Tell me what?"

"It's not important," whispered Tarot. "We need to find the Engine."

"Wait one second," Percival whispered back with more edge than he intended to his words. "I don't like people telling me what's important and what's not. They very often get those two things swapped." Then louder, to the mother, "What is it that you were expecting them to tell me?"

The High Cleric stepped down off the steps and into the cold. Her breath slipped out from between her lips like a trail of ghosts into shadow. "The Rider is a malevolent spirit. A thing of such evil, such pure cruelty that you could scarcely imagine. We tried to destroy it. We tried to banish it. We even tried to reason with it. But the Rider was born at the dawn of all things, and the Rider cannot be denied."

"Yes, yes," Percival threw his hands up in front of him. "I know this part. This is where I came in. 'How do you trap a shadow?' and all that. Illuminari created the boy as a prison for the Rider."

"Illuminari with a little help from his lovely assistant," Mouse corrected.

"Illuminari with a little help from his *wife*," said Tarot.

Percival made no claim to psychic power, but he sensed that he was about to feel very stupid.

"They used ancient magics," said Mouse. "*Deep* magics."

Percival closed his eyes. "I hate metaphors."

"Heh," Um laughed. "And not even a subtle one."

"My husband knew something like this was going to happen one day. Maybe not the exact details. Maybe not the exact shape of events. But he understood. He was prescient," she confessed. "He was prescient, and he was prepared." She allowed herself the saddest laugh. "He always took such care with our son. I actually thought he was a good father. To raise such a kind and loving boy? But he was really just perfecting his ingredient. His Cauldron of pure innocence."

And now the sadness overpowered her. The High Cleric's whole body quaked with each sob.

"He took my son away from me, Mister Gynt! He took my son and stuffed the Devil down his throat and left him an empty husk of a thing."

Percival stepped forward cautiously toward the High Cleric and did something that no one had done for her in eleven years. He gave her a hug. "That's horrible," he whispered. "More horrible than I can fathom."

At first the High Cleric stood impassive in the accountant's embrace, but then she began to cry again, and she pulled him tighter to her chest. "Thank you," she whispered back.

Um glared at Tarot, who had also begun crying, but he felt no urge to hug her. "Yoo knew, and ya didn't tell us."

"It didn't seem relevant."

"Didn't seem relevant that the missin' boy was yer secret brother?"

"What difference does it make?"

"Yoo don't decide what difference it makes! We decide."

"How would knowing any of that change anything?"

"Ya made us think he was a thing," Um growled. "Yer own brother. Ya made me think he was... an object ta recover or destroy."

"Poor baby," Tarot sneered through her tears.

Percival rested his hands on the High Cleric's shoulders and looked into her bleary eyes and said, "They have your son. Even if they never find the Engine, that means something. You need to trust us, so we can put this right. You need to tell us the rest."

"The rest?"

"After the ceremony eleven years ago, you hid your son, and you hid the Engine. Whatever magics Illuminari used to conceal the boy started to fail after his death. How do you know that the same thing won't happen with the Engine?"

"You're right. I don't know that. It's possible."

"So you understand why it's imperative that we get to the Engine before the Space Nazis do. We can't leave it unprotected."

The High Cleric had nearly run out of tears. "You're right, of course. Every sacrifice we made is meaningless if the Engine is restored."

"So you'll tell us where the Engine is?"

"No."

Um slapped his forehead, hard.

Across the room a pleasantly mechanical voice intoned, "Dumbwaiter opening." Then another: "Dumbwaiter opening." Then another and another and another, all overlapping with each other. The thirteen artificially intelligent dumbwaiters that lined the side wall all hummed to life, their panel doors lifting to reveal the dark shafts within.

Before the assembled could manage much of a reaction, a small ceramic sphere dropped down the third shaft, landing with a crack on the dumbwaiter platform. Through the cracks, a red gas poured, rolling over the side of the dumbwaiter and gathering along the floor like the Devil's own fog.

"Not good," Percival assessed with perfect clarity. He pulled his handkerchief from his pocket and wrapped it round his face like a bank robber's mask.

More spheres dropped, two or three to a shaft, cracking and spilling out the same gas. Franklin tried the larder door but found it locked. "Your Holiness!" he shouted as he tugged at the door knob. "I suspect a trap!"

And the red fog continued to pour down from the cracked spheres and to billow outward across the floor, weaving its way between the black slabs towards Percival and the rest with alarming speed. Mouse backed the High Cleric up the stairs. Halla pulled Tarot up onto one of the slabs. Percival took a step forward and tested the fog with his foot to see if it was corrosive. It was not.

"Well, that would have been embarrassing," he muttered.

Um pushed his way past Mouse and the High Cleric and the guard. "I got this one covered," he said. The heavy blade deployed from the underside of his mechanical arm with a thunk. It was an intimidating weapon before it lit on fire, and then it lit on fire. Um set the weapon to work on the door, cracking it and splintering it and, of course, setting it just a bit aflame.

He broke open a goodly-sized whole in the middle, and then bent down to stare through to the other side where, at that precise moment, a small army of Nth Realm shock troopers were gathering, all in black except for their armbands and the red lenses of their gas masks.

Um counted thirty-two with his arm's bio-sensor array. He fired his death ray through the hole. It was green and hot, and there were horrible, melting screams on the far side of the door. He checked his bio-sensors again. Nineteen.

Percival approached the dumbwaiters. Impossibly, gas was still flowing out of the cracked spheres. Percival theorized that the spheres weren't so much releasing gas as producing it through a chemical reaction between the air in the larder and whatever chemical substance was inside each shell. He hatched a simple, one-part plan.

"Dumbwaiters, go back up to the kitchen!" he commanded, and an instant later each of the dumbwaiters was announcing "Dumbwaiter closing," and doing just that. "Um!" he shouted, "I could use you to lock out these dumbwaiters!"

"Busy killin' shock troopers," Um shouted back as he fired off a second blast from the death ray. "Most dumbwaiters are pretty smart. Try reasonin' with 'em!"

Percival sighed. The key to a good negotiation, he'd once read, was to find common ground. The question was, what did Percival have in common with a tiny, computerized lift?

It was barely ten seconds later that the dumbwaiter doors started opening again. "Dumbwaiter opening." "Dumbwaiter opening." And as each did, it belched out another dumbwaiter's worth of red into the room, pent up during the trip from larder to kitchen and back. One such belch caught Percival squarely in the face, stinging his eyes and seeping through his improvised mask to infiltrate his nostrils and open mouth.

He stumbled back and hacked a loud and chesty cough. The gas was to his shoulders now, and as many times as he could send the dumbwaiters away, there would be someone upstairs to send them back down again. He had to override the dumbwaiters.

"Um!" Percival shouted, but Um was otherwise engaged. Death ray! Death ray! Death ray! "One thing at a time, Gynt!" Death ray! Death ray!

Percival grinned. Of course. That was it! Not the "Death ray! Death ray!" bit, but the "One thing at a time!" Percival didn't know how to override the dumbwaiters' programming, but he could do the next best thing. He could give them a command that would take so long to execute that they'd never get to the next order in queue. What did Percival have in common with a tiny, computerized lift?

"We're both so very good at math."

And so he told them, "Dumbwaiters, back up to the kitchen, but this time match your velocity to the curve defined x squared over the quantity four minus x equals y, where x is measured in meters traveled and y in seconds elapsed!"

"Dumbwaiter closing," each dumbwaiter answered in turn, sliding their panels closed, shutting off the flow of gas once again.

The fog was to his lip now and to Tarot and Halla's knees where they stood on the black slab. Percival had only gotten a whiff of the gas, but he suspected that any more than that would have been fatal. As long as he kept his chin up, he felt that he was in no real danger. Which is to say, no real danger except for the mad army of shock troopers massing at the larder door.

"Death ray's spent!" Um called out after his twelfth blast.

"Any chance they didn't just hear you say that?" Percival called back, making his way to the foot of the staircase.

"Unlikely," Um confided as a pair of shock troopers bashed down what was left of the door.

Um caught one with his kung-fu grip and slammed him against the wall. The other pulled a small black pistol and shot Um in the side of the face, taking off a piece of his cheekbone and a bit of eye. The same shock trooper raised up his left foot and kicked Um in the chest, sending him tumbling halfway down the stairs and catching Franklin and Mouse and the High Cleric underneath him.

Percival lunged across the room, opening his umbrella as he ran, but he was too late to block a second shot from the shock trooper, this time piercing Um's right shoulder and, beneath him, Franklin's throat. Franklin's eyes went wide for the first time in many years and then went still.

Mouse, who was trapped under Franklin, whispered a sympathetic "go to the light" charm, and the High Cleric, trapped under Mouse, offered a hushed "Amen."

Percival stumbled to a halt at the foot of the steps. Um and poor Franklin and Mouse and the High Cleric were lodged partway down the staircase, the lowest of them a drop of sweat from the surface of the fog. They were a disjointed mass of legs and hands and helpless faces, and at the bottom of the pile, the High Cleric had wedged her pastoral staff between the walls and was now exerting her every reserve of strength to keep them from falling into the red pool of gas.

And the shock troopers began marching down towards them.

Under cover of umbrella, Percival took to the first step of the staircase and whispered to the High Cleric, "While what you're doing now is incredibly brave and inspiring and all that, I need you to let go now. You need to fall in."

The High Cleric's hands had already begun to shake and her grip was already beginning to slip. She took a deep breath and let go of her staff, and she and Mouse and dead Franklin and Um all went collapsing into the fog, clearing a line of sight between Percival and the shock troopers. The one who'd shot Um took the lead with the one Um had bashed against the wall following just behind. Percival counted five more left beyond them, and then someone in a cape and a sash and an ego at the rear.

"Hullo," said Percival, tugging his handkerchief down to reveal the thinnest and saddest of smiles. "My name is Percival Gynt, and here are three really excellent reasons why you're not going to shoot me…"

11 | THREE REASONS WHY

The shock trooper who had shot Um and killed Franklin and was now pointing his tiny pistol at Percival's head was named Fnn-5. He was only fourth removed from Franco Nicodemus Noon, and he was therefore very good at two things: killing and following orders. So when the Archduke said, "Hold! I want to hear what the man with the umbrella has to say," Fnn-5 grudgingly complied.

Percival had correctly calculated that any man dramatic enough to wear a golden sash to an armed massacre would enjoy a bit of bombast from his victims before their deaths. Percival's ploy would buy his companions the seconds they needed to regroup and possibly turn things to their advantage, if only he could come up with three really excellent reasons why these men shouldn't shoot him.

In that instant he had none, but Percival was confident he could come up with something. He was, after all, very nearly always very good or pretty good under pressure. Or at least passable. Percival could feel the unhelpful claw of doubt clawing its way, claw-like, into his brain. No good. Focus, focus, focus.

Percival knew instinctively that he needed to start big. If he didn't justify their curiosity with this first reason, then they could well lose interest in the game before it had properly begun. He needed a reason that they'd find satisfying on its own, but which would also leave them intrigued to hear whatever came next. For these purposes, Percival considered revealing some shocking personal truth or some secret bit of knowledge that he'd picked up over the years as an accountant to the rich and famous. Ultimately, he decided that a wholly fabricated lie would better serve his purposes. It was risky, of course. What if they knew that he was lying? But only a lie could be shaped to fit the exact contours of his needs. Only the lie would be both satisfying enough in its own reveal and also suggestive of other greater secrets to come.

And so his first reason was this: "Because I can tell you where the Engine of Armageddon is." Lie. But it certainly got their attention.

The shock troopers murmured muffled murmurs at each other through their gasmasks. The Archduke raised an incredulous eyebrow. "Do you? Then where, pray tell, is it?"

Percival didn't respond immediately. Instead, he took a minute to adjust his umbrella so that all the Archduke could see of him was an enigmatic smile creeping out from beneath the umbrella's shadow. And then he announced, matter-of-factly:

"Reason two:"

To the extent that he was making this up as he went along, Percival had felt quite happy with reason number one. For reason two, he wouldn't need to make the same sort of bold claim, but he did need to offer them something that would further stoke their interest in the game, something that would allow him to proceed unchallenged to reason three. If reason two failed to capture their imaginations, they might well cut him off and demand that he return to reason one and answer their questions about the location of the Engine. Which, of course, he couldn't do, because reason one was a big, fat, aforementioned lie.

"Reason two is..." No good. He was blanking.

The Archduke cracked his neck to the left and reached for his saber. "You know," he said, "for a moment, I really thought you had something there."

Oh well, Percival thought. Might as well go for broke.

"Reason two is that my name is Percival Gynt, and I don't have that name by accident. I'm Percival Gynt of Gynt Colony. Percival Gynt, the sole survivor of the Gynt Massacre. The Gynt Massacre, which the newsfeeds tell us was twenty years ago this week. And I alone in all the universe know what really happened that day. I alone know why one scrawny, shivering eight-year-old boy was spared. I alone in all of space and all of time and all of imagination can tell you what foul truth beats within the blackened heart of the Demon Beast of Gynt."

"Wait! What?" Tarot exclaimed from somewhere behind him.

"Not now, Tarot!" Percival called back without averting his eyes from the Archduke. "I'm in the middle of a thing."

The Archduke took a moment to ponder reason two before conceding, "Not *at all* what I'm here for, but I admit that would be a fascinating story to hear in full." The Archduke chuckled. "And you have a third reason on top of all that? You know, I like you, Gynt. I may just have to cut off your legs and keep you in a cage."

"And they say romance is dead," said Percival, and his smile was broad now and gleaming white. Because, if his math held, his people were nearing their positions.

"And reason three," he explained, "is really the best of them all. Because reason three isn't about me, strictly, or the things I know, but rather about the people with whom I happen to surround myself. A magician, a magician's assistant, and a man who just won't die. What do all three of these people have in common? Easy! They can each of them hold their breath for an absurdly long period of time. And though you shot the one of them dead who might have died from gas inhalation by now, our stalwart tower guard has a contribution to the cause to make as well. Because he was armed with a Smith & Wesson AK-71 Stun Baton and..."

Percival paused mid-sentence to tilt his umbrella forward in front of him. "Um?" he asked and/or stammered.

Within the space of a second, Fnn-5 fired six rounds into Percival's umbrella, but Percival had braced himself and the six rounds bounced harmlessly off the umbrella's triple-reinforced microweave. At the same time, a blast came out of the fog, completely paralyzing the shock trooper's left side. He fell sideways against the wall as a second and third blast connected with the shock troopers behind him.

At the far end of the room, Mouse and the High Cleric emerged from the red fog by the thirteenth dumbwaiter. Mouse spoke a "maybe technology works like this" charm and slid open the dumbwaiter door to reveal an open shaft leading upwards. "Out this way," he motioned.

The Archduke saw events slipping out of his control, and the turn enraged him. With a single swipe of his blade, he cut through two of his own men as he marched down the stairs towards Percival and his frog-in-the-bog.

Fnn-5 tried to form words with his half-paralyzed mouth, perhaps to swear vengeance or forebode some grim fate for our heroes, but he was silenced by the Archduke's saber through his left lung.

Percival backed away, collapsing his umbrella as he went. Behind him Um rose out of the fog with Franklin's Stun Baton in hand. He fired two times, but the Archduke blocked both blasts with his blade.

"Perhaps if you tell me where the Engine is, I'll let you and your friends go," the Archduke mused as he stepped down into the fog.

"Ah ha!" cried Percival. "So you don't know where it is either!"

"Either?" said the Archduke with an audible sneer.

Percival immediately realized his mistake. "I meant in the same way other people who aren't me also don't know?" Percival took another step backwards and knocked into one of the black slabs. It was ice cold, and he let out a high pitched "Guhguhgacck!" nearly dropping his umbrella as he did.

With this opening the Archduke lunged. Percival gripped his umbrella in both hands and held it high to deflect the Archduke's falling blade. As he'd hoped, the umbrella's microweave proved too strong for the sword to cut.

Um circled to his right to get a clean shot at the Archduke, but the Archduke saw him and sprang unexpectedly towards him, slicing the stun baton in two with a stroke of his blade. The resulting electrical burst caused Um's hand to spasm, and what was left of the baton slipped through Um's froggy-fingers into the fog.

"I'm not that interested in you," the Archduke confessed, jabbing his blade into Um's open, bloody cheek and twisting. Um stumbled backwards, letting out a long, languishing scream as he did. Percival charged from behind with a guttural yell, driving the dull tip of his umbrella a good three centimeters into the Archduke's back. The Archduke swallowed his pain and whipped around to face Percival. As he did, the umbrella wrenched from Percival's hands and clattered to the ground some distance away, lost to the fog.

The Archduke's breaths were shallow now. He had lost his detached cool. "Did you really think you were going to take me on," he fumed, "*with an umbrella?*"

Percival pulled out his watch and held it up over his head. "Let me think about that for six seconds and get back to you." He tapped the Time Stop app, but instead of all motion in the universe ceasing for six seconds, he got a tiny animated low battery warning.

The Archduke stared at him, confused for a full two seconds before swiping the watch out of Percival's hand with his saber. Percival stared at his empty hand for another half-second, then shouted, "Right then! Halla?"

Halla took a running leap off of her slab, her feet finding the next hidden under the fog, then the next and the next, then as the others watched agape, she leapt high, spun in the air, and came flying down foot first into the Archduke's face. The Archduke fell backwards, and Halla rode him to the floor like his head was the weighted end of a teeter-totter. From the fog Percival heard a loud crack, surely the sound of skull bouncing off stone.

Halla, herself not the tallest of women, disappeared after the Archduke into the fog, and when she did not immediately pop her head up to catch a breath, Percival knew that something had gone wrong. An instant later, Percival's fears were confirmed by a woman's scream and the sound of steel slicing into bone.

Across the room Mouse understood immediately what had happened. He turned away from the High Cleric, whom he had been trying to boost up into the open dumbwaiter shaft, and charged back across the room towards the spot where Halla fell, drawing his Magnum Conflict Resolver from its holster as he ran.

Um, who had lost a lot of blood by this point, steadied himself alongside one of the black slabs. Percival counted to three on one hand and then made a mad dash for the stairwell. Mouse lifted his MCR in front of him and fired four mini-missiles into the ground where the Archduke fell.

Tarot smiled and whispered a "take him down" charm.

Mouse's mini-missiles exploded on impact, shaking the room and sending shockwaves through the fog. Overhead, the hung carcasses swung violently.

Percival was almost to the stairwell when a hand clutched his ankle and sent him sprawling into the fog. Percival's eyes were on fire. If he took another breath, he was dead. He groped forward, blindly, found the High Cleric's pastoral staff, and whipped it round to catch his attacker with a formidable thwack, a hard-enough hit to loosen its grip on him. Percival scrambled up the stairs, drawing a long, deep breath as soon as he was out of the fog. He pulled the gas mask from Fnn-5's dead head and slipped it over his.

In that moment Percival thought perhaps he recognized the man's face, but pushed the thought from his head to focus on the matter at hand. As he'd suspected, the red-tinted goggles allowed him to see through the red fog as if it were a thin mist. He saw Halla pinned to the floor, the Archduke's blade through her shoulder, neatly ringed by Mouse's impact craters. Like a carnival act. But she was bleeding out, still conscious, if barely, eyes squeezed shut, desperately holding on to her final breath.

And he saw the Archduke, now wearing a gasmask of his own, crouched low in the fog, one hand on the back of his head, still reeling from the staff hit. He looked up towards Percival and for a moment the two simply regarded each other, whatever emotions they felt concealed behind their expressionless masks.

Then Percival pointed and shouted, "HE'S THERE!" Mouse fired his last two mini-missiles in the direction Percival indicated, smashing one of the black slabs in two and leaving another crater in the floor. But now the Archduke was loping across the room, first under cover of fog, then leaping from slab to slab as Halla had, and finally swinging from chained carcass to chained carcass before dropping like a cat into the fog at the High Cleric's feet.

He rose, no longer the foppish dandy, but now transformed into the very black-masked, red-eyed visage of Death Himself. A gloved hand caught the High Cleric by the neck and squeezed. "Tell me where the Engine is," he growled, his voice deepened and distorted by the gas mask into something inhuman.

But the High Cleric could not speak, could barely breathe within the Archduke's grip. Displeased, the Archduke lifted her up by her throat and threw her back against the wall. The High Cleric could feel a half-dozen of her bones break at once as she bounced off the wall and fell back down into the fog at the Archduke's feet.

"You *will* tell me," he snarled.

By now Percival had found and recovered the third of the useful items he'd been looking for at the foot of the stairs. He clicked it on, and a sheath of blue translucent light slid over him. The guard's force field belt. "Excellent," he muttered to himself. It still worked, though there was no telling for how long.

Percival tightened his grip on the High Cleric's staff and charged forward shouting, "I'm not done with you yet, Space Nazi!" Percival was instantly disappointed with himself. What a leaden turn of phrase. "I'm not done with you yet?" Really. Ugh. He would have been better off with a pun. Perhaps "The Master Race is over, and you came in last!" or "How did you NOT SEE this coming?"

Or, well, sometimes silence is best.

The Archduke frowned behind his mask and shouted, "Obviously we don't call ourselves that!" as he braced himself to receive Percival's charge. Percival was leading with the pastoral staff's tip, a sort of improvised spear, but the Archduke was faster and stronger than Percival. He caught ahold of the shaft with both hands, jerked the front end down and the back end up, and sent Percival flying over him, past him, and back-first, upside down into the wall behind.

The wall cracked under the impact, and Percival tumbled

gracelessly to the floor, but still his energy sheath held.

He stood to face his enemy.

"That force field belt won't last you long," said the Archduke, advancing towards Percival with the staff.

"I won't need it to." Percival dove low, pushing the Archduke's feet out from under him. The staff clattered to one side. Percival scrambled on top of the Archduke and pounded him across the jaw with a force-field-reinforced punch. Then another. "What is this all about?" Percival demanded. "Who are you working for?"

Across the room Mouse wrenched the Archduke's blade from Halla's shoulder and pulled her to her feet. Up on her slab Tarot leaned and squinted, trying to catch some glimpse of Percival or the Archduke through the fog.

By now Um had shambled to the steps. They'd left a pair of shock troopers paralyzed, but still alive in the stairwell. And at least one more operating the dumbwaiters from the kitchen.

"Ragnarok," the Archduke growled. Then, again, louder. "RAGNAROK!"

Percival took hold of the Archduke's mask and pulled it off. Underneath, the villain's eyes were full of determination and contempt. Percival's energy sheath was flashing red now. The batteries of the old guard's force field belt were dying and with them Percival's brief tactical advantage.

The Archduke drove his knee into Percival's gut and shoved Percival off of him. As Percival recovered from the hit, the Archduke rose and scanned the mists for the High Cleric. And he saw her, cowering behind one of the black slabs, eyes closed, nose and mouth pinched shut. The Archduke leapt up onto the slab overlooking her.

"And there you are, Your Holiness. Hiding, are we? Isn't there a commandment against that? Never flee from judgment?"

Up on the stairs Um beat two paralyzed shock troopers into unconsciousness. He considered killing them, but he knew they might have information he needed.

As he reached the top of the stairs, he was on guard. He very nearly unleashed his flaming heavy blade on the two shock troopers that flopped in front of him before he realized that they were already unconscious. Standing over them at the shattered door stood Esme, white habit discarded to reveal a frizzy brown mane, white dress now splattered with blood, some hers, some not. In her hand, a long serrated kitchen knife, caked largely in blood and a little in cake.

"Esme?" Um asked, not sure if he had her name right, but even more so, not sure he was looking at the same girl.

"I've decided that this is my chicken after all," she explained flatly. "I want to help."

Percival pulled himself up off the ground. He was disoriented, out of breath, and the gas mask wasn't helping. He saw the Archduke up above, ranting, and the High Cleric on the far side of the black slab. The Archduke was clearly stronger than he was and a better and more experienced fighter. He needed a weapon. Where had the staff gone?

"That's the man who stabbed me," said Esme, pointing out the Archduke to Um. "Archduke Gregory-something-or-other."

"And that's Percival in the gas mask," said Um. "He looks confused. Like he's lookin' for somethin'."

Like looking into a mirror, thought Esme.

Percival could hear someone shouting from across the room. A girl's voice. Tarot? What was she saying? "Leave her?" Her own mother? No. No, that definitely wasn't Tarot's voice. And that wasn't what not-Tarot said.

"Cleaver!"

Percival's eyes focused on the meat-stained cleaver at the Archduke's foot. In one swift motion, he snatched it up off the slab and swung it hard into the Archduke's right shin. The Archduke shrieked in pain, instinctively lifting his injured leg up to his chest. Percival grabbed his other leg, pulled, and sent the Archduke toppling down face-first off the slab and onto the larder floor.

The High Cleric, who'd about reached her limit, scrambled up onto the slab and took in a deep breath. Percival circled round the slab and threw his weight against the Archduke, who had taken in a mouthful of gas as he fell. He had a few seconds of struggle and twitch in him before his body gave out.

"And reason number four," said Percival as he stood, "is that I don't like Space Nazis very much."

"You know, I don't think they call themselves that," said the High Cleric, from atop her slab.

Percival shrugged and asked her, "Any chance you want to tell us where the Engine is *now*?"

"Still no."

12 | VARGOTH GOR IS NOT DEAD

They took the dead away in bags. The wounded, on stretchers. The faithless fled when the killing started, but others had to be commanded to leave in the aftermath: the High Cleric's servants, her attendants, her devout Fathers and Sisters and Brothers. With shrill screams and quivering whispers, she bade them all to go.

Even her own daughter. "Leave me," she had said, "and attend to your friends." She spoke of Halla and of Um, who had been taken to a nearby hospital for treatment of their injuries. But Tarot protested. Mouse was there with them already. Their wounds were not so serious. And they weren't properly her friends, if she was being honest. But her mother had a well-calloused heart and would not yield. So Tarot kissed Percival softly on the cheek, and she left.

In the end, it was just the two of them, alone in the tower. The High Cleric and the accountant. Lora and Percival.

"I'd like to show you something," she said, her voice raw and weary. "A thing which is everything, and a bit more."

At the apex of its power and influence, which is to say that final moment before Percival stepped foot into the High Cleric's tower, the Intergalactic Church of the All-Mother numbered sixty-two trillion, seven-hundred thirty-two billion, five-hundred and three million, four-hundred and twelve thousand, six-hundred and ninety-seven members in its congregation. Counted amongst the faithful were many prominent politicians, entertainers, poets, philosophers, inventors, entrepreneurs, soldiers, union laborers, doctors, lawyers, self-replicating protoplasms, robots, instruction manual writers, ninjas, pirates, samurais, zombies, a fair share of self-hating magicians, and at least seven Fummers. The Church's influence extended over three galaxies. Four if you counted the Cinnamon Galaxy, where they had recently established a respectable foothold by preaching the enlightened doctrine of *Ebris Gozo Nuell*, which loosely translated means "That smells delicious!"

All of which is to say that the Church had managed to achieve a staggering level of success in a relatively short period of time. Over the span of a decade it had gone from being a fringe cult to what some would describe as a massive, massive cult. More charitably, one might say that the Church was swiftly and rightly embraced as the true word of a cold and merciless but surprisingly patient God, who had inexplicably sat silent through several billion years of sentients practicing false religions and following false prophets before finally revealing Her true and proper gospel.

No one could quite account for it, but the Church had found and filled a void in the universe and a void in the hearts of men. And of women and of children as well. Also of protoplasms, robots, instruction manual writers, etcetera, though the metaphor becomes increasingly metaphoric as we extend outward to sentients without cardiovascular systems. Put simply, the Church was indispensable.

This despite all efforts by the High Cleric, in her final days, to dispense with it. In the months following her encounter with Percival, in what would prove to be the final months of her life, the High Cleric attempted to lay plain a decade's worth of deceptions. "It's all lies," she announced on MTV3. "I made it up. #stopfollowingme," she tweeted. But the faithful would not believe her. It was a test of that very faith, many speculated. Or perhaps the High Cleric had been suborned to blaspheme by dark powers. Or maybe the High Cleric had been suborned to test their faith by non-dark powers. It was a confusing time for those who had committed everything to an ideal, and no heartfelt confession from the High Cleric, no painstaking point-by-point op-ed *mea culpa*, no explicit video evidence posted to YouTube was going to convince them that the religion they'd devoted their lives to was a lie.

We can take, as a for instance, a man named Wyndham Jung, called Young Wyndham by many, as devout an adherent to the Church as ever there was, a callow young man who lived his life alternately horrified by and terrified of the world he inhabited, the sort who could only manage two unique facial expressions. One that asked the world, "Why did you just slap me?" and the other that asked accusingly, "You're about to slap me again, aren't you?" Thanks to the good word of a well-placed uncle, Young Wyndham found himself in the employ of the Celestial Governorship, first as an unpaid intern, then later as the Celestial Governor's own Celestial Food Tester.

The position was created after a handful of visiting dignitaries complained about a rack of nyorg prepared in the Celestial Kitchens. But what the Governor's men told Young Wyndham was that there had been threats made against her over the past few years and that the first three Celestial Food Testers had died from poisons. Now the Governor and her men laughed and laughed and laughed over this joke, but poor Young Wyndham woke up every morning in terror, prayed to the All-Mother for salvation and went about his duties with all the quivering excitability of a stuttering breakdancer who badly needs to urinate while being struck by lightning. As you can imagine, faith played a central role in Young Wyndham's life.

The news of the Church's dissolution came at the worst possible time for Young Wyndham, following some other traumatic events which we will discuss later within these pages. It was at this dark hour that one of the Governor's chefs decided to play a prank on Young Wyndham, placing a bit of chili powder in the Governor's pancakes. Of course, Young Wyndham was not prepared for the heat that accompanied his first bite. His first instinct was that he had been poisoned, and given everything he'd been led to believe, this was certainly a reasonable conclusion. So Young Wyndham leapt from his chair, knocking aside the Governor's own breakfast plate, and dashed for the nearest water closet where he forced himself to vomit every scrap of food and bile that he could summon forth from his stomach. The Governor's men laughed, but the Governor herself was not amused, if for no other reason than that she now had duck gravy all down her front. And so the Governor got up and went looking for her errant food tester, feeling, perhaps for the first time, an iota of compassion for a member of her staff.

In the water closet Young Wyndham was on his knees, crying and praying and wiping away the vomit from his nostrils. First the Church, and then the unmentionable thing, and now this. He knew he wasn't dying. He could hear them laughing down the hall.

The Governor knocked on the water closet door. "Young Wyndham," she said. Even the Governor called him that. "I understand that these past weeks have been quite the trial for you. Perhaps it's best you take some time off."

Wyndham's chest was heavy, and as he spoke his words came out broken and horrible, like they can when you try to speak and cry at the same time. "But..." he stammered, "what about... the *poisoners*?"

Outside, the Governor sank her head. "That's all rubbish, son. The worst we've ever had is some mild food poisoning. The runs and such."

At that Young Wyndham began to wail, for the true scope of his humiliation had become clear. All the precautions he'd taken, the research, the stories he'd told to others about his bravery in the face of mortal danger. Young Wyndham dabbed his eyes with a trail of toilet paper.

The Governor could hear Wyndham muttering through the door, but she couldn't understand the words through his sobs. "What's that, Wyndham?"

Wyndham rested his head to the door and he repeated, "Why is this world nothing but tricks and trials?"

The Governor sighed and then did something she hadn't done for a number of years. She sat down on the floor, her side resting against the water closet door. "Let me tell you a story, Young Wyndham. A story of when I was a child and of a valuable lesson I learned. Would that be acceptable?"

Inside, Wyndham nodded. The Governor couldn't see Wyndham,

but after a pause of a few seconds, she started her story anyway. "I was born on a world called Second Ifeesia. Don't worry that you haven't heard of it. It was a primitive place, pre-industrial is the polite way to say it, all mud huts and wood fires and the sun and the moon are the eyes of a giant.

"Myself, I could never see it. If the sun and the moon were a giant's eyes, where were its nose and its mouth, and why did the eyes seem to go in circles? I was always asking impolite questions like that. The village elders called me 'The One Who Tempts Fate.'

"We were primitive, but not isolated. Visitors came from the sky now and then to trade with us. Our blue rocks for their sundry goods. Woven blankets, better knives, pocket torches. The elders called them magic. 'Gifts from the giant,' I laughed! They looked up to the sky fearfully and apologized. 'She's just a child!' they told the sky giant. 'She doesn't understand!'

"Then one day a man came from the sky who wanted nothing from us except an hour of our time. He was an entertainer, he said. A magician. And I know what your faith says about magic, but just be patient. There's a point to the story that I think you'll appreciate.

"He came all this way to put on a show. And who were we to refuse him? It was late in the evening, so at his request, we built a great fire in the middle of the village, and we all gathered round it. The magician reached a trembling hand into the pyre, clenched his teeth, swore an oath as sweat dripped through his beard, and finally pulled out a tiny ball of flame. He squeezed it between his smoking palms, grunted, and when he released it, it was a mighty redwing soaring up into the night sky, and then he shouted angrily, gutturally, 'Enough!' and the bird exploded into a hail of red feathers, and as they drifted down, he sang a low, sad song as tears formed in his eyes, and before us the feathers began to swim as fish through the air. When it seemed that he could no longer contain his sadness, as his voice began to falter, his chest heaved and he fell to his knees, he threw up his arms and waved them down again. The fish-feathers turned to red glass, gleaming in the firelight. They swirled and rose, and it seemed as if the light of the fire was growing brighter and brighter, until finally we could see that it was daylight. He had raised the sun up over the horizon!

"Well, the elders didn't know what to make of it. Some of the villagers clapped. Some smiled or laughed. A few cried. But mostly they just got up, confused, and went about their days. It was morning after all, and there was work to be done.

"Personally, I didn't believe it for a moment. I went up to him, I of at most ten years old and not a meter and a half tall, and I poked him in the side. 'How'd you do it, then?' I asked. 'What's the trick?'

"And he looked at me with my churlish scowl, and he snorted. 'That's two questions, child. Try asking them one at a time.' He was just acting superior, I thought, as adults will do. Deflecting. But I humored him.

"'How'd you do it?' I repeated.

"He thought for a moment, then answered, 'Well I reached into the flame and found the part of it that most wanted to be a redwing. I pulled her out, and in my mind I told her that she had as long to fly as till the thunder came. Then I released her into the air, and when she had flown high enough, I invoked the mighty thunder with my shout, and the redwing came undone as a cloud of feathers. And then I sang a song for the feathers to remind them of the fish in the ocean, beautiful in their own way, but so sad, because they will never know the sky, and so they danced for me, in honor of the fish. And once their dance was done, I raised an arm and reminded them that they had always been glass. How silly that they'd forgotten? Then the roaring flames called through the shards of glass to your sun and bid her rise early to meet them. I didn't have much to do with that part. That was the fire acting through the magical glass on its own initiative. Any decent fire would make the same request under those same circumstances.'

"At the end of his explanation, the magician smiled, seemingly quite impressed with himself. I did not yet share that opinion, and he could see it in my eyes. 'Go ahead then,' he said. 'Ask the other question.'

"So I asked, 'What's the trick?'

"'The trick,' he said, 'is to make it look difficult.'

The Governor rested a hand on the water closet door. She imagined that Young Wyndham was resting his hand on the side opposite, though he wasn't. "Sometimes," the Governor said, "the world isn't what we think it is or what we think it *should* be. It's not something greater or different or worse. It is simply the thing that we're presented. If the High Cleric of the Intergalactic Church of the All-Mother says she made it all up, I'd be inclined to believe her, but that doesn't mean we don't live in a world of miracles."

On the far side of the door, Young Wyndham was dead. As it turned out, he was deathly allergic to chili peppers.

But that was all to come. Fifty-eight days earlier, Percival followed Lora silently through the tower halls, their footfalls echoing in the hush. Twice Percival tried to speak and failed, as a jumper whose will has faltered at the very chasm edge. Velocity, he decided, was the key.

"Why me?" he asked finally. "You don't know me. Don't have much reason to trust me. And yet you turn away from your own daughter and a longtime friend, if I can call him that, and you take me into your confidence instead. Is it because you feel somehow indebted to me? For saving your life? Or is there something about Tarot or Mouse that I should know? A reason I shouldn't trust them?"

Lora smiled grimly. "Perhaps, as you say, it's a little bit of both."

There was more than a hint of sadness in her voice, but something else as well. A barely concealed grimace, Percival noted. And perhaps she was favoring her staff more now than she had before? She'd been injured in the fight, he concluded. Perhaps badly. And she didn't want anyone to know. Whatever she had to show him, it was worth putting off medical attention. Perhaps worth risking her life.

They stood, after a time, at her chamber door. "It's in here," she said, and she pushed the door open. Percival let out an audible gasp. All across the room, painted in red and carved into the walls and burnt into the floors were the familiar words: "Vargoth Gor is not dead."

Lora shook her head. "I've been told it's a bit ostentatious, but—"

Percival stepped swiftly in front of Lora, held her back with one hand and held out his umbrella in front of them with the other. He scanned the room for sign of the vandal. "I think he's gone," Percival said, "but we should be careful."

"Who's gone?" she asked.

Percival took a step forward and crouched down by the edge of the High Cleric's canopy bed. He pulled up the bed skirt with the tip of his umbrella. "The vandal, of course."

"What *vandal*, Mister Gynt?"

Percival looked up, correctly intuiting that she couldn't see what he saw. "You don't see it, do you?"

"See what?"

Percival placed his hand on an area of rug where the word "DEAD" had been burnt in. Cold. "It's been like this for some time." He stood. "I can see it, and you can't."

"See what?" she repeated.

"Vargoth Gor and her amazing lack of deadness."

"She didn't!" said Lora with a sort of smirking outrage. She looked around the room, trying to see what Percival could see. But to her eye, her chambers were in a perfect state of order. Not a jot of dust. Not a linen out of place. Not a scratch on the wall or a stain in the carpet.

"Only her enemies can see it," said Percival. "At least, that's what Tarot said. Except I've never met Vargoth Gor, and you have. Which raises the question: Why am I, who's never met Gor, automatically her enemy, but *you...?*"

"Yes?"

"Well, you've seen her villainy firsthand, haven't you?"

"We also saved the universe together. What's that old-time expression? Ah, yes. 'We cool.'"

Percival sighed. "All right, then. Go ahead and show me what you're going to show me."

"Actually, if you could—" Lora grimaced again as she made her way to the bed. There she sat and sighed. "In the top drawer of my dresser there's an object I want you to have. You'll know it when you see it."

Percival slid open Tarot's mother's dresser drawer, feeling quite uncomfortable as he did. Within were the sort of unmentionables you'd expect to find in a lady's dresser, and Percival turned back to Tarot's mother questioningly.

"You need to dig a little," Tarot's mother advised him.

This Percival did, awkwardly sliding away undergarments until he came to a strange, glowing bauble, a tiny orb of silver and glass perhaps ten centimeters in diameter that glowed from within with an unearthly blue light.

"What is it?" Percival asked.

"Illuminari called it the Secondary Codex. A record of the universe as it is today. A complete download of Wikipedia, Facebook, and Google Maps updated in real time."

Percival had been staring intently at the bauble, but now his eyes jerked up suddenly. "Wait, are you telling me that the definitive record of all life in the universe is... peer edited? Couldn't you have used a data source that was, I don't know... better credentialed?"

"Let's not be elitists, Mister Gynt." Lora reached forward with a finger and poked the glowing ball. In response, a series of holographic images fired up around the globe depicting star charts and historical write-ups.

"You said, 'A thing which is everything, and a bit more.'"

"As I suspect you know, there is also a Primary Codex, a record of that which existed before the Engine began its march of destruction. Every time the Primary and Secondary Codices were synched, we downloaded the Apocrypha into the Secondary Codex. Here." Lora tapped the globe again, and the holograms changed, now depicting worlds and histories unfamiliar to Percival.

Lora slid her fingers across the holograms, flicking through images too fast for Percival to process. "The Ifeesians, the Haze, the Torquids, the Amiable Elders of Twern, the Liquid Twin Confederacy. My husband insisted that we memorize their names." Lora smiled wistfully. "But who will remember us?"

"What about the Primary Codex?" Percival asked.

"I don't know," said Lora. "I suspect it's with the Engine."

"And where's the Engine?"

Lora paused as she regarded Percival. "Mister Gynt, would you indulge me a curiosity?"

"It's been a long day, Your Holiness, and you've been through quite a lot. I'd indulge you as many as four curiosities, if it so pleased you."

"A kind offer, but I believe just this one will suffice. Tell me, Mister Gynt, why do you think I haven't revealed the location of the Engine of Armageddon to you or to my daughter as of yet?"

"Well, I couldn't say for certain, but I have a theory."

"I thought you might. I wonder. Do you perhaps attribute it to some estrangement between my daughter and myself? That I would spite her in the face of cosmic calamity?"

"No, ma'am."

"Or that I don't still feel the most debilitating guilt over what was done to my little boy? That I don't yearn for some way to make things right? That it doesn't tear me up inside to see him used as a pawn in this horrid affair?"

"No, ma'am."

"Or that I don't understand the peril we all face so long as the Nth Realm have my son and seek the Engine? That if they find it before you, it could mean the end of us all?"

"No, ma'am. I believe you understand that better than most."

"Then why? You seem to me a sort of detective. Why wouldn't I tell my daughter or you or young Mouse where the Engine is? Why, when I have every reason in the world to tell you, when my heart aches to tell you, why do I instead stay silent? Why do I not do the only thing that my heart and head have agreed upon as right in these last eleven years?"

"Because you don't know where the Engine is."

"Exactly right."

"In his journal, Illuminari said that only one person knows where the Engine is. The one person he trusted most of all. And only a loving daughter could think that that was you. He lied to you, ma'am. Used you. And then you left him, turned against him, started an entire religion to defame him and everything he stood for. You loved each other, I'd wager. But trust? Not a bit of it."

"Very good. But if not me, who?"

Percival eyes darted from wall to wall to floor. "Gor. Has to be, doesn't it? If I had a proper enemy... Someone so diametrically opposed to me that we hated each other to the core of our beings... That's the one person I'd know better than anyone. The one person I'd know as well as myself. And while I would never trust that person to do what *I* wanted, I would most certainly trust that person to do as *she* wanted. I'd trust that implicitly. From the stories I've heard, Gor craves power. If Illuminari trusted Gor with knowledge of the location of the Engine, it's because the secret itself gives Gor power. Illuminari trusted that Gor would never betray his secret, because in doing so, Gor would have to relinquish that power. A lot of supposition in there, but am I close?"

Lora smiled. "I can see why she likes you. Yes, you're exactly right. But let me ask you another question: Do you think it odd that the religion I founded only ten years ago has grown to dominance across four galaxies?"

"Four? Really? I wasn't aware."

"Well, three-and-a-half. But we're making great strides in the Cinnamon Galaxy."

"No, I don't know how. I'm sorry. I suppose if I did, I'd have a religion of my own. Just assumed you struck a chord with certain segments of the population."

"Would that I had such instincts. No, it has to do with the Engine. Or more precisely, to do with the Engine and the Rider and what happened when we separated the two. There was a tremendous amount of psychic energy binding the two together. When that link was severed, the energy dispersed. Like nuclear fission, he said. It washed over us in a wave, transforming us. Elevating us. Making us better."

"It gave you some kind of... super-religiosity?"

"It's not mind control, if that's what you're thinking. But it made me more charismatic. More... empathetic. More able to understand the human condition and speak to it in a language that resonates with the common person."

"And Gor?"

"Gor was much the same. You have to remember, the Engine erased Gor's past. Her long years of villainy were forgotten. No one save the three of us and a few bewitched taggers could even recall her name. No one knew her face. She had a clean slate, as they say. She could have gone on to do anything. And the power that she was exposed to... Enough power to realize her every fantasy."

"Gor seized power somewhere? A fiefdom that she could rule..."

"...as long as the Engine and the Rider remained separated. Bring them back together and the energy gets swallowed back up. We lose everything. That's how Illuminari knew he could trust Gor. It's as you said. He gave Gor exactly what she'd been after for all those years. He let Gor conquer the galaxy."

"Wait. Sorry?"

"Has no one told you? Eleven years ago, Vargoth Gor won. This is her galaxy now."

"You mean that metaphorically."

"No."

"You mean, from behind the scenes? She's a sort of puppet master to the Celestial Governor perhaps?"

"No. Think, Gynt."

"I don't..."

"Think."

"Oh."

"Two terms. Unopposed."

"Vargoth Gor *is* the Celestial Governor."

"And so she shall remain, for all of time, as long as the Engine remains hidden away."

"Governor Zell is not dead."

"Very much not."

"Well, then."

"Well."

"Perhaps I should pay the Governor a visit? I've been thinking tea and crumpets."

13 | RAIN

It was never night in the Holy City, but the storm clouds were gathering and the sky was dark as any midnight. Percival met Tarot at the hospital beneath an archway by the main entrance. "It's going to rain," she said plaintively.

"S'alright," Percival reassured her. "My umbrella is also an excellent umbrella." He reached out his hand, and she took it in hers, and together they walked out into the blustery, pre-storm streets of East District.

The streets were narrow, paved with cobblestone, and they merged together and separated at strange angles. On a different day, at a different hour, these streets would be thick with tourists and street performers and merchants hawking their wares. But at this moment, for all the evidence, Percival and Tarot might have been the last two people left on the planet. Or, indeed, the whole universe.

"I thought we might have a meal," Percival suggested, "if we can find a place." He squeezed her hand in his.

She smiled. "Mister Gynt, are you asking me out on a date?"

"Well... Your mother won't have our new spaceship for a few hours, and Um and Halla could both do with the rest. A lad needs something to do with his idle time."

Tarot slipped her arm around Percival's and brought her head to rest on his shoulder. "You know, I might just have to cut your legs off and keep you," she whispered.

"And they say romance is dead."

Percival and Tarot chose the first open restaurant they came to, a tiny corner bistro with an indecipherable name, and were just settling into their booth as the rain started. It was a hard rain, thought Tarot, and unforgiving. And she did not think it would stop.

Percival watched her, lost in her thoughts, and he frowned. This would be painful for both of them. And then, as she looked up, he forced a pleasant smile onto his lips. "I can't make heads or tails of the menu," he joked. "They seem to specialize in French fusion cuisine, but I'm not sure what they're fusing it with."

Tarot sighed and opened her menu. "I think you're right," she said after inspecting the entrée list. "My French is a little weak, but I think this is *foie gras* of pterodactyl."

"Well, I'm definitely having that."

"You shouldn't. They probably force feed the pterodactyls."

Percival snapped his menu shut. "Just the salad, then."

"I'm sorry. I didn't mean—"

"It's all right, really. The meal's not important."

"It's not?"

"We need to talk, Tarot."

"About pterodactyls?"

"No."

"Because I was finding that part of the conversation really interesting, and if we could just go back to it, I suspect that you could win me over on the *foie gras*."

"Don't you want to ask me?"

"Ask you what?"

"We've both said some things that call for an explanation. Don't you want to ask me about the Gynt Massacre?"

There was a dread in her eyes that Percival hadn't seen since their first meeting on Sanctuary-8, but just for an instant. And then she turned her head and called out to the waiter, "*Garçon*! We're ready to order."

The waiter, a Fummer ex-patriot, all eyes and mouth and floppy tentacles, floated over to their table to take their order.

"Welcome to H'nn'yghl!" he breezed. "Would you like to hear today's specials?"

"Yes, I would," said Tarot with a self-satisfied grin. "And your wine list and your desserts, and perhaps your personal recommendations as well?"

"*Oui, oui, madame!*" said the Fummer, before launching into a prepared speech that was mostly in French and a little bit in sounds-like-cat-is-being-strangled. His recitation took nearly six minutes, and in that time Tarot feigned complete and rapt attention, while Percival merely sat and stared flat-faced at her.

When the Fummer was done, Tarot put on an apologetic smile before saying, "Ooh. I'm sorry. I think I missed the part at the beginning. Could you start over?"

And the guileless Fummer was prepared to oblige before Percival shewed him away with a waive and a "Give us a moment?"

"Yes, of course," said the Fummer, and he backed/floated away.

Percival reached a hand across the table for Tarot's. She frowned before giving it to him, but then he smiled, and she smiled despite her better instincts.

"You knew about the Gynt Massacre?" he asked. "When you met me?"

Tarot shook her head. "I *still* don't know what it is. And more importantly, I don't care. The past is the past. We don't need to—"

"We do, though," Percival insisted, before adding, "You really didn't know?"

"I take it this was a famous massacre?"

"Pretty famous, yes. Not galactically famous, I suppose, but it made the news. They do retrospectives, every now and then. Thought maybe you'd have read about it growing up."

"Oh, well there's your problem," said Tarot. "My parents didn't let me have the internet growing up. Said it'd rot my brain."

"Well, all right then."

Tarot breathed a sigh of relief. Maybe that was the end of it.

"I've never told anyone this before, but..." And there he went again! Tarot tried to pull her hand away, but Percival held fast. "...on the news, they've been saying that the Gynt Massacre was twenty years ago, but it wasn—"

"I DON'T CARE! I DON'T CARE! I DON'T CARE!" Tarot shouted. Percival released her hand in shock. Somewhere in the kitchen, a tray of glasses fell to the floor and shattered.

The Fummer waiter flew out of the back and across the floor, tentacles flapping behind him. "Is something wrong, *madame?*"

Tarot let her head fall into her folded arms as she struggled to hold back tears.

"Um," Percival stammered, "She's having a hard time deciding. Can you give us a few more minutes?"

The Fummer assented and left the two to work through their issues. He'd received an associate's degree in Philosophy from Duke-DeVry University, so he was keenly aware of the ethical implications that came with the selection of certain items on their menu. He certainly didn't want to rush them through such difficult decisions.

"Tarot," said Percival. He rested a hand on her shoulder. She didn't look up. "I need you to talk to me. I need you to trust me. I need you to tell me why you never told me about your brother. I need you to tell me what Mouse and Halla have been planning. And most importantly, I need you to tell me that you're not involved with the Space Nazis."

Tarot looked up from her sleeves with bleary eyes. "What?" was the only word she could form, so she repeated it several more times, though her voice was shaking. "What? What?"

"They knew about your brother. And they've been following us. Tracking our movements."

"No," she said, sniffling back tears. "It's a coincidence. They're just following the same logic we are. First, the station. Then, Mother. Then—"

"Then?"

"When we find Gor, they'll be there too."

"They've been following a homing beacon."

"What?"

"We captured a few of them alive this time. Um pummeled them into submission. And before I came to get you, I stopped off at the local constabulary, and I learned some things."

"What things?"

"Maybe you should tell me."

"I don't know anything. Percival, you have to believe me." Tarot was crying now, staring off and to the side, pulling at the ends of her hair.

"Heinrik Mueller says the Archduke's ship tracked us using a homing signal that was originating from our ship. Now, I know I didn't bring a beacon on board, and I'm confident that Um didn't. That leaves you and your friends."

"I don't—"

"You know, it's awfully convenient that you were able to teleport off the ship right before it was destroyed, but Um and I were left to die."

"I didn't—"

"So, are you the lead Space Nazi or is that Mouse?"

"I—"

Percival slammed his fist against the table, and the table shook. "Stop LYING to me!"

Tarot wiped the tears from her eyes, and she muttered something softly that Percival couldn't make out.

"What?" he said.

"Turn out your pockets," she repeated.

"What?"

"I said—"

"I heard what you said. What I want to know is—"

"Just do it," she insisted, so Percival did, setting out his watch on the table, followed by his wallet, a stray cufflink, his handkerchief, a business card, the Secondary Codex, and a piece of stray lint, all in a line.

"Is there a point you're trying to make?" he asked with an ill-concealed disdain.

Tarot put Percival out of her head, straightened her posture, and waved a hand over the objects on the table. "Beacon revealed," she whispered. Nothing. Then again, "Beacon revealed." Nothing.

Then her hand passed over the business card. "Beacon revealed," she whispered, and the man on the card began to play his electric guitar as the name of his firm flew by in the background.

And Percival could hear a high-pitched tone coming from the card. Beeep. Beeep. Beeep.

"Clay from University," he mumbled, suddenly very angry with himself. "There never was a Clay from University." What's more, he remembered where he'd seen the shock trooper on the stairwell before. The one he'd taken the gasmask from. It was Clay again, or a clone of him. "It was me," said Percival. "I was the mole."

By the time Percival looked up, Tarot was already out the door. He grabbed up the contents of his pockets, even the business card/homing beacon and the piece of lint, and shoved them back into his trousers, and then he grabbed his umbrella and ran out into the rain after her.

Tarot hadn't gotten very far by the time he'd made it outside. The rain was coming down in sheets, and her lavender cloak was getting wetter and heavier with every step.

"TAROT!" he shouted after her. "I'M SORRY! I MADE A MISTAKE!"

Tarot turned, shaking, cloak pulled tight around her. "NO, YOU WERE RIGHT!" she shouted over the rain. "WE DON'T KNOW EACH OTHER! I WAS JUST PRETENDING, BECAUSE THE WORLD IS ENDING, AND I DIDN'T WANT TO DIE ALONE!"

"YOU'RE NOT ALONE!" Percival shouted back.

"WE ALL ARE, PERCIVAL, BUT IT DOESN'T MATTER! BECAUSE SOON ENOUGH, NONE OF THIS WILL HAVE EVER HAPPENED!" And then she turned her back on him and disappeared into the rain.

Percival watched her go, and when he could no longer see her through the rain, he closed his umbrella and tossed it to the cobblestones.

And for the first time in some time, Percival allowed himself to get well and properly soaked.

14 | CASUAL FRIDAYS

It's four o'clock on a Friday, and the salaried employees are starting to pack up. Mr. Glorp sticks his melty green head out of his office and asks Tom if he's going to go see the new *Zorro* movie. Percival, who is still paid by the hour at this point, keeps his head down and keeps working. He's been struggling with the same eleven-dimensional pivot table all afternoon, and he wants to get it done before he leaves. More importantly, he wants to get paid till five, even if that means he's the last out of the office again.

"Pack it in, sailor," says someone behind him.

"Ahoy, Midge," he answers, not bothering to turn around. He's not sure why they're speaking in nautical terms today.

"You want me to come aboard?" she asks playfully. Midge Jha is Mr. 11010's executive assistant, a few years older than Percival, a few pounds heavier than Percival, and possibly a few IQ points smarter. She's died her bob red-red this week to match her new horn-rimmed glasses. And because it's Casual Friday, she wears jeans and a green sweater instead of her usual skirt and blazer combo. She is at ease with herself in a way that Percival has never been.

"Can't ahoy just mean hello?" he asks as he turns to face her. "I thought it was one of those all-purpose words like aloha or shalom."

"No," she replies flatly. "Never become a sailor, Gynt."

Percival salutes. "Aye aye, Captain."

"Better," she commends him. "So, what are your plans for this weekend?"

"Um. Just Sunday dinner with Mum. I—"

"Lovely. I've been nominated to tell you to stop wearing a suit and tie on Casual Friday. It's making everyone uncomfortable."

"You were... nominated?"

"Technically Paul was nominated, but then we remembered the time he made the muffin girl cry, and I decided I better step in."

"I'm sorry. I didn't mean to make anyone uncomfortable. I was just trying to make a good impression."

"Well, the consensus impression is 'I'm weird and overly serious and I'm trying to show up the people who hired me.'"

"Oh."

"Yes. Oh. So lose the jacket next week. And the waistcoat."

"Right. Um."

"And the trousers."

"Lose my trousers?"

"Buy a pair of jeans. Or those khakims with the slider. Stop trying to look like an accountant."

"But I am an accountant!"

"Not yet you're not."

"It's just... I don't..."

"Also, your hat is too serious. And the umbrella?"

"But it might rain!" Percival sputters.

"On what planet?"

Percival shuts up, tosses his hands up in front of him to signal that he's done. And his face registers a hurt that makes Midge feel like Paul-after-the-muffin-girl.

"Don't be like that," says Midge. Then, in a moment of weakness: "You should come and have a drink with us. Tom's almost done smurfing the Taylor account, and then a few of us are going to the Drowning Pit of Despair."

"As fun as that sounds..." Percival shakes his head. "But I've got this pivot table to get sorted. It's still not displaying correctly along the Zomward axis."

"Well, you're not going to be authoring pivot tables all night, so how about you come by when you're done?"

Percival thinks for a moment, taps the save button on the sheet of paper he was working on and slides it aside. "I can't," he says finally. "I have a... thing."

"A date thing?" asks Midge with an incredulous smile.

But Percival shakes his head. "No. No, a different sort of thing."

"Another family thing? Again, with the mother?"

"No."

"A cat thing, then? It's about your cats?" Midge smiles, her confidence welling. "There. I've cracked it."

"I don't own any cats."

"Nonsense. I can picture it now. You have twelve of them. Maybe thirteen. And they all sleep with you in your bed at night, and you set their food out on the dining room table at mealtime so you don't have to eat alone."

Percival frowns. "No, it's a... It's not... I'm going to the library tonight. To do research. There was a murder in my apartment building a few years ago, and I think I can solve the case."

"Seriously?"

"The killer, I think he was leaving clues in the comment section of a number of contemporaneous blogs. The aliases, the post timestamps, and the URLs form the cypher, and then the individual posts—"

"No, I mean, *seriously*? That's the best excuse you can come up with? You watch too much television, Gynt. But I bet that *CSI: Sorrow Point* will survive the Nielsen dip this one week, if you change your mind."

Percival nods, forces a smile. "I'll think about it."

"You need to reach outside yourself, Gynt. That's all I'm suggesting. Now and again, you need to make a human connection."

He repeats, "I'll think about it, I promise."

"Thinking. Okay. Small victories," says Midge. Then, after a brief thought, "One of your cats is named Ms. Pretty Paws. Am I right?" She turns and walks to the elevator. "If you don't watch yourself, you're going to die alone, Gynt!"

Percival spins back to his desk and holds up the piece of paper with his pivot table on it. He shakes it and the table starts to rotate. She's right, of course. Not about the cats or *CSI: Sorrow Point* or the meaning of the word "ahoy" or even that he'll die alone. But it is true that he needs to reach outside himself. He can't solve a mystery by burying himself in facts and figures. He needs to meet his suspect face-to-face. Look him in the eye.

Make him cry like the muffin-girl.

It's a few minutes before midnight now, and Percival Gynt is knocking on the door to apartment 4D, the apartment directly below his own, and the place where Diane Eeps was found dead three years, four months prior.

He waits patiently for the current tenant to come to the door, Alexander Eeps, Diane's son. Percival hears footsteps and then various unlockings and unlatchings and slidings of bolts. He squares his tie and runs a hand, pointlessly, through his mad mop of hair.

The door opens the length of the last chain, enough for Eeps to glare out with one owlish eye, revealing a sliver of a long, disapproving face. "You want something?" he asks in a flat tone that suggests he's already grown bored with the conversation.

"Just a moment of your time," says Percival, fashioning his mouth into an uncomfortable smile. "I'd like to ask you a few questions about your mother's murder."

"You a cop?" asks Eeps.

"No," Percival clarifies. "Accountant."

Eeps looks Percival up and down. He doesn't blink, Percival notes to himself. Curious. Alexander closes the door, unchains the last chain, and opens it wide.

Eeps is tall and broad shouldered, bald with severe features. He is dressed for bed, in a white T-shirt and a pair of gray pajama bottoms. "Come in, then," he says.

The apartment is larger than Percival's, all wood floors and high ceilings and stark white walls. The front hall opens onto a kitchen on the left and, at the far end, onto the main living space. As through the cracked door, Percival can see a sliver of the truth beyond. A plastic cover over the couch. A doily sat upon the table. Nothing in the apartment newer than a decade.

He hasn't redecorated.

Eeps slides the door shut behind Percival. "What's this about?" he asks. "You'd agree it's odd for accountants to make house calls. Particularly at this hour."

"Suppose so." Percival glances around for something to use as a weapon should it come to that. There's a coatrack to his right that he might be able to make something of. "I live in the apartment upstairs," says Percival, in imitation of the sort of small talk he's seen others engage in around the office or on TV. "Moved in a few months back. I've been meaning to stop by to introduce myself."

"Yeah. I thought I recognized you. But why now, I wonder?" Percival is inside now, but Eeps has him penned close to the door. His body language says "stay put till I know what to do with you."

Percival reaches into his breast pocket to remove his handkerchief and dabs a bit of sweat from his brow. He is excited, anxious even, but not scared. Why isn't he scared?

"I understand that your mother was murdered in this apartment some years ago, and that the killer was never caught." Not the sort of thing you'd say to a proper human being, but Percival senses that this is not what he is dealing with. "I was wandering if I could ask you some questions."

Eeps takes a moment before responding, and in that moment he is nothingness. He is neither menacing nor reassuring nor angry nor calm. His owl eyes see through Percival and out into the hall beyond. And then his mouth twitches into an unconvincing smile. "Accountant-related questions?"

Percival nods.

Eeps turns his back on Percival and walks off into the kitchen, around the corner and out of sight. "I'm having a drink, then," he says.

"Are you thirsty?"

Percival stays put, considers whether this would be the rational time to run. "Yes," he calls, "as long as it's no trouble."

Around the corner, Eeps pours two glasses of brandy. "What are your questions, then?"

Percival only has a few questions prepared, but none that he would consider polite. Nothing that doesn't transparently expose his intentions. He briefly considers improvising another, something innocuous to ease the mood, to establish a sense of trust between the two of them, but what would be the use? He knows what Eeps is, and he knows Eeps knows he knows. So he begins:

"Are you CatsAreLOL19999?"

Eeps emerges from the kitchen with a glass of brandy in each hand. Percival recalls that Diane Eeps was poisoned. "Yes," says Eeps with no indication of hesitation or panic or surprise.

"Are you IsWeNongrammaticalNow?"

Eeps hands Percival a glass. "Yes."

"Are you @MaxAdelphiaFTW?"

"Yes."

Percival holds up his glass, regards the color. "Mind if we switch?"

Eeps shrugs and obliges. "I want people to know," he says. "I've been waiting for someone to work it out." Eeps takes a slow sip of brandy. His eyes stay fixed on Percival, even as his head tilts ever so slightly back.

Percival drinks as well, downing it all in one long gulp. A *faux pas*, he would later learn. "You could have called the police directly," says Percival. "If you'd wanted people to know. That would have been faster."

"I'm sorry," says Eeps with no tone of apology in his voice. "Perhaps I misspoke. I didn't mean to say that I wanted to be found out. What I meant was that I wanted there to exist someone with the capacity to do the finding. Someone with a mind like mine. And here you are."

"Yes," admits Percival, though he's not thrilled with Eeps' implication. "I am indeed here."

"Tell me then, Mister…"

"Mister Gynt."

"Tell me, how many of my teachings have you decoded?" Eeps reaches out and plucks the glass from Percival's hands. "Have you made a tally of the dead?"

Percival knows about the mother and has gleaned enough from half-decoded web posts to suspect that there were others. "I know you killed your mother first. It was a murder of convenience, to see if you were capable. And since then?" Percival considers the rate of unexplained deaths in Slidetown Province over the past forty months, factored by how many might be poison deaths, factored by how many such killings might have gone unreported or misreported, factored by how many might be the work of unaffiliated poisoners. "Seventeen, perhaps?" His actual tally was twenty-four, but it wouldn't do to over-estimate.

"And more," Eeps acknowledges. "But never a man before. No specific reason for that. I'm not a pervert. It's just how circumstances played out."

"Never a man *before?*"

Eeps nods. "I had to kill you, of course. If I let you go, you'd just off and tell everyone. And that would spoil the puzzle for everyone else. We can't have that."

Percival stretches the fingers of his right hand towards the coatrack. "There was poison in the brandy glass?" he asks. "In *both* glasses?"

"Indeed. Not enough to kill a man of my size, but more than a fatal dose for the average woman…"

Percival frowns, completing his killer's thought. "Or accountant."

Eeps holds up the two empty glasses in front of him. "I'm going to put these back in the kitchen now. We'll start to feel the effects of the poison in a minute or so, and one of the first symptoms is muscle spasm. I'd hate to break these. They were a gift from Mother, after all."

Eeps leaves Percival in the hallway. "Well, not a gift precisely," he clarifies from around the corner. Percival's hand tightens around the coatrack and then immediately opens again. A wave of pain shoots through every nerve ending in his body and then fades to numbness. He staggers sideways into the coats, can't get more than a wiggle out of either arm, attempts to call out, but can't manage more than a slurred "Blauhhhh!"

Eeps shuffles back out into the hall. "Want to see this," he mumbles. The poison is affecting him too now. Eeps' eyes are glassy and his jaw is slack. Drool trickles down his chin. He is become Frankenstein's Monster in pajama bottoms.

In his head Percival summons a memory of ripped flesh and exposed intestine. He vomits hard into Eeps' face, stumbles into him, knocking against his shoulder, and then past him down the hall. "Blauhhh!" Percival moans. "Blauhhhhh!"

The sick stings Eeps' eyes. He can't see, nor move his numb arms up to wipe the sick away. Instead he turns and lumbers blindly down the hall after his escaping victim. "YOU CAN'T RUN!" he shouts, even as his vocal cords constrict inside his throat.

Percival falls over Eeps' plastic-wrapped couch and vomits onto the shag area rug. In his head, he's back in the cave, scrambling through the dark. Death at his back. Stumbling through muddy water. Blood on his boots. With limp limbs, he scuttles forward, like a beached fish to the sea. The world blurs before him. A voice echoes from all sides: "ISHUDDAFFDUNTHSYEEEEERSAGO!"

Percival reaches white wall, vomits against it. This, he thinks. This is what I am. How did I forget? He wills a finger to twitch. Then a thumb. He forces a smile.

"WHERRARRYOOOOO?" Eeps slurs from across the room.

"Dance for me," says Mother, years before. And then she throws rocks. "Sing for me," says Mother, and then she cuts him.

Percival lumbers to his feet. He turns to Eeps and smiles imperceptibly. "Blaauh. Blaaaauh. Blauh," he says. I'm Percival Gynt, he thinks, and you don't impress me.

Eeps stumbles blindly forward. Percival turns and scrapes his fingers against the window's edge until he lifts it half-open, then he throws himself out onto the fire escape. He closes one numb hand around the ladder, then the other, and slowly pulls himself upwards.

From the open window, Eeps shouts, "GNNNNN-NNNNNTTTTT!"

Forty-one minutes later, Percival trumbles into the Drowning Pit of Despair. He's still feeling the after-effects of Eeps' poison. Feels like his head is operating at half-speed, and the rest of his body's five seconds behind that. His eyes won't focus, and he keeps almost falling over to his right, but he's giddy for whatever happens next.

The pub is thick with scum and hooligans and the sound system blares with cheesy rock anthems from the 19980s. All the things that Percival hates shoved up against him, but he doesn't register any of it, just bounces along through the crowd. No pardon me's tonight. No excuses.

He finds his co-workers at the back of the pub, Midge and Paul and Tom and Mister Glorp and Compubot, all squeezed into a corner booth. They're all of them very drunk or Compubot. Midge and Paul are doing shots of something orange. Mister Glorp is trying to make out with Tom. Compubot, trapped in the corner, is building a pyramid out of Midge and Paul's empty shot glasses.

"Um." Percival stands there uncomfortably for a moment, swaying ever so slightly. The others don't immediately look up or register his presence. He's about to maybe-but-probably-not say something when Midge finally sees him through the bottom of her shot glass.

"Holy poop!" she exclaims, a drunken grin wide on her lips. "It's Percival Gynt in a bar!"

"In a *suit* in a bar," mumbles Paul, who's having trouble keeping his head up or his eyes open. "At least, I think we're still in a bar."

Percival is still smiling. "Midge," he says, "I need to talk to you. The most amazing thing's happened!" He reaches out a hand and pulls Midge up from her seat and away from the table.

Midge giggles. "What's gotten into you tonight?"

"I did it, Midge. I caught a killer. Well, didn't so much catch as ran from. But it was him. I was right. I looked a killer in the eye. Stared him down. Sort of. It was amazing!"

Midge isn't following most of what Percival is saying. He's talking too fast, and his voice is slurred, and Midge can't hear him over the music, but she smiles and nods.

"It was because of you," says Percival. "You pushing me to step out into the world. You know me better than anyone. Better than I know myself."

"Do you want to do shots?" asks Midge, but Percival doesn't hear her.

"I realized something tonight. Who I'm supposed to be."

Midge looks back at Paul, who's passed out now, and shouts, "We're going to do another round!"

"I'm—" Percival waits for Midge to turn back around and places his hands on her shoulders. "I'm in love with you, Midge. I love you."

Midge smiles kindly, takes Percival's hands off her shoulders. "Right! They've got this one that flashes lightning. Do you want that one?"

Percival sputters as Midge slips past him towards the bar. "But I—"

Tom slaps a shoulder around Percival. "Weird night, huh?" With his free hand, Tom wipes bits of goo from his nose and cheek.

Percival stares into the crowd. "I thought—"

"Well, we've all been there."

Percival can feel time beginning to catch up with him. "What happens next?" he asks.

Tom says, "Everything."

PART

IN WHICH THE FATE OF THE UNIVERSE
RESTS IN OUR HERO'S HANDS
AND THEN SLIPS THROUGH HIS FINGERS

Top 5 News Downloads for April 12, 20018

5 [Last of the Silvermoon Clan Executed on Jagrhar-4](#)

4 [Which Dinosaurs are Highest in Cholesterol?](#)

3 [20 Years Later, Soldiers Remember the Battle of Gynt](#)

2 [Bloodbath in the Great Cathedral](#)

1 [Governor Promises Inaugural Ball will be Unforgettable](#)

You may also be interested to know

68 [Parts of 12 N^{th} Realm Shock Troopers Found Adrift in Deep Space, Mostly Dead](#)

Today's Weather

Foreboding

1 | *THE MEAT THERMOMETER*

In the years following his death, the man born Tyree Bell was better known to most as the Mad Architect of Galactic Zero. This is perhaps an unfair appellation. After all, Mister Bell wasn't technically insane, at least not by the standards accepted by the medical community of his day. What Mister Bell was, was a man of epically poor judgment. Or, to put it more finely, he was an epically poor judge of character. For though in later years, long after his death, Mister Bell would be recognized as something of a visionary, in his own time he was simply a man more in love with the New than he was with his own life. A man who stupidly ignored those two ageless maxims:

o the customer is always right
o particularly if the customer has the bigger gun
(or, in this case, all of them)

When the Celestial Governor commissioned Mister Bell to tear out the interior of an old sanctuary world and rebuild it as her new seat of power, she gave only two instructions, the second of which to design for her a capitol city that would be feared and envied throughout the seven galaxies, a capitol that would serve as a fitting monument to the Governor's boundless power and influence.

And Mister Bell was more than equal to the task. He had recently begun experimenting with anti-gravity plating and had conceived for the Governor a planetary core in which gravity bent and folded over like origami, where massive steel spires rose up around the core's interior, rising upwards and inwards to the planet's raging MagmaStar, where interconnecting roadways and bridges met at strange angles, often upside down or sideways or both, where a man could look up from a pedestrian walkway to see a lake hanging overhead, could picnic in a park on the side of a skyscraper, could dance on a transparent ballroom floor, the planet's MagmaStar flaring underneath/above. It was a wonder of three-dimensional design, everything the new Governor had wanted in a capitol, breathtaking in its ambition, staggering in its execution, and unfortunately for Mister Bell, a bit vomitous on first introduction.

The Celestial Governor in fact vomited three times during her first tour of the new capitol. Once, just a little bit in her mouth, and she might have let that go. Second, off the side of their touring skiff, in plain view of the visiting delegation from the Iblis-Yzjzyax Confederacy. And third, and fatally as it would turn out for Mister Bell, out her mouth and nose, sideways, into the face of Ambassador Presidium Hol, crown prince of Iblis, with whom the Governor had very much hoped to have... diplomatic relations later that evening.

"Takes some getting used to!" Bell pleaded. "I'm sure there's something you can take for the motion sickness!" he cried. "And, anyway, he didn't seem that keen on you *before* all the puking!" was the last thing he said before the Governor tore off Mister Bell's lower jaw.

And even in those final words, Mister Bell proved himself the visionary. For as it turned out, the Governor was indeed able to accustom herself to the strange gravity of her new capitol over an extended period of time. And there were indeed pills that she could distribute to her staff and to the citizenry and to select visitors to counterbalance the initial disorientation of the gravity effect. And it was even the case that Ambassador Presidium Hol, crown prince of Iblis, had *not* been very keen on the Governor prior to the puking, nor during, nor immediately after, but he was properly enamored of anyone capable of ripping off an underling's jaw in one go, a proper brew of strength and mercilessness that the prince found quite intoxicating. And so it was that the Governor and the Ambassador conducted diplomatic relations right there on the skiff, in full view of the balance of the Iblis-Yzjzyax delegation, and directly over the lifeless corpse of the Mad Architect of Galactic Zero.

Hence the expression, "Don't jaw off to the Governor."

Eight years and two re-elections later, Celestial Governor Zell was quite pleased with her seat of power. Now called Galactic Zero, it was the metaphoric if not literal center of the galaxy. All essential commercial and political dealings in the region were conducted through Galactic Zero. Galactic Zero was the hub of all great entertainment and artistic and scientific achievement. And if it wasn't the spiritual center of the seven galaxies? Well, Zell would not begrudge the successes of old acquaintances.

And yet it would be wrong to say that Zell was happy. She had everything she'd ever dreamed of, yes. Unchecked power. All the material wealth that one could hope to acquire. Her oldest enemies, dead or forgotten or bound to servitude. And yet? And yet there were the whispers. Rumors. Or perhaps it was simply her paranoia finally getting the better of her. That there were forces moving against her. Illuminari's hollowed-out boy, the Rider, in the hands of fascist revolutionaries. The magician's apprentice, young Mouse, out and about and surely up to no good. And another, barely a name, a curiosity. Gynt? Who was this man to terrify Zell so? There were stories, suppositions, woven through the official record. Was he human or a monster himself? Or was he, as Zell had begun to suspect, the very fist of Fate, clenched and ready to deal that final, mortal blow to the woman who defied history?

It was with this pernicious fatalism roiling inside of her that the Governor carried herself in the hours before her third inaugural ball. It was meant as a distraction, as a bit of frivolity to help lighten her dark mood. But she knew her enemies were circling. They'd already taken down the High Cleric. One act of violence, and she was dismantling everything she'd spent the last eleven years building. One act and a man. Gynt. At the heart of everything, like graffiti scrawled across the stars, "He is coming for you."

One could respond to such events with panic and despair, but Zell prized her dignity above all else. If she maintained the appearance of normalcy, then everything would be normal. Routine was her ally. Protocol, her weapon of choice.

And so, though she very much believed that she'd be dead by Monday morning, Celestial Governor Zell summoned her Celestial Food Tester to her so that the two might tour the Celestial Kitchens together, to oversee preparations for the great Celestial Feast to be held in her great Celestial Honor. And no power in the universe would protect the chef or servant or passing bystander who failed to meet her expectations.

"Young Wyndham," asked Zell as they rode the spiral lift round the tower to the kitchens, "What can you tell me about the feast that the chefs are preparing for me?"

Zell was an imposing presence, just over two meters tall, broad-shouldered, bald-headed, square-jawed, a half-dozen gold hoops pierced through each earlobe, skin gray and hard and smooth like polished granite, eyes narrow and uncompromising. The elegance of her red robes with their gold trim and nouveau styling did little to soften or conceal the hulking physique underneath. Whenever Zell asked a question, Young Wyndham's first reaction was to flinch. His second, to answer quickly and thoroughly and deferentially. And then his third, again, to flinch.

"Well, ma'am," he said, "the main course, ma'am, is goose prepared three ways. Ma'am. First, as chronoton-infused rillettes of goose confit, seasoned with nutmeg, cinnamon and foosh. Then an engorged nyorg appendix, wrapped in goose breast prosciutto and lightly braised in an Armagnac demi-glace reduction. And I believe, ma'am, that the final preparation is liquified goose gizzard over a semi-sweet anti-matter truffle ice cream."

"That sounds hideous," Zell revulsed.

"Hideous-bad or, um, hideous-*good*, ma'am?"

"There's only ever one kind of hideous, Young Wyndham."

"Of course," conceded Young Wyndham with a timid nod. It was coming now. He could sense it.

Zell slapped her food tester on the back. "But there's good news," said Zell with a droll smirk across her lips. "If *you* die, I don't have to eat a lick of it."

Zell laughed, but Young Wyndham couldn't see the joke.

The Celestial Kitchens were over a kilometer long from end to end, running the height of Blue Tower along the interior wall. Blue Tower was Zell's chief residence as well as the tower where she entertained off-world delegations and held all public events. Not to be confused with Red Tower, where she made laws and conducted other affairs of state, or Black Tower, where the military and police were headquartered and where, some whispered, her Celestial Necromancer Corps experimented on the dead and dying.

The floors of the kitchens were orange ceramic tile over the usual anti-grav plating. As elsewhere in the capitol, the plates here emitted a low-pitched hum that only a few intelligent species could hear, but which had the serendipitous effect of pacifying most of the lesser species. This allowed for the easy slaughter of the day's protein, be it fish or fowl or beast or necroblob. That the odd busser or dishwasher could sometimes be found staring into the distance humming/drooling was considered an acceptable loss for every docile nyorg or basilisk brought to the saw.

The kitchens were a maze of appliances: griddles and grinders and mixers and meat saws, walk-in cryo-freezers, sonic sinks, and the ovens! Small ovens, large ovens, narrow ovens, seven-dimensional ovens, convection ovens, rotisserie ovens, gamma-reactive alchemical ovens, coal and brick ovens, anti-ovens... Each chef had to become a specialist, the master of their hundred meters of equipment.

"You know how to operate the deep fusion evaporator?" one asks another.

"Nah, sorry. I'm fillin' in for Ted. You'll need to walk down to Sector 12 to find somebody who does appliances that start with D."

And on this afternoon, the kitchens were alive with activity. Every shift was on hand. Specialists from off-world had been called in. All the

Governor's favorite chefs of the past decade had been reanimated for the occasion. All to ensure that the night's feast met with the Governor's overlarge and unforgiving expectations.

Into this maelstrom of cookery strode the Governor and her food tester. Around them, the chefs and the wait staff and the other servants bustled and bounced off one another with chaotic fervor, but they parted for their master, bowed and scraped and muttered their well wishes then hurried on their way, none eager to incur the Governor's undivided attention.

"This here," said Wyndham, gesturing to a short, trembling, furry chef, "is your goose master. His name is Nevin."

Chef Nevin managed an unconvincing smile, a hasty, ill-considered curtsy, and a mumbled "Your Governorship." He held his toque in his hands in front of him like a holy amulet, now and then nibbling the top nervously with his rodent teeth. The Governor couldn't quite decide if Chef Nevin was a tiny rat of a man or a great big man of a rat. Either way, she was confident that she could fit all of Nevin's head into her mouth if she needed to. Perhaps if the goose wasn't to her liking.

"Liquified goose gizzard?" asked the Governor, an eyebrow raised.

Nevin nodded. "Over a semi-sweet anti-matter truffle ice cream, Your Governorship." Then adding after a pause, "It's what the people expect these days."

The Governor frowned, but the rat was right. Normalcy. Routine. Protocol. Goose gizzard.

"Ma'am," said Wyndham. "There's a man."

Young Wyndham pointed one fleshy finger down the aisle, past frying vats and the towering, stainless steel behemoth that was the Omega Oven™ and onward to an enigmatic figure standing silent some ten meters distant. Between them, all activity had stopped. The aisle was clear. The staff had hushed. All eyes were on the Governor and this stranger.

The other was not a tall man. He was slight of frame, and stood stooped, perhaps pained. He wore no shoes and muddied trousers and worn suspenders over a bloodied undershirt. His right arm hung in an improvised sling. Upon his face, a mask of red and gold with a long beaked nose, a scraggle of brown hair emerging overtop. He swayed, ever so slightly, ever so hypnotically, as if under the power of a divine breeze that blew only for him.

"Who is that?" the Governor growled.

"Perhaps one of the revelers?" Young Wyndham speculated nervously. "Here for the party?"

Behind them Chef Nevin wisely slipped into a workstation cupboard.

"A reveler? What's he wearing?"

"I believe it's a Zanni mask, ma'am."

"A *what*?"

Young Wyndham flinched. "Zanni, ma'am. A sort of jester character from ancient Earth theater. The Zanni character was a wise servant or a trick—"

"I don't need a history lesson, Wyndham. Why is he wearing a mask?"

"The masquerade, ma'am. Among tonight's festivities is a mas—"

"Why is he wearing a mask *in my kitchen*?"

Young Wyndham sunk his head, raised his arms up defensively, took a step back. "I-I don't know, ma'am. I'm just the food tester."

Then, before the Governor could slap her servant's head off, the stranger spoke. He said five words. Or, to be more precise, he said, "Five words."

"What?" said Zell, turning her attention back to the stranger.

"I have five words for you," said the stranger. "You'll want to hear them, but I advise you to clear the room first." The stranger's voice was raw and rasping. "Five words that will change your fate."

Fate. If the Governor still had a heart left within her massive chest, it would have trembled at the word. Instead she snarled and pointed to a line chef who was at that moment handling a grotesquely large silver carving knife. "You're good at gutting fish," she growled. "Gut our intruder like a fish!"

The line chef's eyes went wide with panic but he did as he was told, or rather he attempted to, charging forward towards the masked stranger, knife first, screaming in a foreign tongue. The stranger rolled his eyes, slipped his good hand into his pocket, and blinked out of existence. Appearing again crouched at the line chef's side, he yanked the chef's left shin out from under him. The poor cook's momentum sent him sprawling across the floor. The grotesque knife clattered out of reach.

The stranger stood. "Five words," he repeated. "Clear the room." Behind him the line cook scrambled to his feet.

Zell fumed. "More!" she shouted with stiff-armed gestures. The chefs and servants looked at each other with nervous confusion. A few advanced wearily on the stranger. One held a spatula in his trembling hand. Another, a fryer basket full of steaming tater tots.

"You're not so scary," said the fry cook, who was obviously terrified. "You're wounded! Bleeding out!" He forced a short laugh.

The stranger frowned. "Look closely," he advised. "Is this my blood, or your family's?"

The fry cook hesitated, let out a horrified squeak. The stranger snatched the fryer basket from his hands and flung hot tots into the face of the enspatula'd cook. Said cook recoiled in mild discomfort, though played as if his was the most horrifying of tortures. "My face!" he shouted, before crumpling, he hoped convincingly, to the floor.

The fry cook turned and ran, hard, into Celestial Governor Zell's chest. Zell was properly angry now and took off the fry cook's head with one sharp twist. She held it in her hands as the cook's body dropped to the floor, blood splurting out onto her red robe and the orange tile below.

Now the servants were running. Not Wyndham, because he feared being trampled. But the chefs and the wait staff and the rest were all running as fast as they could to the exits.

"You didn't need to do that," said the stranger plaintively.

The Governor dropped the cook's head at her feet. "You wanted the room cleared, didn't you?" she said with a sneer. Adding, "And his name was Louis, by the way. Louis Quince."

The stranger nodded and sighed and let the fry basket fall to the floor at his feet. He reached into his pocket and pulled out a 19949 edition Apple Watch, turning it over in his good hand.

The Governor smiled. "Ah," she said. "The 19950 edition, if I'm not mistaken. I have one quite like it."

"I know," said the stranger. "Five words."

"Yes, yes," said the Governor, wiping her hands against the clean parts of her robe. Then she thought of Young Wyndham behind her.

"Run," she commanded without turning, and Young Wyndham ran.

The stranger raised his watch to the Omega Oven beside him. Curious. "Are you ready?" the stranger asked.

The Governor scowled, and the stranger responded with a thin, self-satisfied smile. And then he said:

"Vargoth Gor is not dead."

The Governor's eye twitched.

"Those aren't the five words, by the way." The stranger glanced at the face of his watch. Not quite yet.

"WHO ARE YOU?" roared Zell with all the anger of a blaggard who already knows the answer to her own question.

The stranger grinned, pushing the Zanni mask up to reveal his face, his too large eyes, and his hawkish nose. "My name is Percival Gynt," he said cheerily, "and those aren't the five words either."

Zell seethed. At her sides, her fists unclenched and reclenched. "Gynt," was all she could manage through gritted teeth. This was it, then. The end.

Percival consulted his watch once again, nodded, then held it up once more to the Omega Oven. "Right! Where was I? Oh yes. My name is Percival Gynt..."

The meat thermometer app on Percival's watch let out three loud successive pings which echoed through the emptied kitchens like the last beeps from a dying man's heart monitor.

"...and your goose is cooked."

2 | *TWO STARSHIPS*

Um was disappointed. He hadn't died. He'd only suffered a grievous wound and, paradoxically, it was making him feel his mortality again. The quick brutal deaths hadn't given him much time to think. He'd just popped back to life and everything was fine. Naked, in one case, but otherwise fine. But this? This slow grind of pain and disfigurement? This was something else. Throw it fast, and the stone skips across the water. Lower it in gently, and it sinks reliably, inevitably to the bottom.

Um didn't want to go to the bottom.

A chunk of Um's face had been spackled over with something called Archanoid gum, a sort of crystalizing excrement produced by fist-sized spider-like creatures kept in the Cathedral hospital. This left the one side of his face numb, and made it hard to turn what was left of his left eye. He was also having some trouble with some of his consonants. He tried to say "I'm Um," to a nurse, and it had come out, "Ah Uhh."

"That's okay," she'd said. "A lot of men get nervous when they talk to me."

Um found this exchange frustrating, first because the nurse wasn't at all attractive. She was far too pale and curvy and blonde and giggly. But worse, to confuse his name for a stammer?

Unacceptable.

When Percival met him out front in the morning, Um was glad to finally have his back to the place. At least he assumed it was morning. The sun never set the night before, and he was beginning to feel a bit timelost.

"Yuh shuh ih thuh awninh?" he asked Percival.

Percival did not give a direct answer. "We're going our separate ways," he explained as they walked down the cobblestone boulevard. "The High Cleric has agreed to provide us with two ships. You and I will leave in one. Tarot and Mouse and Halla will take the other."

"Hlih uh?"

"Tarot and I came to a bit of a disagreement last night. We agreed it would be better this way."

"Uh ah we goinh tuh thuh say hlace?"

"Maybe. The High Cleric told me where to find Gor. I don't know if Tarot and Mouse know. Though even if they don't, I don't imagine we can keep them from following us."

"Ho whuh hahhen?"

"I just don't think that the two of us can be in the same physical space for a while. And, anyway, I'm not sure we can trust Mouse or Halla."

"Hah! Nah yuh hown hike ee!"

"Don't start," said Percival with the sort of already defeated tone that suggested to Um that he could start whatever he liked and Percival would just roll over and take it. Ideal, if his goal was to emotionally pummel Percival into a sniveling pool of mush. Less good if-and-seeing-as his goal was to help Percival save the universe.

So he stopped, and he turned to face his forlorn companion, and he grabbed him by one arm and pulled him so he had to face him too. His one Archanoid shat eye wasn't quite pointing the right way, but he looked him in the eyes with his other eye, and he said with as much compassion and intensity and sincerity as he could muster:

"Hnaah at ah ih!"

Percival closed his eyes and nodded. "You're right," he said. "Of course, you're right."

Percival had no idea what Um had just said, but this seemed to him the best all-purpose response.

It took over sixty years to construct the enormous complex that now houses the Great Cathedral's Sister 10110001 Memorial Spaceport. Construction on the two interlinked buildings began in 19939, back when the planet was still fully owned, operated, and populated by Fummers. All of the construction work was done by the Fummers themselves, based on designs by the famous Fummer architect, [unpronounceable].

Because the Fummers rarely left their homeworld and because they rarely entertained off-world guests, the Fummers had no need for a spaceport. What they were actually attempting to build for all of those years was an enormous football stadium. Back then, Fummers used to love football, although they called it soccer on account of the fact that they have no feet. Fummers played soccer by drifting as close as they possibly could to the ball, nudging it with their large, floating head-bodies and trying very hard not to accidentally swipe the ball with their willowy floating hand-tentacles. Most Fummer soccer games ended in a 0-0 tie. In this way, they were unremarkable.

There was some resistance in Fummer society to building this enormous sporting complex, which would also include three Chili's restaurants, two Applebee's, a geothermic tesseract, and a Red Lobster. There were those who felt that a sporting complex shouldn't be built with taxpayer's money, that it should be built with private funding alone. Others objected to the location of the complex, which was right next to a public park, an orphanage, and an old Fummer burial ground. Still others wanted the complex to be built bigger or smaller to taller or shorter or to house a *football* stadium instead of a football stadium. Fummers loved football almost as much as they loved football, although they called the game pigskin super-huddle blitzball on account of the fact that, again, they have no feet.

The real hero of the stadium construction project was [unpronounceable]. Through the years, there were many work stoppages. Money dried up for months at a time. There were legal disputes, protests, and strikes. But it was always [unpronounceable] who stepped up with a solution, whether it was a new investor, a renegotiated contract, or a heartbreakingly eloquent speech on the importance of sport in Fummer society. Late in his life, [unpronounceable], who never had any children, said of the stadium project, "This is the achievement of my lifetime, my one great legacy. It's this project that I want the people of the universe to think of, countless centuries from now, when they hear the name [unpronounceable]!"

Sadly, [unpronounceable] died a few weeks before construction of the complex was completed in the year 19999. Some say that it was a blessing that [unpronounceable] died when he did, for surely he would have been devastated by what happened next. A day and a half after construction was completed, the Fummer government approved the sale of their planet to the High Cleric of the Intergalactic Church of the All-Mother. Of course, the High Cleric had no more use for a football stadium than the Fummers had for a spaceport. The retrofitting took a few weeks work, disarming the geothermic tesseract and the Red Lobster was no easy feat, but the stadium's retractable roof was readymade for spacecraft takeoffs and landings.

As part of their negotiations, the Fummers had pushed to have the new spaceport named after the late [unpronounceable], but the High Cleric deemed such a tribute to be "literally impossible."

Instead she named the spaceport after a robot nun she made up on her way to the ribbon cutting.

The Sister 10110001 Memorial Spaceport consisted of two connected buildings: the main dome, from which ships landed and took off, and the smaller screening facility, through which all travelers were processed. Visitors were screened by security for harmful intent, had their luggage searched and returned, and were charged an excise duty for the transport of certain items, lifeforms, or ideals. While waiting for their psychological profiles to be completed, travelers could stop by the gift shop or take a meal at one of the several Chili's or Applebee's.

With the High Cleric's advance word, Percival and Um were able to move swiftly through each screening and on to the dome. They were asked a few perfunctory questions. Um was asked, "I see you have a death ray. You weren't planning on using that on anyone, were you? No? Very good, then." Percival was asked, "I see that you're on our No-Fly list. Can you come with me? No? Nevermind, then. Best of luck to you!"

Inside the main dome nearly three dozen starships were parked in tight proximity. Many were transport vehicles, sleek commercial carriers, tall and thin and pearly white with long red fins. Adverts played across their hulls while the ships idled. "If you don't wear khakims, you'll die alone." Others were cargo ships, squat and squarish and candy-colored, some stacked two or three high. And there were the privately-owned ships, each a curious thing unto itself: a glowing sphere, a robot lion, a cabinet of blue wood. The heat from all of those engines was stifling, and Percival could sense a subtle time distortion. Ground crew stepped in and out of the engine smog, wrinkly old brown-skinned men with cheap checkered suits and bubble helmets and clipboards. Perhaps always the same wrinkly old brown-skinned man, thought Percival.

He approached one of these men with Clay-from-University's business card in hand. "By any chance," asked Percival, "are items left unattended on spaceport grounds vaporized for our protection?"

"Indeed," the man in the checkered suit cautioned, "so best be careful with your possessions."

Percival considered this, nodded to himself, then tossed the business card casually to the ground between them.

"Sir?" asked the man as Percival turned and walked away. "SIR?" he repeated, but Percival kept on walking. A few footsteps more and Percival heard a loud zapping sound behind him. He allowed a self-satisfied smirk to cross his lips.

Um rejoined Percival in the shadow of the robot lion. He patted his companion's shoulder and pointed out a nearby ship. It shared the same design as the commercial carriers, tall and sleek and red-finned, but the customary advert had been replaced by a pure blue sky and long trailing clouds. And the sun, brilliant and pure, peering out from behind. Percival grinned appreciatively. Um shook his head and pointed a second time, adding an extra mechanical finger for emphasis, directing Percival's attention to the young woman who sat in the ship's doorway, her feet dangling over the side, kicking back and forth as she read from the back of a folded sheet of paper.

She had piles of frizzy brown hair, this woman, and the humidity was doing her no favors. She dressed in sturdy traveling clothes, brown leathers, black straps, brass buckles, and pockets anywhere and everywhere. A wrench was strapped to her thigh. Around her neck was wound a long red wool-esque ThermoScarf. Up over her eyes, a pair of brass-rimmed goggles.

There was something about her eyes. Like brown pools of...

"ESME!" Percival shouted as he jogged over. "I almost didn't recognize you without your habit!" Then, in a more conversational tone as he approached, "You kit out quite handsomely."

A smile flickered briefly across Esme's lips as she pocketed her fold of paper. The boarding door was a meter over Percival's head with a ladder beneath. Esme looked down at Percival and Um as they walked up, two strangers to whom she was about to trust her life. But then, Esme had entrusted her life to strangers before. Never with good results, but always wholeheartedly. Esme examined that logic in her head, realized that Percival and Um were staring, and so packed it away for another time.

"I'm coming with you," she said matter-of-factly.

Percival shrugged and looked at Um, who also shrugged. Um also said something hard to understand and Percival nodded. "Fine by us," he said, and he began to climb the ladder.

Esme backed away from the entryway. "Don't you want to know why?" she asked as Percival pulled himself on board. They were standing on the rear wall of the passenger cabin. Artificial gravity hadn't been switched on yet.

"Is it because you just found out that the religion you devoted your entire life to is a lie? And you need something else to believe in? Something important enough, something massive enough, that it'll fill the epic existential void that's opened up inside you? That you've stumbled into an atheistic world view that tells you that simply being isn't enough? That you must be doing something to matter? Something along those lines?"

Esme frowned. "I was just going to say that you seemed like nice people, and I didn't really have anything else to do."

Um humphed as he pulled himself into the ship. Percival gave his nose a good scratch.

"Yes, well, I suppose that's a sort of an existential void then, isn't it? You've got a sort of a metaphysical to do list with a big... existential..."

Um rolled the one eye that would still roll and then began a three-armed climb up the passenger seats to the pilot's cabin.

"The High Cleric," Esme began before correcting herself, "Lora... She said that you and her daughter Tarot had a falling out. I thought you could use an extra pair of hands."

Percival turned his back to Esme, pulled the boarding door closed. "Yes, well, let's not talk about that. Things happen." He took a long sniff, straightened his shoulders and turned. "Where's the other one, then?"

"Oh!" Esme grinned. "Over here!" She motioned, and he followed her over to a side window. "The ship we're on is called the Daylight," she explained, and then she pointed out a second repurposed commercial craft, back behind a stack of cargo pods. The other was very much the shadow of their own. "That one's called the Nightfall." A black sky, full of twinkling stars, and a shimmering crescent moon. "I don't know what it is," she whispered. "But I feel drawn to it."

Percival rested an avuncular hand on her shoulder. "It's the allure of the night," he mused. "It calls to us all. The poet Byron once wrote—"

Then the artificial gravity switched on and Percival and Esme flopped awkwardly to the floor.

Over the loudspeaker, Um let loose a bizarre, consonant-challenged chortle. It was a sort of "hoggahoggahogga" with what was perhaps an arrhythmic knee-slapping in the background.

A hint of fear crept into Esme's skull. "Is he all right?" she asked.

Percival nodded as he slid himself into a sitting position. "A spider-thing shat on his face, and now he can't talk to me. This is the best day of his life."

The starship began to rumble awake. Percival reached out and took Esme's hand and smiled. "I just realized. You've never been off-world before, have you?"

She shook her head and blushed.

Overhead the not-a-football-stadium dome was sliding out of view. All around the ship, ground crewmen held up their hands and their clipboards and motioned for everyone to stand back. Beneath the ship, the time smog whipped round and ignited. The time smog whipped round and ignited. The time smog whipped round and ignited.

And the ship had lift. A crowd of tourists from the planet Pulpactchka smiled and applauded as the ship streaked into the sky, as was their custom. "Safe journey," they each whispered.

"Safe journey," said another looking skyward, a stranger to them, a woman in a lavender traveling cloak. The Pulpatchkins smiled and nodded to her and then piled into the blue wood box.

"Do you think he knows?" asked Mouse as he emerged from the smog.

Tarot turned to him. "Knows what?" she hissed.

Mouse smirked. He pulled his spectacles out of the air, and slid them over his nose. Halla's arms wrapped around him from behind. She let her head rest on his shoulder. Her bright blue eyes watched Tarot as if from some faraway world. As if from a dream.

"That we're the heroes," said Mouse. "The only ones who can mete out justice in an unjust age. The only ones who can rise above sin and cynicism to save the universe from itself."

Tarot pulled her cloak tight around her and stalked off towards their ship. "You save the universe," she called to him. Then quieter, to herself, "And I'll save *him*."

Esme smooshed her face up against the glass. She wanted Percival to understand that she was tough and capable and worthy of his trust, but she couldn't help herself from giggling as the spaceport and the city and the countryside kept getting smaller and smaller below them. So impossibly small. And then they were lost in the clouds. They were *in* clouds! And then above them!

And then it was night. Her first night. Like the starship, or in pictures she had seen. In works of art. But where was the moon? She scanned the tiny window at her seat then, frustrated, stood and rushed across the aisle to another window. Not there either. She wasn't sure why it mattered, but she knew that it did.

Percival watched all this with a bemused smile. This was neither his first nor his hundredth nor his thousandth space flight, but somehow seeing the joy in her eyes stirred something long ago and innocent in him. "If you think this is something," he boasted, "you should see what happens when we shift to—"

Percival sprang from his seat and charged down the aisle toward the pilot's cabin. "UM!" he shouted. "Whatever you do, don't shift to superlight!" And he was going to explain why, too, if given the opportunity. But he wasn't.

Outside the windows reality shifted and folded in on itself. Stars stretched from points to lines to webs of intricate and inhuman pattern. Cosmic nebulae blurred and bloated and opened. And a wave of anti-matter skimmed the side of their craft, shearing off the ship's left fin.

"Because the last foldship is probably still waiting for us," he whispered impotently.

Destabilized, the Daylight began to tumble zomward, end over end. But inside, the gravity held. The Bluedusk Optima 1 swung around for another run. In his cockpit, Ilsum Yott snarled. This would be justice for his brothers-in-arms. He lowered his thumb onto the trigger and...

The Daylight dropped to sublight. Percival leaned his head into the pilot's cabin. "We seem to have a slight tactical problem." Um turned and nodded. "To leave this system, we'll eventually need to shift into superlight." Um nodded. "But if we do that, the foldship will destroy us." Um nodded. "But if we don't, the universe will end." Um gave a mild shrug. "Eventually end." Um nodded. "And we have no weapons, and we're already damaged enough that steering will be a challenge." Um nodded. "Is that it, then?" Um nodded. "Nothing to add? No contributions?"

Um shook his head. Percival looked about the cabin for the best, hardest substance against which to drum his head.

From behind, Esme offered, "What do you think about *this*?"

Three meters and eight dimensions away, Ilsum Yott powered down his weapons and resumed his wait. He'd been parked in orbit for close to twenty-four hours now, stewing in his hatred, desperate for the opportunity to finish off the men who'd killed his friends. That these men had killed in self-defense didn't matter to him. That it was already his mission to kill them before this affront? Also unimportant. He would accept the payment offered to him, yes, but money was no longer his motivation.

The Bluedusk Optima Five had shared many adventures together, fought and lost wars together. Two had died in a dogfight with the Devil Himself, though it was only he and Oolin and Jordan who could even remember that. And now that Oolin and Jordan were dead, who would remember him?

Yott's stomach was twisted into knots, metaphorically but also literally. Inside his hyper-dimensional cockpit, his physical form was more of an abstract idea than a continuity. He was a crumpled-up Picasso painting of a man with nothing left to look zomward to except a long and lonely life of anger and regret.

When he was a boy, he'd always wanted to learn the cello.

A pale blue light blinked to life on his control panel. An incoming transmission. Yott grumbled and switched opened a channel.

"Hullo," came the voice, young and tentative. "My name is Esme. I'm sort of a nun. I was hoping you could not shoot me."

Parts of Yott's fingers gripped his microphone, pulling it close to his lips/knees/exposed liver. "I have no quarrel with you, miss, but there are men on your ship who must suffer for their actions."

"Um," said Esme, then after a pause, quietly, "No, not you." Yott did not understand. "What are their names?" she asked finally.

"I don't know their names," Yott admitted. "The Frog and the Dandy."

Through the channel, Yott could hear muffled clamors. Then, after a moment, "Are you sure they're on my ship? I don't see them."

"I have it on good authority."

"The authorities? They searched the ship before takeoff. I'm sure they would have—"

"Not *the* authorities! I have it *on* authority. Do you think I'm some kind of space cop? You must be a nun."

"Well, then whose authority?"

"I can't tell you that."

"Secret authority?"

"Let's just say yes."

"Do *you* know who they are?"

"I know enough."

"Are you sure?"

"Yes."

"Are you sure you're sure?"

"Yes!" Yott shouted, slamming his fist/knee/femur hard against his console. "I'm not some springity-spring chicken!"

After that it was quiet on both sides of the channel for several seconds, except for the heavy heave of Yott's chest/knees/aorta as he fumed.

"I'm sorry," said Esme finally, in that same delicate tone that she'd learned in her years on the streets of South District, when any offense taken might be the last. It was a tone she'd cultivated during her time in the church, where mortal mercy became the last way station on the pilgrim's path to a cold and unforgiving god. "Which is not to say that I'm apologizing for anything," she added, correctly judging Yott as a man who would not be condescended to. "But rather that I feel compassion for you. Not pity," she emphasized, "but proper sympathy.

I don't know you. I don't know what you've been through. But I can sense a pain in you. A pain you haven't been able to share."

Yott's breath was slowing, becoming regular. Percival looked to Um and winked. Their pursuer was calming down.

"The church teaches that the past is a burden that we carry with us, but we needn't carry it alone. Sometimes sharing your troubles makes things better. Not lighter, but easier to bear. If you'd like, I could do this for you. I could listen."

There was silence on the channel.

"Are you still there?" asked Esme.

Silence.

Eight dimensions away, Yott's tears formed strange patterns across his skin and insides.

"It was..." Yott closed his eyes, tried to recall each sight and sound and smell of that one summer evening, so many years before. "It was Gaston's idea to join the Space Brigades. There were only the four of us at the time. We'd all grown up together on Bluedusk. Me and Gaston and Jordan and Oolin. Oolin wanted to start a rock band instead, but we all knew Oolin was an idiot, and anyway we all knew he'd happily fall in line with whatever the rest of us decided we wanted to do. And Gaston loved the stars.

"We met Newkirk at the academy, but it was like we'd all known him forever. We all liked the same music, read the same internet feeds. Loved the same woman. Eudora Li was our shared crush that first year. She was a year ahead of us and a better pilot than the five of us combined. She also had the tightest—" Yott remembered that he was talking to a nun. "Her hair was very tight. I suppose.

"Jordan dated Eudora for six weeks at the start of our second year. We all wanted to murder him. They broke up because he was too serious for her. So he said. Newkirk got a shot at her later that year. They went out a couple of times, but it never really went anywhere.

"In our third year, her last before graduation, I danced with her. Just once. And you just about had to scrape me off the floor afterwards. 'You're a lovely dancer,' is what she said to me. 'Best of the five.' She kissed me on the cheek and said she'd walk herself home. Next morning, we found out she'd left school early to fight in the Iblis-Yzjzyax War.

"A few months after that, she was dead. We were all of us set on avenging her, but there were conflicting accounts. We didn't even know what side she'd joined. In the end, we flipped a coin and lost. The Yzjzyax were crushed, and we spent six months locked up as prisoners of war until our parents negotiated our ransom.

"But being in a war... Even losing a war earns you a reputation. We did a few scrub jobs, put together the cash for the five Optima-series foldships. We weren't creative. It was Oolin's idea to call us the Bluedusk Optima Five.

"For a while we were living the life. *WMI* is what Newkirk used to call it. That stood for 'Women, Money, Infamy.' Me, I was less about the women. I could never shake the memory of that last dance with Eudora. She ruined me for hedonism.

"Everything changed with the Wilp job. We encountered them on the edge of space, refuges from some timelost civilization. Old, eyeless men. They'd grown paranoid over the years, made a vow never to re-enter Euclidean space. Said the Devil was stalking them. And you can't imagine the fear in their throats when they said it.

"But we were young and stupid and some of us were still nursing a death wish. So we asked them: 'How much will you pay us to kill the Devil?'

"We took their money upfront. None of us really believed we'd find the Wilps' Devil, but there was no harm in looking for Him. So the five of us set out in five directions, and we scoured the nearby systems for evidence of the Devil. It was Gaston who found Him.

"Gaston, who always loved the stars.

"The Devil's ship was not large, perhaps ten meters wingtip to wingtip, carved from the blackest stone, an ugly distorted shape, like a winged horse or a dragon formed of wax and left to melt into the fire. It was a suggestion of a thing that shouldn't be. And at its heart, a burning white eye.

"The whole thing happened at superlight. Gaston died before we could reach him. The Devil had disintegrated the backend of the Optima 3 and left parts of Gaston to drift out, crumpled, into Euclidean space. Oolin and I came in hot from the zom and unloaded our cannons on the Devil's ship. No effect. We streaked past and swung around for another strafe. We weren't really thinking at that point, just channeling wrath.

"The Devil's Eye was gathering power. I can still feel the heat of it on the back of my neck. I shouted to Oolin over channels to target the Eye. We both charged it head on, firing like mad. No strategy, just trying to hurt the thing.

"The Eye flares up, and there's this white burst of light. Like everything, everywhere is white. And for a split-second, I think I'm dead. But then the light recedes and me and Oolin are both still there, still alive, and hurtling straight into the Devil's Eye. I pull up. Oolin swerves, loses a chunk of his aft wing.

"Jordan comes riding in along the yellow-axis, leaving a trail of temporal mines in his wake. He's shouting for us to bug out, but Oolin's lost control of his ship. And the Devil is slowly, slowly turning towards him. And the Devil's Eye is burning hotter and hotter. And Jordan and I are just shouting over the open channel, 'Oolin, get out of there! Activate your eject suit! Eject!'

"But Oolin's having mechanical trouble, can't hear us, and couldn't eject if he wanted to. His internal sensors are all busted up and his command processor is convinced he's got a hull breach so it's pouring sealing fluid into the cockpit, which means that even if he survives getting disintegrated by the Devil, he's still going to drown in his own hull sealant.

"Oolin's maybe got a few seconds, and I only see one option. I slow my engines and dock on the underside of the Devil's ship, then accelerate hard hornward, shoving the Devil ahead of me up the yellow-axis and through the temporal mines. Enough to slow Him down. Jordan gets a tow on Oolin, and the three of us get the Hell out of there.

"Later on, Jordan explains what happened to Newkirk. That big white flash, when I thought maybe I'd died. Jordan was following Newkirk in. Newkirk accelerated, intercepted the blast. And when the light faded he was gone. Completely disintegrated.

"We go back to the Wilps and tell 'em to keep their money. They don't put up a fight about it. But they tell us, 'You are like us now. You will find that pieces of you are missing. You should not go home.'

"Maybe we should have listened to them, but home was all we could think about. We needed to see our families. Someone had to tell Gaston's parents what had happened.

"Except when we got there, Bluedusk had been overrun by the Iblis. And not recently. The planet had fallen years ago. All our cities were in ruins, our people relocated into work camps. I had been there weeks earlier, enjoyed an outdoor concert, but now that park was a pile of radioactive ash. A decade of devastation in the span of days.

"It was Oolin who worked it out. Poor, stupid Oolin. He found his sister working in the Iblis Governor's kitchens. She hugged and kissed him. She'd thought he'd died all those years ago when the Iblis first invaded.

"We'd never went to the Academy. We'd stayed on Bluedusk and started a band instead. Me and Jordan and Oolin. Because there had never been a Gaston to tell us to go out into the stars.

"The war between the Iblis and the Yzjzyax raged on longer than it should have, widened, intensified. When the Iblis came to Bluedusk, we were unprepared. I'm told I tried to fight them off with my cello. I was quickly put down.

"My mother buried me in the countryside, near a rebel camp. I sometimes wonder if I could have found my bones.

"The Wilps were right. The Devil had made ghosts of us. There was no home for us now. We killed as many of the Iblis as we could, and then we fled back into foldspace.

"Over the years, Oolin and Jordan would occasionally go back, but I never did. Every time they came back to me I could see it in their faces. They were a different. A little less the men I knew. Something had changed in the universe and changed in them too.

"I still remember the day that I said... to Jordan..." Yott could barely form the words. "'Do you suppose that somewhere in this twisted universe, Eudora Li is still out there?'

"And Jordan asked, 'Eudora who?'"

Percival slid the microphone from Esme's grasp and raised it to his lips. "Attention, Mister Space Mercenary! This is Percival Gynt AKA the Dandy speaking. I'm going to need you to repeat that story for me, only slower this time, with spatial coordinates and calendar dates for all major events."

3 | EVERYTHING YOU KNOW

Percival stood over his companions, one hand on Um's shoulder and the other on Esme's, as their pursuer told his tale. He gave Esme's shoulder a squeeze to let her know the she was doing a good job. But in truth, it was more than that. Here was a veteran starkiller, and Esme, with a kind word and an open heart, had turned him into a blubbering pool of self-pity. They were defeating their enemy with niceness, Percival reflected. A welcome change from the usual firefights and fisticuffs. He hoped they wouldn't have to death ray him in the back later.

Such was Percival's pride that he almost lost track of what the mercenary was saying. But he heard this: "Said the Devil was stalking them." Percival tugged on Um's shoulder, and Um glared back at him, his one good eye wide. He'd caught it too.

"How much will you pay us to kill the Devil?"

Percival flailed an arm over Esme's shoulder, fumbled for and finally flipped the mute switch. And then he blurted, "Did he just say...?"

Um frowned and tried to shush Percival, but it came out as "Shjshjh!" on a slurry of spittle.

"We need to..." Percival's voice trailed off as he searched the control panel. "We need to record this. Can we record this?"

Esme looked back to Percival, not quite understanding what was happening. "I can't quite understand what's happening," she explained helpfully.

Percival shook his head. "Stupid." Then clarifying to Esme, "Me, not you." He pulled out his watch, swiped to the voice recorder app, and tapped the record icon.

"The Devil's ship was not large, perhaps ten meters wingtip to wingtip, carved from the blackest stone, an ugly distorted shape, like a winged horse or a dragon formed of wax and left to melt into the fire. It was a suggestion of a thing that shouldn't be. And at its heart, a burning white eye."

"That's it," said Percival. "The Engine of Armageddon. They saw the Engine of Armageddon. They saw and survived an encounter with the Engine of Armageddon."

"Wheh?" asked Um.

"Must have... Must have been before Illuminari banished it. But how long? We don't really know how long it was out there, unmaking the universe, before Illuminari and the rest found it. It could have been years..."

"Uh illenihuh..."

"Or that," Percival agreed. He took a deep breath, sank, and sat on the floor behind Esme and Um. "We've been taking Tarot and Mouse at their word this entire time. That only the few of them knew about the Engine. But if it's as simple as anyone sighting and surviving the Engine, then others must know. Anyone could be involved."

"But there's more," added Esme, peering down over the back of her seat. "Listen to his story. The Wilps had reality reshaped around them. The surviving pilots came home and found their planet's history rewritten. But they remembered."

Percival nodded. "Like Gor. Gor was twisted up in the center of a MagmaStar..."

"Aah theh whuh I uh ih olsace!"

Percival frowned. "Um."

Esme shut her eyes tight, wrinkled her nose, and translated, "And... they... were... high... up... in... FOLDSPACE!"

Um grinned from the ungummed side of his mouth and patted her on the shoulder.

"But that—?" Percival sputtered as he jumped to his feet. "If the history wipe effect doesn't work on you if you're in foldspace, then that means millions, maybe billions of people should remember parts of the erased universe! How is that possible? We... We..." Percival leaned back against the cockpit wall, closed his eyes, and took a deep breath. "We know absolutely nothing."

Um nodded. Esme held the microphone up to Percival, and she nodded too. She flipped the mute switch off.

Percival slid the microphone from her grasp and raised it to his lips. And then, after a deep breath, he said, "Attention, Mister Space Mercenary! This is Percival Gynt AKA the Dandy speaking. I'm going to need you to repeat that story for me, only slower this time, with spatial coordinates and calendar dates for all major events."

From the height of foldspace, Ilsum Yott let out a vicious roar and unloaded his anti-matter cannon into the twisted void. Betrayal! Betrayal! Yott trembled in eight dimensions.

In the Daylight's cockpit, Esme leaned over the co-pilot's chair and shouted into the microphone, "Listen! Listen to me. The thing you call the Devil is the Engine of Armageddon. It's a machine..." She corrected herself. "A *weapon* built to unmake the universe. And we believe that the people who hired you are trying to find it and take control of it! Mister Gynt is trying to stop them!"

Yott banged his fist and part of his jaw against his control panel. Lies. Heartless lies.

Percival smirked. "I can prove it," he said, reaching into his trouser pocket for the Secondary Codex. "Drop out of foldspace, and I'll show you the evidence. And if you don't like it, you can kill us, then."

Um shook his head vigorously. Percival smiled and nodded.

"I can't," Yott growled. "Optima-series foldships aren't designed to leave foldspace."

"Oh." Percival shrugged. "Well, maybe we can enter foldspace, and then you can board our ship?"

Um renewed his silent, furious objection.

"No," said Yott. "My ship doesn't use a Euclidean shell. I couldn't board your ship any more than I could drop out of foldspace."

"Oh. Well, Um," Percival stammered. Then adding, "Ohhhhh."

Um raised a brow. Esme looked to Percival curiously.

"What," said Yott. Less a question than a prompt.

"The Engine erases people from history, rewrites time and spaces as if they never were. But you remember your friends."

"Gaston and Newkirk," Esme added helpfully.

"It's not enough that you were in foldspace..."

Esme nodded. "You'd have to be literally *in* foldspace."

"No Euclidean shell. Only a handful of ships use that design. Almost all small fighter craft, one or two lifeforms per craft. Couldn't be more than a few hundred in use at any one time, and only a fraction of them for any extended period of—"

"Nun?" said Yott, interrupting.

"Esme," said Esme.

"Are you really a nun?" he asked calmly, his temper having by now seeped out of him.

"Up until yesterday," she answered. "I quit. It turns out God is made-up."

"Hmm." Ilsum Yott thought about this for a moment. "I have been away a long time. Suppose it's hard to think straight when you've spent the last thirty years of your life twisted inside out and backwards."

Thirty years, Percival mouthed to Um.

"My name is Captain Yott, for what it's worth. Ilsum Yott."

"Well," said Esme with a smile that Yott could hear over the channel, "it's nice to meet you, Ilsum."

Then it was Percival's turn. "Captain Yott, if you're prepared to eject from your foldship, I can show you a record of civilizations that were erased by the Engine. I can show you the history of a hundred species like the Wilps. And I can promise that we will do everything in our power to stop the cretins who are even now conspiring to take control of the Engine of Armageddon and use it to end the universe."

Yott considered Percival's offer. "I made a vow that I wouldn't leave foldspace. Reality keeps shifting. The Devil... your Engine of

Armageddon... it changes you without you even knowing."

"Captain Yott, the Engine was deactivated and hidden away eleven years ago. There are forces trying to find it and reactivate it, but until they do, you're in no danger."

"Eleven years?"

Percival nodded his head. "I'm sorry. Yes."

"I could have ejected from this ship at any point in the last eleven years?"

Again, Percival nodded. "Yes."

"All this time, I lived in fear. No, *lived* is the wrong word. Existed..."

Esme took the mic. "It's time to come home, Ilsum."

Eight dimensions away and with a lifetime's hesitancy churning within his breast/guts/spine/toes, Ilsum Yott pulled the ripcord on his pan-dimensional eject suit.

Ilsum Yott's scream echoed through time.

And then he was back, drifting agreeably backwards through three-dimensional space. Inside his suit, Yott felt as if he'd just stood up from a long, forced crouch only to be punched in the face by his own internal organs.

It was a sensation which Yott found positively invigorating.

An eject suit, when not contorted 2.5ward and frmm, is actually a sleek, sophisticated piece of tech. The innermost layer is respun ThermoCool liquigel, stretched thinnest across the extremities and thick over the core and vitals. Liquigel coats the interior of the pilot's ears, nose, and mouth as well as other orifices. The liquigel is punctuated along arms and spine with reinforced transdermal apertures, colloquially "skin plugs," which serve as conduits for oxygen, nutrients, and other chemicals injected into the pilot's body as needed from the suit's next outermost layer, the manufactory.

The manufactory is a uniform layer precisely three microns thick. This layer is composed of a sentient, telepathic, higher dimensional fungus named Earl that lives symbiotically with each pilot, synthesizing necessary chemicals from the pilot's own biomass and administering them back to the pilot via their skin plugs. Some cryptomycologists theorize that there is only one Earl and that each manufactory is only a three-dimensional extension of the true Earl, a fungus that extends outward from a hyperthetical twelfth, thirteenth, and possibly fourteenth dimensions.

A pilot's Earl dies when the ripcord is pulled, as the Earl fungus can't survive the dimensional descent back to regular Euclidean space. Those hypertheorist cryptomycologists who ascribe to the One Earl Theory call this the Severing, for they believe that these pilots are each slicing off a piece of the One Earl. They believe this angers the One Earl and that one day it will have its revenge. How a higher dimensional fungus locked eight dimensions away from regular Euclidean space would get its revenge is as yet unclear, but the One Earlers insist that that day is coming and that when it finally arrives, there will be substantial ruing of past mistakes by all culpable parties. For this reason, they call their prophesied day of Armageddon Ruesday.

Hence the One Earler maxim: "Bask in ye cleverness and ye excesses and ye soft sofa cushions while ye may! And pray that ye shall die ere Ruesday come!"

This is one reason that most major universities set aside a separate faculty lounge for hypertheorist cryptomycologists.

The outermost layer of the eject suit is hex-strength microweave, bulky and gray and lined with additional circuits and sensors and servomotors, switches and blinking lights, and, of course, the now useless ripcord. A photoreceptive faceplate relays visual information to an attoscopic radio receiver implanted in the pilot's cerebral cortex, and the gravatonic pulse emitters in the pilot's gloves allow for a clumsy method of propulsion while in zero-G.

After a fourth gravatonic pulse discharge, Ilsum Yott was within an arm's reach of the Daylight. He groped along the side of the ship for the boarding door, camouflaged as it was by holographic sky. Finally, he found a recess inside of a cloud and within that recess, a door handle.

Ilsum took a moment for himself. If you're going to do this, he thought, then do it.

And so he did. He tugged, and the door opened, revealing a strobe of red light from within. A trap, he assumed. Still, he had no option but to continue on the path he had chosen. He climbed inside, noting the shift to artificial gravity as he did. "Down," he muttered. "I remember down."

In the moments between darkness, he could see the ship for what it was: a standard commercial flier with no obvious retrofitting, darkness, a main cabin taken up by row and after row of passenger seating, darkness, bins for storage overhead, darkness, and the long straight walk down the middle to the cockpit.

Ilsum didn't need his suit's sensors to tell him there was no atmosphere. It all would have gone rushing out past him when he opened the boarding door. Commercial fliers weren't built with airlocks anymore, because of a certain politician who once speculated that it made the space pirates' job too easy. So Esme and the others had improvised one for him.

Ilsum pulled the boarding door closed, which immediately restored standard lighting. They'd be repressurizing the cabin now, which would take a few minutes. Ilsum walked to a row of seats near the middle of the cabin and sat. He took up a seat-and-a-half in his bulky suit with his legs wedged awkwardly in front of him, but this was still the most comfortable that he'd been in years.

As the atmosphere slowly filled in, Ilsum could begin to hear the mechanized voice that must have been there all along: "Main cabin breached. Repairing. Repressurization at 55%. Rising. Main cabin breached. Repairing." And so on.

As the ship announced repressurization at 83%, a light on Ilsum's suit went green and he began to unscrew his helmet. Inside the suit, the liquigel was already withdrawing from Ilsum's insides, gathering up the dead Earl fungus as it went, and depositing itself into a series of pouches along the suit's interior for easy disposal. Ilsum wrestled with his helmet, finally pulling it free on the third try. Oxygen! Not synthesized by a fungus and injected directly into his blood, but real oxygen flowing down his throat, filling his lungs.

He clicked a button on his armrest and the seat reclined, ever so slightly.

The cockpit door slid open, and Esme stepped out cautiously, goggles on, her wrench at the ready. "Ilsum?" she asked as she walked down the aisle towards their guest.

Ilsum's flesh was pale and hairless and taut, not wrinkled but cracked. His teeth were yellow and crooked. His eyes, wide and empty.

Ilsum Yott was dead.

Percival slipped an arm around Esme's shoulder. "You won't be needing the wrench," he whispered to her.

"Did you know?" she asked as her goggles collected her tears.

"Once I knew how long he'd been in that foldship, I suspected. He'd grown old out there, grown knotted like a tree. I knew that coming home again would be a risk."

Esme screwed her face into a grimace, pulled away from him, and thunked him on the arm with her wrench. He cried out, and Um came barreling into the cabin.

"Whuhs goinh ah?"

Esme holstered her wrench and closed on Yott's corpse. "We killed him," she said, her back turned to them, "just as assuredly as if we'd shot him in the face."

Percival massaged his arm. He wanted Esme to think the best of him, but this moment was the truth.

Esme ran the back of her hand across the gaunt of Ilsum's cheek. His mouth was wide open, drawn back. Was he smiling?

"You're with your brothers now," she whispered, and she kissed him on the forehead, and she closed his eyes.

4 | *THE DREAD ANTENNAE*

No one spoke for some time. Esme sat out in the passenger's cabin with Captain Yott. Percival sat with Um in the cockpit, while Um was teaching himself how to fly the ship without one of the navigational fins. Not impossible, but it required a lot more math. And Um hated math. Meanwhile, Percival was running over scenarios in his head, also a sort of math.

"We're not ready," he said finally. "We don't know enough to face Gor. What we learned from the starkiller changes everything."

"Uhs ih?"

"I thought that no one knew about the Engine but the Conspiracy. Thought we had a short list of three suspects. But if Yott encountered the Engine thirty years ago and lived to remember it, that means anyone could know. More importantly, it means that other people *must* know."

"Ut theh?"

"There must be more information out there about the Engine. Even if it's all bound up in tall tales or rumors. Maybe something that can help us against Gor."

Um considered this as he cross-referenced and adjusted values in the Daylight's nav computer. "Hah Haahs?" he asked finally without turning away from his work.

Percival nodded. "Tall tales, yes."

"Huhuhs?"

"Rumors, yes."

Um allowed the biggest and froggiest of smiles to form along the unshat side of his face, and he flipped the switch for superlight.

Theorist's World was not actually a world, but simply a large asteroid located in the Mormageddu Belt near Sanctuary-2. And if you were to consider the opinion of most mainstream scholars of the day, its inhabitants weren't properly *theorists* either. For these reasons and others, Theorist's World appears on many star charts of the sector under a very different name: the Rock of Paranoia.

The Rock was settled by a small band of Nth Realm sympathizers in the waning days of the Last Great Intergalactic War. An important historical note: One reason these settlers remained sympathetic to the Realm's cause, despite overwhelming evidence that the Realm was engaged in an unprecedented genocide on an unprecedented scale, is that the settlers didn't believe the evidence that said genocide was actually happening. It was their belief that said evidence of said genocide was in fact fake news, manufactured to discredit the Nth Realm, who they venerated as a pious order of intergalactic truth-tellers whose sole object was to expose the vast conspiracy of telepaths, Orthodox Jews, and Ant People who secretly ruled the universe.

After the War ended and the Nth Realm had lost, the rest of the universe had to decide what to do with the misguided settlers of "Theorist's World." And while most found their beliefs execrable, most also agreed that the settlers were fundamentally harmless if left to themselves. The decision was made to lock off Theorist's World. To allow none of its settlers or the settlers' children to leave, and to allow no communication between the settlement and the rest of the universe.

Over time this second restriction was loosened to allow a small contingent of scholars from Harvard-Blorp University-Blorp to periodically visit the settlement to complete an anthropological study. For each visit these scholars, or "The Dread Antennae of the Ant People" as they were known to the settlers, would prepare a long list of seemingly unrelated facts. On arrival they would provide this list to the settlers and then note whatever absurd theories the settlers would devise in response. The settlers proved to be very good at this game, sometimes exposing actual hidden connections of which even the scholars were initially unaware.

After the first study on Theorist's World was published by Harvard-Blorp University-Blorp Press-Gablonk, others became interested in the settlers' curious gift. The first among these were rival universities and ThinkTanks™, each eager for a breakthrough in species cognition or pattern-recognition. But all such lofty endeavors were soon sidelined in favor of larger governmental and commercial interests. Important People found new and devious uses for the settlers in criminal profiling and counter-intelligence and, most sinisterly, product focus testing. "Children like robots, magic, porpoises, and murder," was the fateful conclusion of one such visit.

And so it went. With each new visitation came new, unconnected facts for the settlers to find hidden patterns in. And when each visitor left, those facts remained to be cooed over, nurtured, and delicately deposited within the settler's ever-complexifying latticework of the obscure. "We know what they wanted us to believe," they'd say, "but what were they *really* after?"

Serious scholars will tell you that the "theorists'" predictive powers were never very good, that their reputation was built on a foundation of lucky guesses and wishful thoughts. But somehow, however impossibly, as the years passed the settlers found a way to grow ever-steadily *less* accurate. Because they were no longer considering a simple list of unconnected facts. They were considering those new facts in the greater context of their latticework, absurd theory built on top of absurd theory built on top of absurd theory. "Gibber and blather!" one general famously exclaimed as he departed Theorist's World for the last time. He had just been told that the universe was being devoured by a hyperdimensional fungus named Earl.

It was only in recent years that some clever few gleaned the true virtue of Theorist's World. It wasn't the settlers' theories that were a value, but all of those accumulated, unrelated facts. Generally, the more obscure a fact is, the less likely it is to appear in a given archive of information. On Theorist's World, however, the inverse was true. The more obscure the fact, the more likely it was to have been presented to the settlers and to appear as a part of their latticework. The settlers may not have been able to tell you who the Celestial Governor was, but they knew how she liked her scone buttered.

Or so it was said.

Once they were on their way, Um showed Percival their coordinates and their trajectory, and Percival at once understood where they were headed. "I have reservations," he said without making any effort to dissuade Um, and he got up and went back to talk to Esme.

Esme, who had fallen asleep on the shoulder of a dead man. Percival couldn't quite make up his mind on whether she was an innocent in all this or a genuine lunatic. A question he could save for another day. He made his way to the back of the cabin and lay down on a stretch of seats for a few hours of sleep.

Instead, he thought of Tarot.

"Where are they going?" asked Mouse as he stared into the Nightfall's holographic nav display. "They should be halfway to Galactic Zero by now."

Halla leaned over from the co-pilot's chair, tapped the dot that represented the Daylight, and traced her finger forward along the ship's trajectory. Data for a dozen planets, space stations, and other starships scrolled across the display. Mouse shook his head. None of it meant anything to him.

"Tarot!" he called out without turning back to the main cabin, "Where is your crazy boyfriend headed?"

"He's not my boyfriend!" Tarot called from a row of seats midway back through the cabin, across which she was presently sprawled. "He hates me, and I hate him!"

Halla frowned. "I'm so glad we're all fourteen," she whispered.

Mouse ignored the both of them as he flicked through the list of possible destinations that Halla had called up. "I see Sanctuary-2 on the list. Maybe he had the same thought I did."

Halla raised an eyebrow. "About the MagmaStars? And if so, why there?"

"It's out of the way. If he wants to test a hypothesis."

"You want to follow him, don't you?"

"I want to murder him, blue eyes. With Illuminari gone, he's the one bloke who could ruin this for us."

Halla leaned close to Mouse, ran her fingers through his dark hair. "For us?" she asked.

"For the galaxy," said Mouse, correcting himself. "Finally, after all these years."

Halla flashed a devil's smile, kissed Mouse softly on the lips, and whispered, "Don't you worry, Master Holden. Vargoth Gor is as good as dead."

"ATTENTION, APPROACHING VEHICLE! THEORISTS' WORLD IS LOCKED OFF! UNAUTHORIZED VEHICLES MAY NOT LAND ON THEORISTS' WORLD! ANT PEOPLE MAY NOT LAND ON THEORISTS' WORLD! PLEASE PROVIDE APPROPRIATE CREDENTIALS OF AUTHORIZATION AND NON-ANT-HOOD BEFORE ATTEMPTING TO LAND!"

This was the message that played on loop as the Daylight wobbled its way to Theorist's World through the Mormageddu Belt. The wobble, of course, was the result of the Daylight's missing right navigational fin. At first Um had been able to compensate for this loss by simply re-angling the thrusters, but with each hour the ship seemed increasingly desperate to turn left, and the more effort Um put into keeping her straight, the more the ship fought him. Now, as they neared their destination, Um was resorting to brute force, pulling hard on the yoke with all three of his arms, calling forth every newton of strength from his muscles/servo-motors to keep the ship steady as it slipped between drifting asteroids. Um could feel his grip failing, the insides of his flesh-hands coating with sweat. All it would take was a half-second of weakness or of hesitation, and the ship would tear itself apart, or perhaps spin off into an asteroid.

"THIH HAAH EHHUH HUUH!" he shouted.

In the co-pilot's seat, Esme pulled her goggles down over her eyes and clamped her hands over her head.

Outside, Percival clung to the ship's top fin and caught his breath. He was halfway there. At this distance, he could feel the heat of the ship's thrusters all the way through Yott's spacesuit. And there was also the time distortion effect to consider. And there was also the time distortion effect to consider.

After one last deep breath, Percival scrambled down the side of the ship to the left wing, firing two gravitonic pulses overhead to keep him flat to the ship's hull. He gripped the edge of the fin with his left hand, and with his right reached down to his thigh where he'd strapped the component extracted from Um's third arm.

"This had better work," he whispered.

He pointed the long silver cylinder towards the inner edge of the fin and clicked the manual override button as Um had shown him. The end of the cylinder separated into irregularly-shaped panels and then parted like a blooming flower to expose the glowing green light within. "Death ray," Percival whispered, and a green bolt of plasma melted a twenty-centimeter hole through the fin. At the same time, the recoil wrenched Percival's firing arm backwards. Despite the sharp and sudden pain, he was able to keep one hand tight around the death ray and the other holding firm to the fin.

Percival scowled inside his helmet, repositioned himself, braced himself for the recoil, and began again. "Death ray." Again. "Death ray." Again. "Death ray. Death ray. Death ray."

The left fin fell away from the ship, flapping backwards into its temporal wake. In that instant, all of the resistance Um had been fighting against was gone, and the nose of the Daylight jerked hard to the right. The back of the ship swung left, just as hard, slamming Percival in the side and batting him off in the opposite direction.

Inside, Um was quickly making the necessary adjustments to

thrusters to regain control. As he'd feared, the ship was spiraling towards an oncoming asteroid.

"AAAAAAAAAAAAAAAAAAAAAAAAHHH!" screamed Esme!

"AUUUUUUGHUUUUUUGHUGH!" shouted Um!

The hours of focused physical strain had taken their toll on the Indulian. He could no longer muster the fine-motor coordination necessary from his twitching flesh-fingers to complete the nav update so he was reduced to hunting-and-pecking with his robot-digits while his flesh-arms hung limply at his sides.

The face of the asteroid, which the pair would later discover was called Big Oops, grew large and close in their nav window, and then held steady as the Daylight drew to a sudden halt some three meters shy of impact.

Before she opened her eyes, Esme asked Um, "We're not dead, are we?"

"Ah un thih ho," he answered.

Esme considered this, and then opened her eyes anyway.

Four hundred and fourteen meters away Percival collided into a smaller and thankfully softer asteroid, which he would later discover was called Little Uh-Oh. Percival's impact kicked up a meters-wide dust cloud that briefly enveloped him before dissipating out into the belt. Inside his helmet, Percival was howling in pain. His suit's microweave was thick enough to protect him from the crash landing, but not from the hit he'd taken from the Daylight moments earlier. He'd taken the full force against his right shoulder and upper arm, which he suspected were both broken. At the same time, he'd let go of the death ray, which was now lost to Mormageddu's Belt.

Percival pushed himself to his knees with his good arm and then opened his suit's radio link to the Daylight. "I'm not dead," he announced, "so I will be needing a lift."

Then he shut the link off and resumed howling.

Nine minutes later Percival was back on the Daylight, and the ship was on its final approach to Theorists' World. Percival had removed his spacesuit, and Esme had stripped him of his dress shirt and shredded it to improvise a sling.

Percival managed a reluctant thank you through gritted teeth.

Meanwhile the Theorists' message continued on loop: "ATTENTION, APPROACHING VEHICLE! THEORISTS' WORLD IS LOCKED OFF! UNAUTHORIZED VEHICLES MAY NOT LAND ON THEORISTS' WORLD!" The signal broadcast from an antique radio tower, the last standing structure on the surface of Theorists' World. Decades prior, the Theorists had disassembled the rest of their settlement, abandoned the surface, tunneled down, and made the interior of the asteroid their new home. This, after learning new facts about the capabilities of long range orbital telescopes.

"Why *wouldn't* they be watching?" one Theorist countered, when challenged on their decision.

At the foot of the tower, built into the surface of the asteroid, were two massive, interlocking RetroBrass doors, curved in shape and fitted into a circular aperture close to 100 meters in diameter. When closed, these doors bore a casual resemblance to the ancient Yin-Yang symbol.

"Hmm. Those doors remind me of something," Esme mused.

"Other, smaller doors?" asked Percival.

Esme didn't think that was it, but neither did it seem worth pursuing so she agreed. "Yes, that's it."

"PLEASE PROVIDE APPROPRIATE CREDENTIALS OF AUTHORIZATION AND NON-ANT-HOOD BEFORE ATTEMPTING TO LAND!"

Um reached for the microphone with two hands. Percival batted the fleshy one away. "Let's let Esme do this," he suggested. Um began to protest, remembered his impediment, and nodded sheepishly.

"Me?" asked Esme as Percival passed her the mic.

Percival smiled and rested a hand on her shoulder. "Like you did with Yott."

"Yott's dead."

"Well, that's hardly your fault. Chin up." He gestured to Um, who flipped a switch. Then back to Esme: "You're on."

Esme stared at the microphone as it crackled to life. "Um," she began. "My name is Esme, and I'm here with—"

Percival threw a hand over the mic and hissed, "Don't mention me by name. I'll explain later."

This startled Esme, but she tried not to show it. She was sure Percival had a good reason. Mostly sure. So she nodded, and she continued, "My name is Esme, and I'm here with... I'm here with the crew of the Daylight. Me and the crew would like to land and... meet with you all."

Esme was feeling more comfortable now. She looked up to Percival, who shrugged amiably. And Um gave her a mechanical thumb's up. "We're here on urgent business. Urgent *non-ant-related* business, and our ship's been damaged, and the universe may be ending soon, and we'd really love it if you'd open up your doors and let us in."

Esme paused, hoping for a response. But there was nothing. No response. Nothing but the crackle crickle snap of static.

No response, but also no pre-recorded message. Which meant perhaps that the Theorists were considering Esme's request. Percival grinned.

"ATTENTION, APPROACHING VEHICLE! THEORISTS' WORLD IS LOCKED OFF!"

Esme let out a loud groan. But at least she hadn't gotten anyone killed this time.

"Well, we tried," said Percival, who was frustrated yes, but on a level not so far beneath also deeply relieved. "On to Galactic Zero, then." He sat down in the co-pilot's chair and looked to Um expectantly.

Um pointed a froggy-finger Esme's way. "Augeh," he garbled. "Tah augeh."

"Sorry?"

Percival closed his eyes slowly. "He says to try again."

Esme raised the microphone back to her lips and closed her eyes. "We have facts," she said. "We have secret facts to trade with you, but we don't have much time because the universe will be ending soon. So, make up your minds."

Crackle crickle snap.

Esme shook her head and handed the microphone back to Um. "I'm going to go back to Yott," she said, and she turned her back on them.

Then, over the radio: "Attention, Ant People! We see through your primitive deceptions, but we will play your game for now. The gate opens. Prepare to be received."

5 | THE LIQUID IS RED

Interrago clung to the blissful edge of sleep and waking for as long as he could, a minute or two perhaps, until their ceaseless knocking finally grew too insufferable to bear. In his dreams, Interrago is the winking moon, standing vigil over a starlit moor. In his dreams, Interrago is fluid and timelessness. Awake, bleary-eyed and scratching, Interrago was a slave to other people's watches.

"In a minute," he mumbled to the dark as he slid one leg into last night's trousers and then the other.

And still they knocked.

Interrago swore as he shambled to the door. "I heard you already." He drew back the bolt and pulled open the door to greet his oppressors. "Only been asleep two hours. There's a name for people like you."

Out in the corridor, the youngsters eyed each other nervously. El Contraire had only been on watch rotation for a few weeks. Verity, for a few months. They had practiced for such moments, run drills, but they were still hesitant, still easily cowed.

"Well, out with it," he growled. "I'm awake now."

"It's just..." El Contraire began sheepishly, before losing his nerve.

Verity completed his thought. "The liquid, sir. It's red."

Interrago frowned. "Of course it is. Hell. Hold on, I'll need shoes for this."

Interrago ran a hand along his shorn scalp. Another day, and he'd take a razor to it again. And then again, a few days after that. Unless the liquid said otherwise.

"Are you paying attention, Interrago?"

Interrago looked up and shook his head. "No, Chairman. I was considering the futilities of fate."

Chairman No sighed and repeated himself, "I said the facts are these:"

Interrago waited.

"Just that. That's as far as I'd gotten."

"Well, go on, then."

Like Interrago, the Chairman had been summoned from bed without warning. He wore a beige bathrobe and fuzzy slippers and a jowly scowl. "A ship arrived in orbit around Theorist's World fourteen minutes ago. Self-identified as the Daylight. Claimed to be fact traders. Also claimed that the universe was ending."

"Nothing we haven't heard before."

"Exactly. But then the liquid turned red." Chairman No withdrew a small glass phial from the pocket of his bathrobe. The liquid inside glowed a luminous red. Interrago's phial hung around his neck from a leather cord. Also red.

"I want you to know," said the Chairman, "that I was prepared to leave you out of this. I knew you were coming off a double shift at the Farm. I could have easily woken Factus instead."

"But you hate me."

Chairman No grinned. "How cruel you are. But before the night is over, you will thank me for this intrusion."

"And why's that?"

Chairman No pulled a folded piece of paper from his bathrobe pocket, and he handed it to Interrago.

"We're passing notes now?"

"Open it."

And Interrago did. The page depicted a young woman deplaning from an o'erturned rocket. Frizzy-haired. Wide-eyed. Dressed in leather. "Werewolf?" asked Interrago.

"Not her," said Chairman No sharply. "Tap the page."

And Interrago did. And now the page depicted another, following after. An alien. Rotund. Brownish-green with an overlarge head and big, saucer eyes and a mechanical third arm protruding from his sloppy gut. "The police officer we spoke to last year. The amputee. What happened to his face?" There appeared to be some sort of spackle smeared across one side of it.

"Nor him," said Chairman No. "Tap again. Trust me." And then the old man chuckled. "I'm about to become your new favorite person in the universe."

This was the rare theory that Interrago highly doubted. But Interrago tapped again, and in that moment, learned something new:

Chairman No was indeed his favorite person in the universe.

Percival and Esme and Um were taken to a small charcoal gray room and made to wait. The room had two doors, sliders, the one they'd entered through and another on the wall opposite. By the far door, a dingy white folding table had been set up with three chairs set to face them.

Percival did not like the implication.

He examined his left hand. With his right arm tied up in a sling, he'd need to rely on the other now. But he couldn't shake the feeling that it belonged to someone else. Silly. "If anyone asks," he said off-handedly, "my name is Potumbo."

"Potumbo?" asked Esme, unsure if he was kidding.

But Percival nodded sternly. "Julius Potumbo," he clarified, "And I enjoy fishing and legerdemain."

At the back of the room, the charcoal door slid open, and three Theorists filed in and took their seats. The first was fat-faced and balding with a scowl that threatened to swallow his whole head. He wore a beige bathrobe. Second came a girl, perhaps fourteen, bright-eyed and inquisitive and wearing an Nth Realm dress uniform. The last of them was tall and lean with close-cropped brown hair and beady eyes. He wore a white T-shirt and jeans and a phial around his neck that glowed an inky red.

Interrago smirked at Percival as they took their seats.

"And haberdashery," Percival added softly. "But not too much haberdashery."

Chairman No laid his hands flat on the tabletop in front of him and then slid them outwards as if smoothing an imaginary tablecloth. "Let us begin," he said, "with introductions. My name is No. I am the Chairman of Theorist's World, the 27th man to hold this position.

"To my left," he nodded to the girl, "is Verity Brown. One of our more promising cadets, if I dare risk her ego in the saying."

Verity smiled admiringly at her leader, but not too admiringly, lest she be thought dim.

"And to my right," he nodded to Interrago, "is Interrago of the Blood. Of which I shall say no more."

Interrago eyed Percival inscrutably. Percival returned his gaze with only the slightest sliver of scrute. Keep it together, thought Percival. He can only see you if you let him see you.

"Officer Um we know," continued the Chairman, "but I'm afraid the rest of you are strangers to us. Perhaps you could...?"

The Chairman raised a hand to Percival. Percival nudged Esme. Esme so jostled and never much for deception, blurted out "Potumbo!" before she could stop herself.

"I beg your pardon," said the Chairman.

"...is *his* name," Esme continued with a quick thumb to Percival. "And my name is Esme. And *I* don't like haberdashery at all. Or fishing. Probably. Or a third thing. Which I've... now... forgotten."

Esme looked to Percival. "I really feel like I'm making a hash out of this," she confessed. "Like, even me pointing out how much of a hash I'm making out of this is actually making more hash. And now I think I'm probably saying the word hash too much. I should stop now, right? Not just saying hash, but... Um..."

Um stepped forward. "Whuh ah yuh huhuhs cuhsuhninh thuh Ejjuh uh Auhuhgehuh?"

Verity leaned forward across the table and tilted her head slightly. "I'm sorry," she said. "What is that you have stuck to your face?"

"Hiduh shih."

Interrago dangled his phial in front of him at eye-level. The liquid inside was now a gooey, gleaming white. "I would like to hear from the one you called Potumbo," he said, in the sort of quiet practiced tone that demands the reader's attention.

Percival looked to Um and frowned. Looked to Esme and frowned. Looked around for other people to frown at. He fumbled in his pocket for his pocket watch, but of course he was in the wrong pocket. "I thought maybe we could talk about the End of the Universe," he said finally, "as an interesting diversion."

No smiled and leaned back in his chair. "The universe has been ending for a long time, young man. What else do you have for us?"

"Has it?" asked Percival. He noted that the liquid was once again red. "That's an interesting *theory*."

"Not a theory, Mister... What did you call yourself?"

Percival considered the liquid. "I didn't. Not a theory, but a fact, then? Sounds more like a metaphor to me. Thin gruel, that. Do you know things, or don't you?"

The Chairman wasn't leaning back anymore. "The first star that burned was also the first snuffed. The *Ejjuh uh Auhuhgehuh* has always been with us. How vast might the universe have been, once upon a time? We are most assuredly in the end times, Mister—"

Interrago raised a hand to the Chairman without a look, and the Chairman stopped. "Let me do it," said Interrago. He slipped the phial from around his neck and slid it to the far end of the table.

"Examine it," he said.

Percival stepped forward, bent down, but was careful not to touch it. Red means danger. White, lies. "You have a farm of them?"

"A guess?"

Percival repeated, "You have a farm of them." A statement.

"You know it doesn't work that way. The liquid isn't omniscient."

Percival stood and frowned. "The blood, you mean."

"If you like."

"I don't."

"Don't like blood?"

"Not especially."

"Which means you like blood... somewhat. The liquid isn't white."

"The *blood* isn't white."

"You've seen your fill of blood, haven't you?"

"Have I?"

"Say it."

"I've seen my fill of blood."

"The liquid isn't white."

"We can see that."

"How old were you?"

"How old was I when?"

"I think you know."

"You think I know how old I was. Marvelous. Is there a point to this?"

"When you first saw blood. First heard the screaming of the dead. How old were you then, Percival Gynt, when the witch came?"

Percival bolted upright, turned quickly. "We're leaving," he barked, even as he pushed through his comrades.

"No, you're not," said Interrago firmly as he held the phial out in front of him, "because the door is locked and the *blood* isn't white."

Percival's fingertips were a hair's breadth from the door, but he let them drop. He did not turn. "I'm never going to tell you what you want to know." Statement.

"The blood isn't omniscient."

Percival did not turn. "I am *committed* to not telling you what you want to know."

"You know what I read in *The Daily Internet* this week? That it's the twentieth anniversary of the Gynt Massacre *this week*. And now here you are."

Percival closed his eyes.

"Say it."

"I will not."

"SAY IT IF YOU EVER WANT TO MAKE IT OFF THIS STINKING ROCK!!!" Interrago wiped the spittle from his lips with the back of his hand. He was smiling now, his eyes ravenous.

"Um..." Percival began.

"Yeh?" said Um.

"No..."

"Yes?" said the Chairman.

"No."

"*Yes*," said Interrago.

Percival took a deep breath. Exhaled. "The Gynt Massacre was twenty years ago this week."

The blood was white.

"A lie. But how is that possible? Young Percival was rescued from Gynt Colony twenty years ago this week. The sole survivor of a vicious massacre."

The blood was white.

"Well, the sole survivor with one, obvious exception."

Red.

"The story goes that you called out to her as they put her down. Called her Mother. That you still call her that."

"HO WHUH?" asked Um, whose exasperation with this line of questioning was now giving way to real anger. "IH THAH YUH IG SEE-REHH? YUH IG THEE-REE?" His froggy-lips trembled. Two fists slammed the cheap folding table, and it cracked. And so did Um's face. "IH THAH YER SAD CONTRIBUTION TA THIS DYIN' UNIVERSE? TABLOID GOSSIP???"

Interrago stood. Straightened. "But of course you knew all that. You would have been briefed. But let him answer this: How many years was it that she kept you? How long was it after she *ate* your father that you began to *love* her?"

Um extended the heavy blade from his third arm and set it on fire. "Ask 'im again. Please."

Verity Brown pulled a Smith & Wesson Conflict Resolver from its holster and placed it to Um's breast. "Yes. Ask him," she repeated, steely cool. "Please."

Interrago sat. "It doesn't matter. Was it four years? Five? But what I really want to know is this: Whose idea was it to send the distress call. The Gynt Colonists were separatists. Isolationists. You could have gone a hundred years, and no one would have ever come looking for you. Why did you send that signal when you did? Why after all those years?"

Percival found the handkerchief in his left pocket, dabbed a tear from his eye. "Because she was getting hungry again," he said quietly, "and because she asked me to."

The liquid was red.

6 | MOTHER

Here he is again. He is always here. Alone. In the dark. *With her.*

Her nail scratches his leg. Or? Would it be better said, a talon? The jagged tip pricks blood, and the little boy who's tried so hard to be silent now gasps.

He has broken his promise. He has spoken. He is no longer safe.

"You shall know such joy," she whispers, "in between my teeth." Percival sobs. The pocket watch slips from his hand and clatters to the cave floor, silhouetting the woman-that-is-not-a-woman as she wraps around him. "Or perhaps we shall keep you for a time."

"Take off your shoes."

"Sorry?"

Verity poked the muzzle of her gun into Percival's rib. "Your shoes. And your socks too. Leave them in the corridor." She glared at the rest of them. "And the rest of you, if you don't want your friend here vaporized." Then her gaze settled on Um, who looked the sort who might tolerate the occasional friend-vaporization. "And your arm too, Frogger." She poked Percival again, this time in his broken shoulder, and Percival winced. "Then into the cells with you."

The four of them stood midway down a long hall, up and down of which were lined disused jail cells. The cells were small and charcoal gray like the interrogation room, with one cot and one pot in each. The outer wall was OneWay glass. Intangible going in, but solid as steel out.

There were a half-dozen more Theorists at the end of the hall by the lift doors, teenagers like Verity, armed and appareled like Verity. Um looked to Percival, but he shook his head no, so Um unlocked his arm and set it on the floor. Percival kicked off his shoes and then asked for Esme's help to pull off his socks. He sat down on the floor, and she sat in front of him.

"What is this all about?" Esme whispered.

"They're conspiracy theorists. I'm a conspiracy theory. Lepidopterists press butterfly's wings under glass. These people do this."

Verity shushed them and motioned for them to get up. She held her gun to Esme's head and made Um back into his cell. "Yer all bein' morons," Um groused. "With the three a us in here, there ain't nobody left ta save the universe."

"Who says the universe is worth saving?" Verity hissed. "Now you," she added, staring at Percival.

Percival backed into the cell opposite Um. He winked.

Finally, Verity took Esme roughly by the arm and pushed her into a cell to Percival's left. "There, that's done," she said. "Now why don't you all be good prisoners and go to sleep."

"Yoo ain't gonna keep us here forever," Um growled.

Verity shook her head. "Not forever," she corrected. "Just till the end."

"Look at all the dead," she says. She has made him gather them all in the moonlight. Made him stack them in piles. Made him pull together pieces. And now she holds her gnarled hand over his and makes him run his over them. To feel the textures of death against his skin. "They're simply flesh now. In death, they are our meat."

Percival whimpers. He does not have tears left, but his face contorts with every dry sob. His pain is primal. His noises are without purpose or meaning.

"Ah, there," she says as she strokes his cheek. "Now tell us which of them you liked least, and we shall do the worst to them."

After a time, the prisoners were left to themselves.

"How we gettin' outta here, Gynt?" asked Um.

"Eh," said Percival, and he slumped down onto his cot.

"But yoo winked," Um grumbled. He stood at the glass and watched as Percival wallowed. Scrawny. Tawny. Useless. Um let his head sink until it propped against the glass.

Sometime later, Percival heard Esme's voice coming through the wall, ever so slightly muffled, giving it a strange quality, as if drifting in from another world or time. "Percival," she asked softly, "What was the Gynt Massacre?"

Percival rolled over.

"Gynt's a planet," Um answered, when he saw that Percival would not. "Native species up and vanished maybe ten thousand years ago. Nobody knows much about 'em or what happened, but the story that spread was that the planet was cursed. Evil. Swallowed 'em up or some such. And nobody's too interested in testin' the theory. Not till Gynt Colony. They was scientists, pacifists, sick a the Last Great Intergalactic War and not the types ta be scared off by some fakakta ghost story. Curse hung like a shield over that planet. Gynt was gonna be their refuge from a universe gone mad."

"But?"

"But nothin'. War ends, decades pass, and nobody hears a whisper from Gynt Colony. Now maybe that means the curse got 'em or maybe they're just happy enough on their own. Nobody's proud a what happened during the War, so people figure, 'Let the pacifists have their peace.'"

"But the massacre?"

"Turns out the curse got 'em. Twenty years ago, almost ta the day, a call goes out. A scared little boy tells the universe his family is dead. Everybody's dead but him. Killed by a monster."

"The Beast of Gynt," said Percival. "I called her the Demon Beast of Gynt."

"Was she? A demon, I mean?"

"No."

Um sat. "She's human, kinda."

"How can someone be *kind of* human?"

Um looked to Percival.

"The colonists... My people found the ruins of an ancient Gynt city. And someone had the clever idea to attempt first contact."

"I don't—"

"Their DNA was close enough to our own that we could perform a genetic splice. We could grow something in a lab that was part us and part them."

"And them," said Um, "was decidedly *not* pacifists."

Winters pass until the night finds Percival curled at his mother's knee. She is weak. Her cheeks are drawn. Her gaze, distant. Her lips move, words form, dry and rasping from her tongue, but their meaning is not known to him.

"*Belo azo shaju beh*," she wheezes into his ear.

His fingers tighten around her gnarled hand. "What do you need?" he asks, his voice a reverent whisper.

"*Belo sephius. Belo beh.*"

He is a boy, and except for his mother, he is alone in the world. "What should I do?" he pleads.

Her yellow eyes fix on him. "*Belo sephius*," she says. "The past hungers. *Belo azo shaju beh*. The past must feed."

Percival sees the desperation in his mother's eyes. Feels the tremble of her grip. He reaches a hand down to his waist, and pulls up his shirt to expose his stomach.

"She didn't spare ya, Gynt. She *used* yoo ta get more food. You were her dinner bell. Except, y'know, the other way 'round."

"Parts of me know that."

"What happened when the rescue party came?"

Um snorted. "The Demon Beast a Gynt outsmarted 'erself. She was grown in a lab by pacifists. Claws and teeth she could work out on her own, but she never heard a tanks before."

Mother's body slumps into the mud. From the nearby brush, Percival lets out a sharp squeal. He scrambles towards her, but his path is blocked by soldiers.

"We got another one, commander."

"Nah, it's just a boy. See."

"He's filthy."

"Poor kid musta been hidin' out in the swamp for days."

"What's that on his head?"

"What's that he's saying?"

Percival turns over onto his back, flails his arms, and screams into the heavens.

"I think he's saying 'Mother.' Poor kid misses his mum."

The commander smiles. "That's sweet. Somebody get me my tranq gun."

"There's a question I been wantin' ta ask."

"Yes, Um."

"As long as we're talkin' about it."

Percival stared up at the ceiling of his cell, up into the gray.

"Yoo wondered about the timin'?"

"No."

"Not even a little? It was twenty years ago tomorrow yoo placed that distress call."

"I don't wonder."

"And now twenty years later, here we are. Fate a the universe rests in our hands."

"No."

"No?"

"Fate doesn't rest in our hands, Um. We rest in Hers."

"Yoo really think—?"

"I do."

"Once upon a time, Percival Gynt was a scared little boy, and because a that, the universe's gotta end?"

"No," Percival corrected, "once upon a time, Percival Gynt was a scared little boy, and the universe wonders, 'What is he now?'"

"It's all about yoo, then?"

"Remember the wink, Um. What does it mean?"

"It means yer one a them cheeky types that's capable a anything."

"Tomorrow morning, we're going to escape," promised Percival. "It's going to be spectacular."

7 | THE LIQUID IS BLACK

Percival woke. Beyond the glass, Interrago waited, looming, Verity close at his side. Interrago was eager, rapacious for the dawn and its inevitable confrontations. In the night he had found the presence of mind to shave, to make himself presentable, but not to slumber. For even with his eyes open, he was troubled by strange dreams.

By contrast, Percival was long resigned to his nightmares.

"You're wrong, by the way," Percival offered without getting up.

"Am I?"

"I've decided that the blood is omniscient after all."

"You've decided?"

And then Percival stood and smiled politely. "It came to me in a dream." The liquid was a brilliant white. Percival approached the glass cautiously. Verity had a sidearm, but Interrago did not. That would make this easier.

Interrago scratched his ear, then inspected the tip of his finger. A transparently feigned disregard. "I want to know how long it took. I want to know what techniques she used to break you."

Percival stood opposite Interrago, mirrored his steely gaze and slump-shouldered posture. "The blood's been red since we arrived here. We brought it with us, yes?"

"It's why we let you land."

"'Red if there's danger' goes the rhyme. For most, that'd be incentive enough to send us on our way. But for you lot?"

"Danger... interests us."

"In fact, it's your bread and butter."

"If you like."

"Now me, I'm lactose intolerant with a gluten allergy, but I feel that we're drifting off topic. If the blood isn't omniscient, how does the blood know danger?"

"That's different."

"Is it? What are the blood's other properties? What's the rest of the rhyme?"

"What's your point, Gynt?"

"I'd like you to say it."

Interrago opened his mouth. Closed it. Frowned.

"Come on! Don't tell me you don't know. Interrago of the Blood doesn't know?"

Interrago didn't answer. He willed his nostrils not to flair.

"I can start it out for you, if you're having trouble. It's a children's rhyme, so I could understand if it was a bit beyond you. Perhaps we could say it together, if you're feeling shy?"

Interrago exhaled hard through the nostrils. Verity reached a cautious hand to his shoulder and whispered helpfully, "It's blue in the darkness..."

Interrago snapped his head to the left and bellowed, "I KNOW THE WORDS, YOU COW!"

Verity went ashen.

Interrago whipped his head back to face Percival. "Blue in the darkness. White when you lie. Red if there's danger..."

"Finish it."

"...and black before you die."

Slowly, purposefully, Percival raised his left hand out in front of him. His alien hand, fingers outstretched and trembling.

"What are you doing, Gynt? What are you playing at?"

Percival's jaw was clenched, his eyes narrowed to a squint. Through gritted teeth, he growled, "Just testing..." His face was flush. A vein in his forehead flared. His whole body shook with concentration. His alien hand tightened to a fist. "...a *theory*."

"ENOUGH!" Interrago growled.

At his side, Verity gasped. The blood in Interrago's phial was black.

Interrago let loose with a mad roar. He snatched Verity's gun from her holster and lurched forward through the glass. In the same moment, Percival barreled into Interrago, stopping his forward movement, trapping him halfway through the OneWay glass. Then Percival's palm came up hard under Interrago's chin, held rigidly in place by the glass. The Theorist's neck snapped. His skull cracked against the glass. His eyes opened wide with a final understanding as Verity's gun slipped through his open fingers.

Percival bent down slowly to pick the weapon up, his eyes trained on the girl. Verity could not find the strength to speak or move, barely to breathe. Percival lifted the gun, the Magnum Conflict Resolver, and pointed it at her through the glass.

And fired.

The OneWay glass shattered.

"Take us to the farm," Percival hissed, "or I'll turn yours black too."

8 | THE FARM

Any proper linguist despises deep space exploration. Stick to your own planet, your own solar system even, and you'll eventually reach consensus on this-is-a-chair, this-is-a-toilet, and so on. But the further out you venture, the less certain you can be about anything. You're light-millennia from home, and suddenly a-chair-is-this-other-thing and a-toilet-is-one-of-these. And now you're talking about Earth-chairs and space-chairs or Earth-toilets and space-toilets, and the thing you thought you knew is bigger and stranger and, frankly, less sanitary than your simple Earth-brain can process.

On Earth there were faeries, yes. Elusive, mercurial spirits that flitted about in the deep woods, cast spells on hapless mortals, and occasionally bought our teeth from us while we slept. Earth-faeries were all of these things and probably also fictional, which made the things we found out here in the black of space all the more disquieting. The real faeries. The space-faeries. The void faeries.

No one's quite sure where they came from or how they evolved to survive in the cold vacuum of space. These weird creatures were first encountered within the derelict hulks of war-ravaged starships in the years following the Last Great Intergalactic War. Void faeries are wretched things, all boney and twisted with their flesh-stretched wings and their mouths full of nettles. The early, fevered speculation was that they were scavengers, nested in the graveyards of the space-born dead to feast upon their remains, but the first vivisections put an end to such legend. Void faeries lack any digestive system and, despite a crude array of cognitive functions, are closer in biology to a plant or fungus than to any animal species.

Scientists continued to pursue the question, "What do the void faeries want?" even as commercial interests circled round to the question, "How much can we sell them for?" By now, post-vivisections, it was well understood that void faeries would change color under specific reproducible circumstances. They could illuminate dark spaces, expose lies, predict danger and even death itself! In short, they were the perfect accessory for the morally gray, financially liquid starship captain of means.

It was Franco Nicodemus Noon himself who brought the first void faerie to Theorist's World in barter for facts about the Engine of Armageddon. The Theorists were so enamored of the future Nth Realm leader that they would have gladly given away their facts for free, but Noon insisted they accept the faerie as a reward for their long-held devotion to peace and universal truth.

Chairman No's predecessor, the late Chairman Obscurro, understood the value of this strange creature immediately, and he undertook not simply to breed more of the things, but to farm the very ichor from their veins. "The liquid," as he called it, became a holy substance to the Theorists. The distilled essence of truth. And the vicious machines that tore the liquid from the creatures' veins became the crucible of their faith.

"We're goin' the wrong way," Um groused as the lift sped deeper into the Rock of Paranoia.

"Um's right," said Esme. "Shouldn't we be heading straight back to the ship?"

"Ship won't fly," Percival answered tersely. He was careful not to take an eye off Verity, who he had backed nose-first into the corner of the car. "You do remember how we landed, don't you?"

The Daylight was a sleek missile-shaped ship designed to land upright balanced on her three navigational fins and to take off from that same position, but the Daylight had lost two of her three fins in flight. When the Theorists opened up their yin-yang gate to the Daylight, Um had guided the ship down as best he could, but he'd had to land her on her side. Once he'd touched down, the ship immediately rolled till stopped by her only remaining fin. Being mostly upside down at that point and properly disoriented, Percival and Esme both fell over, even though the anti-grav was still active. This had amused Um at the time but was less funny in retrospect. The Daylight had suffered serious damage and there would be no good way to launch her, even if they were able to fight through every armed Theorist that now blocked their way to the launch bay.

Add to this the fact that they had yet to retrieve their socks or shoes or Um's arm. With Percival's right arm in a sling, they were down to a paltry five arms between them. The situation was grim, and Percival had them retreating even further into the asteroid.

"Yoo got a plan, then?" Um asked.

"In two parts," Percival confirmed. "For part one, Esme, I need you to reach into my right trouser pocket."

"Um..." Esme had received such requests before but hadn't expected such a proposition to come from Percival Gynt.

Um thought perhaps Esme was deferring to him, so he shoved his fatty fingers into Percival's right pocket and extracted his watch. "This what ya want?" he asked.

Percival grinned. "Splendid," he said. "Now I need you to call Agent Fred, apologize, and ask him to come pick us up."

"What?" Um sputtered. "After all this, yer just givin' up?"

Percival shrugged his one shoulder that would still move properly. "Or, if you prefer, you can tell him that I have incriminating information about the Celestial Governor that I will share with the Theorists if he doesn't do precisely as we say."

Verity was listening. "I'm sure we could make a deal," she offered with a trembling voice that betrayed neither authority nor confidence.

She was ignored.

The lift control panel pinged three times, and its doors opened on a vast chamber awash in the blue light of the void faeries. There were tens of thousands of them hung down the length of great metal racks. No, not hung, but skewered through. Cables and tubes and wire frame grew through their arms and legs and chests, their glowing blue blood stripped from them and pumped into massive glass vats beneath the steel grate floor.

Void faeries did not have the power of speech, but they could offer up a low moan or wheeze. Their pained, discordant whimpers were more unsettling than any scream that Esme had ever heard on the streets of South District.

Percival marched Verity down a short, grated stairwell to the chamber floor. The others followed. Each step brought a sting of pain for Percival and Esme, on account of their bare feet.

"What are we doing here?" asked Esme, who couldn't properly contain her unease.

"Order of operations," said Percival. "Are your goggles flash resistant?"

Esme nodded.

"Good. I'm going to need to borrow them." And then he turned to Um. "Um, I need you to place that call now. And please be honest with Agent Fred. He's just trying to do his job."

Percival and the rest took position at the center of the chamber. Percival ordered Verity to sit and take off her socks and shoes, which were unfortunately a size too small for Esme.

Um walked a few meters away and swiped to the phone app on Percival's watch. He tapped in the number for Fred's secure direct line. It rang once.

"Gynt?"

"Um."

"Spit it out."

"This is Officer Um. Sir."

"Officer? Not after the stunt you've pulled. If you're lucky, you'll be hanged for your treasons. But I suspect..."

"Sir, I been instructed ta blackmail ya."

"What? Blackmail me? Have you gone dim? I've never done anything blackmailable in my entire life. My every thought, instinct, and act is devoted to the service of law and to the preservation of galactic stability."

"Yeah, yeah. Yer a real saint, boss. It's not always about yoo. We got compromisin' information 'bout the Celestial Governor yoo won't want getting out. Yoo'll do what we say ta keep it secret."

"You sound desperate, Officer Um. You're not thinking clearly. What kind of compromising information could you possibly have about Governor Zell? For God's sake, she just won re-election unopposed. She's probably the most beloved being in the universe!"

"Um," said Um. "Percival didn't actually tell me that part. Hold on and lemme get 'im."

Um called over to Percival. Percival handed over the gun to Esme. He began to explain how to fire it, but Esme waved him off. "I know about guns," she said.

Percival walked over to Um and took back the watch. "Hullo, Agent Fred. What's your morning been like?"

"Mister Gynt, I feel it's only fair to tell you that even at this moment we are tracking your signal and sending cruisers to intercept."

"Good. That's part of my plan. When they get here, they'll need to give us a ride to Galactic Zero."

"And why would they do that?"

"Because you're going to tell them to. Hold on a moment. I'm going to switch on the video feed and hand the phone back to Um." Percival switched on the phone app's video feed and handed the watch back to Um, and he asked Um to kneel.

"How come?"

Percival pointed up. "For the angle." Um grinned and kneeled before Percival Gynt, angling the watch to capture Percival and the void faeries above him in the video feed.

"Where are you?" Fred asked, straining to take in everything that he was seeing.

Percival slid Esme's goggles down over his eyes.

"There's something you need to know about your beloved Celestial Governor, Agent Fred. But to make sure you believe me, I'm going to need to tell you in the form of a lie."

Just then three pings sounded from the lift doors at the far end of the room. The doors slid open and Chairman No emerged with a half-dozen heavily armed teen Theorists at his back.

"Drop your weapons and throw your hands in the air, or my men will vaporize you!" No shouted.

"What's going on? What's that racket?" Fred demanded.

Percival smiled and spoke: "Celestial Governor Zell *isn't* secretly an evil wizard named Vargoth Gor."

Tens of thousands of void faeries turned a blinding white at once, as did the massive vats of their blood collecting beneath the steel grate floor. The effect was, as Percival anticipated, immediate and overwhelming. The Chairman and his men were caught entirely unprepared. They dropped their weapons and seized their eyes in agony. Esme, who'd worked out Percival's plan a half-second earlier based on the word *isn't*, squeezed her eyes shut and clutched Verity's gun tight to her chest and counted backwards from ten to distract herself from the searing pain. Um, who'd figured it out based on the camera angle, still couldn't get his arms up fast enough to block the faelight that seemed to come from all directions, the sheer intensity of which was magnified through his saucer wide eyes. He let out an awful, alien croak as Percival's watch tumbled through his fat fingers, down through the steel grate floor, and into the vat of brilliant white blood that lay directly below. Verity, as blind and traumatized as the rest, stood and ran in a direction that she estimated was back to the lift, but was in fact towards a faraway corner of the room.

Percival, alone among them properly protected by Esme's goggles, looked down through the steel grate and frowned. His watch was slowly slipping beneath the surface of the blood pool.

He placed a hand on Esme's shoulder, whispered in her ear, and she handed him the gun. Around them, the color of the room was reverting back to blue, but it would still take some time for the others' vision to return to them.

Slowly, cautiously, he advanced on the Chairman and the other Theorists as they scrabbled their way across the grates, searching for their weapons. He fired two shots a few meters in front of them. Not close enough to hit anyone, but close enough that they could feel the heat.

"All right, gentleman," Percival began. "Let me offer you some new facts. In about an hour a small war fleet will arrive at this asteroid and will be expecting to find us in one piece. You will let them land, pick us up, and leave. Or I will kill every last man, woman, and child on this station. Do you honestly agree to our terms?"

The Chairman could not yet see, but he could tell that the light had not changed. He could tell that Percival wasn't lying.

"I promise that you will not be harmed," said the Chairman. And Percival likewise knew that the Chairman wasn't lying.

"Good," said Percival, and then he helped the Chairman up. "Now that we understand each other, I want you to tell me everything you know about the Engine of Armageddon."

9 | BEYOND THE SEVENTH GALAXY

"I thought you were going to save them," said Esme after they were safe aboard one of Fred's ships. "All those poor creatures."

Percival wiped faerie blood from the face of his watch. "I would have liked to," he said distantly. "Still might when this is all over." His watch glowed white at the seams.

"And those things you said? That you'd kill children?"

Now Percival looked up and frowned. "I thought perhaps you'd appreciate the logic of that. I swore to do those things *if* they didn't agree to my terms, but because they knew I wasn't bluffing, I knew that they'd agree."

"But what if they didn't?"

"Um," he began. But there were no more words coming. Instead, Percival bent his head back down and returned to his wiping. And so the two sat silent, side-by-side, in the dark corner where Fred had deposited them. The sign above their heads read "Auxiliary Hold Gamma-Gamma-Four."

"What about these, sir?" A soldier stood at the doorway with a pair of muddied combat boots in hand.

Percival took them and held them to his feet. "Too big," he muttered, and he tossed them onto a pile with the rest.

They had escaped the Rock of Paranoia, had learned what they needed to know about the Engine in the process, but somewhere along the way the Theorists had lost his shoes. Call it the final vengeance of the Racist Laundry Detail.

Um ducked as he entered the hold. He was once again clad in the crimson armor of the Sanctuary-8 province police. "We're nearin' hailin' distance a Galactic Zero. What d'ya want us ta tell 'em?"

"That you're escorting a VIP to the inauguration?"

"And if they ask which one?"

"Do you think I'd pass for the High Cleric?" Percival allowed himself a sad grin.

Um grunted and left.

"Percival," Esme asked with a courage that had been building for some hours, "is it true, then? Are all the things the Theorists said about the universe true?"

The Theorists had long postulated the existence of the Engine of Armageddon, or at least of something quite like it, even before they had any facts that proved their claim. They'd heard tell of men and women returning from superlight only to find their homes and history gone. They'd been told tales of space-wrecks salvaged from the highest dimensions, the last relics of civilizations that never were. For close to a century, they'd known that something was slicing away at the fabric of the universe. What they didn't know, what they couldn't explain, is why.

In this singular matter, the Theorists had no theory.

And then a stranger came to visit them, a student historian and writer. Well, a blogger. Though still a young man, he was quite prolific and not without influence in certain shadowed circles. His name was Franco Nicodemus Noon, and he very much wanted to know why he wasn't dead.

The year previous, Noon had bartered for transport across Yzjzyax space on a foldcruiser called "The Shortest Path." Midway through their journey, they were beset by a coal-black ship that melted through the freighter's hull with a beam of white light. Amid the fire and the screams, Noon killed one of the crew, stole her eject suit, and ripcorded back to Euclidean space. He was the only survivor.

And so Noon drifted in the dark of space, a hundred light years from the nearest civilized world, praying to the Old Gods for rescue. By his third night adrift, Noon knew that he was alone. No distress call had been sent. No rescue party would come for him. On the seventh night, his suit's manufactory malfunctioned and began pumping hallucinogens into his system rather than medicine and nutrients. On the eleventh night, Noon was visited by the gods Wotan and Mecha-Thor. It's said they whispered secrets in his ears.

On the thirty-first night, Noon was discovered by The Wronged Crow, a salvage hauler. The Crow's crew was disappointed to find someone clinging to life inside of Noon's eject suit, but these salvagers were not savages. They gave him a bed and a meal and time to recover from his ordeal. And when they slept he slit their throats.

If Noon had ever known decency or mercy, those virtues were now forgotten for the gods had given him a mission. Wotan commanded that he find the black ship again and that he take it for their glory. Noon searched *The Daily Internet*, but he could find no record of the black ship or of the attack, nor indeed of a freighter called The Shortest Path, nor of any of her crew, nor any of her passengers save himself. According to the official record, he had vanished from space port on Yzjzyax-114 nearly three months prior. "Sometimes a man is simply swallowed by the universe," one of his fellow bloggers opined. "And sometimes the universe is swallowed by something larger still," Wotan answered back.

Noon arrived on the Rock of Paranoia on the 22nd of September, 19964. This was 10,196 days prior to the Gynt Massacre. 19,192 days before Percival met Tarot on the platform at Slidetown Station. Noon knew the Theorists' powers and their politics by reputation, and he found them easy allies. A few kind words, a gift, and a whiff of mystery was all it took. They were especially taken with the name he'd chosen for the black ship. *The Chariot of the Gods*.

Noon spent decades studying the Chariot with the Theorists. They compiled archival accounts, anticipated trajectories, launched drones to track the Chariot's movements, even jousted with it now and then.

From all of this, Noon learned some practical lessons, chief amongst them that the black ship's eye opens downward. It erases anything in its path, and it erases it completely from all of time and space in all dimensions that it touches. But it leaves the higher dimensions inviolate.

And the Theorists say that this is where Franco Nicodemus Noon went when he was done with the universe, to a superluminal palace that sits atop space and time. His own private Valhalla to await Ragnarok and the new world to come. For Noon grasped the truth, even before the Theorists. The truth of his Chariot and the truth his Chariot revealed.

Decades later, over strawberry milkshakes, Tarot would tell Percival Gynt that the Engine of Armageddon had erased a full third of the universe. Three galaxies. But that was only a few years work. Her father and the others, they'd only had pieces of the puzzle, a few variables in the equation. But Noon saw the whole of it, the legends, the theories, and all the maths, and the truth was inescapable. Galaxies beyond count. A universe beyond measure. And an Engine on the move since the very dawn of time.

This then is the riddle of the universe: How could a thing be, in the same instant, so insurmountably vast and so pitiably, piteously small?

Esme nudged Percival awake as their ship emerged from the intraplanetary tunnel and into the core of Galactic Zero. Through the porthole, they could see but a pinpoint of the controlled chaos that was the galactic capital: the massive towers thrusting inward from the core's interior wall, the roadways that wove together at strange angles with no respect for this-is-up or this-is-down, all burnished in the crimson light of the planet's MagmaStar.

Galactic Zero was once Sanctuary-5 before the Celestial Governor and the Mad Architect left their mark. Once a refuge from tyranny. Now a seat of empire. Why, Percival wondered, would Gor choose this world above all others?

The ship touched down on the underside of a public park. The topside, angled pleasingly to the light of the MagmaStar, was all green grass and fountains and cobblestone paths and baby strollers. The underside was smooth steel and shadow.

The metal was cold beneath Percival's naked toes. The sensation, an almost gratifying distraction from the dull throb of his broken arm and shoulder. Percival walked to the edge of the platform, crouched down, and looked out over the side, inward, past the tallest towers and, just for a moment, into the heart of the MagmaStar.

Um crouched down next to him and handed him a chalky blue pill. Percival gulped it down before Um could tell him what it was. "It's fer yer back, in case yoo was wonderin'," the Indulian groused. And then he stood and offered a handful of smaller red pills to Esme. "And yoo should pass these out ta the soldiers," he instructed. "They'll counter the disorientin' effect a the gravitational—" But before he could finish his sentence, Esme had passed a pill to Percival, and he'd swallowed that one as well. "Ta the *soldiers*," Um repeated. "He just took a *blue*. Yoo tryin' ta knock him inta a coma or what?"

"Oh. Um. Sorry," said Esme as she backed away sheepishly. "I'll go hand the rest of these out to the soldiers, then."

Um shook his head and looked down to Percival. "Well then," he said. "Yoo still alive down there? Yoo remember what year this is?"

Crouched at the platforms edge, staring over the side into the light of the MagmaStar, Percival could feel himself falling in place. He could feel the universe spinning around him. And, just for a moment, he could see a darkness stirring amongst the flames.

10 | THE DEVIL'S FACE

By noon, the streets of Galactic Zero were thick with revelers. They drank. They cried. They blew their Ur-Horns and waved the Celestial Governor's colors. For them, there would be no grand banquet. No masked ball. No glimpse of the great dame herself beyond whatever footage the state censors would deign to share through her official YouTube channel. But that could not diminish their fervor. For this was their celebration too. Their victory. "Every vote counts," they used to say, and that meant it was all of them together who had made this day possible.

Percival's soldier escort formed a wedge through the crowd. Some of the revelers responded angrily to being shoved aside, but as many gaped with bleary fascination at the crimson soldiers and their mysterious charge.

"Who's he, do you suppose?" asked one toothless indigent, halfway through his third bottle of blue vodka.

"He's got no shoes," answered an orphan boy, perched atop the crossbar of a street corner signpost. "He must be important, if he don't need shoes."

"Ach!" the toothless one spat, "You ain't got no shoes either. Don't make you king of no Cinnamon Galaxy."

Esme was just a few steps behind Percival, but from the way she carried herself she could have been any other reveler. She hooted as loudly as anyone and brandished a small flag she'd been handed a few blocks before. She was born on the streets, Percival reminded himself. Streets not so far removed from these. Was she simply trying to blend in, or was she properly enjoying herself? They'd all been taken in by Gor, all voted for her, all trusted her implicitly for years to rule over them. Was it too much to expect the others to see through that now? To do what had to be done?

Percival signaled for his escort to halt. The soldiers circled round as Percival pointed out a storefront through the crowd. The shop bore no name, but made its business clear by the three outfits that hung in the window: vampire, witch, and naughty nurse.

"Gentlemen," Percival announced to his escort, "I believe I'm in need of a disguise."

The soldiers stood guard outside while Percival and Esme slipped in. "Are you sure we have time for this?" Esme asked, but Percival wasn't listening.

Inside, the shop was dank and cramped. Just a few racks of costumes and a few crates of masks and the shopkeeper stood behind a narrow counter. The only light came in from outside, in shafts of MagmaStar red.

Esme smiled and said hello to the shopkeeper while Percival rifled through the masks. "Has business been good this week?" she asked. "On account of the masquerade?"

"Not many aristocrats down these ways, love. Just the usual riff-raff."

Percival stood a little too quickly and had to catch Esme's shoulder to steady himself. "You still look a little green," she noted with no small measure of guilt. "Are you sure you're going to be okay?"

Instead of answering, Percival held up a red porcelain mask with a long beakish nose. "What do you think?" he asked.

"As a disguise?" Esme frowned. "It's not exactly inconspicuous, is it? A little too flashy?"

Percival grinned. "Perfect. Help me tie it on." Percival held the mask up to his face with his good hand, and Esme dutifully tied the ribbon round back.

Esme turned him around to admire him. "So, are you the Devil?" she asked.

Percival shook his head. "Not by choice." And then he placed a hand to his stomach. "Oh. That's not good."

Esme looked to the shopkeeper. "Do you have a toilet in back? My friend's been feeling a little queasy since..." She paused. Since I accidentally drugged him, she thought. Not helpful. "Since breakfast."

"Yeah, yeah. Just not on the costumes. Back through the curtain!" He pointed the way.

Esme tried to help Percival in that direction, but he gently nudged her away. "I'll be fine," he whispered. "Just need a minute in the privy."

"You've got five," Esme called after him as he disappeared behind the curtain, "and then I'm coming in after you!"

On the far side of the curtain, Percival straightened and drew the watch from his trouser pocket.

Dear Mum,

I suppose that I should begin with an apology, both for my last, too abrupt email, and for the silence that followed. I can only imagine the fit of worry I must have left you in. "A spot of trouble," I said, with no regard to where your darker thoughts might lead you. Did you imagine me off on another one of my silly-strange adventures? Or could you see me dead at the bottom of a bloodied ditch?

That I should put such thoughts into your head! I wish that I could tell you now that I'm safe, that I'm off on some madcap romp or another, joyful and carefree as the breeze, but that is not the way of things. I do this day contend with grave threats to us all. My life, and indeed all of our lives, are very much at risk. But take comfort at least in the fact that I am not yet worm food. I am not fill for the ditch just yet.

Please know too that I would have written earlier if I could. I have been running, my pursuers servants to the same power as your stewards. Only now that we have resolved our disagreements do I feel secure in contacting you. My own welfare is one matter, but I couldn't countenance drawing you into my misadventures.

And yet, in all this time, there's no one I've more wanted to speak to!

Our grim anniversary is on the morrow, the day that marked the beginning of my life and the end of yours. By what right? Is it enough to pretend myself better than I am? To play the hapless fool or questing knight? Does Fate forget or am I ever damned to be the little monster you made me?

Why now, I ask myself. A silly question, perhaps. I might as easily ask, Why then? Why any of it? Why not the black of night instead? Why not the nothing of never being?

I feel the jaws of a trap closing on my leg. Perhaps if I had been more careful, I would have seen it ere it sprung. They want to see the monster, I think. I have a mind to oblige them. They will not be happy in the end.

I hope your stewards let you keep the extra blankets I sent you.

If this really is the end, I want you to know that I don't hate you for what you were. I love you, and I'll see you on Sunday if I'm not dead.

Your son,

Percy.

The Steward looked up from the printout when he was done and then out into the darkness before him, into the creature's yellow eyes and teeth. "Shall I read it again?" he asked with practiced distain.

"*Belo atah,*" she answered, her voice a slither in the dark.

The Steward sneered. "You'll speak in *our* tongue if you want me to respond. Not your demon gibberish." He lowered a hand to the whip coiled on his belt.

The creature snarled at the threat, but when she finally spoke, she relented. "Repeat," she said softly, cloyingly. "Say the pretty words again."

For four years, the Steward had served in this role as the demon's keeper, the ninth steward in twenty years and the longest serving, the longest *surviving*, of them all. This was hardly by chance. The rest had either been driven mad by the creature's games or... eaten. But this current Steward, the Last Steward as he called himself, he knew how to handle her. Or so he liked to think. He'd taught himself the demon words but would not abide them being spoken. He kept her restrained at all times, naked, and so long as his overmasters would allow, hungry.

He never got too close. Avoided prolonged conversations. Did all the things right that his eight dead predecessors had done wrong.

And still she clawed her way into his skull. Into his nightmares and his dreams. Still she made him sweat and fume and curse the dead gods of his people.

"No," he said finally, after pretending to consider her request for some ponderous interval. "Perhaps tomorrow." He drew the whip from his belt, let it uncoil to his feet. "*If* you can remember the right words."

Esme pounded on the door a third time. "I'm serious, Percival. I don't care if you have your pants on in there or not! If you don't open this door, I'm opening it for you."

No response.

Esme huffed and puffed and threw herself against the door. Too late, the shopkeeper let out a shriek of protest from out front. The door splintered and cracked and fell into the tiny toilet.

Percival was gone. The window, wide.

11 | AS I WAS SAYING

"—and your goose is cooked."

Percival couldn't quite feel his legs or, mercifully, his broken shoulder or broken arm, and the floor felt like it was wobbling beneath him and the universe might soon end, but all that aside, he was quite pleased with himself.

Governor Zell frowned. "I suppose you're quite pleased with yourself," she said.

A good judge of character, thought Percival as he pocketed his watch. And there was something else. He saw the fear in Zell. The same fear he saw in the High Cleric when they were alone together. The kind of fear that only comes from having everything in the galaxy to lose.

"I wasn't kidding by the way," said Percival. "About the goose. It *is* cooked. Well done. I'm no chef, but I expect that if you leave it in too much longer, it may go black on you."

Zell pounded once on the countertop to her right, never taking her eyes off Percival. A tiny little rat-man chef creature scurried out from the cupboard below, darted across to the Omega Oven, and swiped longwise across its touchpad interface to power the appliance down.

The little chef was around a corner and gone before Percival's brain could register confusion. "You have a—?" Perhaps a hallucination? thought Percival. Best not to dwell. "I'm not here for you," he said flatly. "It's not me you need to fear."

"Yes, of course," said Zell. "You are not disaster. Disaster follows in your wake. What cold comfort you offer, Mister Gynt."

"What I offer—" Percival paused mid-retort. The Celestial Kitchens spanned a kilometer end-to-end, and from those distant corners Percival could now hear the clomp-a-clomp of marching men. Were there dozens? Or hundreds? And none so easily dispatched as a fry cook or a *poissonier*, Percival predicted. So he spoke quickly. "Illuminari trusted you with the Engine for a reason, yes? If it's released, you'll lose everything."

"I am aware," said Zell.

As the marching grew louder, Percival could smell a vulgar perfume in the air. Death. "Grimsouls?" he muttered. An army of Grimsouls. "It was you on The Lonely Mutt. 'Call from 001.' That poor man. Captain Klieg."

"As you say, I would lose everything. Illuminari gambled correctly. There is nothing I would not do to protect what is mine," Zell snarled, "and what is mine is everything."

Now Percival could see them, the ghouls in black leather, brains disengaged, boots clacking against orange tile, marching down every aisle in prefect lockstep, hundreds from the right, hundreds from the left, an army of recycled men. "All right," said Percival, raising his one good arm in surrender, "I concede that you have me slightly outnumbered."

The Governor raised a stoney finger at the bedraggled accountant. "Give me one reason I shouldn't rip that arm off your shoulder and feed it to my men."

"Ah!" said Percival, a tired grin forming on his lips. He scrounged deep into his trouser pocket. "Then I couldn't hand you... this!" He drew the Secondary Codex from his pocket and held it out to Zell. "A peace offering. 'Everything,' she called it, 'and a bit more.'"

Zell opened her palm and whispered a "you are mine" charm, and the Codex flew into her grasp. She held the bauble up to her eye and peered into its interior. From Percival's vantage point, he could see the Governor's eye magnified and distorted through the blue glass, and he thought perhaps that he could see a tear forming in that warped, monstrous eye. "Yes," said Zell. "I remember. We called them the Apocrypha, but they were once truth. The last record of the Torquids. The Amiable Twerns. The once proud Ifeesians."

"I once told someone, 'It's amazing how much you miss the people you don't like very well, once they're gone.'"

"Indeed."

Percival shambled forward. "But you said 'last record,' and we both know that's not true. There's another of these, isn't there? The Primary Codex."

"The Primary Codex is lost."

"Lost?"

Zell palmed the Secondary Codex, took a hard sniff, and wiped the damp of tear or perspiration from her face. "Well, inaccessible at any rate."

"It's with the Engine."

"Yes."

"And the Engine is where I think it is?"

Zell looked Percival in the eye, thought, frowned, then nodded. Then she turned her back on the accountant and walked away. "Take him," she growled to her dead soldiers. "Take him to the Black Tower."

12 | *THE BLACK TOWER INTERLUDE*

When Percival woke up, he was very naked.

Now for anyone who is unaware, the difference between being naked and being very naked is precisely the difference between having little dignity and having *very* little dignity. In Percival's case, little dignity might have meant "naked in the corner" or "naked on a couch" or even "naked in the middle of a fancy party." In this case, *very* little dignity meant naked and dangling upside down from an iron chain hung from the ceiling, the chain wrapped tight around one leg, the other leg left to flail and kick awkwardly to steady himself as he swayed, the rest of him just loose and flapping or shouty and indignant.

"WHERE AM I?" Percival shouted indignantly. "GET ME DOWN FROM HERE, ZELL! ZELL! ZELL, WE ALMOST CERTAINLY DON'T HAVE TIME FOR THIS!"

Wherever Percival was, it was dark. That much he could tell. And though he couldn't see walls or floor, he could make out the vague outlines of other men similarly chained nearby. "Hullo there," Percival called to one of the nearest. He'd meant to deliver the line casually, amiably even, but the blood was all rushing to his head and the cold iron chafed against his bare leg, and he feared that he may have come across a bit crazed. When he didn't get an immediate reply, Percival began pumping back and forth, swinging himself closer and closer to the other man. "How long have…" he asked through gritted teeth. "How long have you been here for?"

The other man didn't answer. Or move. And even before Percival had swung near enough to see, he could smell that the man was dead. The other's chain ended in a rusted hook skewered through his half-rotted calf. Percival looked up to his own leg and considered himself lucky. But not *very* lucky.

"Yes, yes," came a voice from the black. "We're all quite dead here. But not you, Mister Gynt. No, the Vargoth has other plans for you."

"The Vargoth?" asked Percival as he snatched hold of the dead man's chain. He worked his way up hand over hand, huffing, till he'd cleared the corpse and righted himself. He took a moment to focus his thoughts as the blood rushed back out of his head.

"She doesn't like when I call her that, of course," said this voice in the dark. "Her name of old. Her name from the before time. It isn't lost on her that she who once mocked Fate now fears its icy nails as no other."

From the black, a sallow man in dark robes appeared. He was wrinkled and balding with deep sunken eyes and hair brittle like white straw. "You must forgive the chain. The other patients the Vargoth tests me with have had no voice to object. And, alas, she provides no table upon which to perform my little chirurgeries."

"Surgeries?"

"You had several broken bones, various cuts and bruises, scrapes, some internal tearing, a mild drug overdose, and two small tumors. The Vargoth asked that I fix you."

"Two... tumors?"

The sallow man smiled through broken teeth. "Small ones, barely noticeable to the untrained eye. And gone now, you're welcome."

"Who are you?"

"Who am I?" the sallow man chuckled. "Would that names still mattered in this darkened tomb. Oh, I was someone once, I like to think. A hero, perhaps. Or monster. I cannot say. Now I am but creature to the Vargoth and her whims."

"You..." Percival clung tightly to the dead man's chain, lifted up his own leg and pawed at the chain around it. "...you know the Vargoth...

You know Vargoth Gor from before? From before she was erased?"

"Forgotten, you mean. And yes. For the better part of our lives. And worst. And for what comes after. She was my student once. And now? But what are we, if not wizards of our word? When the time came, she shook my hand. Ten years seemed quite the bargain."

Percival unraveled the last of the chain from round his leg and used it to swing down to the floor. He landed before the sallow man with a cat's grace. "You said she was your apprentice?"

The sallow man nodded ruefully. "Or so I thought. Though now I have the time to wonder, was I not the student all along? For the lessons she has taught me, such dark truths. What shall we sacrifice of ourselves, Mister Gynt, in the pursuit of righteous ends?"

For a time, Percival observed this sallow, broken man, looked him in his bloodshot eyes and sought to take his measure. "Anything," he whispered finally.

And the sallow man nodded. And then he turned and disappeared into the black from whence he came. And his voice echoed after him, "Wait here, Mister Gynt, for time is short, and I have pants to bring you."

13 | RUESDAY

The crimson of the city's MagmaStar roared in through the glass of the dance floor. White marble steps, cast pink in the lavalight, rose up in concentric circles from the ballroom floor and closed again as gravity reversed itself overhead/underfoot. Above and below, the ballroom was already thick with revelers, the galaxy's richest, most well-connected sycophants, resplendent in their jewels and feathers and velvet cloaks and safe to preen their excesses behind their masks of silver and jet. They clinked glasses, laughed gaily, and whispered of a better, fatter tomorrow.

A string quartet of goblin-men played Brahms from the ceiling well. Somewhere else, on some distant planet or planetoid, church bells chimed to toll the hour.

The Celestial Governor sat on her throne at the edge of the room, arms folded, face twisted into a scowl, tired and bored and thoroughly fed-up and wanting very much to vaporize the lot of them. She was the ultimate authority in the galaxy, and in that moment she had all the good graces of a sleep-deprived four-year-old. She wanted this to be over. Not just the party, not just the goose gizzards still churning in her stomach, not just the night itself, but every night, all of it, the great trap that Illuminari had set for her, the trap of power, the power and responsibility of the crown, of castle walls and taste testers.

"How many of them do you suppose I could kill," she asked Young Wyndham, "before anyone would notice and make a fuss?"

Young Wyndham was having a hard time keeping down his goose. Or was it *up*? The Governor had sat Wyndham above her, right at gravity's turn, where the steps turn inward once more, such that he was upside down relative to the Governor and his head dangled down close enough for Zell to turn and whisper if need be. In this position, the blood was rushing to Wyndham's head and to his toes at the same time, a situation he considered deeply and medically problematic. On another occasion, Wyndham might have asked the Governor sheepishly if he could stand up for a moment, just to reposition himself or perhaps to go for a short once-around-the-ballroom. But he could read the Governor's expression, feel the loathing in her growl, and he knew this was the time to accept his precise and literal place in the universe.

"Many," Wyndham answered after a time. "All, perhaps. To die at your hands would be a great honor for all of them, of course."

"Of course," Zell grunted in assent. And where's the joy in that?

Director Fred and Officer Um walked the corridors of Blue Tower accompanied by four of their men and four of the Governor's former-men.

"Does it rattle ya?" asked Um. "Yoo killed as many Grimsouls as anybody in yer day."

"It's still my day," Fred grumbled.

"And now the Governor's makin' her own and usin' 'em fer personal security. Kinda backs up what Gynt said about her..." Um paused and glanced back at their Grimsoul escorts. Judging by their glassy stare and synchronized robo-march, they were still under remote control. Brains in the off position. Still, no way to know who might be listening from the other side. "...about the Governor *not* bein' an evil wizard."

Fred stopped, frowned, then pulled his radio to his lips to report: "This is Fred. Corridor 10110 clear and secure. Fred out."

"Not even a little?"

Fred glanced back at the Grimsouls. "You want the truth?"

Um glared mutely. He'd learned a long time ago not to answer rhetorical questions.

"I care very little about the past of any one individual, Officer Um. I care a great deal about the future of us all." Fred adjusted the knot of his power tie, then turned the corner into Corridor 10111, adding as an afterthought, "Us, and whatever it is *you* happen to be."

The White Knight dropped to one knee before the Celestial Governor and dipped his head respectfully. Zell dismissed Young Wyndham with a wave and the food tester, fearing any second thoughts, bolted for the nearest toilet.

The Governor considered the man before her. "Short. Obsequious. With delusions of nobility. Young Mouse, is it? How kind of you to visit."

The Knight rose. Under his silvered helmet, he even smiled. "In the end, we're all pretending to be something we're not, aren't we?"

The Governor nodded. "And this *is* the end, isn't it? At long last."

"For some of us." The Knight raised an arm back and ushered forth a woman draped in black linen, her face obscured by shadow. "You saw through my disguise so easily. Perhaps you'll see through hers?"

Zell could make out none of her face and could make little from her shape or stance. She could be anyone or no one, and so Zell shrugged. "This one is not known to me."

The White Knight hung an arm around the woman in black. "Ah, but that's where you're wrong, old one. She and you are good friends. For this is Death, your sweetest mistress, and she has come to take you to her breast."

Instinctively, the Governor reached for Wyndham's neck, something to snap. To grind to powder in her grip. But she'd sent the boy away. Instead, a man would have to do.

She rose.

The Celestial Kitchen stank of death. And not metaphorically. It held the stink of five hundred dead soldiers and a blackened goose. "Can't hold it against me," mumbled Chef Nevin as he wrapped hors d'oeuvres with his delicate rat-fingers. "I didn't march them in here. I didn't force the dignitaries of eleven systems to eat and sicken themselves on contaminated food."

But a true chef objects, Nevin reminded himself. A true chef would have said "no." Could have told them to throw it all out and start over. Could have taken a stand. He would have been eaten himself, but at least he would have been swallowed with his integrity in one piece. And now? Perhaps he had a day or a week? Maybe even a few months or a few years. But he'd caught the Governor's ire, and one day the Governor would come for him and wolf him down. And he would taste like coward.

"Should have voted for someone else this time," he sighed. "Why do I always forget that there's someone else?"

"Excuse me," said another, a beaming young lady with a fright of frizzy brown hair and big brassy goggles that made her eyes enormous. "I seem to have misplaced my accountant. Might you have seen him?"

"Corridor 11011 is clear. Moving on to Corridor 11100." Agent Tullis lowered the radio from his lips and motioned for his men to follow him around the corner.

His men! The very words sounded ludicrous as he heard them in his head. Tullis was nineteen, just a week out of the Academy, and hadn't expected to be put in charge of anyone for years. But when they'd arrived to take over security for the inauguration, the Governor's staff had insisted that patrols be divided between Agency men and the dead things the Governor kept as her personal guard. When the Director was forced to divide his squads in two, he suddenly needed twice as many squad commanders. Tullis was given command of 16-Beta because the Director had heard good things about an Agent Tully, and Tullis didn't have the nerve to tell him that was someone else.

Tullis had read about Grimsouls at the Academy, had even autopsied one as part of an independent study, but had never seen one in its active, un-dead state. He was properly terrified, probably the sane response, but he thought he hid it well.

It confounded Tullis, as he looked back on it, that he could be so brave in one moment and such a coward in another. There was probably some reason for it. Tullis' father was a ship's counselor, gifted in identifying and reconciling just this sort of contradiction, but Tullis had never had that level of insight. "A bit of a dullard," his father had once concluded at the end of a particularly awkward Thanksgiving dinner. That was the day Tullis had been accepted to the Academy. Tullis hadn't even told his parents he was applying for fear he might disappoint them, so now he had to tell them that he'd applied, that he'd in fact gotten in, and that he was scheduled to ship out on the first of the year, all over the same roast turkey. His father was briefly flummoxed by the news. Why would his son want to sell his soul to the Agency? And what would the Agency want with his son of all people? "Perhaps they're *all* dullards," was how he neatly cross-solved the two problems.

The truth was that Tullis' acceptance letter was meant for a promising young applicant named Tully, but once the email went out, the deans of the Academy were too embarrassed to admit their mistake.

During his time at the Academy, Tullis discovered that he had a gift for pathologies and for field medicine. His father understood the mind, but he understood the body. And *you* should not be possible, he thought to himself as he eyed the four dead men in his company.

In Corridor 11100, Tullis and his men found a contingent of latecomers, over a dozen, presumably all from the same club or office, all done up in the same costume, which was in truly poor taste. These costumes were quite convincing, each head-to-toe in black, with the infamous armband, a pair of red goggles, and a realistic-enough pulse rifle hung to one side. Tullis might have been convinced they were the real thing if not for the words "Space" and "Nazi" written across their chests in gold. The revelers laughed as they saw Tullis and his men round the corner. A few carried open wine bottles or champagne flutes which they raised to toast the squad as they approached. A few, the sober of them Tullis imagined, recoiled at the sight of the Grimsouls.

"You know, I don't think they call themselves that," said Tullis, before adding, "Just keep moving. We need everyone to keep to the designated areas." He'd attempted to sound tough. A few seemed properly chastised. A few saluted drunkenly as they passed.

Once the revelers were around the corner and out of sight, Agent Tullis called in his report: "Corridor 11100 clear. I found some stragglers loitering in the hallway, but I sent them along. Be advised that they're dressed as Space Nazis. Repeat, *dressed* as Space Nazis. Please don't shoot them."

Around the corner, the revelers' gait stiffened.

Queegan Fumph was quite drunk, even by his own prodigious standard. And though the little man tried with great enthusiasm to follow his sister's anecdote about the priest, the rabbi, and the indigent necroblob, he found that he was only able to pick out every fourth word or so. The rest was just noise and light and the occasional wave of guilt and regret. Certain that he would feel no worse for abandoning his sister, he promptly did, stumbling out onto the dance floor as the harmonies of Schulberg wafted down from overhead.

He was a squat fellow, barely a meter high and nearly twice that round the waist. He more waddled than walked on the best of nights, and here he fairly rolled. In his feathered cloak of yellow and green, he looked like nothing so much as a soft pillow in a strong wind, a harmless distraction.

When the wind stopped, Fumph found himself at the foot of a gorgeous young woman in diaphanous white. The folds of her dress barely covered her milky white skin. Dark tresses spilled out from behind a silvery faerie mask. And she was pouring herself a glass of rum! He loved her immediately.

"My lady," he said, more or less. She looked down and frowned from behind her mask. What she had heard was "Mahh Luhh." He swiped a fatty paw in her direction, which is to say he offered her his hand, and he asked her, "Meyyuhavtheesdannnnnsss?"

As some number of her floated before him, Queegan Fumph stared back blankly. Queegan thought perhaps to try again, but a taller man, which is to say a man of average height, stepped in ahead of him, clad in red and black leather, the mask of the horned devil pulled down over his face.

"Sorry to cut in," said the stranger, his voice partially muffled by the mask but still a standard of deviation clearer than that of the roly feathered man. He extended a gloved hand to the faerie princess, "But may I have this dance?"

The lady dropped her tumbler, which crashed upon the dance floor to titters and applause. "Percival," she whispered.

"Tarot," he said, taking her hands in his. "Let's dance."

Officer Um chortled as he bounced the Realm shock troopers roughly against the corridor wall. Yes, they wore store-bought costumes, but Um was no fool. To his eye those weapons were real enough, and for all their drunk-eyed weeping, he'd seen better actors in the slums of Sorrow Point back on Sanctuary-8. For everything that lot had put him through over the past few days, he would enjoy cracking them until they cracked.

Um picked up one of their supposed prop guns off the floor and pulled back the primer. The prop gun whirred to neon blue life as surely as any plasma rifle he'd ever handled. He chose one of them, the biggest and the toughest and the least weepy, and jammed the barrel into the back of his neck. "Confess yer sins," he growled. "Or don't. I'm sure the next guy'll be real helpful after I blow yer head off."

To which there were many sobs and whimpers, but none from the big man. He was calm as the void. Calm as a racist, psychopathic, genocidal void.

Then Fred handed him the channel: "—advised that they're dressed as Space Nazis. Repeat, *dressed* as Space Nazis. Please don't shoot them."

Um raised the radio to his sneering lips. "Yer sure? Ya ran their idents?"

A half second pause. Then, "Yes, um, that's standard procedure. They all came out clean."

Um frowned. He was so sure. But maybe his aggression, his desire to find and hurt his enemy, was overwhelming his rational instincts. He looked to Fred, and Fred shook his head.

In that moment, Um realized something about himself. He didn't care particularly whether these were Realm shock troopers or rich, obnoxious blowhards who thought it was funny to dress up as shock troopers. Either way, they were scum, and their lives didn't matter. Particularly in a story near its close. As an officer, he'd had clean kills and messy kills. Before that, kills he didn't like to remember. Ones that still haunted his quiet hours. What would a few more matter? Either God forgave or God didn't. Surely the thousandth sin is no worse than the one before.

"No," said Fred as he tightened the knot of his power tie one last time. "Let's give them their props back. We still have ground to cover."

Um nodded, spun the gun in his hand and passed it barrel first to the shock trooper before him, their grim-faced leader. His compatriots let out sighs of relief, smiled, slapped each other on the back, laughed, and joked as they took their weapons back. But not their leader. Not him.

Fred motioned to the other agents and their Grimsoul counterparts to continue down the corridor. He placed a hand delicately on Officer's Um's arm. "Any one individual," he reminded him, "any five or ten or a hundred, don't mean anything to me. It's only all of us who matter. Only everything."

Um nodded again, turned, and followed Fred down the corridor. "Y'know, the Fummers are makin' me a new suit," he told Fred. "Somethin' nice fer my court martial."

Plasma fire burned through Um and Fred's skulls. Their corpses slumped to the floor.

Grim Leader pulled his mask back over his head and spoke into his radio: "Gamma Company is in position, Commander Noon. We are ready to begin."

Tarot was a gifted dancer, taught by her mother at a young age. Percival still had to count the steps in his head, but he was passably fair.

"So what happens now?" Percival asked as he dipped Tarot low to the dance floor. The question was obligatory. The answer, obvious. Bad things. Only bad things.

"Mouse is confronting Zell right now. They're going to have it out."

Percival pulled Tarot back to him. "Then you know? You know who she is."

"We always knew. That's what this is all about for Mouse. Mother felt guilt and wanted penance, so she invented a God. Gor felt greed and wanted power, so she conquered a galaxy. Mouse felt wronged and wanted justice. All he's ever wanted is to be the gallant hero."

"And the Engine? Do you know where the Engine is?" He spun her away from him. She twirled dutifully.

"No, but Mouse will get it out of her."

Again, he drew her close. "And how will he do that?"

Tarot grinned. "As befitting a great hero."

And then came a thundering slap, and now the White Knight was sailing across the room, and his back cracked against the steps opposite the throne.

The band stopped. The revelers cheered. From her throne, the Governor seethed. Her hand was red with blood and in the cake, shards of the White Knight's silver helm. "Yes," said Zell as she wiped her hand with one sleeve. "I do believe I'm feeling better now."

The White Knight tried to rise, but he was caught at gravity's edge and couldn't find his up. He wrenched off his broken helm and let it drop and made that his down, and then he stood. "VARGOTH GOR," he cried out, and his voice resounded. "I name you warlock. I name you necromancer. I name you VILLAIN." From his side he drew a thin silvered blade and pointed it at Zell's head. "And I challenge you to a duel for the fate of all things."

Percival scratched the back of his head. "What's the point of all this?" he whispered to Tarot. "Does Mouse really think that Gor will accept some schoolyard—"

"And I accept!" Zell bellowed, a monstrous toothy grin stretching out across her jaw.

Percival's eyes darted around the room, from reveler to reveler.

"Where's Halla?" he whispered. Now Tarot looked, but she couldn't spot her either.

Zell leapt out across the ballroom and as she did she roared with laughter, "Yes! This is what I've missed! Challenge! Com—"

Before she could complete her thought, she collided with Mouse, who'd launched himself from the far side of the ballroom sword first. The blade slid through Zell's chest and out the back with a quiet swikk. The Governor's eyes went wide, and a tiny spurt of blood issued from between her lips. The two fell as one onto the glass dance floor. Mouse hit first and the Governor on top, crushing down against him. Mouse let out a shriek and a wheeze as his bones snapped like so many twigs underfoot.

Zell lumbered to her feet and smiled. "Really, little Mouse." She laughed as he pulled the White Knight's sword from her chest and tossed it clattering to the ground. "You should know as well as anyone that I have no heart."

Mouse gurgled and twitched and struggled and failed to rise. Tarot covered her mouth. Percival wasn't quite sure if she was about to scream or vomit. But then she turned to him, tears in her eyes, and she said, "Do something."

"He had to know that it would end like this."

"Percival Gynt..." And she looked at him, and suddenly they were back at Slidetown Station, and she a stranger, and the world was still full of mystery, possibility, and hope. "Do something."

A few meters away, the Celestial Governor raised a booted foot and prepared to squish a rodent.

Percival sighed, then called out, "Wait!" He lifted his Devil's mask. "Zell, wait. This isn't doing us any good. The boy is a sideshow. This isn't the time."

Zell snarled. "Tough." And she brought her boot down.

And Percival stopped time. He walked over to Zell and to Mouse. A few centimeters separated foot from face. He crouched down and grabbed ahold of Mouse's arm. If he timed it right, he'd be able to pull him out of the way. And that's when, crouched there at the Celestial

Governor's foot, he saw them. The Space Nazis, pouring in from the corridor, a dozen or more, their weapons readied. He'd been told repeatedly that they don't call themselves that, but it was spelled out very clearly on their shirts.

Time resumed, Percival yanked, and Zell's foot came down awkwardly against the glass of the dance floor. The Governor stumbled, and in that moment she was hit by three plasma blasts, one to the shoulder, one to the lower back, and one to the back of the head. The Governor snarled.

"Ah, I see that you're plasma-proof," Percival noted as he repositioned himself to best utilize the supreme ruler of the galaxy as a human shield.

The rest of the crowd was, sadly, not plasma-proof. Fumph died with a pop and a spludge. The goblin-players snapped and burned. One by one and five by five they died. Till there was no one but Zell and Percival and what-was-left-of-Mouse and Tarot lurking somewhere in the shadows.

Zell turned to face the Space Nazis. "So, is this it then, Gynt? Your great apocalypse? Your end of all things? Just another band of rabble. Just another pack of men... with *guns*."

Behind the Space Nazis, at last, the dark lady appeared. "No, Governor. Not just men." Halla drew back her hood and smiled.

From somewhere behind Percival, Tarot gasped. "I swear, Percival," she whispered. "I didn't know."

Halla advanced down the stairs with her Space Nazi phalanx. "Assemble the gate," she commanded. The last of the Space Nazis carried three long, unwieldy canvas bags with them. From within, they drew a series of telescoping steel tubes, which they began to bolt together.

"Perhaps," Percival suggested to the Governor, "we might prevent them from doing whatever this thing is that they're doing. Perhaps you might, you know, break them or something."

Zell harrumphed and approached Halla. "And who are you, anyway? Young Mouse implied that we'd met before, but I don't recognize you."

Halla nodded. "We met once. When I was a boy."

"A b-boy?" the not quite dead Mouse gurgled.

Percival shook his head. "Of course. It had to be you behind all this."

"What is this nonsense?" Zell snarled.

"The Theorists told us. When Franco Nicodemus Noon was done with this world, he hid himself away..."

Halla smiled. "Yes..."

"...in Valhalla."

"A lovely name for a daughter, I thought. And poetic. But that's all backstory, and just now I believe we're due for an ending."

Behind her, the Space Nazis had finished assembling what Halla had called their gate, a triangular structure, perhaps a meter high. And between the bars, a pale light swam.

"Halla," Percival began. "Or Franco? Frank?" he asked, inadvertently deadnaming his enemy. "This is a terrible idea. You can stop this. You can stop this right now. We'll all put our toys away and pretend this never happened."

Halla clung to the frame of the gate and smiled a wicked smile. "Do you like my yellow-horn gate?" she asked. "It came to me in a dream."

Zell stepped slowly, determinedly forward. There was something emerging from the gate. A shadow from the light. A memory given form. The boy from the photograph. The boy from the video. The boy who was never named Kevin. Now Percival saw the resemblance. He was Tarot's brother once, all those years ago. But now he was just a hollow thing. A hole in the universe wearing a dead boy's skin.

Tarot lunged forward. "Caul!" she cried out. Zell reached out a trunkish arm and pulled her back.

"Not anymore," Zell told her. Her words were harsh, but not unkind.

"You don't know," she sobbed. "You haven't heard him speak."

Halla crouched behind the boy, wrapped him in her arms, and

asked him, "What do you see, my pale rider?"

"Above us... only sky..."

A single tear ran down Tarot's cheek, but a smile passed across her lips. "That was always his favorite song."

Percival frowned as he pulled Tarot from Zell's arms. "We need to shut this down. Now."

Zell nodded. Perhaps this was the end. Perhaps that was even a good thing. But she would not surrender meekly to oblivion. Vargoth Gor was not dead yet.

The Celestial Governor turned to the Space Nazi and her dead-eyed prize and sneered. "And tell me, girl. What's to stop me from wringing the life from your useless neck?" She advanced slowly, purposefully, letting each step fall with a stomp on the glass of the dance floor, hands raised in front of her, reaching out at neck level, closer, stomp, closer.

Halla, crouched there next to Caul, did not flinch, did not back away. Instead she smiled and said, "You know I had dinner once with the Mad Architect of Galactic Zero."

Zell stopped short, her stoney fingers mere centimeters from the Space Nazi's throat.

"You may be able to withstand our plasma fire, Madam Governor, but..." Halla gave the smallest of nods, a pre-arranged signal, and two of her men trained fire on the glass beneath Zell's feet, melting it to sludge. Before the shock could register on her face, Zell fell down through the hole, and up into the GE MagmaStar that raged at the heart of Galactic Zero.

Ah, thought Governor Zell as a hot wind buffeted her plummeting frame, I see it now. Illuminari's trap. Illuminari's grand joke. The choice, the same as before, all those decades ago. Fall into the MagmaStar and allow herself to be incinerated or speak the charmed words and open a pathway zomway into the singularity at the heart of the star. To trap herself again in that dark silent place, twisted inward on herself, alone but for her agony. The very thought was grim torture. Governor Zell would rather die than face that kind of hell.

But Vargoth Gor chose life.

She whispered the secret words into the wind and space turned sideways and back. Before her, the MagmaStar blossomed like an eleven-dimensional flower. Out of the roaring flames of the MagmaStar, a dark thing rose, an ancient angry shape.

Gor fell against it with a THRACK squikk.

Percival crouched at the hole the Space Nazis had opened up for Zell. The glass, even a few centimeters from the edge, was still cool to the touch. For a split second, Percival's thoughts drifted to the physics of the thing, but then his eyes focused on the dark shape rising.

"Predictable," Halla clucked. "In choosing her life, she chooses your deaths."

Up out of the MagmaStar, the Engine rose, a dark misshapen thing of cold black stone, and on its back, the charred and beaten form of Vargoth Gor.

In Halla's arms, Caul began to convulse. Black smoke spilled from open mouth and nostrils and tear ducts. "Hush, my child," Halla cooed. "Your years of torture are nearly over. Soon you will be back in your proper house."

Tarot wiped tears from her bleary eyes. She was close now. Just a few more lies. She rested a hand on Percival's shoulder and leaned down next to him. "We don't have much time," she explained with a sniffle, "so I need you to listen carefully."

The stone that hung from Tarot's necklace glowed with a golden fire. Percival reached out and took it between his fingers. "This stone..."

"My father made it. It senses—"

"Innocence."

She nodded. "Hope. Purity."

"Love?"

Percival's fist closed around the stone. Tarot unfastened the chain.

"You may not believe this," she said, "but all of those things are inside you, even now. You just need to embrace them. The Rider needs a new host. Before it returns to the Engine. This is your moment."

"Tarot, I'm not... I've seen... I've *done* horrible things in my life."

Tarot shook her head. "I don't care. All that matters is right now.

Are you my hero, or aren't you?"

Behind them, Caul slumped weakly to the floor. The Rider now hung above them, a cloud of oozing black darkness. Halla was entranced. With all the glee of a child, she removed a glove and ran her fingers through the black.

"Um," one of her soldiers stammered, "Do you have any more orders? Should we eliminate the hostiles maybe?"

Percival stood, perhaps taller than before. He steeled his jaw and held his right fist out in front of him, trailing a chain of brass. And he cast his mind back to a time long gone, to find a better version of himself. "When I was a boy," he said calmly, firmly, "my father left me in the dark."

Beneath them, above the tower, the Engine continued its steady ascent. Halla looked over at the accountant in his Devil's mask and smiled. "No," she told her men. "I have no further need of you. Shoot yourselves."

Percival closed his eyes to the sounds of rapid plasma fire, of slumping melted flesh and rifles clacking and clunking against the dance floor. "The dark was to be my cloak against evil. But he also left me with his pocket watch, and as the evil crept closer, fear got the better of me. My tiny hands trembled, and the watchlight spilled out between my fingers."

What game was this? Halla wondered as she circled the accountant. What last amusement did Fate present before her final, inevitable victory?

"The fear of a boy of three." Between Percival's fingers a golden fire bled. "A good boy. An *innocent* boy." The light burned bright now, forcing Halla to recoil, but the inky black that was the Rider lunged for the Accountant.

He grimaced, but he did not recoil.

"I remember," Percival grunted as the Rider dug into his chest. "My fear is pure. A light... in the dark..."

Halla rubbed spots from her eyes with one hand and groped for a plasma rifle with the other. "No," she muttered. "The Rider must not be trapped again."

Through the raging firelight, Percival locked eyes on Halla. "The shadow is trapped..." he growled as the Rider poured into him, "...in a circle of light."

Tarot knelt down over her little brother and scooped his limp body into her arms. "I saved you," she whispered. "I'm a good sister."

Now shivering with rage, Halla lifted her rifle and fired on Percival. The blasts dissipated harmlessly. Like Caul before him, the Rider's power protected this new host. "No!" shouted Halla. "Relinquish this fool! Your Chariot awaits!"

And so it did. The dark of the Engine filled the window of the dance floor, and as it pressed upwards, the glass began to crack. Percival and Halla stumbled. "The Gods spoke to me!" Halla cried to the Rider. "The Beast promised! We will unmake this universe together! This is our destiny! This is Fate!" But the Rider hungered for the light, and in that moment it knew nothing else.

The glass shattered. They were atop the Engine now. Halla found herself on her knees, but she was not humbled. "This is madness," she hissed. "He is no hero! He has lived a life of darkness. He wears the Devil's own face! This is but illusion. A magic trick!" She rose, stood over Percival and Tarot and Caul, squinted through golden flames and inky darkness. "And now I saw the lady in half."

Halla fired once, twice, three times.

Tarot dropped lifeless to the cold black stone, dead with her brother in her arms. And in that moment, the golden fire died.

Percival choked on his own breath. His eyes went wide, moist. Inside him, the Rider twisted and recoiled and withdrew.

Halla turned her rifle on the accountant. "It appears we both of us misjudged you," she told him. "Die knowing that you were both more and less than you believed yourself to be."

Percival bowed his head. Without another viable host to tempt it elsewhere, the Rider descended eagerly into the Engine. Halla placed the muzzle of her rifle to Percival's temple and slowly squeezed back on the trigger.

But before the plasma rifle could discharge its payload, two stony hands closed around Halla's throat, crushing the life from her. Her arms spasmed and the plasma blast fired wide. Vargoth Gor dropped the once-Noon to black stone. Quietly, she repeated the charm. "Vargoth Gor is not dead. Vargoth Gor is not dead."

Percival looked around, broken and confused. The Engine was lowering again, back up towards the MagmaStar. And with it he and Gor and the bodies of Halla and some of her men. Of Tarot and her brother. Percival took Tarot's hand in his and whispered an apology. "You didn't need a magic charm," he told her. "You were never alone."

"We have to go, Gynt," Gor commanded. As she spoke, the Engine was tilting, turning to face the towertop. Percival and Gor steadied themselves as Tarot and the rest slid backwards into the MagmaStar.

"Run!" Percival shouted, and he sprinted up the side of the Engine at twenty degrees, thirty degrees, forty, fifty, sixty. And Gor barreled behind him, whispering a "the Engine has a surprisingly high coefficient of friction" charm as she did.

Percival leapt and caught a marble step by the tips of his fingers. He screamed out in pain. Next to him, Gor caught hold, her fingers crushing into the stone. "Help me up!" Percival shouted. "Quickly!"

Gor grunted. Below them, the Engine was opening its white eye. Gor flung herself upward into the room, then reached down with one massive limb and hauled Percival up after her.

By their side, a White Knight stood tall, denying his pain. "This is it," said Mouse. "The reason I was born. This is my dragon." And he lunged forward through the empty dance floor, shining sword held proudly aloft. "AND I AM THE WHITE KNIGHT!"

Mouse vanished into a tower of light, the Engine's scorching gaze. The white light rose up through the ballroom, through the core of the Blue Tower, unmaking every atom in its path.

Five years earlier, Matthew Holden is agreeably drunk in the darkest corner of the Drowning Pit of Despair. He has lined up seven shots in front of him, each one glowing or bubbling or oozing. Surely one of these will kill me? he thinks, or at least put me out of my misery for another night.

He downs the black. He forgets what the bartender called it. "Them," perhaps. It skitters eagerly down his throat.

An hour earlier, he was still angry. He is always angry, except when the chemicals tell him otherwise. He is always angry because he still believes that Fate can be changed. That good can triumph over evil. That past mistakes can be forgiven.

He had gone to his old master again. He could not remember if it was for the eighty-sixth or eighty-seventh time. And he had begged him to reconsider. It wasn't that the enemy had been a bad ruler. In fact, the first five years had passed in relative peace and modest prosperity. No, it was the principle that most troubled young Holden. That one of such evil could be rewarded with such power. His old master called power a trap, but that didn't make any sense to Holden.

How could it be a trap to be given exactly everything you've ever wanted?

Now Matthew Holden downs another. This time, the red. "The Devil's Spittle," he recalls. And that's what it tastes like.

Around him, everything is noise and haze and vulgarity. He scarcely registers the form cohering at the edge of his vision, a woman, blond and blue-eyed and boyish in all the ways he quietly prefers. She places her hands on the table before him and leans down to speak softly to him.

And as she does, he can hear nothing else. Only her words.

"So tell me," she asks sweetly, "are you my White Knight?"

The moment hangs in eternity for an instant, and then it vanishes.

Percival stared into the column of light. Great chunks of his life were disappearing, rearranging. He clutched his chest. "I'm forgetting something," he muttered.

"Just Mouse," Gor sneered. "Hardly important." Then she hauled Percival backwards up the steps.

Just then, Esme entered from the corridor, dragging a trembling rat-chef after her. "I don't understand!" she shouted down to Percival and to Gor. "What are we doing in the Hollow Tower? What's happening?"

Percival wasn't sure himself. The very facts around him were changing. He had to think quickly. To act quickly. Instinctively, he reached for his pocket watch, but it was gone. "No time," he whispered as he stared into the white light tower. "No time."

He pushed past Esme and the rat-chef, circling the tower of light. The others joined him at the Yellow-Horn Gate. He knelt before it, allowed one hand to pass through the misty portal, to twist and fold back on itself. He grimaced, then pushed his hand further.

Esme had questions, and she knew that if she wanted to keep them, she best not waste time asking them.

Nevin, by contrast, knew no such prudence. He turned to the mighty Zell, and he stammered, "W-What's happened? What is the dark thing in the sky? What is the strange shaft of light that fills the Hollow Tower? What are we doing here? W-What happens next?"

Gor frowned. "It's simple, child. We tried to save the universe. We lost." She looked to Percival, arm-deep into the gate's misty portal, face contorted in agony. "And now we run away."

IN WHICH THE UNIVERSE IS SAVED
(OR DAMNED)

Top 5 News Downloads for June 3, 20018

5 Manhunt for Celestial Governor Continues

4 Galactic Economy in Turmoil

3 Cryptomycologists Offer Dire Warnings, Truffles

2 15 Accounting Tips That Will Change Your Life

1 High Cleric Says All-Mother a Sham, End Times Imminent

You may also be interested to know

213 Hundreds of Nth Realm Sympathizers Apprehended in Void Faerie Trafficking Bust

Today's Weather

Apocalyptic

1 | *THE GIRL WITH NO MOTHER*

Shan Morton, age ten, was born to no mother. How this happened, no one was quite sure. The popular understanding was that baby Shan had simply appeared one day on an operating room table, screaming her infant heart out, umbilical cord trailing off to nothing. Whether this story was true or not none could say, and consequently none had said, and subsequently none would say, for the paradox would prove brief. For in a few moments Shan Morton, age ten, would not exist either.

Shan and her father, Astro-Tobias Morton of the Last West Regalia, lived on the outer surface of Sanctuary-1 in the province of Sensible Fallback Position. It being Sunday, the two were just then returning from church and now found themselves walking the crowded aisles of the Olde Goblin Market. Shan had it in her head that this was her father's idea. Astro-Tobias thought perhaps his daughter had suggested it. But both were happy for this time together on this lazy spring day as the suns flickered overhead and exotic scents carried on a warm breeze.

By instinct, they left a space between them as they walked.

"Excuse me, sir!" a long-nosed goblin-man called, and he beckoned to the pair with a tangle of digits. "Have ye ever seen such wonders as these, I ask ye?"

His stall was simply a dirty red rug thrown down and cages piled to a human eye's height, these of all sizes and designs, all ages and intricacies. And in each, a void faerie, gray and low and hacking and passing miserable.

"What are they?" asked Shan as she pressed up to the cages, entranced by the delightful ugliness of the creatures within.

"Faeries," answered her father. "Monsters. Perhaps not the proper stuff for children."

"Nonsense!" the goblin-man opined. He thought perhaps to pat the child on the head, but he saw the steel in her father's gaze and drew backwards. "They are a sort of magic, yes, mysterious but ultimately benign. Their colors tell ye secret truths. A blue light in the dark. A white light in a liar's presence. And deepest red in times of danger."

Shan smiled. "And what does it mean if they go all black like pitch?"

The goblin-man frowned, leaned closer, and smirked. "So ye already know the stories, I see. Well it's superstitious nonsense if y—" He stopped mid-word when he saw that the girl was pointing.

Behind him, one after another, from left to right, from top to bottom, the void faeries were turning black, the liquid churning below the pale of their skin, passing like one continuous wave through all of them, and in that moment the Faeries smiled their thorny smiles and knew peace. Astro-Tobias dug his fingers into his daughter's shoulder, then shoved her hard away from him, down the aisle, to his right and nearly to her knees.

"RUN!" he bellowed as pure white light bore down from overhead, unmaking everything in its path. Shan looked back and her father was gone, lost to the white. She trembled and cried, but someone had told her to run. Who?

It didn't matter. The light was coming for her. Shan turned and stumbled forward, fell, picked herself up, and ran. Ran as fast as her ten-year old legs would take her. Pushed through the shrieking crowd, darted between feet and tails and pushcart wheels. Ran till her every muscle ached, but still the white burnt at her heels.

And then a hand grabbed her collar, pulled her rough and sideways into an alley. The hand and its owner smelled of grime and desperation, he a ragged fellow in a sweat-soaked vest and tattered black trousers. His hair and beard, a mat of dark curls. His nose, sharp like a beak. His eyes narrowed with a stark intensity.

In his left hand, he held a simple stone bound to a chain of brass. He pressed it hard to her cheek, and he snarled something so queer that she could not at first make sense of it.

"W-what?" she stammered.

"I said," he repeated, "ARE. YOU. INNNOCENT?"

But before she could even dare feign an answer, the stranger and his stone vanished into nothingness, and Shan was alone in the alley, a blaze of white at her back.

It was a peculiar thing. To have no mother or father. No friends, no home, no past, nothing behind her and just the dead end of a cobblestone alley ahead. And then that too was gone.

Shan Morton was a paradox. But just for a little while.

2 | *THE FAR SIDE OF THE GATE*

His foot slipped as the cobblestone vanished out from underneath him. Percival Gynt fell backwards onto his bony ass. "*Belo atah*," he hissed. The floor of the teleport room was cold and hard, and Percival felt like death. "Just one more minute," he grumbled. "One more and I might have found someone."

Esme looked down on him and frowned. "The Eye's turning. Time to bug out. Gor's orders."

Percival lay there, not ready to move, not sure he had the strength or the will.

"Next window, you take a shower, Gynt. You smell like pee and sadness. And maybe shave off that thing that's growing down your face."

She reached a hand down to him, and however reluctantly, he took it. "Let someone else take the next run. Me or Gor. Nevin even. You're pushing yourself too far."

Percival stood and shook his head and lurched to the teleport room door. "No. My fault. I wasn't good enough for her. But I will be."

Esme followed him into their tiny ship's cockpit, a cramped compartment with two faux-faux-leather seats amidst a tangle of cables, under a canopy of counter-polarized glass. They'd wedged the Yellow-Horn gate in between the two chairs, a soup of pale light swirling within its bracketed frame.

Outside and overhead, a planet died.

Esme bowed her head and whispered an empty prayer.

"One other thing," said Esme as they crouched down in front of the gate. "You told me to tell you…"

"…if I start saying the words again."

"Yes, and you have been."

Percival drew his hand slowly, cautiously to the surface of the portal. "Thank you," he said. "That's helpful." And then he plunged his arm into the soup, grimacing, holding back convulsions as his fingers splintered across six dimensions.

Esme looked up, looked for the Engine turning against the black of space. "Tell me what the words mean. '*Belo beh.*' '*Belo atah.*'"

Percival looked back at Esme. His whole body was shaking now. These translations across dimensions were getting harder. Through gritted teeth he told her, "They mean I haven't been right since Galactic Zero." Then he turned back to the gate, tears forming in his eyes, and he threw himself through.

Esme frowned. "Yeah, I got that part." And then she was after him.

A moment later, the ship they called "The Last Best Hope" was gone.

Percival fought off the disorientation, pushed himself to his feet/liver/elbows. "If you'd just given me another fifteen seconds…" he called out to Gor, and his voice echoed yellow and horn.

This place that Halla had left behind was vast and confounding, a maze of empty space, of fractured reflections. A tortuous refuge perched above the lower dimensions. Here they were safe as history collapsed below them.

"Another fifteen seconds," Gor replied, her voice converging from all directions, "and we would not be having this conversation." Vargoth Gor was elsewhere and nowhere, sat balled within herself, pulled fetal and then inside out, eyes closed, but also open, pointed inward. She focused on her breathing. Tried to remember that this was just a moment in time, not an eternity trapped in Hell.

The portal spat Esme out next to Percival/behind him/through him. "We're cutting these too close," she said as she collected herself. "I saw the Eye advancing on us just before I crossed."

"Yes," said Gor. "We are in... *near* unanimous consent on that point."

"How much longer do we have to stay up here?" Nevin whimpered as he huddled in eight corners of the room. "My head can't handle this place."

"A few hours for the Engine to finish off the system," said Gor, "and then we have a few days to plan before the next strike."

"I'm hungry is all," said Nevin. He could feel his stomach rumbling through his rat-teeth.

"Yes, yes. There will be time for all of that," said Gor in an attempt to end the conversation, "*after* the rewrite is complete. Only then will it be safe to emerge."

"Safe?" Percival repeated incredulously. "A strange choice of words, magician. While we hide here, the universe is being scoured clean, one system at a time."

"And every change," Gor reminded him, "ripples through time and space. Consider your home on Sanctuary-8. *Eight.* Today Sanctuary-1 was removed from our history..."

Percival nodded as much in defeat as in consent. Remove one piece from the stack and the entire Jenga tower could overturn. Maybe Sanctuary-8 was never colonized. And with no Sanctuary-8, there would be no Lunar Colony. No summer internship at Henderson, Glorp & 11010. Percival would never have become an accountant. Would never have met the killer in apartment 4D. Never met Um or Agent Fred or Tarot. *Tarot.* Perhaps.

While they were in this space that Halla had built, they were shielded from those changes, cut off. In Gor's words, "Safe." Percival wasn't in a state of mind to fully process this, to fully consider the implications, but he understood that while the Engine struck, he had to hide.

"I'm a coward," he whispered. "In the end, just another feckless coward."

From across the crooked expanse, Esme lifted her goggles from her eyes and frowned. "We're not going to win by being brave though, are we? We're not going to courage the Engine to death. We need to stick to the plan. The Engine was shut down once. We can shut it down again."

"Yes," Gor agreed. "If we can find a proper innocent, we can draw the Rider out of the Engine, and then trap the Engine again. In all the seven galaxies, there must be at least one."

"The sacrificial lamb," Percival whispered. "The best of us, in exchange for all the rest of us."

"Or whoever's left," Neven whimpered. He was a small thing, used to uselessness, but this was unbearable. "Six weeks of this and all we've done is watch as worlds die. Sanctuary-1. Hessius. The Small Brood. Blue Dawn. How much more of this do we have to endure before we admit that what we're doing isn't working?"

"The chef is right," said Percival. "We need a better pl—" Before he could finish his thought, Percival doubled-over and under and around again in pain. "*Belo beh*!" he cried as the pain lanced through him and dark thoughts filled his mind.

Esme rushed to his side. "Are you okay?" she asked. A rhetorical question, she knew, but one she hoped would demonstrate her concern. Since Galactic Zero, since his failed attempt to ensnare the Rider, Percival had been subject to these periodic flashes. The strange words. The excruciating pain. Moments when he and the Rider still felt as one, when he could still feel its hunger.

"Maybe I could say a prayer," she suggested. "I don't really believe anymore, but it's Sunday. What could it hurt?"

Percival closed his eyes/mind/heart and steadied his breath. "Sunday," he repeated. "Yes, Sunday. I should see Mother."

3 | *SUNDAY DINNER WITH MUM*

The planet Six was originally called the planet Het which, roughly translated, means "best planet." The people of Het liked this name, but it didn't earn them any good will from the rest of the universe which, by and large, thought their own planets were also very good.

Then, in the year 19932, a scholar at Duke-DeVry University published a paper claiming that Het was actually the sixth oldest planet in the universe. The people of Het weren't sure if this was true, but it was a rather smashing claim. And since the other five very, very, very old planets were either uninhabitable or very remote or, in one case, very smelly, it meant perhaps, by this one very narrow criterion, that Het really was "best planet" after all.

In 19934 the nations of Het got together and passed a joint resolution formally changing the planet's name to "Six" in celebration of the planet's special place in intergalactic history. The new name had a basis in fact, and was therefore less confrontational, but in every Sixer's heart it still meant "best planet."

When, in the year 19942, a scholar at Oxford FSU published a paper which provided ample evidence that Six was merely the twelfth oldest planet in the universe, the people of Six humbly declined to change their planet's name a second time.

At roughly nine past two in the afternoon, Percival Gynt fell out of a hole in the skies over planet Six and landed in a dumpster in the alley behind the White Castle. As he lay in refuse, he took a moment to reflect back on his life, on the various decisions he'd made that had brought him to this point, and whether there were any lessons to be learned in all of this.

No, he decided. Sometimes life is just this horrible.

He could barely move. The translation to higher dimensional space and back was wearing on him. He felt a bit like someone had stretched him out on a rack and then slapped him with his own kidneys. And in his head, a familiar voice whispered vile thoughts, searing hatred and rapacious hunger.

Looking up, he saw that a wee rat-man was about to crash down on top of him. And then a wee rat-man crashed down on top of him.

Nevin squealed. Percival grunted. Before either could scramble out of the way, Esme fell on top of the both of them with her duffle bag and then Vargoth Gor on top of her. Nevin and Esme were light, at least by people-you'd-want-to-land-on-top-of-you standards, but Gor weighed half a ton. She tried a "let's not crush them" charm as she fell, to limited effect. Her weight drove Esme into Nevin, Nevin into Percival, and Percival down through layers of grime and detritus, nearly to the bottom of the dumpster. There would have been aching moans or epithets, if any of them dared open their mouths beneath the surface.

They'd made this same exit from Halla's hideaway before. It always let out over the same dumpsters. Sometimes they managed the order better, so Gor came out first, but it wasn't an exact science.

Gor was first out of the dumpster. She helped Esme up and out and then lifted Nevin up by the head and deposited him on cobblestone at Esme's feet. Percival scrambled out on his own, weak and woozy.

While she recovered, Gor drew the Secondary Codex out of the air and swiped a thumb across its surface, muttering "synched" softly to herself. After vanishing the Codex, she raised her hands and made a show of barking out a "that smell is Percival, not me" charm.

Percival answered with a deliberate, audible sigh as he picked orange rind off his trouser leg. "So," he asked his companions, "shall we find our next Last Best Hope?"

The merchant weighed the bag of gold that Gor had given him in one hand and smiled appreciatively. "Ya know there are folks out looking for ya," he said. "I won't say nothin', but just so ya knows."

Gor ignored the man. Perhaps he continued to speak, but Gor had turned her attention to the craft. "What do you think?" she asked the others.

"Well, it's..." Nevin began.

"...square," Esme concluded.

It was in fact a cube, perhaps thirty meters to a side, and made from a cheap-looking purple plastic, stood in the middle of a wheat field. There was one obvious door at ground level. No obvious propulsion.

"You're sure it flies?" Percival asked the merchant.

The merchant stroked his long, furry, purple, prehensile nose and thought. "Don't see why not," he offered finally.

"Then we'll take it," said Gor, and the crew approached their ship.

Esme slid a bottle of champagne from her duffle and bashed it against the hull. "Our Last Best Hope," she said as wine ran down the side.

"Our Last Best Hope," the others echoed.

Martian Stacking Cubes are budget starships, originally developed by Doctor Emil Martian Stacking in the late 199th century and later popularized by the MTV2 comedy series *Star Blockz, Yo*. They are powered by MMDs, or Mostly-Magic Drives, which allow a ship to travel at superluminal speeds despite the obvious scientific impossibility. Outright ignoring scientific laws has always been cheaper than circumventing them, but is generally frowned upon in polite society. If you can afford it, you should really consider a CSD, a Completely-Scientific Drive, or at minimum an ASD, an Acceptably-Scientific Drive. An ASD is basically an MMD with more pistons.

The exterior of a Martian Stacking Cube is made of a space age polymer, which is marketing speak for "dating back roughly two hundred centuries," and comes in one of five colors. The interior is standardized. Beige shag carpeting leads up a spiral staircase from the airlock door to the domed main cabin. There, faux-leather faux-white couches surround a charcoal gray George Foreman HoloTable™. The HoloTable provides all ship displays, including star charts, system diagnostics, and Facebook. All ship functions are handled by voice command, except enabling voice command, which is done by raising one's hand and waiting patiently to be called on.

From the main cabin, crew have access to a set of privacy pods for the purpose of sleeping, peeing, or pooping. Esme waited until Percival was secured within one such privacy pod before approaching Gor.

"Why are we going to see Percival's mother?" she asked. "Is she someone important?"

Gor stared past her into a holographic display of their flight path. "Important? I couldn't say. Dangerous, certainly. She's a prisoner in one of my maximum-security facilities." She pointed out a flickering blue dot within the display. "Orpheus Turns. That's where we're headed."

"She's a criminal?"

"No."

"You said she was in prison."

"We don't just lock away criminals, child."

Esme considered this riddle for a moment, and then dismissed it. "Percival's falling apart," she said finally, changing the subject. "He's let himself go. He's full of self-doubt and recriminations. He's weak, and he's tired, and he's been muttering to himself in some weird language. It's not just guilt over what happened to that woman he cared about. I think the Engine did something to him."

Gor nodded distantly. "When you met Mister Gynt, he still wore the façade of a civilized man, but already it's been slipping. What you see now is not a change in the man. It is a revelation of what has always lain beneath."

Esme frowned. "I don't believe that, and neither do you."

"Monsters, Esme. We also lock away monsters."

The last time Percival had gone to see his mum, she had been in a foul mood. More so than usual. Though she hadn't said the words, Percival was sure that her stewards were torturing her again. She'd complained of chills in the night, of persistent pains and sharp pangs of hunger. At times, her words became sobs, and Percival could do nothing to console her.

The chief steward had no pity in him. "It is our prisoner, Mister Gynt, not our guest," was his refrain. To which Percival merely nodded and shuffled his feet, because that was the role he was playing. But inside him, deep down, a creature growled and clawed at the door of its cell. On his way back to the shuttle, Percival thumbed through his apps and ordered his mother an extra set of blankets.

Elsewhere, the steward opened a drawer and drew out his whip.

Fifty-six days later, the new Last Best Hope reached an expanse of space empty but for the Orpheus Turns space station. The station was of modest size, roughly twenty times as large as the Last Best Hope. Its hull was carved from black and green crystal. Its shape, a sort of squashed egg.

Troublingly, the station was dark. There were meant to be exterior lights and illumination from the windows. Instead, the structure was a virtual silhouette on the ship's holo display.

"Looks like the power's out," Nevin noted unhelpfully.

"Would explain why they weren't answering your calls," added Esme, further articulating the obvious.

Percival ignored them, stroking a hand through the tangle of his beard. "Mother," he whispered, "What have you done now?"

Gor stood from her seat on the couch and turned to the staircase. "I'll get the spacesuits."

She readied two suits, one for herself and one for Percival. The others would stay on the ship. If she and Percival failed, the fate of the universe would be down to them. A street rat and an actual rat. Gor shuddered at the thought.

"You're sure I shouldn't come with you?" asked Esme as Percival pulled on his suit. "I have a wrench. I could be useful if you need a nut removed."

Percival shook his head wearily. "Stay with the ship. In case we need to leave quickly." He patted her shoulder and approximated a smile. "Don't worry. Everything will be fine."

He turned away, stopped, then looked back. "But I'll take your wrench just in case."

Together in their suits, Percival and Gor descended the staircase to the airlock. Over vocal transmit, Gor chided, "Fine you say?"

"I should think," Percival answered, "that Mother is almost certainly full by now."

Vargoth Gor used her magics to activate the station's docking clamps and its airlocks. As she crossed over from ship to station, she felt a familiar presence, faded but unmistakable. *Illuminari, my old friend. What were you doing here?* She did not trouble Percival with these musings.

The station airlock opened into darkness. Gor muttered a "let there be light" charm and a pale glow flickered from her glove. Before them, a dead man floated in a mist of his own blood.

Percival reached out a hand and gently rotated the body. "Clawed. Chewed. Signs of a struggle." He leaned forward and poked. "But not much of a struggle. One of the guards, I think. Edwards, maybe? Edmington? Dead at least a week. Maybe two? Three?"

Gor pushed the corpse aside and stepped through the mist into the station corridor. She looked left and then right into gloom. "No power. Life support offline. No gravity, except what's built into our boots." And then something on the far wall caught her eye. "And what's this?" Words, written in blood. "THE PAST HUNGERS."

"*Belo sephius.*"

"Those damned words of yours."

"Damned." Percival nodded. "I think so. I've carried those words with me for twenty-five years."

"Your mother's language."

"Not only. When I was connected to the Rider... They spoke with her voice."

"Are you sure? And you hadn't thought to mention it till now?"

"I thought perhaps that it was because of me. That it was speaking in my truest tongue. But the words linger. Even now, I hear their whispering."

"You think there's some connection. Between your Mother and the thing out there. But how can there be? All this time. The Conspiracy of Days. Your mother was locked up here."

"I don't know, Governor." Percival gestured into the darkness. "Shall we find out?"

One advantage of their spacesuits was that they couldn't smell the dead, but by Percival's count there were hundreds, guards and crewmen, and as he recalled, not all of them unkind, now slashed and torn open and adrift in zero-gravity. Corridor after corridor of them. Percival knew that he should feel something for the dead. Sympathy. Compassion. Anger, even. But for him then, it was all of it a faraway song, a half-forgotten tune.

"Here," said Percival, tracing a gloved hand along the metal arc of a massive wheel set into a blood red vault door.

"Why here?" asked Gor.

"Because this is where we always have Sunday dinner."

Gor gripped the wheel and turned, and the vault door slowly opened. Within drifted the bones of the dead, picked clean and discarded in the dark. Beyond, Percival could make out a familiar slate table turned on its side. And two chairs, one empty.

In the other, hunched at the edge of Gor's light, sat Mother, naked. From certain angles, she appeared human. Beautiful, even. But then she would shift and reveal a fang, a claw, a distended stomach or tumorous growth, the tendrils, the ribs-like-jaws, the crawling fresh. Her eyes turned to them, and she smiled broken knives.

"Atmosphere," said Percival, over vocal transmit, and Gor whispered a brief charm. They took off their helmets as oxygen filled the room.

From her chair, Mother inhaled slowly.

Gor bent a knee. "The Demon Beast of Gynt."

"You are wise to prostrate yourself before us," she replied with a voice like acid and long winters.

"Mum. You look well..." Percival selected his words carefully. "...fed."

"And you, my dear boy. Come let us consider you."

Percival approached her cautiously through the bones. There was no fear, but neither was there trust between them. She slid a black talon down his gaunt cheek and through his tangled beard.

"You've lost your hat," she said finally.

Percival nodded wearily. "A neat summation," he conceded. "You've killed them all this time."

"You didn't visit. You didn't write. *Belo ess*. The past grows bored."

Percival rested his hands on the empty chair. "I've been distracted."

"We know. We can hear your distractions. Out there in the endless black. They sing to us as they feast."

"You know about the Engine?" Gor spat from the far end of the room.

Mother looked past her son to the once and future Celestial Governor. "Oh, lovely simple child," she cooed. "We *are* the Engine."

Percival fell to one knee before his mother, and he took her inhuman hand in his. "You...?"

"The first children of Gynt. They didn't die off. Weren't cursed and swallowed into the earth. They left. They... *became*."

"No. No," he repeated. "Illuminari... Tarot said... even Franco Nicodemus Noon... Everyone agreed that the Engine was as old as the universe itself."

"Our dear boy," said Mother. "Our dear, sweet boy. Noon was insane, a religious fanatic prone to believe the most unlikely faerie tales. And Illuminari? He was worse, a magician, committed to secrecy, misdirection, and whatever lie would best bolster his legend."

"The trick," whispered Gor, "is to make it look difficult."

"You knew them?"

"Noon, of course, was instrumental to my plans to free my brethren. He came to me seeking answers. I told him what he wanted to hear. Pretty stories of Ragnarok and Valhalla and all the glories of the next world."

"*Your* plans," Percival parroted as his hands slipped from his mother's grasp.

Gor advanced through the splinters of bone, curiosity finally getting the best of her instinct for self-preservation. "And Illuminari?"

"The old fool. Oh, yes. He worked it all out years ago. Came to visit us. Came to study us. Poked. Prodded. 'Twas we who told the wizard how to stop us the last time."

"Why?"

"For every liberty he'd taken. Every violation of our person. Of our dignity. Of this body. It pleased us to take from him his son."

"And what about *your* son?" asked Percival. "Was it mere coincidence that I was drawn into this business?"

"Son for son. He turned you into a weapon against us."

"No. Illuminari is dead. I've never even met—"

"Sweet boy. Simple boy. Who set you down this path? Was it someone close to Illuminari? Someone guided by his magics?"

Percival turned away. Tarot's stone was cold in his pocket. *Illuminari's* stone. Was it possible? Was this all he was, finally? A puppet. A plaything. "And the Engine? It was restored on the anniversary of the Gynt Massacre. That... That can't be a coincidence either."

"Illuminari saw fit to install this one as Celestial Governor on that date, to sully our grim anniversary with pageantry. With pomp and circumstance. We sought only to reclaim it for our kind."

"Our kind, Mother? Our *kind*?" Percival walked back towards the doorway. "We are the *unkind*."

"Yes," said Mother, smiling. "We quite like that. Yes. We are the Unkind." She turned a creeping eye to Gor, confiding, "Our boy has quite the way with words. This is why he will be devoured last."

The atmosphere thinned at the doorway. Percival stopped and took a deep breath. "No," he whispered.

Mother reached a tentacle out to stroke Gor's chest. "What did our pretty boy say, Madam Celestial Governor?"

"He said *no*," said Percival, more firmly now, as he stared back into the darkness from which they came. "He will not be devoured last. He will not be devoured. The Engine... The Unkind will be stopped."

"He has some fire now, hasn't he?"

Gor stood rigid as Mother's talons poked through her suit and scratched at the stony flesh beneath. "Perhaps we shall devour this one here?"

Gor was unaccustomed to fear, but this thing before her she did not understand. She found that, try as she might, she could not fix upon the creature firmly with her eyes or her thoughts. Could not summon the right words to turn her into a toad or a pillar of salt. Parts of her were still human, but the rest? A thing born before language. Before reason.

Gor chuckled as a talon pierced her lung. *Damn you, Illuminari.* Fate would not be denied its taste of flesh. Her killer would bear the name of Gynt after all.

"No," Percival repeated as he slapped Mother across the face. He had caught her by surprise, and now she reared up angrily, kicking her chair back behind her, her human form unfolding into something older. Its mouths roared in discordant anguish.

Startled, Percival stumbled back.

"You presume too much, little one," the voices cried out. "We are Mother, but we are not merciful. And our love for you is no stronger than our hate. And no shield against our rage."

Percival raised his arms before him. "*Belo atah*!" he shouted into Mother's hot breath. "The past repeats! *Belo ess*!"

The creature considered. "The past grows bored."

"Yes," said Percival, wiping sweat from his dingy brow. "So let us amuse you! Let us take you from this place. Let us take you back to the beginning. Let you show us how it started, and how it ends."

The creature folded back into itself, withdrew its tendrils from

Gor's chest, sending her slumping to the ground, faint and feebled and gasping for breath.

"Home?" she asked, a sweet coo, a long-forgotten meadow.

"Yes," said Percival. And he laughed, for he could see it now. All of it. The entire tapestry. Past. Future. Fate and happenstance. Hatred. Jealousy. Revenge. It was the wheel on the vault door. A perfect circle, always turning. A serpent, swallowing its own tail.

Percival Gynt had a plan. And it began like this:

"Home, yes. But first I need to shave."

4 | *VARIOUS TOILETRIES*

There was a pounding at the door, but Percival ignored it. Shouts as well, angry or confused. Which, he made no effort to distinguish. For this moment, he was alone with his thoughts and a range of toiletries.

His hand glided over scissors and straight razors, various gels and creams, brushes, bottled scents, soaps and oils. His fingers seized around a small ivory comb. His hand trembled as he lifted it to his brow line.

It was then he noticed the other man, eyeing him suspiciously through the glass. The grim, gaunt waste of a man with the wild beard and sunken eyes. Percival closed his eyes. The Stranger spoke.

"You look like Hell, traveler."

The two of them shared a smirk as Percival drew the comb back through the slick of his hair. "No worse than you," Percival joked. "But I've been told I clean up well."

The Stranger reached for the scissors and began clipping away at his beard. "I've no doubt you can present a pretty surface. It's a question of what lies beneath."

Clumps of hair fell into the sink. "That's the question, isn't it? The darkness within me. Where did it come from? Was I born with it? Was it put there by a wicked mother?"

The Stranger nodded, adding, "Or is it just a shadow cast from far away?"

Percival considered this as he brushed shaving cream across the scruff of his cheeks. "I used to believe that we were all of us the pawns of Fate, lured into strange matters beyond our agency."

"And now?" The Stranger lifted a straight razor to his chin.

"My mother has taught me a lesson. That we are caught up in the schemes of men and women and monsters, of mortal intents, not Fate, and that we are ultimately responsible for ourselves, for our own machinations."

"And our own darkness?" The razor sliced a downward stroke, close to the flesh.

"And our own absolution."

The half-shaved Stranger set down his razor and studied the other through the mirror. "From whence comes this newfound optimism? From outside, the stakes appear as high as ever. Your prospects as dim."

Percival turned a bare cheek to the mirror and examined the smooth of his skin. "Mother ought not to have told me of the link between her and the Rider. I think she thought to break me, but instead she..."

Percival paused. The Stranger frowned. "Yes?" he prompted.

"She gave me ideas. Reasons to think back to a childhood I've spent the better part of my life trying to forget. To consider what my father and the others were doing on that grown over sepulcher of a world. What they were digging for, and why they bred monsters in their basements."

The Stranger reached for his razor with an agitated, unsteady hand. "And?"

"In the years following the Gynt Massacre, I scavenged the compounds a dozen times over. I read through their journals, their research. I confess it didn't mean much to me at the time, their outlandish theories about collective consciousness and genetic memory. But I understood that that's why they bred Mother, an effort to tap into that ancient wellspring of knowledge."

The Stranger drew the razor down across Percival's unshaven cheek.

"But they understood the dangers. They were foolish, yes, but not fools. There was a failsafe in place. They were killed before they could use it, but it was complete. A weapon designed to eradicate Gynt consciousness. Tested. Ready."

The razor pricked Percival's skin. Blood dripped down the Stranger's cheek. He tossed the razor into the sink before him.

"They called it... the Cauldron."

"*Belo azo shaju beh*," the Stranger snarled. The thing with a man's face placed its hands firm against the glass, pressing until the skin went pale white and the glass began to crack.

Unfazed, Percival wiped the blood from his cheek and flicked it against the glass. "There was a traveler once... Do you know this story? He came across a strange old man on a long and lonely road. 'The Devil walks these paths,' the old man warned. 'Take me with you, for it is better that no one walks this way alone.' The traveler wasn't one for company, but he agreed that this made good sense, and the two continued together till nightfall. 'The Devil roams these parts,' the old man reminded the traveler. 'Let us camp together, for it is better that no one sleeps alone this night.' Reluctantly, the traveler agreed that this made good sense, and the two made camp together till morning. As the sun rose, the old man prepared breakfast and entreated the traveler to break bread with him. 'The Devil is surely near,' the old man said, 'so let us sup together while we can.' To this, the traveler frowned. 'We walked together on the road for a day, and did you see the Devil? We slept together in one tent, and did the Devil disturb your slumber? Perhaps you are just a lonely man. Perhaps there is no Devil.' 'Perhaps,' said the old man as he knelt before the traveler. 'Or perhaps the Devil will show mercy to the man who cooks his breakfast.'"

Percival Gynt smirked into the mirror. Something horrible lay on the other side, barking, slobbering, clawing to get out. "Do not be confused," Percival whispered, "about which of us is the old man and which of us is the Devil."

Percival placed a palm to the glass and closed his eyes. *Are you my hero, or aren't you?* When Percival opened his eyes again, the Stranger was gone and the mirror showed a perfect, unmarred reflection.

5 | PLANET OF THE UNKIND

When colonists returned to the planet Gynt, a respectful sixteen years after the Massacre, they made their settlements on the far side of the planet, a world away from the ancient ruins and the mass graves of what they called "the haunted hemisphere." But Percival Gynt was not afraid of ghosts. He was here to make peace.

The Last Best Hope touched down outside of Compound Fourteen at twelve past two in the morning on June 5th, 20018, some fifty-seven days since a mysterious woman stole Percival's hat at Slidetown Station. Weeds grew up through cracks in the ceramic tile of the landing pad. Exotic strains of ivy overtook the walls of the compound.

Five sentient lifeforms exited the craft, the first to set foot on this side of the world in decades. First among them was Vargoth Gor, once Celestial Governor Zell, now a weary shell, shuffling and wheezing and spitting curses into the wind. She used a telescoping steel tube as a walking stick. In her shadow followed Nevin the rat-chef, timid, anxious, but ultimately thankful for this brief escape from the world of cramped spaceships and inside-out pocket universes. Behind him, Sister Esme, goggles down, hair pulled back, wrench in her white-knuckle grip, resolute, determined that the current crisis was just another logic problem to be solved, that the monster at her back was a pawn to be played and sacrificed. This despite the rumble in her stomach and the hot breath on the back of her neck. She had faith in Percival Gynt. Fourth came the Demon

Beast of Gynt herself, smiling her jagged teeth, home at last for the end of all things. Free. Her tendrils stretched out towards the sun joyfully.

And then, finally, the last of them. The accountant. Percival Gynt had found for himself a new suit, a summer tan, two-piece, single-breasted, off-the-rack but well-fitted, with a copper-threaded tie and silver cufflinks. After weeks ground down to nothing, Percival was once again standing straight, clean-shaven, smirking, with a magic stone in one pocket and a plan in another.

His feet crunched against the broken tile as he stepped out of the ship. "Yes," he said. "I believe this will work."

When he was a boy sent scavenging by his mother, Percival had found a backway into Compound Fourteen, through a window in the rear kitchen that had been partially pried open. He was too large to fit through the gap now, but their rat-friend was perfectly proportioned for the task. Esme boosted him up to the sill, and Nevin skittered through the break in the wire mesh.

"Of what purpose is this subterfuge?" asked the Demon Beast. "Mama Alecto could tear the doors off their tracks as easily." Of this the others had no doubt. Even now, they instinctively recoiled with every syllable the creature uttered. Gor, more than the rest of them, still nursing her wounds from their last skirmish.

Alone among them, Percival maintained his cool. "This was my first home, Mother," he reminded her. "Some good manners are all I ask."

"Of course," she cooed. "For you."

A moment later the kitchen door slid open to reveal a trembling, dry-heaving rat-person. The phosphorescents glowed overhead. The climate control hummed, circulating fresh cool air through the compound. The fusion reactor that powered the compound had enough raw materials to run for tens of thousands of years. If not for the dead, it would have been a perfectly nice place to stop for an afternoon visit.

There were three of them in the kitchen, barely skeletons now, their meat long ago harvested to feed ancient appetites. They lay flat, arms at their side, arranged respectfully between the counters. Each lay in the tatters of their old clothes, in a dried splatter of their old blood.

"There will be more of them," Percival confessed.

His mother smiled her approval. "We had no idea you were so precise, my child. You did wonderful work here."

Esme tapped her wrench against her thigh three times so she wouldn't bark out loud.

Percival asked the others to split up and canvas the compound for the Cauldron device. He gave a vague description, explaining that it was large but not too large, metal or plastic, with lights or switches or sensors or glass panels, and that they should absolutely not touch it if they find it.

He knew that Mother would simply go on a rampage, destroying anything that bore a passing resemblance to that description, and that was fine. That would keep her occupied.

He only needed a few minutes.

Through the haze of memory, Percival Gynt navigated to a small out-of-the-way room in the third subbasement, living quarters to one of the compound's many support staff. This was the room he always found himself in when he came to scavenge the compound as a child. It was a refuge from his mother's wrath. A place for him to hide away, to pretend he was something other than he was.

The room was sparsely furnished. Just a bed and a footlocker and a shelf with some personal effects. Percival picked up a framed picture and wiped the dust from it:

A beaming young man in hospital scrubs holds his newborn son in his arms and nuzzles him with a scratchy beard.

Sit still, he told me. Don't move from this spot. But I went away, didn't I? So far away.

Percival set the picture back down. "You too will be forgotten," he whispered, his voice threatening to break.

Beside the picture lay the pocket watch he'd left behind all those years before. He lifted the watch by its fob, allowing the face to dangle at eye height. An Apple Watch, 19949 edition. Round, like a circle.

Gingerly he slipped his father's watch into his inside coat pocket. He was almost finished now. He sat down on the bed for a moment to catch his breath. To center himself. At the edge of his awareness, he could hear the Unkind, their fingernails clawing through the ether, whispering, cursing, salivating for their next meal.

"*Belo atah*," he said softly. "The past repeats..." He took a deep breath and then stood. "...until it does not."

Percival Gynt turned off the lights on his way out.

"Mother!" Percival shouted, this time louder than the time before. She looked up from the destruction she had wrought with a sneer on her lips. If this fabled Cauldron was to be found in this particular laboratory, she had certainly smashed it or crushed it or melted it with her acid spittle by now.

Percival was flanked by his companions. Mother took a piece of broken machinery and flung it uselessly across the room. "Where is it?" she howled from every orifice. "Where is the device?"

In that moment, Percival could feel the Engine draw into orbit overhead, readying its eye. Besides the hatred and the hunger, he could feel new emotions emanating from its dark core. Fear.

And desperation.

"It's here, Mum." Percival raised a hand and let the watch slip down from its chain to dangle before her. Like bait. "I'm afraid I lied to you. The Cauldron was actually quite small. In the end, I hope they'll note that it was the little things that mattered m—"

Mother lunged for the watch, but Percival was ready. He stopped time and stepped out of the way. He was on the far side of the room when time started back up, and Mother fell to the floor.

High above, the Engine's white eye opened.

"It's no use, Mother. One swipe of my finger and the Cauldron will turn you and that damned Engine off, and this madness will finally be at an end."

Mother growled and pounced again, but there was no stopping time again. The battery was too low. Instead Esme ran and hurled herself onto Mother's back, whacking her wrench repeatedly against the Demon Beast's head. Gor attempted a "wrenches are deadly" charm, but choked on her own words. Mother picked Esme off of her with a free tentacle and sent her crashing into the far wall. She hit with a crack and slid down to the floor limply.

Mother turned her attention back to Percival, advancing slowly now. "My dear boy," she cooed. "My sweet boy. You wouldn't do this to your mum, would you? You wouldn't harm the woman who loves you most in all the galaxies?"

Percival stood firm, thumb on the watchface as it blinked "Low Battery." "The woman who loved me most was named Tarot, and she's dead because of you. Perhaps you can apologize when you see her."

Mother was still, looming over Percival, calculating. With the least of her strength, she could shred her son to pieces. High above them, the Engine was fully charged and ready to strike. Now, thought Percival. If you're going to do it, do it now.

From the far end of the room, Esme let out a broken, pathetic laugh. She spit blood to the floor. "I get it now," she said weakly. "That's a wonderful plan. Really good."

Vargoth Gor looked to Nevin helplessly. Percival turned to Esme and slowly shook his head no. Please. No.

"It's here, isn't it? The Engine. We lured it here. And it'll erase the planet to stop you from using the device..."

People had always told Esme she was too smart for her own good. She had never understood what that meant.

"...and erase itself in the process... like a serpent swallowing its own tail."

Percival slumped down to the floor and let the watch clatter down beside him. High above them, the Engine understood and closed its eye and turned away. Nevin rushed to Esme's side as her eyes rolled back.

Gor advanced cautiously towards the Demon Beast.

"You tricked us?" Mother whispered, not fully understanding the words. "You... You lied to Mother. Tried to *forget* Mother?"

Gor spoke no charm. Silently she reached her hands around Mother's head and turned until it snapped off. The rest of her fell into a pile on the floor.

6 | *THE DROWNING PIT OF DESPAIR*

Esme never knew her parents. Never knew the story of how they met and fell in love. Never knew that her father was a charming smuggler who fell in with a dangerous gang of thieves and killers called Silvermoon Clan. Never knew that her mother was a Silvermoon herself, a thief among thieves and heir to the family's gift and curse, a single drop of werewolf blood stretched and nurtured over eleven generations of directed breeding rituals.

Her father helped her mother escape that fate, and for that they were hunted across the seven galaxies. They were married in secret. Their daughter was born in the hidden compartment beneath their cargo hold as Silvermoon assassins searched the rest of their ship.

Her parents knew they couldn't outrun the Silvermoons forever. When her mother's gifts emerged under the light of a full moon, her family could track her over any distance. And so it was with Esme. For this reason, father and mother chose to give her over to an orphanage on the planet Fum, where the sun never set and the moon never rose. Where Esme would be anonymous and safe.

But then the planet was sold to the High Cleric of the Intergalactic Church of the All-Mother, and the Fummers were exiled to the dark side of the planet. They had no choice but to leave Esme behind to fend for herself. As a child, she cursed whatever parents left her alone to that fate.

Till the day she died, she never knew the truth.

The ship once called the Last Best Hope crash landed onto the surface of the moon a quarter kilometer from the bubble dome of Lunar Colony. The purple cube bounced once, twice, three times, tumbling end over end, kicking up massive clouds of dust, stamping the surface, and finally gouging a trough for forty meters as it skidded to a halt.

Inside, the artificial gravity held. Percival, Nevin, and Gor sat still but coiled on their couches, watching the holographic display spin between them. Gor held Esme's dead body in her arms. All of them in their spacesuits.

When the holographic display finally came to a rest, Percival called out "NOW!" over vocal transmit. They stood as one and ran down the staircase. Percival threw open the door and emerged on top of the ship into a cloud of moon dust. Gor passed Esme up to Percival, and then she and Nevin climbed out after.

"As we discussed," Gor rasped.

Percival laid Esme down between them and unscrewed her helmet. "Are you sure?" he asked. Gor nodded, and Percival pulled the helmet off.

Her skin was pale. Her eyes, wide beneath her goggles.

In the moon dust Gor traced the symbol of the Deathward rune. Nevin sat beside Esme and held her hand. "Please," he prayed to the All-Mother. "Please let this work."

As the dust settled a ray of light pierced the cloud, lighting Esme's face, casting a glare off her goggles. Her whole body shook, and Percival and Gor found they had to hold her down.

Her mouth opened in a snarl, revealing sharp teeth and finally a silent howl. And then she couldn't breathe, and she was dying again.

Percival quickly snapped her helmet back in place.

"When did you know?" Esme asked an hour later as they worked their way through the evening crowds of Business District.

"There were clues," said Percival. "You barked now and again. Seemed fascinated by space and the night sky."

"Also, I could tell by looking at you," said Gor, her voice still ragged.

"Mostly that," Percival clarified.

"Normally the Deathward rune has no effect," Gor explained, "if the victim has been dead for more than a few seconds, but your latent lycanthrope gave the magic an extra boost."

"And thank goodness for that," said Nevin, "because now we can all die together."

Percival slapped a hand on Nevin's tiny shoulder and said in all seriousness, "Yes, my little friend. But first we drink."

Before them stood a ramshackle blight of a building, crooked from the foundation on up, paint peeling off the walls, garish with neon signage against smoky black glass, pulsing with the sound of horrible, ancient musics.

"Ladies and gentleman, I present to you: The Drowning Pit of Despair."

Inside, the four squeezed into a booth. The crowd was particularly rowdy that night. Loud and drunk and groping and ready for a fight. Do they know? Percival wondered. Can they sense it in their bones that there's nothing left for them but tonight?

"We tried, right?" asked Nevin. "That should count for something."

"There will be no prizes given out for effort, little chef," Gor replied before descending into a fit of coughs and wheezes.

A waitress came, and they ordered shots of something it recommended called Karma. Before and after it brought them their glasses, the four sat together in silence as the bar thumped around them. Finally, it was Esme who spoke.

"I'm sorry, by the way," she said to Percival. She considered reaching out and holding his hand, but decided not to. "About your mother, that is. She was an evil, disgusting, flesh-eating monster, but I understand that you loved her, so I'm sorry she's dead."

Percival considered this, nodded, and drank his shot.

"Percival? Percival Gynt?"

There was a woman now standing at the side of their booth, pretty, lightly buzzed, with purple hair and horn-rims and an incredulous smirk. Helpfully for this narrator, and for reasons that shall not be delved into here, she was wearing a T-shirt that said, "REMEMBER ME? IT'S MIDGE!" in big blocky holographic lettering.

"Midge?" asked Percival as he attempted to stand from the inside of the booth. Gor had him trapped and was in no hurry to get up to get out of his way.

Midge answered Percival's question by tapping her shirt. The letters danced for emphasis. Eventually, when it became clear that Vargoth Gor was not moving, Percival sat down and gestured to the opposite side of the booth.

"Please join us," he said, and Midge squeezed in comfortably next to Nevin and Esme.

"Where have you been?" asked Midge after she downed Gor's shot. "Compubot was telling everyone you won the lottery and moved to Planet's Core."

"Did anyone believe that?"

"Of course not. Everyone knows Compubot is a habitual liar."

Nevin nodded. That's what he'd heard as well.

It didn't take Midge long to pick up on the fact that, Percival's momentary joy to see her aside, the mood at the table was sour. And so she leaned in and, with a conspiratorial smile, asked him, "Who died?"

"Many people," Esme answered flatly, before correcting herself. "Most people."

Midge chuckled at that. She really didn't get Esme.

"We have a problem," Percival explained, "that appears to be intractable."

"An *accounting* problem?" asked Midge.

"That's one way of putting it."

"Hit me."

Percival leaned back for a minute in thought, finally offering, "We have a... large sum of money... and it needs to go... somewhere? But we can't find a *bank* that will take that much money."

Nevin whispered to Esme, "We should talk to Gor about that. She can probably find a bank for us."

"I assume the reason you're having trouble finding a bank is because that amount of money raises questions you don't want to answer?"

Percival shrugged. "Let's say there are special requirements."

Midge caught their waitress by its sleeve as it passed and asked for a pitcher of water and five glasses.

"I think we're fine," said Percival, to which Midge rolled her eyes.

Gor began coughing, a desperate wheezing cough. When the waitress came back, Midge asked it for a "Them" for her new friend. "With extra crawlies," she stressed. "It'll help put your throat back together," she told Gor. "Or rather, I should say *they* will."

Gor was not known for her graciousness, but she thanked Midge with a nod as she coughed blood into her napkin.

Then Midge turned her attention back to Percival. "Percival Gynt," she asked, "are you an accountant, or aren't you?" She held up the pitcher of water, pointed at it, and then emptied it into the five glasses.

Percival Gynt had a very bad thought. The kind that begins in your chest and works its way down into the pit of your stomach and up your throat and behind your eyes and leaves you anxious and empty and trembling.

And yes, yes, he was an accountant.

7 | THE FINAL ACCOUNTING

"Smurfing."

"I'm sorry," said Esme, because that's a thing she heard other people say at times like this, "but what?"

They stood on the roof of the Drowning Pit of Despair, fairly bouncing as the bass pulsed through the concrete beneath their feet. Nevin crouched near the edge, looking down to the crowd below, still thick and boisterous at two in the morning. Gor was scratching a symbol into the concrete with her finger and a "sharp as steel" charm, while Percival and Esme talked money laundering.

"It's a simple concept," said Percival. "If you have a lot of money, and maybe you came by it... *dishonestly*... You can't just deposit it in the bank, can you? One lump sum would raise too many questions. So you break the one lump sum up into lots of little lumps, well below the regulatory limits, and deposit them in lots of little bank accounts. It's called smurfing because smurf is an old word that means... um, bank account or... something."

"Okay, I think I've got it," said Esme guardedly, "but do you want to explain the rest anyway?"

"I do! We've been thinking of this problem the wrong way. The ritual to pull the Rider out of the Engine is simple and Gor knows how to do it, because she's done it before. The problem was that we didn't have an innocent soul to bind the Rider to. I tried, but even in my best moments, I'm just sort of fleetingly and very loosely innocent."

He pulled the stone from his pocket, hung from its brass chain. It glowed from within with a weak, flickering golden fire.

"Illuminari made this for Tarot, to seek out that one perfect innocent who could replace her brother. But she found me instead. Whether that was chance or Fate or Illuminari's masterplan... It taught us something. If even I, after the life I've led, the horrors I've seen and in my worst moments been made to perpetrate, have a shred of innocence that can be kindled..."

Gor looked up from the magic sigil she'd carved into the rooftop and completed Percival's sentence for him. "Then multiply that out across the population of the universe, and we have ourselves a shadow trap."

Nevin looked back from the edge with dawning horror. "You're going to put the Rider into... everyone?"

Percival nodded. "Just the smallest bit of it, but yes. And it will eat away at their best selves, leave them just that fraction sadder, that fraction darker. But we'll all be alive. The universe will keep going."

"And when we die?" asked Esme, "will the Rider stay trapped in our bones, or will it slowly start to reconstitute itself?"

Percival shrugged. How could he know? "We buy ourselves these days. We're only ever buying ourselves more days."

Percival threw Gor the stone. Gor sat down in the circle and began to chant. It was an "evil wins" charm.

Percival joined her in the circle as they'd discussed and removed his father's watch from his pocket. He placed a hand on Gor's shoulder. For the spell to work, it was important that the vessel stand perfectly still. In six seconds, Percival Gynt and Vargoth Gor would damn the universe.

Percival activated Time Stop.

8 | *THE CONSPIRACY OF DAYS*

Six months later, Percival Gynt arrived at Galactic Zero via Ubiquitous™, the new planet-to-planet teleporter service that was suddenly, unironically everywhere. It was the first day off that he'd allowed himself in weeks. Setting up his new detective agency-slash-accounting firm was taking more time than he'd anticipated, a fact for which he was secretly grateful. After everything that had happened, after everyone he'd lost, he needed the distraction, and now that he was taking this day for himself, he couldn't help but feel a pang of guilt.

But his friend called him, so he came.

He joined Nevin on one of those impossible park benches that hung upside down over another park with a pool of zero-G water floating between. The MagmaStar cast the pool in a beautiful sunfire red as it oozed across the sky.

In the distance the Hollow Tower served as a grim reminder of their time together.

As they sat together Nevin pulled a brown paper bag from his tiny rat-coat and handed it to Percival. "It's tuna fish," he said as Percival opened the bag.

Percival unwrapped the sandwich and took a bite. It was easily the best tuna sandwich anyone had ever made in the current version of the history of the universe. He groaned appreciatively, and Nevin wrinkled his nose in pride.

By the time Percival finished his sandwich, Nevin worked up the courage to ask, "H-Have you noticed a difference?"

Percival balled up his trash and set it next to him. "No," he said. Then, after further consideration, "Yes." Then, "I don't know."

Nevin nodded. "I saw a man bump into another man on the street the other day. The other man shot him this look. Not angry, but... intemperate? Unkind. A perfectly ordinary reaction, but I wondered..."

As did Percival. For so many years he had thought of the traumas of his childhood as something separate from him, as a beast to be locked away and buried and denied. In doing so, he had perhaps given those feelings more power than they deserved, a life apart. But ultimately all of that was metaphor. This, the thing they had done, it was not simply the idea of the beast. It was the beast itself. It was real. It was there now, at home in that familiar hole. There, in him, and in all of us. Every sentient being in the universe, living out Percival Gynt's childhood nightmares. Forever. Perhaps no one would notice.

"We did what we had to do," was all the answer that Percival Gynt could muster.

"*We*." Nevin shifted his posture uneasily. "I went back to work almost immediately afterwards. Gor... I mean, *Governor Zell*... She put me straight to work on this 'Return to Greatness' dinner. So I'm back in the kitchen, plucking and gutting, same as before. Same as always. And I had this moment where I thought, 'Yes, but we saved the universe, didn't we?' So that's okay. Except *we* didn't, did we? I didn't do anything. Just followed the rest of you around and stated the obvious and occasionally cowered from things. And it got me thinking. Be honest, Percival. Do I even matter at all?"

Percival forced a smile across his lips. "Of course you matter," he answered, a hand placed gently on Nevin's tiny rat-shoulder. "You made me this sandwich."

"That's true," said Nevin as he twiddled his tiny rat-fingers, and they sat together a little while longer.

Vargoth Gor arrived promptly at 2 p.m. aboard a touring skiff, a round, golden platform with jewel-studded handrails, a familiar rune carved into its underside. The gravity distortion pattern beneath the skiff kicked up tiny gusts of wind, one of which sent the balled-up trash from Percival's tuna sandwich flying off across the city.

"Governor," Percival said coolly.

"Accountant," Gor replied, and she offered Percival a hand up onto the skiff.

"Are you the real reason I'm here?" Percival asked as the skiff lifted up past the zero-gravity pool.

"You weren't returning my Facebook pokes."

"I don't like to think about what we did together."

"I've offered you money. Fame. Robots."

Percival turned away. "I also don't like to think of the things you did separately."

The skiff began descending towards the MagmaStar, and as it did Gor whispered a "this skiff has excellent heat shielding" charm.

"Midge says hello, by the way," Gor offered as an attempt at small talk. "We had tea and crumpets on Sunday."

Percival stared glumly down into the MagmaStar and thought about what he'd lost to it. "Why am I here, Gor? I get it. You won. You won the galaxy. I would have thought that gloating was beneath you."

"No," said Gor. "Redemption is beneath me."

Percival looked to the Celestial Governor curiously. "I'm not following," was all he could muster.

"I have done and will do great evils. For this reason and others, Illuminari saw fit to trap me within this MagmaStar for what at the time felt like an eternity. And perhaps he was right to do so. But now from this star that took so many years from me, I can return something to you."

Could it be possible? Percival did not dare to speak the words aloud. Deep down he could not entirely escape his conviction that Fate was real and petty.

Vargoth Gor spoke the secret words, and the MagmaStar bloomed across eleven dimensions. And from within, Tarot rose, preserved to within a few seconds of her death, three plasma bursts burnt through her body. Percival placed a hand over his mouth and stifled a sob.

Slowly the skiff turned until the MagmaStar was overhead and Tarot came to a rest on the platform at their feet. Percival knelt down over her and took her hand. "I'm sorry," he whispered.

Gor rolled her eyes at the sentimentality. And as she did, Tarot's wounds began to knit back together. Percival shouldn't have been shocked, but he was. And he began to cry.

"The Deathward rune," he whispered.

"The Deathward rune," Gor repeated.

When Tarot opened her eyes, Percival was the first and only thing she saw. "Hey there, stranger," she whispered. "Where have you been?"

"Where have I been?" Percival asked incredulously through his tears. "Where have I been?"

He hugged his best friend.

"We're alive?" Tarot asked, and Percival nodded.

"What happens next?" the one of them said to the other.

"Everything."

PERCIVAL GYNT WILL RETURN IN

PERCIVAL GYNT AND THE UNEXPECTED PORPOISE

"...and a bit more."

9 | *THE SUSPECT*

Esme slipped into the interrogation room while the two arresting officers were on their cigarette break. Inside, she found their suspect shackled to an adamantine table with a custom set of cuffs that secured each of his three arms. Behind him on the wall, the words "VARGOTH GOR IS NOT DEAD" were written in actual-magic marker. For now, she thought, suppressing a growl.

The suspect scowled at her through wide green lips as she sat down opposite him.

"Oy," he said, "and I suppose yer good cop?"

"Do I look like a *good* cop?" she asked, genuinely curious. The new clothes that Percival had picked out for her were overly serious, a gray pinstripe blazer and skirt over a beige blouse with thin frameless GoogleGlasses, but she didn't think they read as either good-as-in-above-average-at-her-job cop or good-as-in-kind-to-her-fellow-sentients cop. Perhaps there was a third meaning to the word that was in that moment eluding her. Not important.

She slid her business card across the table. It read:

GYNT & KLIEG
<hr>
ACCOUNTING

The suspect stared blankly through saucer wide eyes. "Yoo gonna do my taxes fer me?"

After a brief moment of confusion, Esme apologized and tapped the card twice. The word "ACCOUNTING" slid to the left to make room for the words "AND DETECTION."

The suspect frowned. "Yoo gonna *detect* my taxes?" he asked, now genuinely lost.

Esme made a little BLURGH sound as she snapped up her card. "No, no, no," she said. "We're not going to do anything to your taxes. Unless..." She thought for a moment. "You weren't arrested for a tax crime, were you?"

"Nah. Murder."

"*Tax* murder?" she asked, just wanting to be sure.

He shook his froggy-head no.

Esme considered this news for a moment before deciding what to do next. Percival had warned her that this individual might not be in all ways who she thought he'd be. "Not the suspect I'm suspecting?" she'd asked, which made her laugh then and also now as she was remembering the exchange.

The suspect now looked uncomfortable and passing frightened. Esme stopped laughing and apologized, considered explaining the joke, but thought better of it. "My name is Esme Klieg," she said finally. "I'm the junior partner at Gynt & Klieg. In addition to being fully certified and accredited accountants, mostly, we're also detectives. And we're interested in taking your case."

She paused, then corrected herself. "Or, rather, we will be, depending on your answers to the questions that follow." Esme tapped the side of her right GoogleGlass lens and questions began to scroll across her field of vision.

"Questions?"

"Such as: Have you ever been a police officer?"

"Do I look like a police officer, lady?"

"Subject argumentative. Have you ever left Sanctuary-6?"

"What's that gotta do with—"

"Subject evasive. Have you ever been to the Hollow Tower on Galactic Zero?"

"Huh? Nah. Listen—"

"That's enough." Esme tapped the side of her lens again, and the questions switched off. She had what she needed. "You fit the criteria. Gynt & Klieg will take your case. Do you accept?"

Esme waited for the suspect's response, which did not come readily. He needed time to process this offer and the strange woman who offered it. They sat in silence for what felt like minutes and was also actually minutes. Esme attempted a polite, bemused smile for much of the duration, although it waivered periodically. Now and then she glanced nervously at the door, wandering how much time she had before the two officers returned from their break.

Then, finally, the suspect asked, "Why me?"

"Why you what?"

"Why me?" he repeated. "Do ya even know who I am, lady? I'm a zero. Just some slob off the street who's seen too much and been pushed too far. Yoo don't know if I'm innocent or if I'm guilty. Ya didn't even know I was facin' a murder rap when ya strolled in here. Are ya that desperate fer clients? Is that yer racket? Ya just slink through police headquarters, snooping fer the first yutz ya can squeeze a few credits outta?"

"Ah. No. You'll find that we don't charge for our services. Also, you weren't chosen at random. You may call yourself a nobody, but my partner believes in you. I believe in you. You've had a hard life? I can relate. But here's the thing."

Esme slipped off her glasses, looked her client in the eyes, and smiled softly.

"Times change, Mister Um. But sometimes, when the stars align just so, you can change time back."

PERCIVAL GYNT WILL RETURN IN

ACKNOWLEDGEMENTS

At some point in the mid 70s, my father bought a spiral notebook. This was not a casual purchase. He was already a husband and the father of two with one more (smartass of a) child on the way, and how he was going to support all of these people and their current or eventual mouths was still an open question. And a spiral notebook meant one less can of beans. Probably. These acknowledgements were not exhaustively fact-checked.

So my father opened up that notebook, and he wrote down his three best ideas for making money, and then he rated them in three categories: Difficulty. Satisfaction. Financial Return. Those ideas were:

- o Start a small business. [Difficulty: Medium. Satisfaction: Low. Financial Return: Medium.]
- o Write a science-fiction novel. [Difficulty: Medium. Satisfaction: High. Financial Return: Low.]
- o Invent a perpetual motion machine. [Difficulty: High. Satisfaction: High. Financial Return: High.]

Years later, I found an old shoebox in some dark corner of our basement full of business cards for something called Melbourne Enterprises. "What's this?" I asked.

No science-fiction novel. No perpetual motion machine. Except this family of his.

My father died in 2014, a few days before Thanksgiving. He did the hard things. Thank you, Dad.

My mother did write a science-fiction novel called *The Unicorn Ring*, which sat for many years in her drawer and now sits in mine. Mom taught me to be kind and curious and creative. She's still alive. My sister Sarah takes good care of her. Thank you, Mom. Thank you, Sarah.

My brother John, who is eight years my senior, did everything in his power to program me into a little version of him up until the day he decided to become someone slightly different and less jackassy. It's because of him, for better or worse, that I love comics and *Dungeons & Dragons* and sci-fi and writing books like this. Thank you, John.

Thanks also to my friends who were there for me at the beginning of this project. I wrote the first few pages while crashing at my friend Nick Daniels' apartment. (I was on my way to Comic-Con, not homeless.) My old college roommate, Daniel Fienberg, read the first chapter and gamely confirmed, "Seems like a novel." At the time I wasn't so sure. And my friends Jeff Furletti and Gabriel Ramirez, the other two sides (or angles maybe?) of the fabled Writer's Triangle, provided encouragement and feedback during a crucial period in the writing of this novel. Thanks, guys.

Special thanks to my mother-in-law Victoria, who helped out with copy editing but has not seen this paragrap. I'm sure it'll be fine.

Most of all, I thank my wife Laura, my most faithful reader and kindest critic, and my son Sam, who is still at age two tragically illiterate. They are the two great loves of my life and, if I may be crude-adjacent, the precise kick in the pants I needed to finish this monstrosity. Thank you, thank you, thank you.

ABOUT THE AUTHOR

Over the years, Drew Melbourne has been a stand-up comedian, a corporate stooge, a school teacher, a comic book writer, a web columnist, a slightly higher-paid corporate stooge, and an inventor of odd holidays, but the job he enjoys most is author-of-this-book. No. Wait. No. Checked with the wife. The job he enjoys most is husband and father. Then author. Then fugitive that travels from small town to small town solving mysteries. Then those other things.

Drew was born and raised in the Philadelphia suburbs. He graduated *magna cum laude* from the University of Pennsylvania and, after a short eighteen-year stayover in New York City, has recently returned to the Philly suburbs with his wife Laura, son Sam, cats Leia and Ninja, and the fast-talking fifth dimensional imp who helps him solve crimes.

He (the author, not the fifth dimensional imp) can be found online at www.drewmelbourne.com.

"There are
OTHER STORIES
of Percival Gynt...

"The crimes of ALEXANDER EEPS,

the CHRISTMAS MACHINE heist,

the haunting of the HARTFORD,

and MORE..."

www.drewmelbourne.com/otherstories

CPSIA information can be obtained
at www.ICGtesting.com
Printed in the USA
LVHW032047131218
600349LV00005B/738/P